D1011005

Free Radicals

Free Radicals

LILA RIESEN

 Nancy Paulsen Books

NANCY PAULSEN BOOKS
An imprint of Penguin Random House LLC, New York

First published in the United States of America by Nancy Paulsen Books,
an imprint of Penguin Random House LLC, 2023

Copyright © 2023 by Lila Riesen

Nancy Paulsen Books & colophon are trademarks of Penguin Random House LLC.
The Penguin colophon is a registered trademark of Penguin Books Limited.

Visit us online at penguinrandomhouse.com.

Library of Congress Cataloging-in-Publication Data
Names: Riesen, Lila, author.
Title: Free radicals / Lila Riesen.
Description: New York: Nancy Paulsen Books, [2023]
Summary: "Afghan American Mafi's sophomore year
gets complicated as family secrets are exposed, putting her
family back in Afghanistan in danger"—Provided by publisher.
Identifiers: LCCN 2022040278 (print) | LCCN 2022040279 (ebook)
ISBN 9780593407714 (hardcover) | ISBN 9780593407721 (ebook)
Subjects: CYAC: Secrets—Fiction. | High schools—Fiction. | Schools—Fiction.
Family life—Fiction. | Afghan Americans—Fiction. | Afghanistan—Fiction.
Classification: LCC PZ7.1.R537 Fr 2023 (print)
LCC PZ7.1.R537 (ebook) DDC [Fic]—dc23
LC record available at https://lccn.loc.gov/2022040278
LC ebook record available at https://lccn.loc.gov/2022040279

Printed in the United States of America
ISBN 9780593407714
1 3 5 7 9 10 8 6 4 2
BVG

Edited by Stacey Barney
Design by Nicole Rheingans
Text set in Narevik

For Manuel.

Here's to writing *our* story, one day at a time.

1

I HAVE four rules as Ghost.

Don't get caught rooting around in the SOL tree. Never reveal my identity. Ensure justice is served without police involvement. And most important . . . don't get emotionally invested.

In the fall of my sophomore year, I broke every rule.

———

Rafi has *It* over again. America and its paper-thin walls.

Mom and Dad are downstairs and I know they can hear it, too. But Rafi's the firstborn male in our Afghan family, so when the chandelier shakes in the living room, Dad pretends it's Mr. Meowgi galumphing upstairs, orange belly swaying. And it's not like Baba notices much; he's nodded off on his pea-green rocker listening to ancient rubab music on his equally ancient Walkman.

Chunky as he is, the cat can't make the chandelier shake like that.

Mom drowns the noise by vacuuming the Daulatabad rugs with the circles, triangles, and tassels, lost in her own

Geometric Daulatabad Dimension of Denial, soon rousing Baba and cueing his usual "Watch the fringe, the *fringe*! Your baba brought the rug all the way from—"

"Kabul, yes, yes."

Mom's thinking about her son, upstairs, yesterday only a smiley squish splashing in the kitchen sink, now seventeen and untamable, putting his girlfriend's *my body my choice* into action. *It.* And *It* chose Rafi.

I say *It* because she's basically this thing that's attached herself to my brother. It wasn't always like that.

God forbid if I brought a guy over. No boy—friend or no—has been allowed past the threshold and upstairs to my room. They can only sit on the curb, like stray dogs.

Baba usually means *Dad* in Farsi, but in our house, Baba is my grandfather, Father of Fathers. Being who he is, it's *Baba's way or the highway*, and Baba thinks dogs are nejin. Unclean.

Tired of Mom's obnoxious vacuuming, I fill Dad's colossal UC Irvine Mathematics Dept. mug with jumbo marshmallows and homemade hot cocoa, my favorite fall creation. Then retire upstairs to my room, slather on one of those clay face masks, and shut-ish the door, since Dad gets mad when our bedroom doors are closed. Rafi's ignoring the *door open!* rule tonight, and thank god.

I rummage for my headphone case in a pile of dirty laundry, pull up Spotify, and wheedle out the dog-eared California DMV manual from underneath my A&P textbook. Baba likes to remind me he failed his driver's test twice before he got his license. I cannot, *will not*, follow in the old man's footsteps. Because driver's license = freedom. And freedom = boys.

One boy in particular.

Honestly, the DMV should've failed Baba on his third attempt. When he backs out of the drive, he putters onto the wrong side of the street, flamenco music blasting from the blown-out speakers.

"California's Basic Speed Law says . . ." I read aloud, then gingerly tip the mug to my lips; spongy marshmallows tickle my nose.

Tap! Tap!

Blergh!—cocoa dribbles down my chin. Through the window's sheer curtain crouches a stooped silhouette.

About the no-guy rule: Cole Dawicki is the only exception. Not that he counts. First, he's my neighbor. Second, he's a pubescent.

Cole brings me letters once or twice a month, depending on the season, maybe three times. Especially come fall because that's when everyone at Santa Margarita North crawls over each other like the undead looking for a beating heart in a pile of bodies. So fall is cheating season and winter, breakup season. Why smash the piggy bank to buy a gift for your S.O. if you're gonna call it quits anyway?

My classmates, whatever shenanigans they get up to, they leave the Final Ruling to the Ghost.

Me, Mafi Shahin.

And if found guilty, Ghosting—my brand of it, anyway—is worth shattering the piggy bank for.

2

IN THE glow of the desk lamp that pours onto the roof, Cole's face is splotched in the telltale reds and purples of exertion. He's panting from tearing around on his bike and climbing the oak tree. Wind turns his XL gray sweatshirt into a parachute. Cole wants to be a baller like Rafi, but Coach Gordan told him he needs to grow before high school. So his rationale is if he sizes up, the Baller Genie will help him fill out his clothes overnight like she did for my big brother.

I know Cole'll be a heartthrob one day but I feel pervy thinking about it. The kid's twelve.

"Beavers?" he says with a snide look at my pajama bottoms.

He doesn't say anything about the witchy green clay mask.

Cole smells like rain and smoke. Mrs. Dawicki's cigarette smoke's inlaid in all the furniture in his house. His bedding. His dog. In Cole, too. Smoked while she was pregnant with him. I overheard Mom gossiping about it with my big sister, Kate, when she visited from UCLA.

According to Grandma, Kate is not a proper Afghan name. Dad chose it.

But now it's only Baba who wants us to be Afghan, anyway. Just say *Afghanistan* out loud and Dad will turn into a turnip. Meanwhile, Mom wants us to be whoever we want, but says *life is easier without men, without boyfriends.* Whatever that means.

"Note, Coleslaw." I cinch my robe, suspicious of Cole's downturned chin—where those big eyes might be looking from underneath his rain-spattered hood. This is a drive-thru transaction. Get the notes, hand over the cash, and buh-bye.

"*Note—s,*" Cole says.

His scrawny sweatshirted arm slips through the window, clutching two folded notes.

"*Two?*"

He doesn't let go. "Ten dollars."

"Hell no!"

I let go so quickly he has to catch himself. The little gremlin.

"Heavens," he says, hand fluttering over his heart. "I'm just a child, you know. Let's break it down . . . five extra for climbing the tree," he says, matter-of-factly, like a lawyer. A learned tactic from watching Mr. Dawicki prepare for court. "With this flimsy branch, I could get you for negligence. I mean—" He tugs on the branch and it creaks. "*And* you've got me going into the woods in the middle of the night. Trespassing on school property, you know."

"It's eight thirty!"

"Bedtime's nine." He flashes his gap-toothed smile. Cole's mom nearly put him in braces but Cole talked her out of it; he said the gap gives him an edge. Twelve-year-olds are already worried about being edgy these days.

Cole knows he's got me. I *need* those notes. If he reads them, my life as I know it—*Ghost* in the shadows—could be over. If he connects the dots, that is. The kid's smart, and even though he doesn't go to SMN yet, I can't chance it.

I've made being invisible a superpower. But Cole doesn't need to know any of that to be my efficient sidekick. And no one can know about our Courier-Ghost arrangement.

"Jesus. Fine." I pray my voice is steady. These kids can sniff out fear.

Cole's changed. When he was in sixth grade, he was my doe-eyed courier. He'd get the notes from the SOL tree and bring them to me, no questions asked. He's wising up as a seventh grader. Money won't satisfy him forever.

It's called the SOL tree because if your name ends up in the knot . . . you're Shit Outta Luck. Everyone knows it. Karma has spoken. Karma being me. I'm the Ghost of Santa Margarita North. Only no one at SMN knows it's me doing the pranks.

A light flicks on across the street and streams through the branches. With an anxious look toward home, Cole snaps his fingers. "C'mon, Mom'll notice."

"Ughhh." I open my desk drawer and slip him ten dollars. Cole flattens the bill on a roof tile, then holds it up to the moonlight. His hood slips off to reveal straight black hair.

"It's not Monopoly money," I say. "I'm good for it."

Without donations left in the notes, I wouldn't be able to pay Cole. I don't know what he's saving for, but I've never seen him spend a dime. He keeps everything in his Velcro wallet with the black butterfly on front.

He gives me a sideways look. "You know, you can have it back if you tell me who's writing to y—"

"*Notes*, Coleslaw."

With a *your loss* shrug, Cole pockets the money and flings the notes into my room. I catch them in midair, cursing.

One is written on heavy paper, the expensive kind from Paper Source. The other, composition grade.

I turn my back to Cole. I don't want him to see it, this energy that runs through me whenever I've got one in my hand. Excitement. Fear. Who will be next?

Cole's shoes squeak, heel reflectors winking in the dark. Perched at the edge of the roof, he makes a move for the tree branch, swaying in the breeze.

There's a chill in the air tonight. November's almost here. We're about to go on the holiday roller coaster. First, Halloween. Thanksgiving. Christmas. New Year's.

Cole used to say bye. Not anymore.

I miss the kid I used to babysit. The one who didn't straighten his hair. The one who squealed when I chased him with the garden hose. The one whose second-grade showcase project was about the conservation of monarch butterflies, something he felt so passionate about he cried when a girl stamped on the paper wings we'd cut together with serrated craft scissors.

Every year, I've gotta get to know the kid all over again. Is this how it is to be a mother?

There's a weighty bonk and a muffled giggle on the other side of my bedroom wall.

It is still here. And Cole heard it, too.

His hand falls from the branch. "Oh, *brother*," he says, amused.

"Cole, don't—"

He crouches, crab-walking past my window . . .

"Oi!" My arm flails. There's the brush of his sweatshirt against my fingertips. I can't go after him. I'm barefooted and the contractors left nails half-hammered all over the roof— toe mines. Sometimes I wonder if Dad told them to do it on purpose to prevent us kids from sneaking out.

"It's a no-go anyway," Cole whispers below Rafi's window. "Curtain's shut. Wait . . ." He's spotted the old silver BMW in the driveway. *"It* again? You must be haaaating this." He laughs in a chorus of pubescent croaks and squeaks.

Cole says *again* like that because my bro and *It* break up like every other week.

Before last year, Raf was nothing but a benchwarmer and *It* ignored him. He was put on the radar when he basically became a giant (the dude grew a foot in a year) and Coach Gordan tripped over himself to put Rafi in the starting lineup.

Now six foot eight and a center, Raf's King of the Court at Santa Margarita North—along with the other Ball Giants.

But Big Bro leaves skid marks on his tighty-whities, and that's knowledge no one can take from me.

Cole's laugh swells in the night.

Downstairs, the vacuum's concluded its fringe-chomping quest. Every time *It* comes over, the rug fringe looks like Meowgi when he had a showdown with Nutter Butter, the squirrel that lives in the tree outside my window. He got his name after I woke to the thief helping himself to a Nutter Butter left on my desk.

If the wind carries Cole's laughter into the living room window . . . Dad's a *no weapons* type of guy, but Baba does have some ancient pulwar sword mounted above his bed.

"Shh! Damnit, Cole!"

"Reeeelax," Cole says. "It's nothing I haven't seen online before."

"*Ew.* You're like—eight."

As his former babysitter, a burning rises in my chest. I've got an urge to scold him for watching porn at such a young age. But I was twelve, too, when I first watched it with my best friend. Well, ex—best friend now.

Cole won't budge from Rafi's window, hopeful the curtain will miraculously swish. There's sniggering coming from the other side now, which means it's likely over.

There's another *thump* and I cringe.

Part of this is Dad's fault; he bought Raf a king bed since his calves stuck halfway off the twin like hairy tree trunks. More space, more room to romp with *It.*

"Ope, it's a boob!" Cole squeaks in his maniacal voice, to get a rise out of me. "I saw boob!"

It works.

"*COLE DAWICKI!*" I whisper. There's nothing worse than when a kid disobeys orders and there's not a damn thing you can do about it. He hobbles past my window again, fist-bumps my head with a "*Pew,*" and leaps for the branch.

I want to tell him to stop swinging like an orangutan, to be careful. Instead, I say, "I can find another courier, you know."

"Just say *messenger,*" he says, anchoring his foot on the branch below. "You're turning into Kate."

"You take that back!"

"You're turning into Kate, Rafi's sis! Accept it!"

"*Rafi's sis?*"

Cole shrugs. "Jalen says it sometimes."

"He talks about me?" I place a hand on the ledge.

Cole snickers and rests his chin on the branch. "Not you, too."

"What?"

"You like JT."

Jalen Thomas.

Aka walking thirst trap. Junior. And to top it off, hella smart. A ball player at SMN, so a quick thinker by nature.

"I don't"—then realizing I don't need to explain myself to a middle schooler—"you're the one who follows him everywhere."

"We're friends," Cole says in a *duh* sort of way.

"Uhhh, seventeen-year-olds aren't friends with middle schoolers."

"Jalen's not like other guys, Rafi's sis."

I've got nothing.

Jalen's invited Cole for sleepovers, and vice versa. It's not weird. It's just—Jalen.

"Don't call me *Rafi's sis*, Coleslaw!"

But he's still singing his little jig as he shimmies down the tree. *"Rafi's sis, sis, sis."*

I hold my breath. The tree shakes. Then there's the unmistakable *fwump* of shoes against dirt. I exhale.

Shoulders hunched, Cole's scrawny figure skulks across the street, sneaker reflectors flashing with each step. One, two. One, two.

3

COLE'S INVOLVEMENT in the SOL tree was an accident.

Getting to the SOL tree is tricky. It's on this steep slope covered with slick leaves that'll sweep your feet if you don't edge down sideways. On one letter run, someone followed me. It's difficult muffling footsteps with so many twigs underfoot.

I pounced, pinning my shadow to the forest floor.

Damn you, Cole Dawicki.

And it was an either *I'll tell you but then I'll have to kill you* or *Bring me the letters from now on or I'll kill you* sort of deal, and Cole chose the latter—especially when he found out there'd be money involved.

How I got him to promise not to read them was easy. I know the kid. He worships Jalen. He worships ball. So I told him if he read them, he'd never grow taller, never get to the NBA. Like lots of athletes, Cole's superstitious.

That, and I threatened to tell Dad *he* was the one who broke his rubab spinning a basketball on his finger. It cost one hundred dollars to fix.

I take a swig of cold cocoa as Raf's door creaks open. There's giggling in the hall, and I imagine *It* fixing her hair in the bathroom mirror to look presentably innocent on her way out.

I stick the notes inside my diary.

According to my big sister, Kate, since *It* and my brother are in a relationship, they're free to do as they please. Kate tells me there are two types of girls in high school: *Girlfriend Material* and *Hook-Up Material*.

I wanna be *Girlfriend Material*. This year, I've pledged an oath to myself, which is the highest of oaths. It's written in my diary, in ink: *Jalen Thomas, this year, you will be mine.*

My first boyfriend.

Sure, I could go after someone easier. Someone, I guess, *on my level.* A sophomore like me. Someone who doesn't stand out, maybe. But when I think about dating anyone else at SMN, a manor of thousands, my heart's not in it.

Some people fall into stuff, like Raf and his ball popularity, and others have to make stuff happen for themselves. That's me. On my queen bed. Thinking about throning me a King of the Court.

I wonder if Jalen has a king bed?

Mom's wrong, life isn't easier without a boyfriend.

With Rafi's sporadic climb up the social ladder, perhaps there *could* be hope for me. He's living proof wishes do come true.

But my big bro's existence is also the reason I'm doomed. *Protective older brother* is an understatement. Case in point: Annalie's homecoming party freshman year. Raf called in a noise complaint after he heard I'd gone into the basement with three skater dudes from San Viejo Prep.

I became popular in the worst way—labeled *Hook-Up Material*—then just like that, invisible.

Shine a spotlight on a Ghost and you won't see anything. But just because they can't see me . . . doesn't mean I'm not there. Making an impact.

I stuff my diary underneath my blankets, for later. I can't read the notes while anyone's awake. The heat kicks on, rattling from the vent above my bed. Baba misses the Kabul desert and oppressive summer heat. That's why he treats us like we're bread rolls in need of baking.

Inside the vent is the jewelry box Baba gave me for my thirteenth birthday. All the notes Cole's ever delivered from the SOL tree are inside, crusted at the edges from enduring the constancy that is Baba's furnace.

If Rafi finds out what I'm doing. If anyone does.

There'll be no rising from the dead.

4

LATER THAT evening, once *It* takes the West Wind with her, there's a knock at my door. My phone sails across the room in surprise.

"Go away, Beelzebub!"

"It's Mom." Her fuzzy slippers are visible from the crack in the door. "And please don't call your brother Beelzebub. Can I come in?"

"Hold—hold on!" I crawl on elbows and knees like a leg-chomping zombie, grab my phone from a pile of dirty laundry, reverse my caboose, and hide it under the blankets. I don't know why. Mom would never go through my phone.

I cast a nervous look to the vent above my bed.

"Okay!" I call.

My door opens a sliver. "How's your head, Mama?" I feigned a headache when the vacuuming started.

Mom calls me *Mama*. Ironic, I know. It's weird the pet names parents have for their kids. First it was *Maforama*. Then *Moo-Moo*. Then *Mama*.

"Better *now*." Mom catches my meaning. She knows I despise *It*.

Dad and Baba call me Gojeh Farangi. *Gojeh* actually means *plum* and *farangi* means *foreign*. Together, that somehow equals *tomato*. I was nine pounds as a newborn and came out, according to Baba, red as a tomato. I'm different from the other tomatoes on the familial vine. Rafi and Kate were both premature. Baby tomatoes.

Mom sits on my bed and gazes at the photo of us kids on my wall.

Looking at the photo, you'd think Kate, Raf, and me were strangers. We're passed out in the same hotel bed at Universal Orlando, three side-facing spoons. Well, two tablespoons and one teaspoon: me. We three share only one Mongoloid feature, that's Baba's eyes: Baba's half Hazara, an ethnic minority in Afghanistan. Grandma was full Pashtun, the Afghan majority.

I like this photo because Raf's not jerking me into a headlock (his go-to brotherly pose) and Kate's not fussing, telling Dad photos are *tedious* or something.

From my Afghan side, I got excess body hair (at least three hairs per pore) but I'm basically all Mom, with pale skin and dark blond hair that I bleach blonder. Mom's not Afghan. She's as pale as they come, born and raised in Michigan.

Dad's family was driven out of Kabul in 1979 by Soviet tanks, and though he's got a U.S. passport, he recollects the sleek black cars with government plates that skulked down our street after 9/11. I wasn't born yet, but I've heard the stories. I get why he tells us to "Act American. Look American." I just wish he weren't so paranoid all the time.

Mom's gaze shifts to the watercolor on my wall, the one she calls *the troubled teen* because the girl's in some dark alley with her hood up and foot against a wall. Mom misses all my old posters, ones with glammed up models in dresses.

Mom forces enthusiasm into her voice. "I was thinking, Mama, how about some new outfits for your birthday?"

I roll my eyes. "Why?"

"Sweatpants and hoodies . . . You don't want your teachers to think you don't care . . ."

"My grades speak for themselves, Mom. Well, except synchronized swim. But to be fair, swim's the only class I *can't* wear a hoodie. Those school-issued swimsuits . . ." I shudder.

Mom's enthusiasm fades. She grabs my hand. "Has something happened at school, Mama? A teacher? Or a bully—"

"Because I like sweats?"

"And you haven't had Annalie over in a long time."

I scratch my forehead. "She's busy with track."

"Which you pulled out from."

"I still run sometimes!" It's been months.

"And then there's this 'tude, miss lady—"

"I'm really not feeling the full daughter audit right now, Mom."

"Okay, okay. But Mama, whatever it is"—she reels me in and gives me a squeezing shake—"remember, high school isn't forever."

I never did tell Mom about Annalie's party. How me and Annalie are history. *Or* what Rafi did. Mom would probably hear *I went into the basement with three guys* and go momentarily deaf.

Maybe before Annalie's party I was into dresses and contouring and eye shadow and stuff, but sweats and hoodies are hella comfortable, so what's the big deal?

Still holding me, Mom thinks aloud. "I don't understand what it could be. High school years were some of the best of my life."

I've *seen* pictures of Mom in high school. Mom developed early, had a booty, and in those tight plaid pants, there's no question she was popular.

Cheek still squished against her shoulder, through fishy lips, I blub, "High school is overrated. How about starting a beauty school at the salon, and I'll—"

"Nope, my youngest daughter is going to be a scientist," Mom says. "Or a judge. But before you grow up and leave me, too, let's practice your parallel parking before the big test, mm? Tomorrow, before school?"

As if starting school at 7:45 a.m. isn't early enough.

My reluctance is palpable, so she goes, "Unless you'd like to go with Dad or Baba . . ."

"Negative."

Dad takes after Baba in the driving department. He never looks at roundabouts, stresses when I'm at the wheel and we get honked, and there's a lot of noisy gum chewing and looking out the window.

"Oh!" Mom lifts a finger, scurries into the hall, then comes back and places salon shampoo and conditioner on my desk.

"If your father asks," she whispers, "it wasn't more than five dollars for both."

Mom's sneaky. Like daughter like Mom, I guess.

"Thanks, Mom. Okay, love you!" I know I shouldn't use those words to get Mom to leave, but I have notes to get to.

———

When the house is still, I pull the new notes from my diary, the ones damp with Cole's sweat.

Then prop myself up. I have to be ready. The things I read aren't always pretty. You know when you read a good book and it's like a movie's playing in your head? It's like that. And I'm a good librarian—I know when to file as *fiction* or *nonfiction*.

How? Might be some SOL magic. Or maybe Afghan djinn magic.

Composition-grade note first. I take a deep breath and sever the tape with a blue polished nail. A twenty wilts onto my lap like a leaf. A weighty donation.

The words are scrawled in big block letters. The note's about some freshman, how she's a backstabbing bitch for having sex with Tommy Lewis last weekend when she knows this other girl likes him.

The heat kicks off. Meowgi bats at a scrunched water bottle on the floor.

Ink's pooled on the words *had sex*, as if the author spent a lot of time there, dreaming up the offense. That, and Tommy Lewis was at Lake Havasu last weekend with his dad.

Fiction.

People are always wanting revenge for stuff that never happened. To start rumors. For reasons I'll never know.

Dirty money is donated to Heart to Paws Rescue down the street. There's no return to sender or I'd blow my cover.

I crumple the note and toss it; Meowgi takes chase as I slice the tape from the heavier note. No donation. It's written in pretty cursive.

From the dented crease, it's clear the writer has folded and unfolded it over and over, reading and rereading, wondering if it should be sent. The heat's on Fallon McElroy, whose name is underlined three times.

Fallon is just generally an asshole, and generally gross (he's a known classturbator, for one). He's that popular guy who no one knows *why* he's popular. Maybe it's because he won this surfing contest in Huntington Beach once, *once*, in elementary school. He also appeared as an extra in *Blood Jurors*, this sexy vampire TV series. But I think Fallon's the definition of "peaked in high school."

There's a tingling in my fingers. That's how it always starts. Then a fluttering in my head, as if Cole's paper butterflies are flapping in my brain . . . I read the first sentence. *Nonfiction.*

Fallon has been dating Josefina for a year . . . but the author says *they've* been sexting Fallon for a month. They even made out once.

Fallon invited the author to a movie. Instead of driving the author to the theater, he drove them to Black Star Canyon and tried feeling them up. When the author said no, Fallon called them *a goddamn tranny* and took off. For thirty minutes the author waited for their ride with waning cell service, listening to the raspy shrieking of mountain lions skulking in the canyon.

My jaw drops. I know who wrote the note. *Brit.*

Brit Rossi.

She's transitioning, and has over five hundred thousand followers on Instagram as this badass activist.

That this could happen to someone like *Brit* . . .

Us sheep are doomed.

Mountain lions aside, everyone knows Black Star Canyon is haunted. Some school bus crashed there in the '70s, killing all the kids inside. Last October, there was an article in the paper about some guy who was stuck in the neck by a needle dart while visiting. To this day, hikers have reported gray shadows stalking them through the trees. It's also a known hook-up spot for high schoolers. I guess we like the danger.

My cheeks burn and my fists clench.

Oh, *Fallon, Fallon, Fallon.*

I'll get confirmation at school tomorrow. As a future judge, I've gotta be objective. Gotta know the facts. And *when*—not *if*—I do, Fallon's going down.

5

HOW I became the Ghost goes like this.

When I was nine and Kate fourteen, she convinced me there were fairies living in the forest behind SMN. We used to leave Wish Notes for them in this tree knot that looks like a swirly treble clef.

The notes had always disappeared by the next day. Granted, it was probably the wind, or one of Nutter Butter's squirrel relatives, but I wanted to believe it was fairies. That between track and piano lessons, *reality* was not the only plane of existence available to my nine-year-old self.

After Kate decided she was too old for fairies and took up figure skating and sneaking out to meet boys, I visited the Fairy Tree on my own.

I had to create my own magic.

But growing up is not always so magical.

I left a wish in the tree. *I wish I was popular. I wish I was seen.*

My wish was granted at Annalie's party freshman year. But I didn't know the winds had shifted in the boughs; the fairies had turned on me.

It was the first party of freshman year and Annalie's parents were out of town. We agreed it was time to reinvent ourselves. No longer gangly track-and-field middle schoolers, we were morphing into dateable freshmen. Okay, so even if our bras were padded, we would fake it till we made it. And making it meant getting boyfriends.

All SMN freshmen were at the party. One or two sophomores, too. Even these cute skater dudes we met at Starbucks that afternoon came through. From Viejo Prep, these dudes were seniors! So by those standards, our party was a success. Maybe even cool.

Mikey, the skater with a lip piercing and sideswept hair, had hurt his shoulder doing some skate trick called the *laser flip*. Probably because his hair skewed his vision. I offered to give him one of my famous back massages on the couch. Kate and I used to nab the egg timer from the piano and practice our massage skills before bed. I always had to give Kate a massage first. Whenever it was my turn, big sis was (conveniently) too drooly and noodly to reciprocate.

The couch in the living room was occupied, so I suggested the futon in Annalie's basement. Two of Mikey's friends followed, wanting to test the Ping-Pong table Annalie kept bragging about.

But trouble was brewing upstairs.

These other dudes Mikey invited had turned up, and they were in the backyard, making a sport outta throwing empty beer bottles at Annalie and our friends.

And someone else unexpected was at the party, too. A mole in a hood. A junior, from the baseball team—a spy, sent by Raf after he got wind of the party. Being six foot eight, Raf knew *he* couldn't go; he'd stick out.

The mole texted Raf I was in the basement with three dudes.

Thirty minutes. That's all it took to set the trajectory of freshman year.

I missed tons of SOS texts from Annalie. The beer-bottle chucking had escalated. Annalie and the others took cover in the tree house; the bottles kept coming like torpedoes. Soon, blue and red flashed outside the basement windows. Then an amplified voice saying, *Party's over, everyone out.* Raf had called in a noise complaint.

Pushing and shoving, Mikey and his friends bolted out the basement door.

When I emerged upstairs, the cops were gone. Annalie, she was pissed. Not so much about the torpedo bottles, the mess, or the vomit in her knockoff LV purse. She was mad I went into the basement with Mikey, the boy she'd deemed *hers*.

There's no such thing as BFF. Annalie proved that soon after.

She started a rumor, and for the rest of the year, I was CJ.

Circle Jerker. That one freshman who jerked off three seniors from Viejo Prep in Annalie's basement.

I lost my crew, all six of them. I quit track because, well, what was I sprinting for anyway?

My soul had left my body. I'd effectively become the Ghost.

I *did* fix Mikey's shoulder with my killer massaging skills. After he graduated, he went off to college in Virginia and I haven't heard from him since.

There was a solution, to undo the last wish I'd left for the fairies: *I wish I was popular. I wish I was seen.*

I'm a math girl, and it was simple.

Rumor (x) x (0) always = (0), so I started my own *nothing* rumor, to nullify the other one. To get them to forget.

My rumor—

—has it that SMN injustices are taken care of with a little help. Letters left in a tree knot on school property. No longer the Fairy Tree—*that name was kids' stuff now*—it had become the SOL tree. Sole purpose: vengeance. Because being CJ sucks. I never wanted anyone else to feel that.

6

ON THE way to school the next morning, it's raining. The teensiest of drizzles is lethal in California; you'd think it was raining baby oil. Even SUVs with all-wheel drive won't chance going over thirty on the highway.

Parallel parking's no biggie in the Tesla, but Mom insists I learn to drive a stick *in case of an emergency where there's only a stick shift available.* So we've been using Dad's beater car, an old Honda.

In addition to my bro leaving the pathetic loaf butt for my PB banana toast, we're already running late, my period cramps are having a goddamn rager, and I was hoping to cover the pimple farm budding on my chin in the visor mirror. I tell Mom, "Forget the lesson," but she says, "Nonsense, you need to learn to drive in all weather!"

It starts out fine, albeit a little clunky. I don't have to go on the highway, thank god, because SMN is only a mile away.

"Turn on Covenanter," Mom says.

"But—" I'm not used to taking Covenanter. I usually take High.

"Calm, *Mama.*" Her eyes are wide like Meowgi's when he spots Nutter Butter. Mom knows blinking could mean life or death; she can't miss a moment as copilot. "Just put in the clutch, brake, downshift, and turn the wheel."

That's all, is it? It's like math class, maybe geometry, because a triangular shape is closing in—

"Yield sign, Mama. Clutch and slow down!"

I put in the clutch with a trembling foot. The car cranks as I downshift. I turn the wheel—

"Okay, Mama, now brake. *BRAKE!*"

I'd like to say the yield sign never saw me coming. I roll at a snail's pace into the sign, toppling it with an awful crunch. Ol' Honda lurches and dies. Mom spits her annual curse word.

Cars *shhk* by, people gawking. With my luck, classmates. Did I just see *It*'s silver BMW?

Stray pieces of Mom's golden hair have dislodged from her braid. She holds a hand to my face. "Are you all right?"

"Fine."

She exhales. Her cheeks flush from pale to red. "These things happen," she says, though her voice shakes with irritation. "The signpost has holes for a reason."

Yeah. So it'll topple easily when a fifteen-year-old snaps it in two.

"Let's call Dad," I say in a rush, and Mom gestures for me to breathe. Mom's more of an *I can do it myself* kinda person but usually does more harm than good.

Smoke emanates from the hood in black wisps.

"Did I—damage the car?"

"Don't think so," Mom says, "we weren't going fast." But the engine won't fire when we switch places.

Mom's tapping wildly on her iPhone. "We'll Uber to school, call in a tow, alert the city about the sign, then I'll Uber to the salon, and—"

Mom yelps. Her phone's tapped out. Mom never remembers to charge her phone at night. She looks at me expectantly and I go: "Yeah, hold on."

I root through my backpack, only to have dread shoot through my arms and legs. Rain clobbers the roof like pebbles in a tin can.

Mom doesn't hear me when I tell her the bad news. Or maybe she does and doesn't want to believe it.

"You what?"

"My phone's on my bed. I left it at home."

Walk of shame, I think, is more aptly used for times like this, times you've left your dad's car sitting atop a broken yield sign and have to trudge one mile to school behind your mother like a pathetic duckling.

"You don't have to walk me, Mom." *Aka, Don't.*

Mom turns, wind whipping blond hair in her face. "A girl your age was abducted in Sherman Oaks just last week." Her eyes skim my sweats and hoodie.

"Sherman Oaks is like an hour from here, Mom."

"Not in the mood, Mafi." No more *Mama.* She's pissed. "What, are you hurt?" she asks, noticing me hobbling like Quasimodo.

"Cramps." The sudden burst of movement has reawakened the beast. In addition to my phone, I also forgot to pop a Midol this morning.

Headlights flicker behind us. Then there's the roar of high revs.

Beep! Beep!

God. Whoever it is, go away . . .

Ford Raptor.

Jalen.

Vroom. The Raptor pulls over onto the shoulder. Down rolls a tinted window, and my face is swathed in cologne-tinged warmth and rap music. Next to Jalen, Cole's a runt in the leather bucket seat. I forgot: Mrs. Dawicki *just can't* with the rain.

Jalen and Cole met at Hoops for Hope, an after-school program for those with busy or absent parents.

Cole's thrilled to see me: hair frizzy, mascara dripping, pimply. He's vibrating with silent laughter, face hidden in the sleeve of his overlong sweatshirt.

"Morning, Mrs. Shahin!" Jalen shouts over the rain.

"Jalen, you grew again!" Mom accuses in amazement.

She's fishing. I mean, Jalen's sitting down, for one. Mom notices Jalen's stopped coming around and wants the goss—some insight into her own teenage son's head—which has been progressively off-limits since puberty.

"It's been a minute, Mrs. Shahin," says Jalen.

Mom puts her hands on her hips. "So which salon's stolen my favorite client?"

Jalen gives his half smile and sheepishly rubs his hair, styled in a bleached, textured high top with twists. With Jalen's smoldering eyes, angular face, and thin, curved dimples like parentheses, people at SMN say he looks like Kelly Oubre.

"I'm just kidding, honey," says Mom. "That style suits you. Remember, sulfate-free shampoo only."

Mommmm. Shut uuuup.

Jalen's eyes flick my way and I automatically feign a nose wipe to hide my pimply chin.

Mom swivels her head. "Is that Cole I see?" Cole emerges from his sleeve, red-faced. "Hi."

Someone honks and Jalen waves the driver on with a "Go 'round, damn!"

Rap booms from the Raptor's speakers and Mom frowns. I raise my brows at Cole; he catches my meaning and turns it down.

A sin, really.

Mom and Kate hate rap. I think it was Kate who told me rap puts the *-rap* in *crap*.

"Need a ride, Mrs. Shahin?" says Jalen.

Mom must see hope rising in my face, because she says: "Thank you, hon. It's handled. You just get yourself to school, mm?" She grabs my elbow and we walk.

The Raptor lurks after us, tires *shhk*-ing in the rain.

Go! Just go! I will. But Cole's voice cracks over the drizzle. "That the Honda back there—the one sitting—uh—on top of a yield sign?"

We stop. The windshield wipers sploosh water onto Mom's pants. "We've got help on the way, Cole."

"You sure?" asks Jalen at the same time Cole asks, "Ew, Ma, what's on your chin—?"

"Just go! *PLEASE!*" I scream—no, *implore* it with the ferocity of a Shakespearean actress. Jalen's elbow hits the horn, double startling us all.

After mistaking the windshield washer for the blinker, Jalen guns the Raptor. Rap music blares at the next stop sign.

Jalen's stunned face replays like a GIF in my head. *Scare your crush to death, Mafi. That'll work.*

I haven't said more than two words to the guy in years. When Jalen used to come over, he and Raf would plunder the pantry and take their spoils upstairs to Raf's bedroom, the floor glittering with Pop-Tarts cellophane and chip bags. Meowgi took care of any crumb-age.

I open my mouth to ask Mom why we couldn't hitch a ride but she swoops in: "Because you can't rely on men to save you, that's why."

"So walking in the rain is better—?"

Mom's voice fights the downpour. "You've got to learn to take care of yourself, Mafi."

We walk the rest of the way without speaking, me shuffling ten steps behind this impossibly proud, proud woman I call my mother.

———

When I finally do get to the white-brick manor that is SMN, there's a hubbub in the hall. A mob blocks my locker, moving slowly through the corridor. Over the uproar, Principal Bugle's nasally voice shouts: "Now wait just one second, Ms. Rossi—!"

The crowd parts and there's Brit Rossi, skipping backward, flipping the bird. Her eyes are narrowed in bold cat-eye makeup. *TRANNY* blazes across her chest in glitter.

She passes Fallon, open-mouthed. He slams his locker door and mumbles something, maybe a prayer. Or a curse. Either way, it's the confirmation I needed.

Brit would stick it to Fallon like that. Flip the script.

"Off—take it off this instant!" yells Principal Bugle, bald head speckled with red and white.

Brit shrugs, crisscrosses her arms, and grabs the bottom of her shirt. Principal Bugle dives in front of her. Brit laughs. "I wasn't actually going to do it, Principal B."

With an eye roll, she follows Principal Bugle's crooked finger to his office.

7

FALLON WILL be Ghosted for his crimes against Brit at Josefina's Halloween party. Saturday.

I've got five days to figure out his punishment. Right now, it's one of my four favorite parts of the day, each correlating to the times I see Jalen. After he's got gym is my second favorite, because his arms are extra veiny. I mean, my god. Veiny arms are a thing.

There he is.

Hot-pink pants. Teal shirt. Red Jordans. A candy choker necklace and a longer metal chain behind it, a gold bullet hanging on the end. Jalen can pull off anything. Except the beard he attempts to grow every month. The last few days it's looked like he's got pubes growing from his face. He's shaved today, thank god.

"What's good?" Jalen says, chewing on the necklace.

He doesn't say it to me, of course. To his teammate Tommy Lewis, and they do the fist-bumpy-slappy-snappy-whatever handshake athletes do.

Jalen's easy to spot not only because he's tall. He and Tommy Lewis are the only two Black students at SMN. The city where we live, Rancho Santa Margarita, basically consists of sixty+ white men and their golf carts, so Jalen stands out in town, too.

I'm in Jalen's Dolce & Gabbana slipstream. Well, it's more a drip than a stream. His pace is relaxed, with a cool up nod to teammates and a respectful down nod to teachers. Jalen's not a walk and scroller like the rest of us.

I envision swinging my arms around his middle from behind, calling him some nickname—maybe Pookie. Or something less cringey.

My hand would probably cling to his back. The 91 on his shirt's all wet. Shower sweats—must've been a hard workout.

Tommy says something and Jalen laughs, and when he turns I see it's the smile that shows the bejeweled canine tooth. He went to Germany last summer to see his mom and the dudes there had an *accent tooth*, a diamond stud glued on.

Jalen would've gotten a nose piercing or two like Dennis Rodman, but I know for a fact he's afraid of needles.

I pass the entrance to the girls' bathroom on the second floor, the local watering hole for all the gossips at Santa Margarita North. *It* is there—with Josefina, her best friend. With Josefina's big butt and *It*'s fashion sense and sewing skills, it's no wonder they're the most popular, well-dressed girls in school. I even overheard the gym teacher asking *It* for wedding dress alteration advice.

Okay, yes, *It* has a name.

Bian Hoa.

She's a senior, like Rafi. Last year, when she was a junior and I was a freshman, Jalen made the half-court shot at the pep rally. Bian kissed Jalen in front of the whole school. Rafi told me that was Jalen's first kiss.

He didn't need to tell me. I knew.

Bian didn't care about Jalen. She's the type that needs to be liked. Needs to be seen.

Jalen blabbered about Bian to Rafi for *months* after that. I'd hear them through the wall, laughing, talking, swiping through her Instagram. When Rafi was put on the radar as this star ball player, Bian freeloaded on his success like a suckerfish hitching a ride on a sexy new shark. Like a fraying rubber band, Jalen couldn't really hold it together. Stopped wearing colorful Jordans for like three months and coming around as much.

It, Raf's Iago, continues to spin lies in his ear so that she. Remains. His. Everything.

Jalen's fine now. He bought rainbow Jordans the other week.

I pass Fallon and our eyes meet. It's like I've taken one of Baba's niacin pills by accident again because my cheeks flare with a prickly flush. I know Fallon's secret, how he deserted Brit at Black Star Canyon.

"All in good time, my love," I murmur when he passes, a promise. Niacin now tickling my ears, I see Brit Rossi at her locker, staring at me. Today, she's wearing pigtails, pearls, and hoop earrings. She looks away.

Can she read minds? Does she know?

"Hey, Jay-Jay!" Bian yells.

I stifle the urge to bark at her; she's already a damn tick on my brother's neck.

No, Bian's not a cheerleader. Tennis captain. Cheerleaders are out and athletes are in, apparently. Someone posted some TikTok in Michigan and it became this thing. Amazing how something so small can completely change the name of the game. Some girls even quit cheer. Social media is powerful.

It pushes past me. Her tan leather backpack whaps me in the shoulder. Then she goes, "Nice job with the yield sign, CJ," and flounces off before I can say anything. I *knew* I saw her BMW this morning.

I hate her.

I hate hate hate her.

Especially when her hand's at the small of Jalen's back—

What in the actual f—?

I narrowly miss running into Principal Bugle. "I'm fine," I say to his hairy crossed arms. "I mean—sorry."

8

MY CRUSH on Jalen is age-old.

Age ten, to be exact. He and Raf had been on the same basketball team growing up and were instant friends. Sometimes, if Mom had a client at the house (before she opened her salon), she'd ask Raf to let me tag along to Rose Park while they shot around.

Raf was always trying to shake me. Once, I used the restroom by the courts and when I came out, the boys were gone. A hollow tingly feeling settled into my calves. Did I even remember the way home?

I called for my brother inside the boy's restroom. When only my own voice echoed back, I started to cry.

That's when Jalen came out of hiding from behind the facilities. "Raf!" he hollered. "It ain't funny no more!"

I tried to stop blubbering but couldn't. Until Jalen put an arm around me and told me, again and again, that I was all right. Feeling his touch, I was suddenly more focused on jump-starting my delighted heart than this *silly crying business*.

Raf emerged, huffy Jalen had prematurely blown the prank. A flicker of concern crossed his face when he saw my puffy eyes until he spotted Jalen's arm hanging over my shoulder.

Jalen walked by my side the whole way home. Raf was his usual ten steps ahead.

———

It has come over every night this week.

On Wednesday, I'd taken a bubble bath and returned to my room only to be subjected to her annoying TV show commentary, like *OMG, NO!* and *Wait, who is she again?* And the worst—*Teehee, Rafi, stop!*—on the other side of the wall.

On Thursday, I was standing on my bed, about to reach up to the vent to reread Brit's note, when I caught a swish of glossy black hair beyond my door. It's hard to relax with Baba's rubab music, Mom's loud soap operas, and Rafi's video games in this house as it is. Now I've got to worry about an evil spy, too? I'm not about that *keep your friends close but your enemies closer* crap. I need me a can of *It*-repellant.

School feels less chaotic than home. At school, I can see Jalen. Daydream about Jalen. And . . . talk to Jalen?

No. Never talk.

It's Friday, the day before Halloween and Josefina's party, and my favorite part of the day: AP Anatomy and Physiology. Not only because it's the last period of the day.

Jalen's in it with me.

Or—I guess—I'm in it with him. I did so well on my placement tests freshman year they put me in with the upperclassmen.

Even though I'm missing the parade of costumes in the hall between periods, I get to class early because Jalen's at the whiteboard doing his postgame analysis with Tommy. Mr. A doesn't mind. Dressed in a vampire cape, he's playing phone games with his feet up on his desk.

The *athletes are stupid* stereotype is just that. A stereotype. Jalen shows Tommy a video of Rodman explaining the Bulls' triangle offense and from what I can hear, it requires some insane basketball IQ.

Tommy only seems half-interested. His nose is hidden in another steamy romance novel, the type of corny stuff Grandma used to hide in her sewing kit. This week, it's *Sense and Sensuous.* I swear, the dude flies through a new one every week.

Jalen backhands Tommy across the chest, like *pay attention!* and Tommy snaps his book shut and crosses his arms like *proceed!* I love watching Tommy and Jalen because they've got this nonverbal language that cracks me up.

As Rodman's talking, Tommy goes, "*Damn*, that dude. Wish he wasn't friends with a dictator."

Jalen says, "For real," then, "That shit's got me torn."

I'd like to say I gawk at Jalen from the back of class and am so distracted I get bad grades or whatever, but that's just not me. I love anything STEM. I love expounding the processes that make up our everyday lives, things we use every day and take for granted. Like how the hip's a ball-and-socket joint. *I just got chills.* That's why you can go three-sixty with it. The shoulder, too.

But I *do* watch Jalen when class begins, his gold-polished nails drumming the desk to some silent beat, winking in the sunlight that streams from the ceiling-to-floor windows.

You can tell Mr. A's got kids because he starts class by telling some dad joke about vampires. We all groan, but we secretly like his jokes. We're not five minutes into the lecture about free radicals when Fallon McElroy disrupts class.

"So, carpenter McElroy," Mr. A says. Fallon's tossing his pencil into the air at the back of the room. He's trying to lodge it in the ceiling. "Can you tell me what a free radical is?"

"Pass, Mr. A."

"There are no passes in life."

I bubble-circle *free radicals* in my notebook, waiting for Fallon's response.

"How about breaking down the words to glean some meaning," says Mr. A, vampire cape flapping around his shins. "Though this is A&P, folks, when in doubt, it's smart to go at it from a linguistics standpoint. So"—he underlines <u>FREE RADICALS</u> on the board—"what does *free* bring to mind?"

Fallon sits for a moment, mouth open.

Free . . . means cruising in Jalen's Raptor, window open, one of his hands on the wheel and the other inching toward mine . . .

"I dunno, not being imprisoned in class, for one," says Fallon.

Mr. A writes *untethered to an institution* next to *free*.

"And *radical*?" Mr. A goes on.

"Afghanistan," says Fallon, and I sink into my seat. Jalen's jaw tenses. Tommy gives him a look like, *Here we go again.*

Mr. A removes his glasses and rubs his eyes. "I'm losing patience, Mr. McElroy."

"I'm just saying," says Fallon, "like radical Islam."

"Or like—a radical idea?" says Brit from the front row, shooting Fallon a look.

"You've brought up an interesting point, both of you," says Mr. A, to which Fallon rolls his eyes. "The word *radical* itself is negatively charged, mm?"

So is the word *Afghanistan*, I think. Or the phrase *Allahu Akbar*, which simply means *God is great*. A phrase used to celebrate life.

"The hope and future of the U.S., of the world, even—lies with its radicals. Those who think outside the box and *believe what they say*. Look at history. The suffragettes, at the time, many thought them destructive to the social order. Universal health care . . . there's a radical idea, yes? Some would argue it's a basic human right! People fear those who go against the grain, who are agents for change. Who *think*. But radicalism is the only path toward liberation. Toward freedom, yes?"

"So you're saying you're cool with terrorists bombing the U.S.?" says Fallon.

A chair screeches and I feel it in my teeth. "Mr. A, for real?" says Jalen, standing. "Enough with this fool."

"Mr. McElroy," says Mr. A, gesticulating kindly for Jalen to sit. "Hall. Now."

I'm only a sophomore, but I swear, Mr. A is on the U.S. President Aging Track. Every month, his salt-and-pepper hair recruits more salt.

Here's a radical idea: Teachers deserve better pay.

Fallon follows Mr. A out the door. His voice echoes from the hall, something about how *vampires don't wear capes*, that he knows 'cause he was an extra on *Blood Jurors*.

"Every goddamn time," says Tommy in Mr. A's absence, and Jalen's *tshh-tshh-tshh* laugh makes me swoon. Fallon brings up that he was on the show every day.

A minute later, Mr. A returns without Fallon. "Moving on," he says, voice still taut with reprimand. He scans the class. "Book away, Mr. Lewis."

Tommy had cracked open *Sense and Sensuous* in Mr. A's short absence.

"The scientific definition of *free radical* is that it is *a highly reactive and unstable molecule that can damage cells in the body*. Interestingly enough, we still feel *radical*'s negative connotation here, don't we, evidenced by the words *highly reactive*, *unstable*, and *damage*? Back in the early twentieth century, anti-suffragists, both men and women, thought the suffragettes unstable molecules of a sort that threatened to do damage to society, a society where gender roles were concrete. In fact, in 1905 many suffragettes began to break windows, handcuff themselves to railings, and went on hunger strikes to garner a public response. Fast-forward a few decades to the fifties and sixties to the Civil Rights Movement, where Black women arranged sit-ins, marches, and grassroots campaigns, and fought sexism and racism while under the thumb of the patriarchy . . . All free radicals in their own right, wouldn't you say?"

There are a few indistinct murmurs.

"So. From the reading, name some free radical–generating substances."

"Pollutants, pesticides, smoke, and alcohol," says Jalen, twirling his pencil.

"And what, then, *neutralizes* a free radical?"

"White men in Rancho Santa Margarita over the age of sixty," says Brit.

Everyone laughs.

"*Antioxidants,*" I blurt, subconsciously emboldened by Brit's comment. I *never* answer Mr. A's questions. Whenever I raise my hand, my mind goes blank when he finally calls on me.

Don't get red.

Don't turn into a gojeh farangi.

DON'T!

"Exactly, Ms. Shahin," Mr. A says. Then adds, "Rafi's sister!" and claps his hands like teachers do when they remember I'm related to the Prodigal Brother.

Someone across the room whispers, "I thought her name was CJ?" Brit shushes them. I flip up my hood—for two seconds before Mr. A signals for me to remove it.

"Mr. A," says Tommy, saving me from further humiliation, "tryna put two and two together, but what's women voters gotta do with science?"

"Pathways, Mr. Lewis," answers Mr. A, looking pleased with himself. "Pathways! I want you all to *think.* Now you'll have a pathway to the term, and one rooted in history, at that. I dare you to forget the definition."

Bzz. Bzz.

Our phones vibrate with the bell's dismissal.

In class, we answer surveys with our phones, play interactive educational games with our phones, and are dismissed by them, too. Seems Principal Bugle's given up on the no-phones rule.

Mr. A yells over the chatter. "Two paragraphs on free radicals due online by end of day. You're free! Go be radicals! Change the world—no pressure! And for ghoul's sake, come back alive on Monday, okay? Safety first!"

Mr. A gives Brit a stealthy low five on her way out. At the door, Brit stops and winks. At me.

9

WHEN I get home from school, our pastry chef neighbor, Cam, with his loud, yappy, floofy dogs, is on our doorstep. Dad's American flag whips Cam in the face and his dogs go wild when he punches the fabric.

"Ogh—gah!" He breaks free. "Found this in the trash again—*shut up, you three!*" Cam shouts over the barking. He's got a crumpled *Wiggs for Mayor!* campaign sign in his hand. "I know it's your grandpa. I *know* it's him."

I'd heard a yelp coming from Cam's lawn at 4:00 a.m. when the sprinklers started up. I thought it was a coyote till I saw the crumpled sign on one end of Cam's yard and Baba on the other, shrinking to the back of our house like a wet spider.

The curtain swishes. Dad's watching, a mug of black tea steaming in his hand.

Cam's eyes follow mine but the XL American flag curls, shrouding Dad's face. The flag's Dad's dream catcher for ICE. They can't take away his American dream.

It's Dad's usual post, that spot. He's always watching. Waiting.

Waiting for what, I dunno. From the look on Dad's face, something bad. Something worse than Cam.

Unlike Dad, who's mostly broody and quiet, Baba takes after old Afghan men: Opinions galore. In Kabul, he was some governor or something, so he's got lots to say about how the U.S. is run. He's not shy when it comes to stealing lawn signs from the neighbors, either. Baba hates Wiggs because of his anti-refugee sentiments.

There's a lot of heat on Wiggs because he's been accused of sexual assault. Didn't even deny it. Said it was a different time, he was a kid and that's what kids do. I'm fifteen and know not to grab my classmates between the legs.

Ghosting classmates is fun and all, but a part of me wishes I could go bigger. Stick it to someone seriously vile.

What I'd give to Ghost a big fish like him one day.

"Must be the djinn," I tell Cam with a shrug. That's Baba's response whenever something unexplainable happens.

"What was that?"

"Djinn," I say slowly. "Evil spirits. They grab your ankles on the stairs."

"*Tchh.*" Cam stalks off, his dogs jumping at their leashes.

As I unlock the door, a gust of wind catches the flag and it nudges me inside. I swear the flag's working Home Security for Dad—

—who rounds the corner as soon as I'm in, slurping his tea.

"School?" He's asking if it was a good day.

"Fine, Padar."

I bend to take off my shoes. Dad hovers.

Something about my relationship with Dad feels formal, like I'm in a display case at the store and he's observing me through the glass. Attempting to find a flaw, a reason not to take me home.

The Quran's out, on the side table.

Before Baba moved in, it used to live in the storage bench with the shoes. Once, Baba asked why the pages smelled like cheese and I had to excuse myself to my bedroom to laugh it off.

I still see him sniff it now and then, hairy nose wrinkled.

Even though Baba spends most of his octogenarian existence preaching in the YMCA Jacuzzi, he's what I'd consider a *conditional Muslim*.

He skips most of the events. Like Ramadan. And he prays namaz once or twice a week instead of five times a day. He used to go to the Sufi Center until someone pissed him off and now he only goes every once in a while.

And Dad stopped going after an Afghan told him he was a traitor for "marrying white." When the man started popping up on Dad's Facebook suggestions, he was convinced the man was out to murder us all.

I close the bench and Dad stalks off, American Eagle jeans popping.

Dad's my guarded guardian. *Guarded* 'cause I can never tell what he's thinking. And *guardian* because he's removed, somehow. A stand-in parent.

Two things are clear about my father: One, he's super sus of other Afghans. Two, he's adamant we "Act American, look American."

Maybe it has to do with some story Mom told me when I was younger. How some guys followed him home when he first arrived in the U.S. Nipped at his heels with their car bumper, laughing, so he'd walk faster.

That's probably when he started to dress differently. No perahan, and he never let his beard grow. Started to buy stuff from stores with *American* in the name, like American Eagle or American Apparel.

I don't have the heart to tell him the clothes are for people Cole's age.

Dad's "Act American, look American" doesn't fly *inside* the Shahin home, an explosion of reds, maroons, and golds. And you can't miss the abrasive elderly Afghan in his perahan tunban, pakol hat, and thick leather shoes, sleeping with his mouth open so wide you can see the gold fillings in the back.

"Baba, you're a badass," I whisper into the old man's ear, backpack tugging my shoulder as I bend to kiss his cheek.

10

IT'S HALLOWEEN. Saturday, the night of the party.

Mom and I are putting dinner on the table. Raf's just back from a run. Since the NBA prioritizes speed and shooting accuracy over muscles and size, Coach G has assigned Rafi extra running homework.

Raf's pretending to help but he's picked up and put down the same plate three times. Probably busy messaging *It*.

"Watch what you post on that social media," Dad says, peering behind him. Raf jumps at Dad's sudden appearance. "Anyone on the globe can read what you post."

"Sorry, Padar." Raf pockets his phone at lightning speed.

Raf is different around Dad. On tenterhooks and desperate for his approval. We learned the term in psych: Raf has a father complex. Or was it father hunger?

Dad uses the alias Sam Hill for his Facebook account. He likes it for the math groups.

When Dad walks into the kitchen, Mom doesn't acknowledge him. On the weekends, it's hard not to notice how separate Mom's and Dad's days are. Dad spends them on the deck, reading, or in his room, napping. They used to go for coffee on Saturday mornings, but that stopped after Baba moved in. I avoid asking Dad questions if I can. He's like a glass pan left on top of a hot stove: Any second, he could explode.

All of us have learned to let him be. Except Baba, who doesn't mind having one-sided conversations. He'll keep trying. Talking.

I really do wonder what goes on in Dad's head.

At the stove, Dad tends to the Kabuli pulao: rice, carrots, cinnamon, beef or lamb, and—*erk*—raisins. I prefer my rice without cinnamon and squishy raisins. But it does flood the house with a homey aroma.

I overhear Dad tell Mom he wanted Pizza Hut, and she huffs and tells him Kabuli's what Baba wanted. Dad prefers American food.

I remember Bian's fingers at Jalen's back, and ask Rafi: "Trouble in paradise?"

"None of your business, Gozeh Farangi." He tosses the plate.

One of my brother's nicknames for me. *Gozeh* Farangi instead of Gojeh Farangi, which roughly translates to *foreign fart*.

"Son Rafi—my Kush Giant!"

Baba shuffles into the room in a flurry of wispy hair that lags as he walks, gold rings with red rubies, and a sheet of paper. Baba started saying the Kush thing after Raf grew. The Hindu Kush mountains surround Kabul and Baba says giants live in the peaks. *Kush* means *Killer*. So Raf's just a Killer Giant, which he sort of is, if you see the way he plays ball.

Baba moved in after Grandma died last year. I think that's why Mom and Dad spend a lot of time parked in the driveway, arguing. They think I don't see them but I do. Meowgi does, too.

Baba claps a liver-spotted hand onto Rafi's shoulder and says heartily, "Do some math for your baba, mm?" Baba likes to refer to himself in the third person. "Solve something."

Baba places the paper onto the tablecloth. And his Diet Coke.

"Maybe later, Baba."

Mom puts a basket of hot Afghan naan onto Baba's paper. "Rafi, how many times do I have to ask you to keep your things upstairs? Every time I clean, they find their way—"

"It's mine, You." That's Baba's name for my mom. *You* or *Hey You*. Doesn't sound kind, but it's actually said with affection. For many years, she was "the American." Grandma's name for Mom. Among others.

"Rafi was about to show Baba some math," Baba says.

Baba's never asked *me* to do math for him.

"That's nice," says Mom in a tone for toddlers, one of forced patience.

"Gojeh Farangi," says Baba, "why don't you help Hey You with the dinner, mm? And watch the Kabuli—so it doesn't burn."

Baba has a lot to say about the way Mom cooks rice. Before he moved in, it was basmati rice and Crisco. Afghans take poorly cooked rice as a personal insult.

The doorbell rings and Dad, staring longingly at a frozen pizza, closes the freezer. Dad despises Halloween.

"I'll get it." I grab the bucket of candy next to the Quran. I wanted to get the Kit Kat, Butterfinger, and Snickers mix, but

Dad insisted on the jumbo bag of Tootsie Rolls since they were five bucks cheaper.

I open the door.

"Trick or treat!" three ninja princesses shriek.

"Sweeties." Baba squeezes in front of me and squints into each young face. "You know, where Baba comes from, there is no Halloween. Baba and his brother, Habib, used to poke at real bones in graves—"

The girls wail and book it to their mom, who's on the sidewalk talking on her phone.

Dinner chat goes as per usual. Grades. Assignments. Who was in Mom's salon that day. Baba tears into his meatballs like a wolf, yogurt and sauce decorating his stubbled jowls. I don't like sitting next to Baba. I'm in the splash zone.

Every time there's a trick-or-treater, I've gotta convince Baba not to follow and dish out one of his stories, which he argues *is* a *treat*.

Dad tells me the bill to fix the old Honda was one grand. Luckily, the mechanic's in Baba's water aerobics class, so he gave Dad a discount. Dad says I'll work it off with chores. I don't ask him the final cost—I just nod and hope I won't be doing chores till I'm thirty.

The phone rings and I get it so Mom doesn't have to.

Only old people call the landline. And bots.

The line's crackly. It sounds like the man on the other end's calling from 1920 or something.

"Baba," I say, "for you."

———

Baba wipes his mouth on the tablecloth. He's shouting into the receiver in Farsi, but he's not angry. Afghans are loud by default.

When Baba's done, I switch off the phone. He always forgets.

Baba looks at me like he's just noticed I exist. "Like gold," he says, patting my blond head. "You know, fair Afghans— no phenomenon. They just don't fit this Yankee stereotype of *those people over there*. Some are blond like Gojeh, or redheaded with the pickles"—Baba taps his face; he means *freckles*—"especially those from Nuristan."

Raf nudges me with his elbow and whispers, "Postman's kid" into my ear. I stomp his foot. Mom and Dad are too busy having some nonverbal exchange to notice.

"And how is Habib?" Dad asks Baba after a moment. Under the light of the chandelier, the dent that splits Dad's forehead down the middle is pronounced. It does that whenever Baba's brother, Habib, calls.

"Habib found his neighbor," Baba says, voice scratchy like corn husk, "by the road."

Whenever Habib calls, a new guest sits silently at the table, skeletal fingers folded. The Grim Reaper. News of Afghanistan always carries with it news of loss.

And behind news of loss lurks survivor's guilt. Felt by Baba. Felt by Dad. Felt by Mom and us kids, too.

Baba's brother is a farmer just outside of Kabul. His wife, Yasmoon, a singer.

She was, at least.

Habib calls whenever he can, and *wherever* he can, and always with a different Skype number.

When I was five, Habib visited. Rafi took to him, but I thought he smelled funny, like burning wax. He told us mythical stories about djinn, giants, and scorpions and made us shirpera, Afghan milk fudge.

Before Kabul was taken by Talibs, Baba was arranging a visa for Habib and Yasmoon so they could relocate to the U.S. The problem was, he had to convince them, first. They refused to leave Afghanistan's pristine mountains, cobalt-blue lakes, wildlife, culture, food.

It was *home*. And for the moment, there was peace. Habib repeated: *As long as the U.S. is here, brother, we are safe.*

But the base was active one day. Vacant the next. The troops vanished overnight.

When the Taliban closed the borders and grounded all flights, Baba hit the C-sharp on the piano so hard it snapped. It's still muted when you play it.

"Even though Afghanistan dropped from news headlines after a week, Baba will *never* forget how America turned its back on the Afghan people." He makes a fist. "Never. For two decades, they promised peace, democracy, education, music, humanity, a life for the girls, and then"—he waves his hand, like, *poof*—"left them to the dogs."

"What happened to Habib's neighbor?" Raf asks.

"He was a Hazara." That's all he has to say. Baba says the Taliban have been systematically killing Hazaras for years. Ethnic cleansing. Since Hazaras are Shia and not Sunni, in the Taliban's eyes, they're heretics.

Outside, an Amazon delivery truck beeps in front of Cole's. Maybe a new PlayStation. Mr. Dawicki compensates for his late nights at the office by buying Cole stuff.

"So, Gojeh," Baba says, after the truck drives off, "tell your baba what you've learned."

He means school. That it's Saturday doesn't matter. Baba's always demanding to know what we're learning.

"We—I guess we learned about free radicals."

"Aha. And what did you learn about this free radical?"

Rafi's texting under the table, smirking. Damn Bian.

"It's a highly reactive and unstable molecule that can damage cells in the body. Short-lived—but destructive."

"A disruption. An illness."

"The science term, yes. But we need radical people and ideas to change the world for the better. Like the suffragettes."

Mom says, "Agreed, Mama," and lifts her glass.

Baba tears his naan and a nigella seed tumbles onto my napkin. In the silence that follows, I flick the seed in his direction.

Shooting a dirty look at Mom's wineglass, Baba goes, "Rafi, give your baba some examples."

Rafi starts and looks up from his phone. He rubs his forehead, exhaling. He took Mr. A's class last year.

"Eh, air pollutants, pesticides, alcohol—all can create free radicals in the body."

"Phone, son," says Dad, and Raf pockets it with a "Sorry, Padar."

"You know"—and Baba glances once more at Mom—"alcohol itself isn't haram, but once it trickles down the throat—"

Haram. Sinful. *Good Muslims* abstain from wine and pork. But Mom was raised in Michigan by atheists, so she pours herself another glass of wine. "Have you read the study, Baba, about Diet Coke and dementia?"

"*Emily,*" Dad warns.

"Where are you going?" Mom says. Rafi's gathering his plate and glass. Mom sounds more jealous than anything else.

"I've got plans with Bian."

"Bian Ho, Bian Ho," chants Baba, in his own world.

"Bian *Hoa,*" corrects Rafi.

I get up, and the same question's fired at me by not one, but all three adults.

"I've got plans, too."

With? all their faces prompt.

Truth is, I've got to blackmail Raf before he leaves. I need an invite to this party to Ghost Fallon. And to, maybe, see Jalen.

"Whoever with," says Dad, "no." I freeze.

"But"—my throat constricts—"I didn't mean to crash the car—"

"And yet," says Dad, shoulders frozen mid-shrug, "you must learn the value of owning a vehicle."

"Padar is right," says Raf, sitting down. He leans back with his arms crossed. I think he's returned just to have a front row seat for my sentencing. I wanna smack the smug look off his face.

"Your daughter crashed the car?" Baba sticks out his gummy bottom lip. "This is news to Baba—"

"Mafi crashed the Honda," Mom says. "We told you yesterday, Baba."

Every muscle in my body tenses, restraining the words *It's not fair!* Rafi, with his basketball scholarship. His girlfriend with the perfect hair. And just generally having a penis, which means he's co-master of the house.

The furnace roars against the nape of my neck. *Why does Baba insist on cooking us in this infernal house?!*

"Rafi's having sex with Bian!" I blurt.

The room deflates like a balloon.

With a sweeping eye roll, Rafi slams his head on the table like a big baby.

On top of his dirty fork.

Shrieking, he tugs it from his forehead. Baba unearths a dirty handkerchief from his pocket but Mom's there first, dabbing blood and tomato sauce from Rafi's four-pronged skin with her napkin. Baba mumbles he'll get "the paste," the green one from his stinky mason jar collection. He says it will stop the bleeding. Mom shouts, "Pressure will do!" but Baba's already creaking his way to his lair.

Mom cradles Rafi's head, though one eye's on the vacuum in the corner, wishing to escape to her Geometric Daulatabad Dimension of Denial.

She can't drown the noise now.

Dingdong-dingdong-dingdong! goes the doorbell. Three frenzied goblins wave their pumpkin buckets at the door.

"NO!" screams Dad. "ENOUGH! GO AWAY!"

Then he points a finger at me. Takes off his glasses, so I know he means business. His dark brown eyes narrow, eyebrow hair curling over his lashes.

"You're excused," he says, voice taut.

Those two words mean I'm excused from all happy things in life. Like the party. Completing Ghost duties. Showing Jalen I exist—and not just as *Rafi's sis.*

11

ALL RAFI got was *the talk*, which lasted a whole five minutes. I know because I was listening, empty glass sandwiched between my ear and the wall.

But I did hear Rafi woofing about something. If Raf can't go to the party tonight, I can't, either. I should've thought everything through.

There's a *thwump* at my window and a hiss. Nutter Butter the squirrel skitters across the roof in circles. Mr. Meowgi's furry face is smushed against the glass, a low vowel-less *rrwrr* emanating somewhere in the recess of his throat.

Weird day to be envious of a squirrel, free on his tree, living his best life.

———

Later that evening, the garage door judders shut and the car pulls from the drive. Nutter Butter jumps onto the tree and watches with Meowgi and me as my parents, dressed smartly in scarves and suits, *euuuu* down the street in the Tesla like a quiet spaceship. I think that's why parents get electric cars. To sneak up on, and away from, their kids.

Rafi doesn't knock; the door's nearly kicked down with his Titan foot.

"You screwed me, you know."

"No, that's Bian."

His fork wound's still bubbling green with Baba's paste. It stinks like the algae growing on the Santa Ana River.

I stifle a laugh. I want to tell him sorry but jabbing at him is easier.

Raf takes up the whole room like that gray wizard in that nerdy movie he likes to watch. The one who keeps bonking his head on wood banisters.

I take a guess. "Calm down, Ganondorf."

"*Gandalf*," he says. "Ganondorf's in *Zelda*." He peers into my vanity mirror and goes, "Damnit, I'm Frankenstein."

"*Frankenstein's monster.*"

He jeers, flops onto my computer chair, and spins around.

"Where're Mom and Dad going?" I ask.

"To Monterey for the night."

"What? Why?"

"It's their anniversary tomorrow."

"Oh." My stomach sinks. Usually I do something nice for them the morning of. Like waffles or something. Maybe spending the weekend together for once will do them some good.

Mom and Dad's wedding pictures are in the peeling photo album in the attic. Mom doesn't bring them out because they remind her *life is constantly changing*, whatever that means.

They got married at some country club up north. Dad thought it'd be cool to have jack-o'-lanterns line the walkway. It was a nice idea until Grandma's skirt caught fire.

Baba snapped a photo and blamed the mishap on the djinn. Ironically, Grandma burned the photo after Baba kept showing people who came around to dinner.

"So what's your punishment?" I ask.

Rafi shrugs.

"Nothing?"

He's calculating. He gives me the look like when he's hooping and the other team's running at him and he's gotta make a choice—where to pass; at what angle to shoot—basketball's all about math.

"They said I can't go to Josefina's party tonight. That I need to . . . *take a long hard look at my future.* Dad's threatening to pull me out of basketball again."

Raf stares at me and I know what he wants. I'm no ball player but I used to run track; I'm two steps ahead.

"So. You know if you don't bring me to this party, I'll sell you out."

Heads cocked, we have a stare-off.

We're both thinking about *the party*. Annalie's party.

For one year, we've made a point of not discussing it. After he called in that noise complaint, there was no big blowout. I knew if we fought, he'd just go snitch to Mom and Dad. Or worse, Kate, and I'd have to hear my sister's favorite cautionary tale about Gina: the most popular girl in her year, who "went wild" after graduation. They found Gina under a bridge on the Santa Ana River. Overdose.

"No drinking," Raf says warily, "and you'll be home by eleven."

"But—"

"We leave at nine forty-two. Baba will be asleep by then."

Forty-two. Such a Rafi response. "Fine."

"And you're walking in ten seconds after me."

"Fine. Wouldn't want to be trampled by your groupies. Or shame you."

He makes a face. "Not ashamed of you. But you're *Mafia*, and things have a way of going wrong when you're around. Stuff gets blurted. Yield signs get knocked over . . ."

And people get what's coming to them.

But that part's on purpose.

———

Fallon's punishment was born out of the four-pronged-fork wound on Rafi's forehead.

Baba's green paste that stops bleeding—it also has pretty *shitty* side effects. I know because Baba left it out once and Jalen dared Rafi to eat it. Raf didn't come out of the bathroom for two hours. It's all natural, made from some Afghan plant, so I'm not worried it'll kill Fallon or anything.

It's not like I'm leaving Fallon to the mountain lions, like he did Brit.

———

"Why do you like Bian, anyway?"

The car's in neutral—engine off. Me and Raf coast to the end of our street before he starts it up.

Rafi's wearing an Enes Freedom jersey, green and black, with a white headband. The basketball team's pretty unoriginal, going as their favorite NBA players. But Enes means something to Raf. He's this Turkish guy who also plays center and is all about human rights.

Raf fires the engine and winces.

The Honda's fixed but Dad refused to replace the belt that screeches like a pterodactyl when it's first turned on. The 'rents get the stealthy Tesla. We get the screeching Ptero car. We can't risk waking Baba.

Once the screeching fizzles out, Raf says, "I dunno, Mafia. There's more to Bian than you think. She's got a good heart." He waits a beat before adding, "She's applying to IU, too."

"NO!"

"Mafia."

Soon, Raf'll be off to Indiana University. Some sweaty dude came to the door in a red shirt smelling of chili dog and basically kissed my brother's feet to get him to commit.

Mom was thrilled. But Dad? A son in the spotlight was the last thing he wanted. Wants. Dad wants Raf to go to UCI, but Raf says IU is one of the best D1 schools.

And Baba, well. He pulled the scout into the kitchen by the elbow and explained his grandson's prospects were brighter as a mathematician. Then he offered him a stale walnut from his pocket.

"I swear to god you can do better than her! Don't let her— trail you to Indiana. It's bad enough that—" I pause.

"That—?"

"You're leaving, too."

By now, I should be used to That Hermit Life. Who cares if the librarian puckers his face like *aw, sweetie* when I spend lunch period studying by his desk? Sophomore year, finding a new crew . . . let's just say nobody's taking applications. CJ wouldn't get past the vetting.

As annoying as my siblings are, being the only kid in the house doesn't sound ideal, either. Mom's comment that I'll soon grow up and *leave her, too* . . . I can't be responsible for Mom's happiness like that.

"We all have our paths, Mafi." It's weird to hear Raf use my real name. "You'll find yours."

"And you think yours is basketball—and Bian?"

"Right now, yeah. And you need to accept that. We're siblings but we're gonna have our own lives. We're only under the same roof for childhood. That's it."

God, I hate how cool he is. I have the same squelchy feeling in my stomach like when Raf deserted me in the park. Or when I was four and Kate told me *we're too old to take baths together*, shutting the bathroom door in my face.

Raf stops off at the Golden Arches for dinner number two. He chucks me the grease-splotched bag with uneaten fries. Raf hates McDonald's fries and I love them. I wonder if he'll keep ordering the combo when he's in Indiana. If he'll just . . . toss the fries.

12

JOSEFINA'S HOUSE is at the end of the cul-de-sac in Sherwood. These are rich-people homes. Walls of glass. There's bass booming at least ten houses down.

Sherwood's famous for dishing out cash instead of candy on Halloween. When I was eleven, I cleaned up: forty-two dollars.

By the time Rafi parks behind a procession of svelte cars that look like they're from some Marvel movie, the time on the dash reads 9:50 p.m. "One hour," he says. "Then I'm driving you home."

"And then . . . ?"

"I'll come back."

I fwump back in my seat, but Raf's already out of the car. He holds up ten fingers to tell me to wait at least ten seconds, and is greeted by dudes chilling in a haze of skunk smoke on the lawn. Giving them the up nod, he walks inside.

A group of girls in glittery short dresses and cat ears walk by. Like gophers, every dude on the grass looks in turn.

I wore a dress like that to Annalie's party. It was the last time I wore a dress, actually. *I thought her name was CJ?* resounds in my head and my hands twist on my black sweats.

Maybe I'll just wait in the car till Raf gets back.

But then I see Brit Rossi in a red dress with checkers up the sleeves.

I'd kill for Brit's legs. And the defined tummy she flaunts on her socials, too. Brit's frowning at the Jeep that's just pulled up in front of the house. Fallon McElroy hops out, arm in arm with a brunette.

No. I place my hood over my head with resolve. *I've got a Ghosting to do.*

WHAM! Something makes impact with the trunk; I scream and hit the lock with my elbow.

Jalen.

He flips the white veil from his head. He's wearing gold Air Jordans, clip-on earrings, and a form-fitting wedding dress. He's Rodman, that one time he married himself.

"Rafi's sis?" His voice is muffled through the glass.

"Er—yeah," I shout through the closed window. Raf has the keys. I can't roll the window down.

"You Rafi's DD?"

"I'm not sixteen yet."

"But you've done driver's ed and all that?"

I nod eagerly, maybe too eagerly.

He crooks a finger. After fumbling with the lock, I take my time skirting around the car, ducking under tree branches, talking myself up. Jalen . . . *Jalen Frikken Thomas* is asking me out of the car. *I wonder what his real middle name is?*

Also, I hope I don't smell like fries.

"Where's Big Time Recruit at?" His breath—fruity and sour—rains on me. I wonder if he'd still be talking to me if he hadn't been drinking.

"Huh?"

"Your bro."

Jalen's so tall, I could rest my head on his chest standing up. The last time I stood *this* close to him was a few months ago when Rafi held a team meeting at the house. I was baking cookies and Jalen leaned over me to toss his empty protein shake into the recycling under the sink.

It made my night.

I nod toward the house. My tongue is useless and my heart's a drum.

"I heard a rumor, Rafi's sis."

I wince. Jalen looks both ways, then whispers in my ear: "They say . . . you a stone-cold killer."

"Wha—?"

"Yield signs, stop signs—even traffic cones—they're terrified when they see Shahin coming."

Relief floods me. I laugh. "The sign's back up now. It's aliiiive!" I say, and with jazz hands, for some reason. *What am I doing?*

He looks at my sweatpants and hoodie. "What're you supposed to be?"

"I, uh." I shrug. "I dunno."

"Well, imma raid the liquor cabinet. With a house like this, bet they've got the good stuff." He scratches his hair and his gold nails make that *ckk-ckk-ckk* noise against his scalp. I love the sound. "But imma make it quick, not a lot of sleep lately— and this Ghost stuff . . . only a matter of time till the next victim get theirs. That SOL tree, you seen it?"

I nod.

"It's got a vibe." He shudders. "Ever left a letter?"

"Um. When I was younger. Kate and I used to leave Wish Notes in the knot—for the fairies."

Jalen's eyebrows reach his hairline. "Fairies, huh?" He shifts his stance. "Not buzzed enough for this." But his furrowed brow tells me he's thinking of his next question. "So did your—shhhttt!"

Jalen gasps as he's tackled from behind with a "Boo!"

Tommy Lewis. He's cracking up and massaging Jalen's shoulders, telling him to chill.

Jalen clutches his heart. "Oh, I see, Tommy Lewis got jokes! Damn!" But there's still fear in his eyes.

"Think I was the Ghost?"

"Ain't playin' with this Ghost stuff," says Jalen. "You ever see *Becoming*?"

Jalen *hates* scary stuff. Especially ghosts. In the eighth grade, Raf hosted a sleepover. While the boys watched some horror movie in his room, I went downstairs to get a glass of water and found Jalen asleep in the living room. He'd pulled my teensy baby quilt from the back of the couch and draped it over his growing legs.

If possible, Jalen was even more beautiful asleep than awake. Something about his lips. The way they parted.

Jalen takes a step back, observing Tommy's Steph Curry jersey.

"Baby-faced assassin?" The diamond on Jalen's tooth winks in the moonlight.

Tommy says, "That's my boy!" then notices me and goes, "Hey, you that sophomore from A&P." It's not a question. Or a greeting.

"Rafi's sis." Jalen shoots Tommy a meaningful look. "And before you interrupted, we was having a friendly conversation."

My stomach flips. The Tommy buffer gave me a minute to breathe.

"All right," Tommy says, "but get your ass ready for flip cup. You move in that dress?"

"Better than Curry."

Tommy skips backward. "Cap and you know it!" Then he hollers at some devil on the lawn.

Jalen slaps his face, trying to jog his memory. "Uhhh. Fairies, right?"

I nod. "Fairies."

Jalen puts a long arm past me, on the car. His veins pop and I lean on Ptero for support. But then I think it's to block others—other people walking by—from seeing he's talking to me.

"That wish. The one you left for them fairies. It come true?"

I wish I was popular. I wish I was seen.

I swallow hard. "Yes."

Jalen nods. His mouth stays open when he thinks. A breeze fills me with D&G cologne and I'm giddy.

Frenzied hoots break the trance.

The devil's tail is on fire. Tommy's chasing him, shriek-laughing at him to *stop, drop, and roll!*

"Witching hour," mumbles Jalen. "You driving me home in thirty, Rafi's sis."

"But—"

He points a finger to hold me to it as he backs away. "Ten thirty . . . at the Raptor."

Dress tight around the ankles, Jalen shuffles up the path to inspect the devil. The fire's out, but his tail's smoking.

Jalen's truck is hopped up on the curb across the street.

Baba says whenever a man and a woman are alone together, the devil's the chaperone.

Alone in Jalen's truck? Haram.

13

RAF WILL kill me if I drive Jalen home. That's one scenario.

Or I'll get stopped by the police and Dad'll chain me to his workbench.

Maybe I'll wreck Jalen's truck and he'll hate me forever. But the Raptor will place me above traffic . . . that'll probably be easier to drive.

He asked *me*. No one else. Driving Jalen home would bring me that much closer to my goal.

My first kiss was with Blaine Rothstone at the movies. He tasted like Coke and pizza and his tongue felt scratchy, like Meowgi's when he licks my hand. I haven't talked to Sandpaper Tongue since.

Plus, a sophomore and a junior isn't unheard-of, though upperclassmen don't usually date younger. But I *will* be sixteen next week, driving and functional—basically an adult.

And Raf? He'll be gone next year anyway.

The answer is clear as I prowl through skunk smoke across the lawn, passing a Wiggs sign, into the foyer. I'm driving Jalen home. But first—

Ghost duties.

Rafi's in the kitchen talking with the rest of the Baller Crew, back against the counter all cool. Bian's taking selfies with two other tennis girls, using filters till they don't look like themselves anymore.

No one notices me in my hoodie, pulled low over my eyes.

"You!"

I turn and sidestep Fallon McElroy, dressed in a ski suit. God, I think that's what he wore as an extra on *Blood Jurors*.

He pushes past me, giving some dude a fist-bump hug. He fills a red SOLO cup with whatever's in the punch bowl. He takes a sip and almost chokes on a spindly veined toy eyeball, lobbing it back into the bowl.

The dude almost drank an eyeball. This'll be easier than I thought.

Fallon stumbles into the backyard, arm in arm with Josefina. They sit at the pool's edge.

I write *Wait thirty mins. Justice will be served* on a napkin and ram it into a drunk guy's chest.

"Hand this to the girl in the living room—the one in the red dress with the checkered sleeves." I incline my head toward Brit. "Don't say it's from me." I tug on his arm before he can walk away. "And tell her she looks beautiful." Because she does. I never could get the hang of French braids.

"Yes, ma'am."

Drunk, these people are pliant as hell.

I slink outside and squat behind the bushes next to the gas meter, waiting for Fallon to set down his cup.

He kisses Josefina. *Yes!* His hand's off the cup and on her boob.

I crouch behind them. With a flick of my wrist, the paste plops into the cup and fizzles. Before I can flee, however, a weight rests on my shoe: Fallon's hand.

"What the—"

He squints up at me. Blue light from the pool shines in his eyes.

"Who are you?" says—

Hold on. The girl he was making out with, that's not Josefina. She's Asian, for one. My brain tells me to get out of there. It also warns me this means something, but I can't piece it together just yet . . .

I blast by a gaggle of football players into the house, turning at the door to glimpse Fallon as he downs the contents, crushes the cup, and tosses it into the pool.

Damnit, I got sloppy. *Never* get sloppy.

I find the nearest bathroom and shut the door. It's painted like the rain forest, with trees, butterflies, monkeys, ferns. I need something to do with my jittery hands, so I fix my hair. Sniff my armpits. Check my breath. If I'd known I'd be driving Jalen home . . . I'd have showered. Definitely wouldn't have eaten fries. My teeth are stale.

You can do this. You can drive Jalen Frikken Thomas home.

I hadn't thought about what I'd do *after* I'd driven him. Walk home? Text Rafi to get me? Jalen doesn't live too far, but walking home in the dark alone . . . Or maybe he'll invite me inside, and . . .

I brush my teeth with my finger, just in case.

I lock the door from the inside on my way out. This looks like a five-bathroom house. Mission: Find the others and lock them, too. The paste will start working in T-fifteen minutes.

A sweep of the area reveals there're 5.5 bathrooms; there's a half bathroom in the pool house. I edge through the main house, the music so loud it vibrates a cough from my lungs.

After locking the bathroom off the pool, I enter the main house through the kitchen door, head down. There's Raf with Bian, Bian fussing over Raf's fork wound, and—

Josefina's on the counter, legs wrapped around Jalen. He's so tall he has to stoop to kiss her.

I realize what my brain was trying to warn me. Josefina and Fallon are broken up. Earlier, Bian's hand at the small of Jalen's back—she was trying to play matchmaker for Jalen and Josefina!

And I'm swaying, eyelids heavy.

I overheard Mom telling Kate once to compartmentalize her life. Kate's in med school and after she saw a dead body for the first time, she couldn't cope. I didn't know what the word meant at the time, but now it makes sense.

I'm putting Jalen in a compartment and sealing it. That gives me time to focus on the compartment at hand. Fallon and his soon-to-be-spastic bowels . . .

Wandering the hall, I stumble upon Josefina's bedroom. It must be, because the wall is plastered with photos of her and *It*. Sticking out my tongue, I stumble into the last bathroom.

It's occupied.

Two dudes, one by the sink, the other by the towel rack, pass a joint.

"Oh—"

And I try to dip out, but there's a third lounging in the tub, nursing a bottle of tequila like a big muscly baby. He looks me up and down through bloodshot eyes. "Wait—I know you. You're that girl. CJ."

The music sounds so far away now. There's barely a vibration in my feet.

Muscly baby gets up, swaying. He reaches around me for the door. A draft tickles the fine hairs on my neck, standing in alert.

He's closed the door.

"My brother's looking for me." I hate. *Hate* that I need him.

"Who's your brother?" says muscly baby. He burps through his nose and it smells like ketchup on steak.

"Rafi Shahin."

"He's big," says the twiggy guy by the sink, "he could mess you up."

Muscly baby juts out his chest. "I could take him." He looks at me like guys used to when me and Annalie would dress up and go to the outdoor mall.

Like *I* was the steak. Annalie liked the attention, but I never did.

The door bangs open. It's Cole, holding a wobbly pink dildo, looking just as confused as the rest of us.

"I found this," he mumbles. His eyes travel from one stunned face to the next.

Wheezy laughter echoes against the tile. Muscly baby says, "Let's dip, this is getting weird."

"Yeah, who brings their kid brother to a party?" says twiggy guy. "That's like—statutory or whatever, CJ."

They're gone. I tell Cole *hold on*, and half shut the door.

I take the moment to myself to look in the mirror. "Damn, was a close one," I whisper, hands on the sink. My reflection smiles humorlessly. "But the Ghost always slips away. No biggie. All good." My legs disagree, vibrating to the bone.

Exiting, I lock the bathroom and fight the urge to take the kid up in my arms. Instead, I say, "Coleslaw, what the hell are you doing here?"

Cole's pretending he's a Dildo Jedi, waving the thing around. "Jalen posted a story. His location's on."

"That's not an invitation." I sigh.

"Why did they call you CJ?"

"Would you—sheathe your weapon, please?"

Cole rehomes the dildo in Josefina's bedside drawer and I direct him by the shoulders into the hall.

"You seem weird," says Cole as I readjust my hood.

"Why?"

He runs a finger along the wall. Why do kids need to touch everything?

"Your voice, it's high and wobbly."

And my heart's still pounding. "I'll deal with you later, Cole."

"You never have time for me. You or Jalen. He's making out with some chick." He delivers mini—moody kicks to the wall.

"I know." I'd like to join his wall-kicking, but it's showtime. Something's changed. The music has stopped. Is that yelling?

"*JT*? Jalen Thomas? You waste no time, do you, slut?" It's Fallon, mouthing off drunkenly at Josefina in the kitchen.

Jalen, Tommy, Bian, and Raf are all there, too. I'm obviously not the only one upset to find Jalen and Josefina kissing. Josefina and Fallon *did* just break up.

I join the back of the crowd, rocking on my tippie toes to watch. Cole whines that he wants up, but I'm not lifting the kid.

"You watch your mouth!" warns Jalen, with a step toward Fallon. Tommy grabs Jalen protectively around the chest, tells him Fallon *ain't worth it.*

Jalen curses but it's Bian who's suddenly in Fallon's face.

She backs Fallon into the wall like a lioness cornering dinner.

"Don't act like you haven't been sexting some girl called Bree. Josefina saw the texts."

Fallon's cheeks have got that alcohol glow. He leans on the kitchen counter. "Josefina wasn't good to me . . . She was."

Josefina's cheeks flush. Next to me, Cole rubs his hands together and goes, "Things are getting juicy."

I scan the room for Brit. For a guilty look that verifies Fallon put Brit into his phone as Bree. I find her by the punch bowl, playing with a toy eyeball. She peeks up, cautiously, perhaps to see if anyone knows her secret. I do.

Next to Tommy, Jalen's eyes lock on mine. He nods.

Holding Josefina, Bian goes, "One day, Fall, you'll get what's coming to you."

"I—" Fallon brings a fist to his mouth. Burps.

Someone says, "He's gonna vom!"

It's like CNN in here. iPhones point at Fallon, everyone waiting to see what will happen next, rocking socials come daybreak.

Fallon's expression spins through emotions like a prize wheel. He settles on shock.

Clenching, he elbows through the crowd and down the corridor.

Eyes wet, Josefina rushes to the pool deck. Bian follows.

The crowd's parting, and soon, there's a hand at my back. "Time to go." But it's not Jalen, it's Raf. "Cole? What the—?"

Cole takes off, screaming like a banshee. The Kush Giant says *Wait here!* and bounds after the kid.

There's the hurried *clop-clop* of shoes on marble. Finding all possible stations of relief locked, Fallon zooms into the living room, past the throng, outside. SMN's paparazzi follow him to the side of the house.

I look for Jalen, but he's no longer standing in the kitchen. One look out the living room window tells me he's not on the pool deck with Josefina, either. I trip over somebody's *Blood Jurors* staff as I'm jostled out the front double doors in a sea of sweaty bodies to the lawn, after Fallon.

Where is he?

Across the street, there's an electronic *chirp-chirp!* and the flash of lights. Leaning against the Raptor, Jalen chucks me his keys as I approach. "You're up, Rafi's sis."

14

IT'S MY first time in a boy's car.

But there's no thrill. No electricity, wondering if our hands will touch, no suggestive smirks at stoplights or whatever.

First off, Jalen was literally just exchanging spit with Josefina.

Second, for sparks to fly, the boy needs to be, like, conscious.

As soon as the Raptor roared to life and Jalen gave me a garbled rundown of critical Raptor mechanics (blinker and lights locations), he turned up some '90s rap, folded his arms across his chest, and passed the hell out.

Mafi Shahin, you fool.

You're obviously nothing more to this boy than a chauffeur. An Uber driver who doesn't charge.

But if he really cared about Josefina, wouldn't he be back at the party, consoling her?

I buckle him in and he groans, veil flowing over his shoulder. I drive.

My phone's vibrating so much my leg's numb. But I won't take my eyes off the road. Yeah, Raf'll be mad. But so will Jalen if I crash his Raptor.

The weight of the truck roaring beneath me, and the responsibility, Jalen at my side . . . Uber driver or no, I'm grinning in disbelief.

At red lights, I don't peek at my phone like most Californians do. I glance at Jalen, making this humming noise in his sleep. His lips still part the same way. Peaceful.

Jalen shifts and his leg muscles pop through the dress silk. *Thighs on guys.* God.

In ten minutes, we're in front of his ranch. I've never been inside, but I've been here lots. When Mom used to pick up Raf as a kid, I'd tag along, hoping to glimpse my crush.

The lawn is shaded by a massive oak tree, beat-up and knotty, sap oozing like blood. I always thought it looked like a Witch Tree or something. Raf told me it's because the kid who lived in the house before practiced his baseball swing on it.

I shift into park and kill the engine, leaving the keys in the ignition. Jalen starts with an "Mm?"

He stretches. "Rafi's sis . . . you an angel."

I wish he'd call me Mafi. *Mafoorama* would even be an upgrade. *Rafi's sis*—I'm like some appendage of my brother's. I can never get out from under his shadow.

Jalen reaches for the door. For a second, he pauses and I think he's going to ask me inside. Then he goes, "How you getting home?"

Silly, ignorant Mafi.

"Uber," I lie. It'll show up on Mom's card.

"Well, hit me up when you get back." He motions for my phone, and soon he's squinting in the screen's white glow.

"Missed calls." He puts his digits in my phone. "Eight, from your br—"

Jalen's head snaps toward the ranch. He rolls down the window, shushing me when I ask, "What's wrong?"

My stomach drops. I hear it, too. Throaty wailing, coming from inside the house.

Jalen tosses my phone into my lap. "Go home." His voice is charged and rigid, like telephone wire.

When I don't move, he shoots out an exasperated sigh. I'd like to move, I want to—but I've frozen.

Jalen reaches across my lap and yanks the keys from the ignition. Pushes open my door and shoos me from the seat with an "Out, c'mon!"

My knees tremble as I step down from the truck onto the street, dark except for orange pockets of lamplight.

Jalen kicks the air, tearing the confines of his dress. Cursing, he dashes up the walkway, muddy veil dragging on the concrete.

———

Hours later and I'm still awake.

I called Raf and told him I'd gotten a ride with this girl from class. Bian was bickering with Cole in the background—Raf felt obligated to take Cole home—so he was distracted and didn't pry. But he *did* come home for two seconds after dropping Cole before heading back out, just to see if I was there.

I didn't Uber. Or hitch a ride with a classmate.

Hood up, I fast-walked all the way home, heart leapfrogging whenever headlights didn't pass me quick enough. When I saw the white brick facade and Nutter Butter's oak tree, the American flag waving me in, warm relief swept over me. But I ducked behind a parked car when I saw Baba slinking across Cam's lawn, gloved fingers wiggling for the newly sprouted *Wiggs* sign.

———

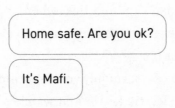

Home safe. Are you ok?

It's Mafi.

Now in bed, I stare at the texts I sent Jalen hours ago. Unread.

I've filled out his contact card to a T. I do that with everyone; it's just something I have to do. His full name: Jalen Thomas. I've still got to find out his middle name. Address, on Brandywine. Basketball #91.

Meowgi's purring next to me. His fur is prickly, like a broom. I don't want to close my eyes to sleep. If I do, I'll relive seeing Jalen's pained face in the Raptor, my existence in that private moment an insult I can't take back.

Raf's not home yet and #JJ is trending on Instagram. Jalen and Josefina.

People online are theorizing Bian's the Ghost after she told Fallon *someday, you'll get what's coming to you* and he sprinted off, clenching. *It* doesn't even deny it. She commented on the post with a winky face.

My cheeks prickle with heat. She's already taken Raf. Now Ghostings, too?

I hate *It*, but I'm jealous how she publicly, bravely, calls people out. Commands respect.

When the CJ rumor tore through SMN, I got tired of defending myself fast. My resistance was as effective as a bent garden hose in a wildfire.

Still refusing sleep, I go downstairs.

I raid the pantry for Oreos and snatch up the peanut butter, ready to twist, dip, and lick, when slippers shuffle into the kitchen. The stove light casts a warm glow on the old man attached to them.

"Gojeh," Baba says, rumbly voice soothing like a chai latte.

He fills the electric kettle and watches as I lick a gob of peanut butter off an Oreo.

"Hungry," I say unapologetically. Baba laughs through his nose.

"All this exercise you and Rafi jan do," he says. Jan = dear. "Some fat is good. In case you get sick." His face sours. Grandma was so frail before she died. "Why jog? Who do you run from?" Baba jogs in place, humor in his eyes.

I shrug. "I don't jog anymore."

"Mm." Baba pours steaming water into his mug.

"Baba, you've *got* to stop trespassing on Cam's lawn."

Baba pretends to spit. "Your baba will never bow to the establishment." Then he hums happily. The fact he's not going on a political rant right now is baffling.

"Baba . . . what's up?" I cram two Oreos into my mouth.

"A plane, Gojeh. A plane is up! Your baba just heard from Habib. There's a flight soon—very soon—to Qatar. He and Yasmoon will be on it. The first step, mm? From there, they can fly to the USA, to be with Baba." He taps his lips, like *shh*.

"I ffought de Saliban veren't leffing planef take off?"

After decrypting my Oreo-laden words, Baba says, "Your habib did translation work for the U.S. military, Gojeh. There are ways. Finally, help has come. You will see, Inshallah."

———

I wake before the sun's up, to the sound of Ptero screeching off.

Baba's headed to his Sunday water aerobics class at the YMCA. Seems the older you get, the less sleep you need. Or maybe it's something else keeping him awake.

My head spins with a hangover that has nothing to do with alcohol.

I knock my phone off the bedside table.

There's a read receipt under my text to Jalen.

No response.

15

I DON'T know a lot about Jalen's parents.

Before Jalen could drive, Mr. Thomas used to drop him off at our house. You could tell he used to be handsome like Jalen, with impressive shoulders, cavernous eyes that charm, and an angular face. At Raf's games, he always dressed younger than the other dads. Ripped jeans with gold cloth peeking through, and a backward cap.

He always had this wary look, kinda like my dad. Like the world, it's not what he expected.

Mr. Thomas never misses Jalen's basketball games. Once, Mom sat next to him and chatted his ear off. He excused himself after the first quarter and didn't return. In line for popcorn at halftime, I saw him sitting on the other side of the bleachers, camouflaged, cap pulled over his eyes. He'd put in orange earplugs, too.

I didn't tell Mom. She offends easily.

Jalen's mom? She lives in Germany.

Last night, the look on Jalen's face told me I'd crossed a boundary, stumbled on a land mine he'd thought was hidden.

———

An hour or two later, there's a thump outside my door.

"Oh my god. It's Sunday," I groan. My mouth is mossy but I'm too lazy to brush my teeth.

"I'm coming in, Mafia."

"I'm naked!"

"Ew." Rafi stops. "Pull the covers up, then."

"Nope. I sleep naked. And as it's seven thirty a.m. on a Sunday, I will be naked for two more hours at least. Wait—I've got a dude in here!"

Rafi opens the door, a hand over his eyes. He moves two fingers to look. "You're not naked. And there's no dude."

"There could be a dude."

"You're so weird."

"What do you want?" I have that fuzzy early-morning-head feeling, like I could melt into the mattress if he'd just let me.

If #JJ is really going ahead, I'm done for. Josefina's the long-relationship type.

"Someone's coming in half an hour and I don't want you walking downstairs in your pajamas with your hair all crazy."

Who the hell could be coming over at eight o'clock on a Sunday morning? And why does Rafi care about my hair?

"Ugh, not *It*."

"Not *It*."

I sit up. I've never heard Rafi call Bian that. Never. I rearrange the sleep pony sprouting from my head.

"Bian broke up with me last night."

"Oh." I should've known. His hair is in a man bun; she hates it like that.

"Wow, don't look so cut up about it."

I can't hide my grin. "I'm sorry, Raf."

Actually, I am. Bian's dangerous when she's single. Wild. And the boys act wild, too: strutting the halls like emus with chests puffed, challenging each other to duels.

"If it makes you feel better," I say, "Baba said Habib and Yasmoon have got a flight to Qatar."

Raf's face brightens. "Seriously? When?"

"Very soon, Baba says. People are helping them behind the scenes, I guess. Wait, so *who's* coming over?"

Rafi looks me squarely in the face. "If you care about me . . . you'll keep out of it." He knocks on the door like *that's that*. The shaver goes in the bathroom.

Keep out of it? "Double standard much?" I say it to myself.

My question's answered when a yellow Honda Fit rolls up to the front curb, the man inside paying careful attention not to scratch the rims. He doesn't look like he belongs in a yellow Fit.

The car is most definitely a rental.

It's the same sweaty balding scout from Indiana University, just a little balder. Dale . . . or Devin or something. He was here last year.

Dale checks his teeth in the mirror and gets out of the car, straightening his burgundy shirt with the IU emblem on the chest. His binder bursts with paper; he's got the look of someone selling home protection products.

The doorbell rings and Meowgi shoots underneath the bed.

Rafi . . . *that scheming little* . . . He knows Mom and Dad won't be back till noon. And Baba—not for another three hours. Baba's probably talking politics with the old men in the Jacuzzi. Not *with* them, per se, but *at* them. Baba might be the only anti-Wiggser over sixty in Rancho Santa Margarita.

16

SURE, I care about Rafi.

But I also wanna know why the secret meeting with this IU scout?

I guess it makes sense Rafi scheduled this with the adults gone. He doesn't wanna be embarrassed by Dad's overprotectiveness or Baba's insistence that basketball's just a "hobby."

I sit halfway down the stairs to listen, telling Mr. Meowgi, chirruping at me, to be quiet.

Dale starts off talking about traffic, the usual small-talk topic of choice for Midwesterners visiting California.

"My baba thinks the answer is to only allow those who can drive stick on the road." Raf forces a mechanical laugh and I cringe.

There's the sound of labored breathing and the unsnapping of Dale's binder. In the silence that follows, I imagine him dabbing at his face with a handkerchief.

"Thanks for meeting—IU's excited to have you." He clears his throat a number of times. "Your parents, are they—"

"Out."

"And, eh—the small fellow with the hat? Your *baba*, was it?" Dale asks, likely remembering the stale walnut incident.

"He's out."

"Aha." Dale sounds relieved. The labored breathing dissipates a bit.

"You're eighteen—" And I hear the rustle of papers as if he's checking to be sure.

"Yes. Eighteen now."

What, liar! Raf's a young senior. He won't be eighteen until August.

"Well, we'll just get straight to it." Dale *ahems* some more. "Like my email said, I'm here for your player profile, but there's something else to discuss—we'll get to it in a second."

Minutes pass where they talk about boring stuff like Raf's average of eighteen points and nine-point-bla-who-the-hell-cares rebounds a game. I'm swinging silently on the wooden banister, but plop on my booty when Dale says: "But more importantly, let's talk about your multicultural background."

"Oh," says Rafi at the same time I whisper: *"Ohh."*

The catch.

Dale goes *ahem-hem-hem* in a way that'd put Baba's old man throat clearings to shame. "Let me first note Indiana University is committed to advancing diversity, equity, and inclusion in all its forms." I can tell he's reading from the paper verbatim because it comes out all drone-y. He clears his throat again, then apologizes, gruffling something about Diet Coke phlegm. "We foster individuality, leverage the educational and institutional benefits of diversity, and support our athletes to ensure they thrive.

"With that said, Rafi Bakht Shahin, we'd like you—the first ever Afghani to play for us—to be the face of our athletic diversity campaign.

Baba hates when people call Afghans *Afghanis*. Afghani = currency. Afghans = people.

"For sure, for sure," says Rafi, in a voice of pained interest, "but the thing is—I'm American."

"But your dad was born in Afghanistan."

"Can—can I ask how you know that?"

I'm wondering, too. Dad's anything but fast and loose with his heritage. I rack my brain. On UC Irvine's mathematics department website, there's nothing that reveals where Dad's from. If Dad *was* here . . . Dale'd be sprinting to his Honda Fit arms a-waving, papers flying.

"A story you posted about your grandma's Afghan meatballs. They did look mighty good, too. One of the interns took note."

Damn. The kofta. I remember. Dad made Rafi take it down.

"And—I mean. Your baba—" Dale does a high-pitched *let's just be honest* whinny.

Rafi's tone's changes. "I mean—yeah, Dad's Afghan, but I was born here."

"So you're Afghan."

Rafi and I had this argument the other day. He says he can't stand people who say they're Italian because their grandpa's from Italy even when they were born in the U.S., say *expresso* instead of *espresso*, and think pineapple pizza from the Hut is the epitome of fine Italian dining.

"I mean, it's my heritage . . . but I'm not like Afghan-Afghan. I don't practice Islam or anything."

"Look, son," says the man, "see this as an opportunity. A way to put yourself on the map. There's a big appetite for diversity right now. Might as well tap into that. There's a Korean fellow as well. And a Black fellow. Parents are from Somalia." For some reason, Dale whispers when he says this.

He goes on, "I know the season's about to start and you're busy with reading and fractions and stuff"—Dale's clearly trying to remember what high school is like but fails—"so we'll getcha a photographer nearby so you can stay put. How's mid-November sound?"

"For what?" I can hear the panic in Rafi's voice now.

"For us to shoot you. Er—with the photographer. I mean, the camera."

"Just so we're like, on the same page . . ." *Good, big bro. Ask questions.* "This is for my player profile, right?"

"Yup! Nothing out of the ordinary. And you'll be sporting your IU jersey, stitched up nice and early for you. You can keep it after the shoot."

"My jersey?"

"Red's gonna look great on you, kid." Dale's *good.* "So— just your autograph, then. First of many. Where's that slippery little . . . ?" *Rustle-rustle.* "Ah!" The couch creaks, and I imagine Dale leaning forward to give Rafi his pen.

After a few seconds, pen scratches on paper.

"Good. We're hoping to launch the player profiles by the end of fall semester." Dale snaps his binder.

"I, uh, thanks for coming, Davis." Ah, *Davis.* That was his name. "Always a pleasure."

Which is a weird thing to say, and Rafi knows it, too, because he's clearing his throat as he walks Davis out. He's only met the scout once.

In the car, Davis dabs his forehead. Checks his mirrors no fewer than four times before pulling from the curb.

Rafi sees me on the stairs. We have a moment where we stare wide-eyed at each other, amused.

"Padar's going to ki-ll you," I say in a singsong voice.

Rafi's nose scrunches. "I told you, *stay out of it*."

"He doesn't want us telling anyone we're Afghan."

Raf points to his face, like *c'mon*. "I think the cat's out of the bag." He struts into the kitchen. I follow.

"But we don't need to . . . *broadcast* it."

"Okay, Dad," says Rafi with a sigh. "But why? Whenever I ask him, he freezes. We were born in the U.S. Our family here is safe. He's just paranoid—for no reason. Nothing bad has ever happened to us." As Rafi says this, a chill ripples up my spine. I silently knock on the kitchen cabinet. "And as you said," he goes on, "Habib and Yasmoon have a flight out. Everything's fine."

"IU's just using you," I say. "They're exploiting your Afghanness—to *pretend* they care."

"They care."

"In the same way shoe companies care about diversity? *You're* the product, Rafi. You're an *Afghani* to him, *currency*."

"It's just a player profile!"

I think of Mr. A's comment, that radicals *believe what they say*. Right now, it's clear Raf doesn't.

"Didn't you hear how he whispered about *a Black fellow. Parents from Somalia.* That guy Dale—"

"Davis—"

"Is racist. And how're you gonna explain it to Dad?"

"I won't." His face flushes. "And you won't, either. I'm tired of Dad saying I'd be better off with some math degree, like him."

"Tell him, then."

Raf stares. When it comes to Dad, Raf hates confrontation. He crams an entire Nutter Butter into his mouth like a gerbil.

"Hey—that's not on the approved list Coach gave you." I point at the nutrition plan on the fridge. It's crumpled from Rafi balling it up and Mom fishing it out of the trash.

He kicks the pantry door and it flails off one hinge. Then the Kush Giant looks down at me, nostrils dark abysses. Raf unsticks the Post-it with chores from the counter and slaps it on my forehead with his palm.

"I'll handle my stuff, you handle yours." Raf shoulders past me with the box of Nutter Butters.

"Hypocrite!" This time I say it loud.

He stops. Turns. "We really gonna do this now, Gozeh Farangi? You wanna open Annalie's Party file?"

I wipe my eyes, pooling with liquid, and stare at my chipped toenail polish. My head wags. A dull pressure settles in at my temples. If I was Bian, I'd tell him to go stuff it. Why's it so hard to look him in the eye when we fight?

It's just that Raf doesn't realize his stuff *is* my stuff. He's my brother.

Maybe *that's* why he did what he did at Annalie's party.

Raf exhales like a whale clearing its blowhole and thunders upstairs. We're out of Oreos, so I eat PB from the jar until my headache becomes a stomachache.

17

IT'S WEDNESDAY, and I'm a bloated popcorn kernel in a mustard-yellow school-issued swimsuit. Besides the popcorn suits and whistle-happy Ms. Hawkirk, synchronized swim is my least favorite class because you can't go ten minutes without choking on a Band-Aid or hair tie. This pool needs a service. And a heater.

Sweet Sixteen indeed.

I wanted to skip swim, but Mom refused to write me a note. Not even on my birthday, because she said discomfort = growth.

Mom *did* make my favorite yogurt banana pancakes for breakfast. Baba gave me eighty-one dollars. Since I was a kid, he and Grandma have given us however old they were in cash. I put it in my drawer so I'm not tempted to spend it. It'll probably go to Cole for courier services rendered. Dad ate his oatmeal on the deck this morning listening to some podcast, and when he came inside, he gave me a birthday hug. Dad's hugs are a rarity. He hugs from far, and always one-armed. You could fit an oversized beach ball between our middles.

Ms. Hawkirk puts us in groups of two or three and we're supposed to throw together a choreographed routine to perform next class.

All sophomores have to take synchronized swim. Even the boys.

Annalie's in it, too. *And* the old crew. There used to be six of us, and we were all inseparable.

One day your best friend's room feels like a sanctuary, a cave, as you run your fingers through her freshly cut hair, talking long into the night.

The next, the pool might as well be an ocean and you pretend the other doesn't exist.

Even if the CJ stuff is slowly fizzing out (I drown the thought of the dudes in Josefina's bathroom), it's on my permanent record. Forever. *Unless* I can get a boyfriend and go from *Hook-Up Material* to *Girlfriend Material*.

Now, in synchronized swim, I'm partnered with two boys who startle every time I talk, googly-eyed as they attempt *not* to ogle at my chestal area. All attempts fail; my boobs are home base.

I wonder if Annalie remembers it's my birthday?

"Oh, wow," says one of the boys, crossing his skinny arms over his chest.

I'm about to say *Okay, eyes up here,* when I realize his attention's elsewhere. My forearms ripple with goose flesh. It's not the cold.

My eyes follow Jalen's long torso down to his muscular quads as he hops into the water. No ladder needed.

Seeing the source of the distraction, Ms. Hawkirk yells, "Class—*CLASS!* Focus!"

"His abs look better than my face," my partner says.

The other one agrees and notes, *"I think he's dating Josefina now."*

Ms. Hawkirk asks Jalen why he's here, and he says, *Coach's orders*, something about water high-knees, tuck-jumps, and wall push-offs to improve explosiveness. Aka: It'll help his hops.

It's the second-to-last period of the day; Jalen's supposed to be in English right now. Class schedules, for athletes, are more of a suggestion.

I can barely hear my partner's idea for the last choreographed bit over the *tshh-tshh-tshh* of Jalen's high-knees down the lane. The final flourish is a dip-back and somersault. I'm getting a chlorine headache from all this water up the nose.

An echoey voice comes from my right. "Hey—Rafi's sis."

Of course I know who it is, but I duck underwater.

Unable to hold my breath any longer, I pop up, spluttering. Ms. Hawkirk blows her whistle. Class is over. My googly-eyed partners swim off, one of them giving his own chest a dissatisfied prod.

"You good?" Jalen says, leaning on the lane marker buoy. He's so tall his knees are on the pool floor.

"Um."

Jalen chews on his beaded necklace. It's hot pink and looks like something a second grader would make with one of those home beading kits.

I'm suddenly hyperaware we're only separated by the lane marker and thin-fabric swimsuits. My popcorn-kernel suit floats around me like a parachute. I'm glad it leaves a lot to the imagination, because I'm self-conscious about my tummy since I quit track.

"Look," Jalen says, necklace plopping from his mouth, "about the other night . . . sorry I rushed you like that. Pops, he—" Shouting reverberates off the walls, drowning his voice.

"Sorry?"

Jalen's doing one of his open-mouth thinks. "Nothing." He half smiles at me. "Hey. Left a wish in the tree."

"You did?"

His nose dips into the water. Bubbles fizz on the surface when he laughs.

"Not tellin' you what it was, though. You know the drill. It'll never come true if I do."

"Right."

"But you said yours came true, so." He clasps his hands, like *here's hoping.*

"I did?"

"Yeah." He looks at me funny. "C'mon, was you drinking that night, or me?" My brain's lagging, stuck on the idea that Jalen's wish resides in the tree. Right. Now. That, or Coleslaw has it—and—"Hey, I said, you tell Raf you drove me?"

I shake my head.

"Cool. 'Cause if he or Coach knew some fifteen-year-old drove me home, I dunno."

He means Josefina. *Josefina* would be pissed if she found out.

"Oh—there it is," says Jalen, cupping a used Band-Aid and launching it onto the deck. "Spotted in the wild." He beams at it. "Never thought I'd see the day when they'd make them for my skin. Damn. A small thing, but gets me every time."

"It's not a small thing."

He scratches his neck. "Anyway, thanks for the ride, and uh, should get back—"

"I'm sixteen," I say, before it's too late.

"Huh?"

"Today. I'm sixteen. You, uh—you said I was fifteen."

"Oh, word?"

"I'm getting my license soon and everything." I don't know why I tell him.

"Whew . . . Remember when we was kids and those geese went after Raf? Six years ago now."

"I remember." Rafi's still got the scar on his butt. When it comes to Jalen, I remember everything.

Jalen's chewing on his necklace again. He grins. "You grew up, Rafi's sis."

That smoky voice, those smoldering eyes—*is Jalen Frikken Thomas flirting with me?*

I suddenly feel naked. Very naked. My chest tightens and I cross my arms. Baba's voice plays in my head: *Nipples are haram. Haram!*

"Well, bye—"

"Happy birthday—" Jalen reaches across the buoy—I think—to nudge me in the shoulder. But then Ms. Hawkirk's voice blares, "NO BOY-GIRL TOUCHING IN THE POOL!"

I turn, only to have Jalen's fist smack my left boob—

I slap his stubbled cheek, a reflex. Not too hard, but hard enough for his Cool Boy Look to wash off with the water.

"Oh, sh—!" says Jalen, hopping back. "I wasn't tryin'—I didn't—"

And I gabble something like *"Tshokay!"* and the next moment, my wet feet are slap-slapping on the pool deck and onto those holey feet-hating rubber mats that lead to the locker room.

I dress so fast I put my sweatpants on inside out. My arm gets stuck in my hoodie and I scream.

"What's all this woofing about?"

I say it in a rush, without breathing: "Ms.-Hawkirk-I-need-to-go-to-my-car-because-I-left-my-homework-in-my-A&P-textbook-and-I'm-gonna-be-late-for-next-period—"

She eyes me suspiciously, but scribbles a note that says she's held me up for Mr. A, nonetheless.

I hurtle toward the armed guard posted at the quadruple doors in SMN's foyer, then slow when it dawns on me hurtling unannounced toward anyone with a gun is not the smartest. I flash my pass at him and he takes out an earbud, nodding and doing those annoying little chewing-gum pops as I mumble between breaths: "Car . . . homework . . . right back!"

I sprint to the parking lot, verify that no one's watching, then dive over the median and barrel down the leafy hill. My Converse *jud-jud-jud* all the way to the SOL tree.

"Please, oh please!" I shove my arm into the tree knot. My hand grazes cool, earthy mud, scabrous wood, and—

It's empty.

I stop, drop, and sweep the forest floor like a truffle pig foraging for mushrooms.

A candy wrapper, a tissue, and—*dear god! A condom*—but Jalen's wish is nowhere to be found.

Bzz. Bzz. My phone vibrates. A&P has begun.

Looking up into the tree boughs, waving in the sunny breeze, I curse at the hidden winged thieves, the fairies, who must've stolen it.

———

Before heading to class, I dip into the bathroom to clean the mud stains from my pants. When I finally get to A&P, sweating chlorine and salt, I hand Mr. A the crumpled pass as he's writing something on the board. He glimpses at it and tells me to sit.

I force myself not to look at Jalen as I search for an empty seat. All desks in the back are taken.

There's only one, right up front. Next to Brit.

As I unpack my A&P book, a hand hovers over my wet ponytail. I don't acknowledge it. I'm sticking to this downward gaze for the rest of class. Maybe forever.

Brit sighs. Her hand lowers, bracelets chinking on the desk. Between Brit's thumb and forefinger, something crimson draws my eye, twirling like a color guard flag.

A leaf.

Mr. A starts the lesson on the anatomy of the legs.

Funny, I don't feel mine.

Brit places the leaf on my open textbook and I forget how to exhale.

My eyes strain at their outer limits. When I look at her, what'll be written on her face? Wrathful, smug accusation?

I close my eyes. When my eyelids lift, so does my fear.

Her face is blank. The hint of a smile, maybe.

I return it.

Exhale.

———

Never get caught rooting around in the SOL tree.

Did I just break my first rule?

18

LATER IN A&P, there's a knock at the door. Rafi says, "Mr. A, I'm gonna need my sister."

Mr. A gives me a look, like *really?* In thirty minutes, I haven't taken in a word of the lesson. He looked so disappointed when he asked me where the *biceps femoris* was and I said the arm. It got worse. *Fallon* corrected me.

Mr. A waves me out and I pop up like a gopher.

Athlete privilege, I tell you. No questions asked.

Raf mouths: *Take your stuff!*

Backpack slung over my shoulder, I don't turn to see if Brit or Jalen are looking.

I know they are.

———

I'm in the passenger seat of the Ptero car, a beautiful November breeze lifting my hair. We roll past the guards at the entrance by the SMN tulip arrangement. It's still so weird to see them, guns bulging from their belts. But this is America. My Insta feed has ads for bulletproof backpacks juxtaposed with lip-plumping kits.

"So. We're going to the Spectrum." Raf eyes my sweatpants. I got most of the mud off in the bathroom before A&P, but they're still wet.

The Spectrum is my favorite outdoor mall in Irvine. They've got the *best* macaron shop called Honey & Butter. The Oreo macaron is my favorite. Saliva pools behind my teeth.

"Aren't you like—mad at me?" I ask.

"I told you to stay out of it and you did. *And* you fixed the pantry door before Mom and Dad got home."

"Yeah."

"And Dad hasn't killed me yet, so I assume you haven't told them."

"Not yet."

He punches my shoulder.

But it's November, the month of the photo shoot. The IU stuff will rear its ugly head soon enough.

"So we're cool," says Rafi, but his rigid posture suggests this wasn't his idea. Mom's work. Has to be. She was the one going on about how my teachers won't take me seriously in hoodies and sweats.

Raf throws on his Ray-Bans and readjusts his man bun. He only wears it up when Bian's not around. She says it makes him look *Asian* and doesn't like it. The irony. Bian is Vietnamese.

———

"Sweatpants, again?" After devouring one birthday cake and two Oreo macarons each (Rafi's treat), we're at the snaking checkout line at Brandy Melville. I made a beeline for the joggers, pushing my way past silky dresses and skirts.

"*Joggers*, not sweatpants."

"You used to be like—girly."

I shrug.

I'm about to tell Raf to forget the joggers when my phone buzzes. A number I don't recognize.

I pocket my phone before Rafi reads over my shoulder; the guy's a kite, observing everything from his own stratosphere.

"You've gotta be like six foot four," comes a twang from behind us.

The man wears a Fox Motocross tank and has got two bras slung over his arm. He hawks spit into his empty McDonald's McFlurry cup.

"Something like that." Raf's used to it by now. Randos commenting on his height. He half turns, thinking the conversation over, but the man says, "Play ball?"

"Yup." Raf pops the *p* on the end, a signal he wants to stop talking.

"Where at?"

Rafi rolls his eyes before doubling back. "Not here. In LA."

Why didn't Raf say SMN?

The cashier waves. We're next. I trip Raf and he pulls me in with one arm and gives me a noogie.

"You two are so cute," the cashier says as I place my joggers on the counter. "How long have you been dating?"

"Ugh."

"No."

We say it in unison, a reflex. Rafi nearly tosses me across the counter in an effort to disprove the clerk's theory.

"She's my *sister*," says Rafi.

The cashier's drawn-on eyebrows almost reach her hairline. "But she looks so—and you look—"

I say, "We're both Afghan."

"American," adds Raf.

Rafi shoots me a dark look, but it's my birthday, so he doesn't say anything. I can almost hear Dad's *Shush!* in my ear over the line chatter behind us.

Rafi hands the clerk Mom's credit card and she asks for his ID. She checks Rafi's license, then the credit card.

"But the card says Emily Shaman? Er—*Shahin*? And the license says Rafi Shahin."

"Emily is my mom."

"Sorry—the names have to match." She slides both ID and credit card across the counter.

"I've never had this problem before." Raf fingers through his wallet. He doesn't have any cash, and my birthday money's in my desk.

Fox guy exhales obnoxiously. "I don't need the joggers," I tell Raf.

"You're getting them."

"It's fine, seriously—"

"It's her birthday." I yank on Raf's elbow. He digs his heels into the rubbery floor, pointing accusatorily at the clerk.

Exit in view, Rafi's pointed finger is holstered till Fox guy mumbles, "Terrorists!"

My brother tears from my grip and doubles back. "What did you say?"

Rafi's chest to chin with the man, eclipsing him by miles. The spit hawker's looking up and down, maybe thinking picking a fight with a Titan isn't so smart.

"I said you 'n' your sister are *terrorists*. I tell people all the time . . ." He sidesteps Raf. "We ain't running a charity."

He pauses, perhaps expecting applause from the line. His face drops like a befuddled troll's when he doesn't get it.

Instead, phones are out. Filming. Waiting. It's America.

"We spent trillions on Afghanistan, training your so-called army for two decades, and you handed over the keys and ran, tail between your legs—no balls between 'em—when the Taliban came back."

"*Sir,*" says the cashier, but he tut-tut-tuts her into silence. "Go back to your country, Abdullah Whateverthefuck. Clean up your own goddamn mess."

I wedge myself between them. It smells like armpit and peppermint down here, but I'll stay here forever if it means my brother's safe.

The man steps back, woofing something about my *terrorist hair* getting in his mouth.

"Basketball," I say, pulling Rafi's face to my own. I say it again and again. *"Basketball."*

Raf closes his eyes. Nods. I guide him from the store. He's chewing on his lips like he does whenever he's in pain.

On the court, Rafi'll get beat up. Torn down. Blood, sweat, tears—he'll leave it all on the floor. But this is real life. Your opponents aren't known, true colors aren't paraded for all to see with some jersey color. Red. White. Blue. There's no asshole uniform.

This is America.

19

ON THE drive home, I swipe away the Birthday salutations, brunch Saturday? text from Kate. I try opening the text I got in line from that random number but my finger slips with Raf's lunky driving and the message disappears. Probably a scammer anyway.

Rafi pulls into the drive next to the azaleas and I see Cole, dribbling a basketball, walking into his house. Just back from school.

Jalen's wish! Maybe Cole has it?

I need to get rid of my brother.

"Some birthday," he says. No matter how badly I want to sprint to Cole's, it's like I'm glued to my seat with paste from one of Baba's jars. "Thanks." He doesn't have to add *for what you did back there.* He fake-out slugs my cheek, then rests a hand on my shoulder. His fingers are so long he can palm a basketball. Grandma used to say he had pianist hands. That he was wasting them shooting a ball through a hoop.

"It's just—" Rafi drums on the steering wheel. There's the *tink tink* of the engine cooling, the metal shrinking. He laughs, but it's a self-deprecating type of laugh. "If I'm honest, sometimes I wish I looked like you. It'd be easier. You can pass everywhere, you know?"

"It's not easier," I say. "I'm the postman's daughter."

Color rises in Rafi's face. Like he might laugh but thinks better of it.

"You look Afghan *and* you've got an Afghan name," I say. "Me, I'm a blond Mafi Fazela Shahin."

"I'll raise you one." He lifts a finger. "Whenever I tell the guy at the international market I don't speak Farsi, he looks at me like I'm some fake. I guess sometimes I get why Dad calls himself *Sam* at Starbucks . . . life's hard enough, right?"

What happened at the mall is a common occurrence. Some ignorant douche says something decidedly unwoke and Rafi loses his temper. Maybe this is why Dad wants Rafi to remove *Afghan* from the *Meatballs*.

"I just want you to be safe." Raf stares at me, dead in the eye. "If anyone hurt you . . . I'd fucking kill them."

I laugh, one single exhale of exasperation. Not because it's funny. It's not. The way he looks at me, the sheer conviction in his brown eyes; it scares me.

Mom appears from around the back of the house in her floppy sun hat. She waves and trips over the gardening hose. When I look at Raf, we're wearing the same goofy smile. Probably wired in us from when we were babies and Mom would pull faces so we'd forget what we were so fussed about.

"Can, uh—" Rafi starts, as I collect my backpack.

"What?"

"I know it's your birthday, but can I ask a favor? Will you go to the shoot with me? It's next Friday, the thirteenth.

"Friday the thirteenth. Sounds promising." Raf rolls his eyes, and I add, "Admit it. You neeeed your little sister."

Raf smiles, and goes, "Psh."

"*And* you feel bad about going behind Dad's back and know I'm right about Dale."

"*Davis.*" He chews on his lips again. "Never mind. Forget it."

I hang my head. "Ugh. Fine. I'll go."

"Cool." I count a few golden strands in Raf's man bun. "Now you get to spend the rest of your sixteenth listening to Baba's spiel about how the naan Mom gets isn't legit because it wasn't made in those clay ovens in the ground . . ." He whistles, like *bad day.*

I glimpse Cole's double doors, the lion knocker shining in the sun. A beacon. It could turn up just yet.

Inside the house, Dad's watching from the window, cloth stars and stripes billowing in the breeze, obscuring his face.

When I get to the doorstep and push the curling flag out of the way, he's gone.

20

MR. MEOWGI turned up after Baba moved in. I was washing the shorwa pot after lunch, watching rain splash onto the sidewalk, when a glint of orange drew my eye. I squinted at the strange bird perched atop our mailbox. Surely birds didn't have stripes—or a tail?

It was a kitten, shivering in the drizzle. The pot clanged in the sink; I tugged on my boots and propelled myself into the rain.

The scrawny thing clung to my shoulder when I gathered him up, emitting a sullen meow that indicated neither fear nor relief, but the recognition of another living, breathing being.

After I had convinced Baba, peeking over my shoulder, that it was definitely *not* a *wet garbage rat*, the old man trailed me to the kitchen sink with cautious interest.

I gave our new guest a flea bath, preening the skittering menaces from his matted fur with a fine-toothed comb. Fleas sprang into the water in droves, which had turned burgundy with blood.

"He will live, Gojeh?" Baba had whispered, his chai rumble of a voice now a gentle blow on a dandelion.

The ginger feline stared ahead while I massaged, sleepy, apathetic. I winced as my fingers traced the bark-like scabs underneath his fur. "I think so."

"He has no home?"

"No." Then I asked Baba the question that had burned in my throat since the whiskered being attached to my shoulder. "Think Dad will let me keep him?"

Baba shook his head and my heart broke. But he was adamant we immediately rehome him. He called local rescues to see if someone could take him, woofing when they all said no, they were full, it was kitten season. "But he has nowhere! Nothing!" he'd repeat.

Baba observed the kitten as he dozed, swaddled in a washcloth, by the electric fireplace. The cat had triggered something in my grandfather that day, a memory he'd tried to forget.

My eyes met Baba's. *He's got to stay!*

He wasn't a fan of *wet garbage rats*, but we'd come to an understanding.

Baba'd convinced Dad by the time he'd shaken out his umbrella at the door. When Dad clucked at him, Baba told Dad the cat had *nothing, no one,* and that was that.

Baba was Baba. A born leader.

———

Inside, Baba's asleep on his pea-green rocker with a much fatter Mr. Meowgi on his lap. No matter how much the old man tries to push him away, Meowgi won't take *No, pishak!* for an answer. He's a two-track-minded feline: *Make old man love me. Catch nemesis Nutter Butter.*

"Gojeh," says Baba, woken by Raf thundering up the djinn stairs. Baba blows in Meowgi's face and he skedaddles off his lap. "Gift for you."

"You already gave me a gift, Baba."

"This is not Baba's gift." His lips curl into a cheeky grin. "This is the Magic Man's gift."

I groan, waiting for what usually comes next: Baba magicking stale M&M'S from my ear.

He crooks his finger and I sit on the armrest. "Let's see what the Magic Man has for Gojeh." He waves his closed fist past my ear, then uncurls his fingers in front of my nose. "Oho, look!"

Draped across his lined palm is a silver necklace with an evil eye amulet. It was Grandma's. The charm is supposed to ward off evil.

"To protect Gojeh from ill wishes."

"Wow, this is—" *Not what I was expecting.* I'm speechless. Touched, actually. I wrap my arms around Baba's neck.

"Also, Gojeh's about to drive on the 405 . . ." He curses in Farsi. "She will need luck in California traffic jellies."

"Jams?"

"That's what Baba said, Gojeh." He rests his head and snores within seconds.

———

I power out the door just as Mom's coming inside.

"Mama?" she asks, wiping soil from her cheek. "Are you *jogging*?"

"Oh—uh—yes." I needed to get out alone, and jogging was the first excuse I could think of. "Don't look at me like that, Mom. I'm *not* rejoining track."

"Okay, okay," she says, but her face looks like Christmas morning. "Just—happy to see some of my daughter's spark back again."

"Okay, bye!"

"Keep your phone on!" she shouts. "And stay in the neighborhood!"

"Yeah-yeah!"

"No *yeah-yeah*; promise!"

"Okay, *promise*!"

———

I jog past Cole's house.

Twice. Three times. My lungs are overdrawn bagpipes and my shins prickle. I keel over to breathe.

If Cole sniffs out my desperation for Jalen's wish, he'll definitely make a game out of it. Throw the note in the garbage disposal to get a rise out of me or something. I'm already flustered thinking about it. But I can't not ask. The anticipation is literally killing me. Jogging used to be so easy. I don't recognize my body anymore.

Finally, rounding the cul-de-sac for the third time, I come to a halt. There's a new development: Jalen's Raptor in Cole's driveway.

"Fuuuuudge!" I give moody kicks to the curb in a Cole-like fashion.

"Mafi?" a far-off voice sounds.

Cole's living room window is open. Rap booms onto the street. No chance of escape; my legs are zapped of energy.

The kid opens the front door. He's got a Supreme cap over his straight black hair.

The smell of Mrs. Dawicki's secondhand cig smoke snakes sightlessly out the door. "What are you doing here, Rafi's sis?"

"Don't call me that, Coleslaw!"

There's squeaking coming from the television. Rubber soles on hardwood. Elbows on his knees, Jalen's on the couch livestreaming on Twitch. He's playing *NBA 2K* on Cole's new Pity PlayStation.

Jalen's getting big on Twitch. People from all over the world watch him play. Jalen and Cole are entertainers. They yell around, cuss each other out. Once, Mom asked me what the appeal was. I guess it's this *insider* feeling, like you're their friend, hanging out.

"I was on a run, and—" Like a roaring train pumping the brakes, I nearly blurt *have you collected lately?*

Cole lifts his eyebrows like *and? "Ohhhh."* He jumps to some conclusion. "JT! Visitor!"

I flail my arms like *nooo!* But when Jalen does a lightning-speed glance over his shoulder at me, I'm propped coolly against the door.

"Hold up," Jalen tells his viewers.

Cole bounds over the back of the couch, taking Jalen's spot without missing a beat. Jalen's player, Dennis Rodman, blocks a shot and Cole squeals in triumph.

Jalen's wearing a long black T-shirt with *DEFY* on the front, sucking on his candy necklace.

"Birthday girl." He closes the door behind me.

Cole's house is the biggest in the neighborhood. The ceilings are easily twelve feet high. I'm jealous because the Dawickis could get a ten-foot Christmas tree. But it's always small and plastic.

I breathe in D&G. Jalen goes, "Just the person I wanted to see."

"You—what?"

Cole's dog, Melisandre, a red Lab mix, whimpers from the crate in the corner.

"Aww, Melly Belly," I whisper, walking the long way around so I'm not on camera. "Why is she—"

"Don't open that door!" Jalen and Cole say in unison. "She gets too excited."

Melisandre is a humper. The trick to get her to stop is to play dead. For some reason, only a fleeing target is hump material. The pooch likes a challenge.

I stick my finger through the crate and she licks it. "Dude, train her already."

"Yeah, Mom keeps saying she'll—*AGH, MOVE YOUR FEET, MY GUY!*—do it." Cole holds the controller suspended above his head, as if it'll help the players move faster.

I watch the comments stream in on Twitch, so many I can't keep up. *LOL. WTF. WE WANT JALEN! DEAD. DAMN COLE. WHERE JALEN AT?*

"C'mon. I need you," says Jalen, waving me down the hall. The sugary excitement I feel starts to turn. Panic. He *needs* me?

He leads me to the back of the house. It looks different from four years ago, the last time Cole was young enough for me to babysit him. He used to run the halls, arms flapping, insisting he was a butterfly while I pretended to catch him with a net (his towel).

It's gloomier now. Someone's tried to mask the cigarette smell with lemon Pledge and I'm nauseated.

Cole gallops after us. I hate to say it, but the kid's presence calms me.

"CD," says Jalen, chucking his phone over my head to Cole. "You on cam duty."

"Cam duty?" I ask.

There's the same dusty bowl of potpourri resting on the toilet tank that's been there for years. On the sink is a needle.

Jalen tips the toilet lid over and sits. Queasy, he takes deep breaths. "You're gonna pierce my nose—and CD gonna film it."

21

"BUT YOU'RE afraid of needles."

Jalen gives me a *how would you know that?* look. He steril-izes the needle with a vodka-soaked cotton ball. Cole doesn't have rubbing alcohol. "Would go to a shop, but I'm not eigh-teen. Pops won't sign the consent form."

"What about Josefina?" I make the mistake of looking into the mirror, and it's obvious what I'm trying to accomplish.

"Ehh, doesn't wanna pierce me. Says it'll look bad."

Already bored, Cole's punching the hand towel like a boxer, fast-mumbling some song.

"So why me?"

"Yeah, why her?" whines Cole. "I wanted to do it!" He swats the towel a little too hard and the whole rack crashes to the floor.

"That's why," says Jalen, shaking his head.

This is my chance to prove to Jalen I *am* cool. That I *can* and *will* do something Josefina won't. Something Mr. Thomas won't let him do. Something Cole *can't* do.

"And," says Jalen, "MageLayer12 on Twitch bet me a hundo I'd be too chicken. Here, or here?" He hovers a Sharpie over his right nostril, then left.

"Doesn't the right one mean you're gay?" says Cole.

"Right one it is." After Jalen marks the spot, he swivels on his heel. "Nothing wrong with being gay, CD. Don't say stuff like that."

"I know," says Cole, reddening, "I'm just saying—it'll look ugly."

"*Gay* and *ugly* aren't synonymous. See what you doing?" Cole screws up his face. "*Cinnabons?*"

"*Synonymous,*" I say.

"Okay, Kate," mumbles Cole.

I throw a handful of potpourri at the kid's face.

———

"When I say *when*, start streaming, but don't get her face in it, CD." Jalen nods at Cole, ready to film. "Don't want Big Bro comin' after me," he says to me. "Ain't tryna mess with that Afghan fire. Seen it come out in practice."

Afghan fire? Maybe I'm less hesitant to jam the needle in his nose.

Afghans are kind by nature. Baba says they'll serve tea to their enemies. He showed me this video of a boy in Kabul making naan once. When the boy saw the camera was on him, he nodded, smiled, waved. Something in my soul shifted, seeing him. He looked like Rafi as a child.

Our knuckles brush when Jalen hands me the tongs. His skin's warm. A little sweaty. "Gentle now, it's my first time."

Jalen's trying to be all suave but I can see the fear in his light brown eyes, watering in anticipation.

"Tongs?" I say, snapping them, and Jalen winces.

"No piercing clamp, so tongs'll have to do. Keeps the skin tight."

Jalen extends his arm like *hold up*, woozy. "I'm good. Start the stream, Cole." He looks at the camera. "Okay, MageLayer12, get ready to cough it up. JT keeps his promises. Let's go, baby. *Woo!*"

The feeling of pushing a needle through flesh—not as bad as you'd think. There's this satisfying little *pop* as it breaks the skin.

After the stud's in and the blood's wiped off, Cole and I lift Jalen off the toilet seat and prop him against the wall, waiting for his *oh shh*'s to fade out. The setting sun's shadow on the turquoise shower curtain has snaked its way to the toilet with an orangey glow.

"Okay now?" I ask. Jalen nods. "I should go . . ."

"Rafi's sis." Jalen blocks the bathroom door with his super-humanly long arm. He swallows hard, then looks up at me. "Happy birthday."

His piercing *does* look good. It suits him. I did that. *Me.*

And to effectively ruin what was gonna be a cute moment, I say, "You too."

———

After a shower (Baba asked why I smelled like cigs and I told him I'd jogged through a smoker circle), dinner, and triple chocolate cake with PB M&M'S, Habib calls with an update. Their flight to Qatar is on November 13.

I'm replaying the afternoon in my head, every look Jalen gave me, every word exchanged, not really listening to Baba's update till I realize Raf's jaw has stopped working on his naan. *The thirteenth.* The date is significant, somehow.

That's the day of Raf's shoot.

I swallow hard, hoping Dad doesn't have mind-reading powers. Under the table, Raf taps my foot, like *be cool*.

———

After I'm forced to sit for tea for thirty-two and a half more minutes, I'm finally excused from the table.

"Mafi," says Dad as I grab the stair banister. I turn. Without his glasses, the shadows underneath his eyes are pronounced. "You don't tell anyone about your relatives in Kabul, do you?"

I freeze.

Shake my head. If Dad doesn't want Afghan meatballs rolling out on Insta, imagine if he finds out we told anyone we have family in Afghanistan.

"So if someone asks you if you have family in Afghanistan, what do you say?"

Sleepy-eyed, Baba observes me, hands clasped. On the mantelpiece behind Baba's head sits the wooden donkey Habib carved for him when they were kids.

I reach for my birthday necklace around my neck and hold the eye charm in my hand.

"No, Padar."

"For their and our safety, you must *never* tell anyone. Is this clear?"

I nod.

Dad inclines his head, releasing me.

Afghanistan's far. But for Dad, not far enough. Every time Habib calls, I can see it in his eyes. He's back. In Kabul.

22

MY SIXTEENTH birthday is drawing to a close. One and a half hours left and still, no Cole. Granted, Cole only brings me letters one or two times a month . . . but I had *really* hoped . . . Maybe I didn't look hard enough? Maybe I'll sneak out, go with a flashlight . . .

The oak tree's been tapping my window for the last hour, faking me out. Darn wind. Mr. Meowgi looks up from the comforter every time, too.

I wish Cole had social media or a phone. At least his parents are strict about something . . .

Tap. Tap. Tap.

"Stop it, you infernal tree!"

"Huh?"

It is Cole. My eyes search his hands. No letters.

"What about Josefiiiiina?" he mocks, a line I'd said to Jalen before I pierced him. Cole shimmies his shoulders.

"Shut up, Coleslaw!"

"Mm, Jalen, kiss me, want me, love me!" Cole clutches his heart, laughing.

I hold my breath. *Don't engage.* "What do you want?"

"Forgot to give this to you," Cole says. "Got it last night." He pulls out a folded note from his hoodie pouch and I spring to the window.

Seeing my desperation, Cole juggles it with an: "Oh, oh, oh!"

"Coleslaw, I swear, I'll smack a kid, seriously!"

"Okay, okayyyy." He pitches the note inside.

I narrow my eyes. "You read this."

"No, I didn't!" Cole nearly screeches it.

"But it's not taped."

"This one didn't come taped, Rafi's sis."

I raise an eyebrow.

He raises his hands. "No cap!"

I shake the note at him. "Remember, if you've read it, you're not gonna grow! No NBA for Cole."

"Agh!" Cole plugs his ears. "Don't even put that into the universe!"

I do think the kid's telling the truth. Somehow, Cole still hasn't figured out that I'm the Ghost. If he knew, he'd definitely hold it above my head somehow.

I deal out five dollars from the eighty-one Baba gave me for my birthday.

Just then, "COLE!" echoes into the night. Then the sound of a door slamming.

"The beast has awakened!" whispers Cole.

He leaps onto the tree like a flying squirrel. The branch cracks a little lower and I murmur, *"Be careful!"*

The leaves are still shaking when my door swings open all the way. I step on the note to hide it with a slippered foot.

"Um, hello?" I tell my big brother. "Just because Dad doesn't want us shutting our doors doesn't mean knocking can go out the window, too!"

Raf eyes me suspiciously. Maybe *out the window* wasn't the smartest word choice. "Thought I heard something."

I cock my head. "Are you wearing silk pajamas?"

"Maybe." He gives me a head bob. "Night, Mafia."

"Yeah, whatever, night."

He half closes the door.

———

I don't read the note until midnight. I'm at war with myself, playing with my evil eye necklace, wondering if I *should* read it. I know Jalen. At least, I already know his deepest desire, his biggest wish: to get to the NBA.

Anyway, I'm the Ghost, not a fairy. I'm not a wish granter. I'm a vengeance seeker, snuffing rumors before they catch fire. This is not my territory.

Plus, Jalen said if he told, his wish would never come true. But he's not telling me, is he? Is there a loophole? I flip through a library-borrowed law book but my eyes immediately fuzz over . . .

What if his wish doesn't come true and it's my fault? Do I believe in this superstitious stuff, or is it just fairy nonsense—make-believe?

But how can I not read it? What if it helps me understand him better—win his heart?

Fat chance. He's with Josefina, my brain retorts.

I light a candle, because this feels sacred somehow. One

whiff tells me the note doesn't smell like D&G. After spending twenty-four hours at Cole's, it reeks of ashtray.

Like a relic excavator with her fossil brush, I take my time unfolding it. I know it'll be a doctor type of scrawl; I've seen Jalen write answers on the board in A&P.

My heart leaps, seeing words there. I haven't let my brain assign meaning to them yet, but the scrawl is definitely his.

It takes a while for it to sink in that *I wish I was an NBA player* isn't what's written. Nothing like that.

I bite my lip. Then read aloud, "I wish Pops would get better."

23

ON SATURDAY morning, I wake to something massive jumping on top of me. Too big to be Meowgi. Guava shampoo fills my nostrils. There's only one explanation.

"What the hell, Kate?" I shove my big sister off the bed.

When we were kids, I used to shake her bed in the night so she'd think there was an earthquake. Kate got back at me by sometimes jumping on my bed to wake me. Twenty-one, and she still does it.

My head spirals, dropping me into reality. I was dreaming. I don't remember what about, but my stomach's in knots. What was I doing before I fell asleep?

The note! For the last three nights, I'd fallen asleep with it on my chest. I couldn't get myself to put it inside the jewelry box in the vent with the others. It's not like the other notes, out for blood . . . I pat the bed—

"What's this?" Kate's curly head emerges, hair swished over her face from the fall. I commandeer the note at lightning speed.

"That's private." Not for her eyes. But maybe not for mine, either. The stomach knots tighten. "Why are you here?"

Kate scans my room, probably deciding what to carp on.

"You really need to close your mouth when you chew." She's referring to Nutter Butter cookie crumbs on my desk. The squirrel must've conducted another night raid. I look to Mr. Meowgi, observing me adoringly from the comforter.

"Your security systems are faulty, dude," I tell him.

Kate puts the wrapper in the trash and lines up my pencil case with my laptop.

"I texted you. *Birthday brunch.* You didn't respond."

"Do we have to?" I'm not in a brunchy mood.

"Not like I drove one hour to see you or anyth—"

"Okayyyy. Your hair's curly," I say, though I look at the cat when I say it.

"I decided it looks more . . . grown-up. Better not to straighten the life out of it all the time. And you? You're letting your natural color grow out?"

"No." Mr. Meowgi stops purring. I guess my darker blond roots have grown out a bit. I haven't bleached it for a while.

"Well, you don't want to look trashy." Kate rifles through my closet. "Here, wear this." She picks out this frilly purple thing from Brandy Melville.

Annalie has one just like it, in yellow. She wore it yesterday. I don't even like purple.

"I'm good." I stand and shrug into an SMN zip-up. With my back to Kate, I place Jalen's wish in my zip pocket.

"Ooh, this one's so pretty." Kate's holding a red flowy skirt that Yasmoon sent me a few years back. Annalie said it looked too *culturey* and I haven't worn it since. "Maybe with a crop top . . ."

"I'm ready."

Kate's natural curls bounce like a shampoo ad when she glances at me. The guys at SMN used to call her the *hot hybrid*. She feigned offense but I know she liked it. "Mom did say you were basically married to sweats nowadays. C'mon"—hangers squeak on the rack—"I'll pick you out an outfit—"

"Nah."

She pulls a cute frown, but it won't work on me. I'm not some dude trying to get into her pants.

"It'll be fun to dress up, and—"

"I said no!"

Meowgi sprints from the room. Kate withers. I feel kinda bad, until: "Well, I hope you're at least wearing underwear." She sighs into my chair.

"Why?"

She makes a *ckk* noise at the back of her throat. "Have some self-respect!"

I dish out a thong from my drawer, whip her in the face with it ("EW, THAT BETTER BE CLEAN!"), and shut myself in the bathroom to put some *self-respect* on.

I hate this feeling, like I want to smack her, hug her, and impress her all at the same time.

———

Outside, it's a sunny, blue-skied, cookie-cutter California morning. A thin strip of smog sits over the "mountains" in the distance, if you can call Cali's dunes mountains. Sometimes it's so polluted I'm claustrophobic, and I imagine all the free radicals the smog's generating in my body.

If the free radicals don't kill me, Kate's driving will.

Mirror check.

Lipstick check.

EDM FULL VOLUME.

Gun the engine.

Rage Kate engaged.

The road is the only place Kate colors outside of the lines. Today's a *green means gun it, blinker optional, cut everyone off* sort of day, my sister's red lips cranking out a steady torrent of half curses.

I don't wanna be the next dead body her classmates dissect for practice, so over the thumping music, I tell her *slow down!* I swear the electronic dance music makes Kate drive faster. It's like being in one of Cole's racing games.

After she zooms into this old woman's parking spot and yells at *her*—"For duck's cake, Miss Gran-ola, move any rod yam slower?"—Kate finishes the flourish by flipping the woman the bird. Kate's SUV used to be Mom's. It's hard to believe that this is the same car that used to take me to piano lessons.

We finally take our seats at the Filling Station.

"Oh, how lovely—right next to the firepit!" Kate says, clapping daintily like a queen, when the server shows us to our seats. "Thank you so very much—Ian, is it? How's your day going so far?"

When the server—"It's going" Ian—leaves, Kate sighs. Then looks at me. "What's with the stink face?"

"How's compartmentalizing going?" I ask her tentatively.

———

Kate orders a mimosa, because she's Kate, and flexes her twenty-oneness. I get a hot chocolate. When Kate raises a disapproving eyebrow, I tell Ian *extra cream* to really ruffle her feathers. I get the waffles with brown sugar butter and Kate, granola with vegan yogurt and blueberries. Vegan's her new thing. Last year, she went paleo and was into CrossFit, scoffing when I refused to eat the wibbly pile of egg whites she put in front of me. *But you need protein!*

"So?" Kate says, shaking my wrist from across the table. "How does sixteen fare?"

My sixteenth birthday was . . . an event.

"Yeah," I say, "cool." I scarf my waffle. Not because I'm particularly hungry, but because I know eating like this will bother Kate.

"You know," she says, "you shouldn't take the next bite of your food until you've swallowed your last. You're prone to ingest more food if you eat fast."

Prone. Ingest. Who does she think she is? Note to self: Never use snooty words when you could use simpler ones. It's annoying.

I eat a handful of Kate's blueberries—antioxidants—to neutralize the effects of the smog.

Spearing the second waffle, I tilt my head at Kate like *cheers*, and cram the entire thing in my mouth like a hamster.

"Lovely." Kate folds her hands on the table. "People are looking," she says in an undertone.

"Oof za fruck carefs?"

More than anyone, my sister brings this side out of me. The free side. The radical side. The side that wants to push back, go against the grain. Ghosting gives me a rush, but this is *almost* better.

A thin shadow darkens our table, blocking the sun, and a breeze.

"*You.*"

The voice sends an involuntary shudder down my spine.

I look up. It's Josefina and *It*.

Bian's hands are on her hips. Her hair is set in beachy curls and her white teeth glint in the sun.

I don't spit the waffle out. *A waste.* I chomp away, taking my time.

"Friends from school?" I've ignored them for so long Kate's all awkward and feels the need to say something. Her face has turned a shade of scarlet.

I shake my head, and the waffle filters an emphatic curse or two.

"We know your secret," says Bian.

For a second, I don't move. Up until this point, *leaf shmeaf*, I've decided Brit can't have figured out my secret. Nothing bad happened after my birthday. Until now.

Bian doesn't speak for a while, wanting me to fess up. But to what? I'm still chewing. Chewing, and thinking about what she's going to say next. I clutch my evil eye amulet, willing it to do its damn job, to keep Bian's evil glare from hurting me.

I swallow.

"What's my secret?" I say, pleased when it comes out level. Smug, even.

Bian taps angrily at her phone with a nail so long I wonder how that's functional for butt wiping, and plays the video of Jalen, a hand forcing the needle through his nose. She pauses the video as Jalen starts to holler, then grabs my wrist and turns it over. "Same nails." Chipped blue nail polish. I should've removed it days ago.

Maybe a small part of me *wanted* her to see the video.

I look to Kate for help, but she has her lips sucked in, all crinkly. They look like Meowgi's asshole. Why does my sister hate me so much?

"You stay away from Jalen," says Bian. "Right, Jo?"

Josefina finally speaks. Her voice is soft. "His nose looks *so* bad. It's infected, too."

"Infected?" Guess the vodka sterilization didn't work. Poor Jalen. I take a swig of hot chocolate and say, "I think it looks badass."

"Stay away from Jalen, homewrecker," says Bian. "And"— she swishes her hair back, as if to think for a moment—"tell Rafi hi."

"Oh, I *knew* I'd seen you before!" says Kate, and she perks up for the first time today. If I were more like Bian, like effortlessly pretty and more like—I don't know, stuck-up?—would Kate like me? "You're Beyong, right?"

"*Bian.* You're Kate?"

And they do this little wavey-jumpy thing I hate.

Kate leans over. "Rafi *really* likes you."

I let them talk, using the opportunity to sneak looks at Josefina. With her dainty nose, long hair, and seemingly pore-less skin, I get it, she's pretty. She's wearing a blazer with a green bandeau that hugs her chest. She made an Insta post about the bandeau last week. She sewed it with Bian.

Cute, but not as comfy as a hoodie.

". . . Well, you know, *he* broke up with *me*."

"What?" I say, coming to. I thought it was the other way around.

"Yeah," says Bian, though she tells it to Kate like I don't exist. "He told me he needed to *focus* on basketball."

"Basketball *shmasketball*," says Kate. "It's just a hobby. He'll be back."

"Um, no. It's not like our brother's playing in some YMCA basketball league, Kate. IU basketball is D1; they only recruit the best. After college, he'll—"

"Join the real world like everyone else," offers Kate. "What are the chances of getting into the NBA anyway? Must be like—"

"—one point two percent," says Bian, tapping away at her phone. "Just googled it."

"See?" says Kate, pleased. My blood starts to boil, acknowledging a sisterly blowout on the horizon. "It's a pipe dream. Besides, it's not like he's any better than the other IU—"

"He is! He's doing this campaign and everything!"

Oh. Oh no no no.

"*Campaign?*" says Kate, eyes narrowed. Bian looks interested, too. Josefina's not. She's smiling at a passing butterfly.

"What campaign?" Bian says sweetly. She's jealous and wants in; she can't stand not being the center of attention.

"*Camping,*" I say. "The team's going camping. Some bonding ritual."

"Mafi," warns Kate, in the same voice she used when we were kids and I swore a bird stole her diary.

Backed into a corner, I bump my glass with my elbow. Ice water splatters onto Bian and Josefina.

Yelping, they vamoose; my goal. But not before yammering some more about me being a homewrecker.

Kate's like an angry balloon. *Rage Kate* re-engaged. Lasers will soon shoot from her eyes. Wouldn't be too bad. If she aimed down, she could reheat my hot chocolate.

"Why do you have to be such a—a—rogue."

Kate rips her purse from the chair and I say in my most regal voice: "Excuse me, dear sister, I believe you've neglected to settle the bill?"

"Happy birthday," she says, scribbling her signature so hard on the receipt it tears. She screams in frustration and thunders off, not apologizing after she whaps the same old lady whose spot she'd stolen in the head with her purse.

I follow her to the car, keeping a safe distance of six feet, texting Rafi. I've gotta warn him I might've spilled the beans . . .

In the car, Kate looks at me.

"What happened to you?"

I guess I've run out of jokes. I stare at gray-white bird poop on the windshield.

Kate exhales, running a hand through her brown hair. Guava releases from the follicles. She still insists on kiddie no-tears shampoo.

"Remember what I told you about high school." Kate's voice is level. Serious. "Do you want to cast yourself as a home-wrecker? *Hook-Up Material*? Guys with girlfriends are off-limits! Reputations stick, Mafi. *Have some self-respect,*" she murmurs for the second time.

My thong has crept up my bum and I've got the itch to fix it, but I'll wait.

Maybe I have some self-respect after all.

24

AT HOME, we're in the backyard on the hammock. Our feet thump the earth with each push off, a cool breeze pushing and pulling the hair from our faces. Whenever me and Kate fight, we get quiet for a while, but still enjoy each other's company. I at least like that about her. The companionable silence.

Dad's on the deck, reading. He hasn't turned the page in a while and I wonder if he's asleep, or just resting.

The Prodigal Brother appears, palming a basketball.

"Where was my brunch invite?" Raf says to Kate.

Kate crooks a finger for Rafi to bend down so she can kiss him on the cheek. "Apparently, you need all the sleep you can get so you can prep for this camping trip of yours?"

"Camp—" Rafi shoots a look at Dad on the deck. But we're across the lawn; Dad's too far to eavesdrop. Raf spins the basketball on his finger, thinking.

"*Rafi.*"

Spinning. Spinning so fast it's making me dizzy.

"*Rafi Bakht.*" Kate stops the ball. Grabs his arm. "*Do not* upset Dad. Mom and Dad have enough on their plates."

"Like what?" I ask.

Kate looks at me like I'm a gnat on her fruit. "The separate beds, for one."

Two full-size mattresses arrived a few weeks ago. Honestly, I get it. I'd hate sharing a bed, too. I didn't think anything of it. It's not like they have separate rooms.

"That's only because Mom kicks Dad in the night," says Rafi.

Or"—Kate raises her eyebrows meaningfully—"they need *space*? I'm just saying. First it starts with beds. Then separate lives. It's our duty to take care of our parents. And Baba."

"Baba's always been cranky and ancient," says Rafi. "Only time he's happy is when I do math for him."

"Spend all the time you can with them," she says. "Baba's done a lot for this family."

"You talk like they're all dying or something."

She frowns. "So what about this campaign?"

Raf does a mock pass with the basketball and does a little turn. "Eh, you know, I was gonna do this *guys against sexual harassment* thing at SMN but decided against it. Conflicts with practice."

Kate looks at me for verification. I shrug.

That's enough for her. For now.

"Basketball isn't everything, Rafi jan. You need to think about what you want to do when you've exhausted that route."

"Rafi's going to the NBA," I say.

"This is between me and my brother."

"*Our* brother."

Kate says, "Rumor is *your* sister is over at boys' houses, piercing noses and wrecking homes." What happened to companionable silence?

Rafi passes the ball; I'm not ready and it whaps me, hard, in the chest.

"The hell, Raf?"

"That was you, Gozeh Farangi?" he says. "I heard it was this"—he looks at Kate—"new girl he's into. From San Viejo Prep."

There's the sound of the basement door closing.

"Kids!" shouts Baba. He putters across the lawn, paper in hand. He sees Rafi. "My Kush Giant! I've got some calculus—"

And I'm up to the safety of my room within seconds. As I open my DMV manual to cram for the last time, the walls are buzzing with this energy. This warm light. Is SVP a front, like Bree for Brit, in Fallon's phone? *Could* Jalen Frikken Thomas be *into me*?

25

MONDAY MORNING, Mom excuses me from school so I can take my driving test.

Besides the fact the examiner has breath like old dog treats and curdled milk, the exam goes without a hitch. I don't bump the curb when I parallel park and only miss two questions on the written version.

After, Mom takes me to lunch at Board & Brew to celebrate, and then I drop her at home so I can drive to school *alone*, strategically arriving *after* synchronized swim.

I back slowly from the drive and pull down the street, bug-eyed and smiling. My first time driving solo! Leaning on his shovel, Neighbor Cam watches me from his yard, likely thinking, *Lord help us, there goes another one.*

With rap music bumping from the rattly speakers and wind in my hair, I get so amped that I roll down the window and *woot!* at a jogger. Interpreting the surge of emotion as encouragement, he pumps his fist. He's still smiling when I look in the rearview.

I arrive at SMN in sky-high spirits. Till I pass a wet-haired Annalie and my old crew in the hall, whispering, giggling, behind their hands.

Now functioning on a lower wavelength, I unearth my A&P notebook from my locker. I glimpse some junior dudes in my periphery and when I turn, their eyes make unwanted contact with my chest, my butt. One bites his lip and winks, and I stalk off to A&P, hood up. I forget about the car and the license and the freedom, 'cause I'm not free. Not really. I'm still chained to CJ.

Maybe I'll poke Mom again, push the homeschooling card. Sweatpants and hoodies can't hide everything.

———

I get to A&P fifteen minutes late.

I hand Mr. A the pass from the secretary. He says, "Pop quiz today," like *good luck*. Then warns he *won't tell me again* to remove my hood, but he probably will.

I scan the desks in the back, finding my hiding spot taken. Holding my breath, I slide into the seat next to Brit and she chuckle-sighs at me. But she says nothing, does nothing, to indicate she knows my secret. Maybe she doesn't know I'm the Ghost after all.

The quiz is on spinal anatomy and it's easy. When I walk it up to Mr. A's desk, he marks it in front of me with a red *99/100*. I whine a bit when I see the blunder but he shrugs. I forgot my damn name.

After the quiz, Mr. A announces we'll be going on a field trip after Thanksgiving. Hiking with an oral exam format, with questions about physiological processes and anatomical stuff along the way. The exam component will be answerable as a group, which has its pros and cons.

"Props to Mr. A for breaking us free from this joint," says Fallon. No one laughs. I hate to silently agree with the dude— till Mr. A reveals Black Star Canyon's our host. The haunted place where Fallon left Brit to the mountain lions.

Fallon's quiet.

Brit shifts in her seat.

Does she notice the pencil trembling in my hand?

We watch an educational video called *Muscles in Motion* on the projection screen for the rest of class.

A silver fingernail taps my desk.

Brit leans in, staring forward. Her hair smells like honey. "You didn't answer my text."

"Huh?"

"I sent you a text." The spam text on my birthday, that was her?

"How'd you get my number?"

"Jalen."

I didn't know the two were friends, but Brit Rossi's an It-girl. Like in the good way. She gets what she wants.

I glance at Jalen and Tommy. Jalen's veiny arms are folded across his chest. Tommy whispers something to him, then flexes his bicep, mirroring the spindly biceps anatomy on the screen. Jalen tips his chair back and picks up Tommy's romance book of the week, *Pride of the Navy*. To the shirtless hunk on the cover, Jalen makes a face, like *not bad*.

Noticing me staring, Jalen's lips curl into his half smile and my heart flip-flops.

"I saw you at Josefina's party," whispers Brit. "The note that drunk guy gave me, *Justice will be served*, that was you."

She stares ahead, smirking as she talks. "After the leaf in your hair, I wasn't sure if you were the haunted—a letter writer out for blood—or the haunter, the Ghost. You have the look of both." Her voice is silvery, and all I can think is *Siren*, the mythological enchantress who lures sailors to their death. No wonder Brit's got so many followers.

Our eyes meet. I hang on her every word.

"But it's transparent now," she says. "I know who you are."

Mr. A shushes us with a "Shahin! Rossi!"

My arms tingle with electricity. She could tell me I'm Queen Elizabeth incarnate, or that life is a game and we're all simulations, and I'd believe her. That poise, conviction—

When Mr. A is distracted by Fallon's feeble attempt to start a fire, Brit whispers: "Later I'm going to send you a text. This time you'll answer."

I stare ahead. Nod.

So the Ghost meets the Siren.

Where will she lead me? You can't kill a Ghost, something that's already dead.

———

I show Baba my temporary license after dinner when he and Dad are watching the news. It's nothing special, just a folded piece of paper I'll stick in my wallet.

But to me, it's everything. Freedom.

My permanent license will come in the mail in a few weeks. I hope my photo's not a disaster because I'll be stuck with it for years.

Baba's turning Habib's wooden donkey in his hands. He glances at the paper with a distracted "Mm," one eye glued to the TV. There was another mass genocide in Bamiyan. The Talibs massacred one hundred Hazaras this time.

Dad clicks his tongue and stalks off to the bedroom, probably to read.

He doesn't want to see it.

The news footage shows bearded Talibs waving their guns. Chanting.

This is why Jalen can't say stuff like *Afghan fire*. These men—they're not Afghan. They're not us. Baba says in the 9/11 attacks, not one of the hijackers was Afghan. That the Afghans' terrorists . . . are our terrorists, too.

"What are they saying, Baba?" I ask.

Baba's lips move soundlessly, translating. He looks at me and says: " 'Death to Hazaras; Hazaras to the grave.' "

Baba's gaze falls to the wooden donkey in his hands. His thumb runs along the smooth curve of its back. I know he's thinking of Habib.

About the dangerous journey he and Yasmoon are about to take.

I feel guilty for bothering Baba in the first place. For being excited about a silly piece of paper.

26

ON TUESDAY evening, I've just finished my homework and queued up *Blood Jurors* on Netflix when I get a text.

Brit. My fingers dance across the screen to create her contact card.

> Be at Fro-Yo Emporium on Grand at 8:30pm.

I literally *just* got my license. I doubt Mom and Dad will let me drive in the dark, and am surprised when Mom tells Dad to let me enjoy my newfound freedom.

"Who are you meeting?" says Dad, dent in his forehead forming.

I play with my evil eye necklace. "Annalie."

Because lying is easier. I don't know what Brit and me are yet. I can't say *a friend*, because . . . is she? I try to swallow but my mouth is too dry.

Mom brightens. "Mama, I'm *so* glad you're hanging out again!"

———

The lone drive to Fro-Yo Emporium is less *woot-y*.

Finding a lucky spot right up front, the doors *bingbong* as I walk inside, my nose assaulted by the sweet fragrance of fro-yo and waffle cones.

It's 8:25 and Brit's not here yet. I sit in the back and stare at a glob of fro-yo stuck to my table. Periodically, I peer outside or watch the workers in low visor hats refill toppings behind the counter.

The sweet smell usually makes me hungry, but a dull ache between my eyes is forming. I'm twirling my hair when headlights shine through the window, blinding me.

A Mercedes-AMG. Raf's favorite car. I know Brit's wealthy—she lives in Newport Beach—but she can't be *that* wealthy.

I squint. Freeze.

It's the Wiggses. *Mayoral Candidate Rolf Wiggs* and his wife.

They hobble toward the door, Rolf first. Wiggs's sunken peepers freak me out, like his body's decided he's so vile he's being unmade and his eyes are the first to go.

Wiggs doesn't hold the door for his wife. She catches it with her knee, nudging it open with a scowl.

Wiggs dispenses a swirl of fat-free vanilla into a large cup. Then shifts to the toppings and snaps at the worker, ordering a "ridiculous amount of Twizzlers" on top. Even his order is gross.

It's then that I realize Brit *is* here. Beneath her Fro-Yo Emporium visor, Brit gives me a cat-eye wink, then gives Wiggs his change. The Wiggses eat at the holey metal tables outside in silence.

If this is what marriage is, I'm out. I wonder if Mom and Dad will be like them when they're old.

Five minutes later, when they're gone, Brit walks over, hip-checking chairs out of her way. A small cup of peanut butter ice cream with chunky Oreos slides onto the table. "*Every* Tuesday at eight thirty," she says, by way of greeting, "they walk in." Her cat eyes hold my own. "Your work on Fallon was—" She wags her head, like *damn*. She maneuvers her sinewy frame into the chair. Only Brit could make a stained fro-yo uniform look badass. She's wearing her big hoop earrings and has tied and knotted her polo shirt to reveal just a hint of flat stomach. Brit leans in. "You are the Ghost." It's a statement, not a question. But she pauses. Waiting.

There are different levels of quiet, and Brit's on *quiet magnetism*. It's not the quiet people default to when they're shy, guilty, or merely don't know what to say. Brit's the sky before a tornado, green and deathly still. The coiling of the snake before the strike.

So this is where you will lead me, my queen? I *will* impress her. Show her I'm worthy. An equal.

Leave it to the Siren to see through the Ghost.

With one tiny nod, I break my second rule. *Never reveal my identity as Ghost.*

Then she says, "We're Ghosting Wiggs. Together," and my head snaps up.

The blender's going. I lean back in my chair; I'd been subconsciously moving toward the Siren as she spoke.

"For you," she says, because I'm in glitch mode, staring at the Implicit Contract in a Cup, like I'm trying to magic it to speak for me. When Brit asked me here, I was expecting . . . what was I expecting?

Not this. Isn't this what I'd wanted? To take Ghosting to the next level, catch a big fish like Wiggs? My dread melts with the fro-yo when Brit says, "Don't worry, I won't tell anyone our secret." *Our* secret.

You'd think after not speaking this long, I'd have something cool, perhaps amusing, to say.

Instead: "Yum yum, Oreos and peanut butter. *How'd you know?*"

Brit regards me from beneath her visor. "Like you're the only one who studies people." She bites her tongue with a teasing smile and I swoon a little. I'd only ever seen her do that for social media.

But this time, it's for me.

When Brit goes back to work ten minutes later, I spoon-feed myself the melted slop, our edible contract signed.

————

I'm just tossing my hair in a bun before bed, full of fro-yo, Oreos, and sugary excitement, when Raf knocks on my door. It drifts open.

He puts a foot up against my wall. *Eff, he's here to annoy me.* "Who'd you go meet?"

Mom's given him a haircut but I won't tell him it looks dope. Messy bun on top, shaved on the sides, one strand of hair down to frame his square jaw. My siblings drained the good-looks well and by the time I was born, there was none left for me.

I twist my hair, staring into my vanity mirror, a gift from Annalie. I haven't switched on the bulbs in forever. "A friend."

"Who?"

"Brit Rossi." I don't need to lie anymore because I don't have to. The Ghost and the Siren have joined forces.

Raf scoffs, like *yeah right.*

"Seriously!"

The way he looks at me hurts a little, like why would *Brit Rossi* waste her time with me, CJ.

"When'd you two start 'hanging out'?"

"We're not 'hanging out.' We're *hanging out.*" I put a bobby pin in my mouth, fixing my bangs.

Rafi reaches to the top of my doorframe and stretches. He's feeling himself right now and it's annoying. "I want you to stay away from JT."

I remove the pin. "Excuse me?"

"Don't act all innocent. Been obvious since we were kids. Bian's still mad you pierced him."

"Why do you care?"

"He's my friend."

"Why's he never come over, then?"

He shrugs. "We've got different interests."

"Or the *same* interest," I mumble. Heat prickles from my cheeks to my hairline. "Wait. *You're talking to* It *again?* Don't tell me you're back tog—"

"We're just friends."

"Is she the one that got you those ugly silk pajamas?"

Still stretching on the doorframe, he twists his torso. "Maybe."

Iago is grooming him with silk . . . not long till they will be back together.

Raf points to the photo of us in the hotel bed, above my head. "Remember Universal, when you were too short to ride the Forbidden Journey and cried for like a week?"

"I cried because you chased and hit me with the broom when we got home, saying it was basically the same as flying behind Harry on the pitch."

He titters with arms crossed, watching a fly on the ceiling. "Good times."

"Is that all?"

I grab a pillow from the bed and nudge Raf from the room.

Raf catches the door. "*Promise me.*"

"Why?"

If he brings up *the party*, I'll scream.

"You don't know how guys talk about you." My teeth clench, reminded of the guys in Josefina's bathroom. The whispering, the looks in the hall. "I can't keep defending you, Goze—"

"*Stop calling me that!*" I throw the pillow. Raf ducks and it hits the wall. Meowgi's eyes dart to the pillow, crumpled in the hall.

"It's mine now," Rafi says, like a preschool teacher confiscating a toy.

I can't sleep without at least four pillows and Raf knows it. But I won't give him the satisfaction. He stomps to his room.

Minutes later, my phone vibrates.

> Want McDonald's french fries?

I'm in the process of thumbs-downing Raf's text when the second text *whoops* in.

You're still driving me to the shoot, right?

I fwap my pillow over my face.

———

On the way to school the next morning, Mom's quiet but her frequent, worried glances are loud.

"Mom, what?"

"It's only . . ." And when she parks in front of SMN, she places a folded crusty note in my lap, embalmed through a process of washing and drying.

Jalen's wish.

"I found this in your zip pocket," she says. "It went through the laundry, I didn't snoop!"

I wish Pops would get better runs red in my mind like a news headline. Old news. And yet—current news. The kind of news that makes your tummy turn.

"Your dad is *fine*," Mom says. "What would make you think otherwise?"

Not what I was expecting.

"It's nothing," I say, gathering up my backpack.

She places her hand on my shoulder. "Please tell me, Mama."

I've gotta give her something. "Well, I guess it just feels lately like—like Dad doesn't want any of us around. He's so serious all the time, and he always shuts himself up in the bedroom or disappears to the deck. And now, you guys sleep in separate beds—"

Oops. Too far.

Mom's hand falls from my shoulder. She clears her throat, stung. "Lots of couples sleep separately these days."

I only know if I dated Jalen, I'd never want to be separate. For like. Anything.

Mom's mouth twitches into a smile. "When'd you start calling your dad *Pops*, anyway?"

I shrug, afraid Mom's daughter-auditing skills will reveal the truth.

"Your dad's a quiet soul, Mama. But never doubt his love for you. For all of us." She waits a beat, then says, "We'll work out the logistics once Habib and Yasmoon move in." She doesn't look happy at the thought. Not at all. I inherited my lack of poker-face skills from Mom.

I stash the note in my backpack, a wad of guilt lodged in my esophagus. That's *two* people who have read Jalen's wish.

———

That evening, a Beamer pulls into the drive. The Wicked Witch is back. *It.*

I scream *noooooo* into my pillow and Meowgi, displeased, swats at my head. His claw catches my pony and by the time he's free, he wants nothing to do with me and his periscope tail darts out the door.

I hear Dad tell Raf *door stays open!* so at least there's that.

27

FRIDAY THE thirteenth, the day of the shoot and Habib and Yasmoon's flight, actually starts out pretty lucky.

My braids don't have flyaways for once, and it's the first time Brit insists I join her table for lunch. She also asks me to Photography Club, *so we can scheme*, she whispers later in A&P, biting her tongue in that seductive, Siren way of hers. I try in the mirror later and look like Mr. Meowgi when he's grooming and his tongue goes *blep*.

After school, Mom has a late client and Dad's subbing, so they ask me and Raf to drive Baba to water aerobics. We say no problem, that we'll go work out, too, but instead we'll drop him off and head to the shoot. Davis told Raf it wouldn't last more than two hours, so we'd be back in time to pick up Baba.

Dad started hiding Baba's keys after he mowed over Cam's mailbox—*by accident, apparently*. "You're lucky it wasn't a child!" Dad told Baba. Baba waved a hand like *pah!* and stalked off.

We're just pulling into the long slope that leads to the YMCA parking lot when Baba announces he's forgotten his swim trunks. This morning, I also found three untouched cups of black tea around the house.

I think Baba's forgetful because today Habib and Yasmoon fly to Qatar.

By the time we've gotten Baba's trunks, dropped him off, and pulled into the Convention Center in Anaheim, we're ten minutes late.

"Building C-AF. Where the hell *is* that?" Rafi's frantic. We've been circling, trying to find the building, for what feels like ages.

"Building C-AF, exhibition hall two. *C-AF*, Raf. Building Cool as F—"

"No jokes. Just look."

"I'm the one driving, here," I say. "Google a map!"

"I'll get carsick!"

Huffing, I pull to the curb, put the car in neutral, yank the hand brake, and fetch a map of the Convention Center. "You're useless sometimes," I mumble, pinching the screen to zoom in.

And I feel kinda bad when Raf agrees.

"Okay, look, it's around the back. See?" I shove the phone in his face.

He waves me off, like *just go*.

When we finally park and find exhibition hall two, set up with a basketball court, the crew's collective gaze says *You're late*. The camerawoman from IU, Florence, gives Raf a pat on the shoulder and offers us water. It smells in the hall, like heat. Like lamps. Dozens of massive studio lights face a white backdrop.

"Armand," a thin man in a maroon suit says by way of introduction. He looks from me to Raf through oversized gold designer glasses. "The director of this whole operation, to which you are now late." He glowers till he gets his apology, then scoffs when we give it. Armand would make a scary principal.

"No makeup." Armand sends the makeup artist away, holding a bottle of foundation. "There's no time. He'll just have to make that . . . *monstrosity* work."

Raf's hand jerks to his face. The monstrosity (*pimple*) must've said hello during the parking stress. These zits move fast.

"At least your hair looks good, bro?" *Too little too late.*

Armand snaps his fingers. "The jersey, quickly."

A pretty girl introduces herself as an IU intern and presents Rafi with his early-made jersey. Forget about blush, Raf's olive skin is purpling. He gets giddy around attractive girls, smiling with top *and* bottom teeth.

Raf brings a hand to his pimple and Armand tells him touching will only make it angrier!

Funny. I've never seen Raf act that giddy around Bian.

———

Rafi with ball extended. Rafi with ball to chest. Rafi with ball overhead.

Yeah, Rafi's having a damn ball, giving Armand everything he wants.

I can't sit still. Maybe I'm more nervous about Raf's shoot than I thought? Or maybe I'm anxious about something else? Intuition tells me to get the hell out of here, to get back to Baba. Has he heard from Habib or Yasmoon? I close my eyes. My brain imagines the smell of jet fumes. Habib and Yasmoon, hearts pounding, as they board a cargo plane. My stomach churns.

Get out of here. Now.

Fifteen minutes later, Armand calls for a water break and I spring up to meet Raf. "Can we go?" In thirty minutes, Baba will be done with water aerobics. Depending on how long he spends talking politics in the Jacuzzi after . . .

Raf's brown eyes ask: *What's wrong?*

"Go?" says Armand. "Not before the last wardrobe change."

"Huh?" Raf tightens his arms to his sides, clinging to his jersey as two assistants attempt to pry it off. Wardrobe's pushed a clothing rack with Afghan garb Baba wouldn't even wear between us: a hairy brown hat called a karakul, like a pakol hat but fancy, and a thick shawl called a patu.

"Rafi." I pull him aside. Raf's hugging his now naked chest, and I choose to ignore the hickeys over his nipple. *Damn Bian.* He knows what I'm thinking. The whole outfit: It's political. The karakul hat is worn by monarchs and diplomats in Afghanistan. And the patu bears the colors of Afghanistan's flag—black, red, and green. The one the Taliban removed to replace with their own.

"This outfit will make a statement," I tell him. "What would Dad say?"

Hair and makeup fuss over Rafi, dabbing on what they can.

Armand hustles over, Florence at his side. "Is there a problem?"

"I'd like to call Davis . . . ?" Raf says in his best *I'd like to speak to the manager* voice, but it's not convincing like when Dad does it.

Armand sticks out his head like an owl. "Who?"

"Uh—"

"Thirty minutes and they've got some fitness influencer coming in here. If we don't snap the shot, who knows what will happen to your scholarship."

"You don't understand," says Rafi. "Wearing this—it could be bad for me. For my family."

The pretty intern girl grimaces, intrigued.

"Why?" says Armand.

Raf turns to me for help, and I'm like *what, don't look at me.* All Dad's ever said is not to broadcast our Afghan heritage, to lay low, *for everyone's safety.*

Is parading in an Afghan flag safe right now?

Impatient, Armand snaps his fingers and Raf's yanked by the elbow, his shorts stripped off by a slew of assistants so that he's standing in his boxers. Is that even legal? He's not eighteen, like he said . . .

"Girl, here. Stand here."

Armand ushers me aside. Cameras are shoved in my face, flashing—blinding me.

"What the—"

"Testing the shot. Need a model."

"Model?"

"Oh, honeybunch, don't flatter yourself," he says. Someone with a little metal thing clicks it near my face.

"Now try it with the turban—" Armand tosses a flowery hijab from the rack and I catch it. "And twirl, we need to practice motion capture for when we give Big Bro the ball."

"It's a hijab," I say, "not a turban. And I'm not putting this on."

When I wore it to the Sufi Center with Baba, it was one thing. But this . . .

Rafi's proffered up at this moment, hobbling, feet stuffed into jandals two sizes too small.

"Are you wearing eyeliner, Raf?"

"No, that's all me." He's nervous, but he's still got jokes.

"Give him the ball, too," Armand says to Florence. "Now, both of you smile—"

There's a rapid-fire of fancy camera clicks, and I duck. "Wait, I'm not in this." I shrink my way from the lights like an alley cat, leaving Raf up there alone. I fold the hijab, place it on the rack.

"Florence," orders Armand, "move that light—yeah—right there. Take some shadow from his nose. Don't need to make it look any bigger than it already is, eh?" He elbows the makeup artist, who gives him a scandalized look.

"All right," Armand says, "shoot him."

———

A crowd's formed outside, snapping photos with the fitness influencer, some shredded girl in Lululemon leggings. Her assistant, a buff dude with a clipboard, storms in and yaps at Armand to clear out. Armand says, "Five more minutes."

Rafi's phone buzzes. *It*, asking if he'd like to hang out. Probably so she can leave more leech marks on his chest.

Armand then announces, "Wrap it up!" and the cute intern struts over to Raf and pats his arm, like *you were great*.

I'd love to snap and send a photo of Raf to *It* right now but I don't know his pass code. It looks like he's telling the intern something important. She frowns and rubs his arm, sympathetically.

Sweat and Axe announce Raf's arrival.

"So let's go then," he says, in a tone that suggests *I* was the one holding *him* up.

"What now?"

"Armand said I can't have the jersey. That *I'll get it when I get it.*"

But I know it's not only the jersey he's upset about.

His phone buzzes again. "*It*," I moan. "Here. Take it."

"That's not Bian. Don't know who that is." Raf picks up. "Uh, yes? This is Rafi, not the Kush Giant, but . . . oh. He what? . . . Jesus. Okay. Thanks for letting me know."

"What? What is it?"

"Baba," says Raf. "I'm listed as his emergency contact. He fell and smacked his face on the pool deck at the YMCA. When they tried to clean him up, he ran off."

Nerves rattle me to the bone. I had a feeling something was off.

"We should call Dad," says Raf.

"No." I'm an accomplice now. If Dad finds out why we weren't there—

I take Raf's hand. "C'mon, Baba can't have gotten far."

28

THE SUN'S gone down.

We drove to the Y, scoured the lot, and when we didn't see him, drove our usual route back to the house at a Cali rainy-day pace, eyes peeled.

I call Baba's phone and it rings and rings. He's *always* got it. At water aerobics, it sits on his towel, ringer full blast.

We pull into the drive without Baba.

Inside the house, it's quiet and dark. The grandfather clock ticks. The fridge taps. Meowgi trills, weaving between our legs. And a pair of eyes, half-mast, glint from the pea-green rocker.

"Baba—?" Relief washes over me. "Oh, thank god."

The old man's hairy nose is caked with blood. It helixes in red rivers to his chin, dripping on the faded gym duffel that sits on his lap.

"Baba, how'd you get home?" Raf asks.

"Baba app'd one of those Zoobers." His chai voice is bodiless, no more spice. "But the driver saw Baba and turned around. So. Baba walked."

The blood probably scared the driver off. And the bare, hairy chest and swim trunks.

"What happened?" says Raf. I go to the kitchen to wet a paper towel.

Baba drawls in a long, slow breath. From the kitchen, I hear him say, "There was no plane." I turn off the faucet and hang my head. *Not again.*

Like I'm a real ghost, Baba looks through me when I tend to his face. I dab the blood and he wiggles his nose. "Habib called Baba when he was getting into the pool."

My brother and I exchange grim glances. There have been *four* false hopes to date. Each time, the flights, the buses, the people who swear they've got some foolproof way out for our relatives . . . they've fallen through.

"Habib and Yazzi left home. Sold it. Now, they stay with another family in Kabul. This time . . ." Baba grips the armrest, voice tense. "Baba was sure. But Allah—he did not will it."

"They can't buy their house back?" says Rafi.

Baba unearths his handkerchief from the duffel and blows his nose. One loud *poot*, then a smaller one. It's always two.

"Talibs are knocking on doors, Kush Giant. They asked your habib"—he stops, looks at us both—"questions. Painted an *X* on his door. He cannot go back."

"What questions?" I ask Baba.

Baba flashes an unconvincing grin, brandishing his gold fillings. "*You kids*, leave Baba to worry, mm? Baba has had a long day. Now, rest." Baba reclines, folds his hands over his gym duffel, and drifts. His nose sounds stuffed, but not broken.

Raf goes upstairs. I hear the bath going. His think tank.

In the dim evening light, I google *X*s and *Taliban* on my phone. I find one BBC article that confirms it: *Taliban are going door-to-door marking the houses of those who pose a threat to their leadership: politicians, teachers, musicians, female business owners, female bloggers, female tattoo artists, female* . . .

I stop reading.

What questions did the Taliban ask Habib? And what did he answer?

I lean back on my hand and accidentally switch on the TV. There's a KTLA segment about how this medi spa in Corona Del Mar can give you abs. It only costs ten thousand dollars.

I'm flipping, flipping, flipping, unsure what I'm looking for, till Baba wakes and grumbles, *End the noise.*

I switch off the TV.

———

Dad takes Baba to urgent care but he refuses both doctors on staff. The first, because he's Pakistani and *probably a Taliban supporter.* The second, because she was wearing an American flag lapel on her white coat: *most definitely a Wiggs supporter.*

Baba doesn't tell Dad he walked home.

I almost wish he would; I've got a ball of guilt the size of New Hampshire obstructing my gullet. Baba insists he's fine, like Mom insists Dad's fine. That their marriage is fine. Baba said after Habib's news, he lost his balance. He blames ear crystals. And the djinn.

———

Later that evening, I can't sleep, so I peruse old photos in the attic.

Mom in her twenties when she'd just met Dad. And standing, miserable, with Grandma at some Halloween party.

Something creaks in the attic and I jump.

Baba squats next to me. Grabs a discolored photo album from the stack. Photos from his childhood. And we both flip through the pages in silence, Baba pointing at this or that person, grinning in recollection. He shows me a picture of him and Habib as boys. Habib looks so much like Dad. Same squashy nose and forehead dent.

Baba fixates on a black-and-white picture of a man wearing a karakul, the kind Raf wore at the shoot, and a long perahan. The man sits at a table with two other finely dressed men and a little boy, having tea in what looks like a field. Armed guards stand behind him.

"Who is that man, Baba?" He looks familiar.

Baba points to the little boy instead. "This is your baba."

"No, Baba . . ." I point again. "The one in the karakul. Who is he?"

Baba strokes his thumb over the man's face. Sticks out his gummy lip. Then turns the page without a word.

Soon, it's time to pack up the past and confront reality.

I direct Baba's feet on the attic stairs. He takes the steps gingerly, feeling his way down. He hobbles to the end of the hall, and I hear his chai voice before I walk into my room. It's got a bit more spice back now. "Gojeh." Baba holds my gaze. Places a hand over his heart and nods.

A heartfelt, Afghan salute.

When I was a kid, I was shy. Grandma taught me not to look people in the eye; she said it was disrespectful to be all *in your face*. Baba trained me out of that. He'd lift my chin and say, *Hello, Gojeh. Up here.*

29

IT'S MONDAY and Jalen's sitting on the curb after practice, basketball duffel slung over his shoulder. Shorts, white socks, and black sandals.

It's the first day of Photography Club and me and Brit are outside shooting edgy photos of railings and staircases. Mostly, we use the time to talk Wiggs strategy. His socials show he's out of town, so the Ghosting needs to wait till he gets back.

"Just put the paste you used on Fallon in Wiggs's fro-yo," she suggests. Brit ruffles her chestnut brown hair and it falls messily over her shoulder.

"I don't know . . ." I hate to turn down the queen.

"You're right, it needs to be something—bigger."

"Definitely."

Brit tells me she despises Wiggs because his win would mean she has to use the boys' restroom.

"It's like an animal shelter in there," she says. "Tommy told me there was a poo in the sink last week. A *poo*, Mafi." She shudders. "I can*not*."

"I can't imagine."

"But it's so much more than restrooms."

It is for our family, too. It's guys like Wiggs who prove Dad's insecurities right.

I think aloud. "So we know he comes in every Tuesday."

"Yes."

"And he drives that Mercedes."

I peer up at her, stairs above. We share a grin. She snaps a photo of me and I go, "What?"

"Wanted to commemorate this stroke of genius we're about to share." Her enthusiasm, approval, only amps me more.

I laugh. Jalen looks our way, then ahead.

"Key the man's car," I growl.

Brit slides the stair railing and hugs me. "Bad. Ass." Then she does her silvery laugh. "A badass who's afraid to talk to her crush. C'mon, you're basically drooling when you look at Jalen in A&P. Go. We'll percolate later."

Brit ushers me forward, and soon I'm behind Jalen, saying, "Oh, hey!" It comes out pubescenty, like I'm Cole or something.

Jalen turns.

"There she is," he says, "Rafi's sis." His lips pull up quarter way, not even half, like usual. He pats the yellow curb and I plop down.

"Where's the Raptor?"

"Broke. Pops got into an accident."

"*What*—is he okay?"

He smiles. "Raptor needs a new bumper is all."

"No, I mean your dad . . . ?"

He looks across the parking lot, into the forest. "Sure."

I think about Jalen's wish. *What is Mr. Thomas struggling with?* But I could never ask. Never pry. It would be foolish to think I could ever grant Jalen's wish.

Instead, I ask: "Do you want a ride?" Raf *just* told me to stay away . . . but I've got the car today. And Jalen looks so beat. He's wearing boring sandals, for god's sake.

"*Know what*, I'll take you up on that." He cancels his Uber.

"Let's go, then." I cast a nervous look at the rectangular window in the gym door. Rafi's working overtime with Coach G but he'll be out soon.

Jalen gathers himself up, knees popping, and we walk into the parking lot. I share a brief look with Brit from across the lot like *OKAY, NOW WHAT?*

She coolly waves me on, and I remind myself to channel her Sirenness. The seductive bit. Not the drowning-sailors bit.

"We've gotta pick up CD, though. He at Rose Park doing drills. Promised we'd go to the Spectrum before all this. That cool?"

I shrink a bit. *Cole?* Then again . . . driving alone with Jalen gives me panic flutters in my gut.

We duck inside the car. I get why Jalen likes the Raptor. Sitting down, his hairy knees eclipse Ptero's gearshift like mountains. "Rose Park? Cool. As long as I'm not picking him up at his house. I can't have Dad seeing me with—"

"Mr. Shahin don't trust Black guys, either?"

It confirms a rumor I heard: that Josefina's mom didn't want her dating Jalen because he's Black. Makes sense, they had a Wiggs sign in their yard.

"No, that's not it," I say, mind whirring. "He doesn't like boys. Like. Any boys. Of any color. Baba says I can't date till I'm forty."

Jalen gives his *tshh-tshh-tshh* laugh. "Hope that's not true." I look at him. "For your sake and all."

Focus. Foot on the brake. Key in the ignition. Hand on the gear stick. Shift to the right, then back to reverse; I can't think when Jalen's next to me, smelling like D&G. But there's another smell, too. Like festering meat. Bian's right—his nose *does* look infected. If I were bossy like Kate, I'd tell him we're stopping at CVS first.

Gosh, the sight of his naked knees is distracting—

"Heads up!"

I slam my foot on the brake but forget the clutch. The car shudders and dies.

"You almost killed Principal B!"

Bald head sweating, he peers inside the cockpit to see what teenager almost leveled him this time.

"Sorry, Principal Bugle!" I shout through the closed window.

He sighs and keeps walking.

Jalen goes *tshh-tshh-tshh* and Ptero sways with his laughter. "I would offer to help but I can't drive stick. Aminata showed me in Germany, it's all manuals there, and—"

"Hey—"

Jalen gazes at me like *huh?*

"Can you like—only talk when we're at stoplights? I need to think."

Some of that sparkle comes back. He gives me his bejeweled smile and I forget to exhale. "Stick shift calc?"

"Stick shift calc," I echo.

And we're off. Just when I'm thinking what to say next, Ptero's *screech* slashes through the air. Jalen throws his weight into the door, hand fumbling for the latch—

"It's just a bad belt!" I shriek. "Jalen—*it's just a belt!*"

Wide-eyed, Jalen shuts the door.

"I was gonna dip." His chest heaves. "Right onto the pavement." He puts his head between his knees—he doesn't have far to go. Then his parenthetical dimples broaden as he laughs and laughs. I join him, but I'm embarrassed. Wish Dad would let me drive the Tesla.

"You holding on to the grab handle does nothing for my confidence," I tell Jalen as we stop at the light on Covenanter, next to the graveyard.

Jalen points to his bubbled cheeks. He's holding his breath. He used to do this when Mom drove us around as kids, too. Said it's so the ghosts don't get jealous.

The light turns green and he exhales.

He notices me laughing at him.

"Common courtesy, Rafi's sis. They ain't breathin' and I am. And seeing as I don't wanna end up over there anytime soon, imma hold the oh-shit handle 's long as I'm ridin' in this death trap."

And because we're busting up with laughter, I start shifting without worrying too much.

"Who's Aminata?" I ask him once the laughter fizzles. "Before, you said Aminata started to teach you to drive in Germany—"

"Mom." Then he stares out the window, closing the Aminata file.

We pass the weathered sign for Rose Park. Cole's hanging from the jungle gym when we turn in.

Jalen rolls down the window. "SLAW!"

Cole yips like a coyote and hurtles across the grass. "Better open that back window," Jalen says, humor in his voice.

"Wha—?"

Jalen leans over me and commandeers the controls, brushing my nose with D&G and peppermint gum. I've got a full-body tingle going on as his skin touches mine. I wonder how it'd feel if he actually, purposefully, desiringly, touched me . . .

Whizz-wham! An orange backpack catapults through the window in the back and falls onto the seat. Cole parkours inside. The car wags, and I'm trying to find the *bejeezus* that Cole scared outta me.

"COLE!"

Lounging, legs open, Jalen rests his thumb over a close-lipped smile, like: *Told you!*

"Lemme guess," Cole says, flashing his gap-toothed smile between us, "we're stuck with this tin can 'cause Jalen won't remove the piercing from his nose so Pops took the Raptor?"

Jalen avoids my eye. It's clear he doesn't wanna talk about the real reason: his dad's accident. "Yo," he says to the kid, "don't diss Raptor's friend Ptero. They're both dinos."

"If it weren't for you," Cole says to me, breathing hard, "I'd still be rolling up in Jalen's leather seats. These—what are they? Multicolored scratchy shit that looks like something my grandma could've knitted?"

"Since when are you cussing, Mr. Butterfly?"

"*Butterfly?*" says Jalen.

Cole gives me the Pubescent Peril look, like *imma murder you*. I actually feel kinda bad. He worships Jalen. It's unlikely Jalen knows Cole's first love was the orange monarch.

"Look, Coleslaw," says Jalen, "Rafi's sis got rules. If we gonna make it to the mall in one piece, you can only talk at stoplights."

I'll correct Jalen soon, tell him to call me Mafi. But I don't want to blow this . . . Jalen in my car, hanging out like we're chummy.

"It's the rule," I chime in, turning around.

"Well at least turn on some rap, damn," says Cole. He scrunches his nose. "Why's it smell like rotten meat?"

I shift into first and the car lurches forward. Grasping the oh-shit handle with one hand, Jalen spins his crusty nose piercing with the other.

30

WE'RE THE Pan Flute Crew, descending in height: Jalen, me, Cole.

Next to Jalen and walking through the Spectrum, I feel like a movie star. Old people with Wiggs hats shoot us dirty looks, and others—girls, mostly—mouth *OMG* behind their hands, marveling at Jalen's tallness. Hotness. Cole touches *everything*, as usual, saying *no fair* when I tell him how much stuff is, and he lists all the things he'll buy when he's a millionaire. At Foot Locker, a worker in a referee shirt tells Jalen, *Bruh, I don't even gotta ask if you play ball!* and Jalen launches into his NBA plan, beaming.

He floats out of the store.

———

"There it is."

We're at Nixon looking at watches. It feels like some VIP club inside, with dim lighting and velvety plum-purple armchairs. Only, the staff doesn't agree we're VIPs.

A saleswoman in a suit reluctantly struts over. She gives us all, Cole with his blue slushie, me with my hoodie and sweats, and especially Jalen—in shorts, socks, sandals, and his home beads and bullet necklaces—a judgy once-over.

"Special-edition Nixon blue face," she says, following Jalen's eyes. She taps a long red polished nail on the glass. I think she's faking a British accent. Is that part of the job description? She lifts an eyebrow at the blue slushie Cole slurps over the counter. "Three hundred and fifty dollars."

Velcro rips. Though Cole's back is turned, I'm like a kite in my own stratosphere over Cole's shoulder. He's counting the bills in his butterfly wallet, money he's made as Ghost courier. Cole doesn't have enough, but he counts again.

"Lay it on me," Jalen says to the woman, sticking out his wrist. "Please."

Her eyes rest on Jalen's dyed hair. His infected nose.

"We encourage only *serious buyers* to try on the watch."

He leans in. Unsmiling, he says, "I *am* serious. I'm big on Twitch."

"Twitch?"

The whole thing is uncomfortable and I fight the urge to leave. When Jalen doesn't budge, the woman obliges.

He slips on the watch and does up the clip. He gives a little "Oo!" and shimmies his arm in our faces. "Rodman has this one. Can I see them other ones, too?"

Jalen selects four others, and the woman places them carefully on the glass for him to try.

Cole peers over the watch Jalen's got on and goes, "Sick!"

And it looks like the *saleswoman* is about to be sick because Cole has regurgitated blue slushie onto the watch face.

Ms. Imitation Britain, minus the Britain (she's suddenly lost her accent), chides Cole and takes the watch to the back to be cleaned.

"Is that a TAG Heuer?" says Jalen, spotting a poster on the wall opposite.

"Doesn't that bother you?" I whisper, palms sweaty as we cross the store.

"Huh?"

"The way she treats you?"

"Nah." Jalen pinches his shirt, showing me the strikethrough *WPC* across his chest. "I ain't playing the game."

"What's *WPC*?"

"White people comfort, Rafi's sis. Or as Ms. Kameka taught us"—SMN's American history teacher—"Uplift Suasion. I'm not gonna dress, act, or look any type of way 'cause white people are too fragile to handle the real JT." The lighted display case glimmers in his eyes. "Here, people cross to the other side of the street when they see me coming." He clicks his jaw. "Might be the *bad* sorta radical in their eyes, but I've gotta be me."

"I get that."

"I'll go for the Nixon after all." Jalen looks up. "Where Slaw at?"

"Maybe Cinnabon, he wouldn't shut up after we passed it." I scour the shop for a short kid in a Supreme cap as Jalen heads for the exit.

Before I can take my next breath—

Cole emerges from around the case and dashes for the door; Imitation Britain screams, "Stop him!"; I go, "Watch out!"; and in an instant, the security guard's whipped Jalen in an arm bar, torquing joints I know from A&P *shouldn't* be torqued—

I scream at the guard, "What are you doing!" while Jalen tells him he doesn't have anything and to *chill, chill, chill.*

"Not *him*!" says Imitation Britain. "The little one!"

The security guard unhands Jalen with a feeble apology. Jalen stares him down and massages his torqued arm. All eyes round on Cole, frozen at the entryway.

The guard beckons to Cole. "Give it here, son."

The kid unearths the blue-face Nixon from his pocket and hands it to the guard, cheeks purple like the armchairs. "I just wanted you to have it," Cole murmurs to Jalen. Jalen's shivering so hard I'm afraid he'll puke.

The guard kneels and cups Cole's shoulder with his stubby paw. "Did this man tell you to take this watch, son?"

"I'm a teenager," says Jalen. He wants to make it clear to the guard. Very clear.

Cole's eyes glisten. He wipes them with an overlarge sleeve. Two seconds pass. Then three. A red light blinks on the CCTV camera anchored in the corner, pointed straight at us.

"No."

"Are you *sure*?"

"What the hell do you want?" I say. "The kid said *no*!"

The guard stands. Places his hands on his belt.

"Randy, he's given it back," says Imitation Britain, sighing. "You three, take your business elsewhere.

Jalen dips without a word—

And power walks all the way to the car, his long legs placing me leagues behind, and Cole, worlds.

31

ON THE way home, I remember a story Ms. Kameka told us about a Black man who got thirty-six years for stealing fifty dollars from the bakery where he worked. After the man had served his full sentence, the bakery owner came clean, said she'd lied.

In Nixon, the watch lady said, "Stop him!" and the guard booked it for Jalen. If Cole had said Jalen told him to take it, what then?

One nation. Divisible. With liberty and justice for some.

I chance a look at Jalen, hood up, parenthetical dimples accentuating his frown.

No traffic-light rule needed for any of us. It's dead quiet till we come to a halt at the light next to the graveyard on Covenanter. Jalen scowls at the headstones. This time, he doesn't hold his breath.

When he speaks, the hairs on my arm stand on end.

"The guard asked," he says, looking out the window, "if I asked you to steal it for me, and you paused."

Jalen shifts his gaze, unblinking, to Cole in the rearview mirror.

Cole wipes an eye. A squeak pops at the base of his throat.

"Nah. Nn-mm," says Jalen, and Cole releases a wounded howl, hugging his knees. Jalen slaps the middle console and twists around. "A pause is all they goddamn need, Cole! It ain't the same for you like it is for me!"

Cole's stock-still, but his eyes and nose run, run, run.

Someone honks. The light's green. My foot slips on the clutch and Ptero convulses. Cole lets out a surprised wail that morphs into sobbing. Jalen shuts his eyes and rests his head on the window. "This kid needta shut the hell up," he mutters. Cole hears. Jalen meant him to.

Hood pulled down to his chin, Cole shakes with muffled sobs all the way to Jalen's.

———

Ptero idles in front of Jalen's ranch. Pollution colors the sunset in a palette of purples and pinks.

"Are you okay?" I ask him. He's still massaging his arm.

"Huh? Yeah." He blinks for the first time in minutes. Then swivels to look at Cole, swallowed by his oversized sweatshirt. He yanks the hood from Cole's head. *"Stealing, CD?"*

Cole repeats, "I j-just wanted you to have it."

Jalen shakes his head. Turns to me. "Thanks for the ride, Rafi's sis."

"*Sure* you're okay?" I ask.

"Lucky he didn't snap it off and I can still play. Not the first time . . . won't be the last. But tell you what, never gets any easier." He uses the grab handle to get out, then leans inside the window. "Uh . . . keep it quiet? People love they rumors at SMN, know what I'm sayin' . . . don't need any heat."

"Of course." No one knows that better than "CJ."

Jalen raps on the passenger door. Walking up the front path, he peers at the Witch Tree, branches silhouetted against a dying sunset.

32

JALEN GONE, I lecture Cole the rest of the drive. I tell him he owes Jalen an apology but he only sniffles. I keep pressing the point till we're one block from home and he squeals, "It's hard to say sorry, okay?" I go, "Well, tough!" and am on the cusp of another rant when the kid parkours out of the window and darts off.

I roll down my window and catch him up. "Grow up, Cole!" Ptero rolls in line with him as he runs. He flips me off and I blaze past him.

By the time I swing into the driveway, heave the hand brake, and hop out, Cole's jumped over his fence. I can't yell now unless I want the entire neighborhood to know our business.

So I stomp the pavement and let out a growl.

Inside, I sling my backpack on top of the shoe bench. The furniture has adopted the smell of grease. I've missed dinner. Whenever I'm not home, Mom forgets to switch on the stove fan.

"Hi, Mom."

Mom's book-shopping on her Kindle at the dining table. I glimpse the title *Reboot Your Life* before she switches over to some hair magazine.

"Have fun with Annalie?" She sounds sleepy, too calm after the afternoon I've had.

Mom texted when we were at Foot Locker and I told her I was having dinner with Annalie at the Spectrum and could I come back in an hour or two?

"It was fine."

"What'd you eat?"

"Food." Mom grimaces so I go: "Burritos, extra guac."

The tablecloth is dotted with ketchup stains and a lone french fry. Guess Dad got his way tonight. Homemade burgers.

I don't have an appetite. *Missing dinner* seems trivial after the events of the afternoon.

"Dad?" I ask.

"Grading exams." Her wrist rotates like a weathervane, like *somewhere in this house.*

Baba, asleep on the pea-green rocker in the dimly lit living room, wakes. He fixes the pakol hat askew on his head. "Katie," he gruffles, shaking a finger, "you know better. It is too late to walk the Kabul—Kandahar Highway." I don't have the energy to correct him.

"Brownies, Mama," Mom tells me. "In the fridge."

"Hey You," says Baba, "your baba would like another."

"Baba is perfectly capable of getting his *own* brownie," she tells him.

Baba looks at Mom from across the room, skeptical. *"Baba supposes, Baba supposes . . ."*

The phone rings. Baba snaps awake. "Gojeh!" he says, because he can't move fast enough.

I answer. "Shahin household." There's crackling on the line. "Habib?"

There's a long inhale, then a husky voice in my ear: "With whom do I have the gladness of speaking?" The speaker's tone is amicable, but there's something amiss, like salt in caramel. Oranges in chocolate. It leaves a bitter taste in my mouth.

"Mafi," I answer. "Are you looking for Bakht?"

Baba's toddled over. "It is Habib!" Baba paws eagerly for the phone.

But the phone is yanked from my hand.

In a voice like a punch, Dad says, "Who is there? *Mm? Who?*" Then hangs up. The shadow of his voice leaves the glass vases singing.

Dad's brown eyes land on mine, black pupils darting behind thick glass, trying to find reason in my eyes.

I murmur, "It was a wrong number, Padar."

But Dad doesn't believe in wrong numbers.

"What did they ask?"

"Um—"

"Fast!"

"Sarafat, *you're scaring her!*" says Mom from the table, to which Dad waves her off.

"He asked who he was speaking with." My voice is surprisingly even. Just a wrong number, right? My brain screams *nonfiction!*

"You said Baba's name," says Dad, lips pursed. *"Bakht."*

Dad and Baba share a grave look.

"Padar, what's wrong?"

"Go to bed, Gojeh," says Baba, holding Dad's gaze. Mom stares at the table.

Dad and Baba retire to the den, and me, to bed. Their low, apprehensive voices flow with the heat through the rattly vent in my room.

———

Just before midnight, right as I'm drifting, my phone vibrates.

It's Jalen.

My eyes can't believe it.

"Hello?" I say, expecting a butt dial.

"So," and the chill in my heart is replaced with butterflies at the sound of Jalen's godly low voice, "rumors, they travel fast."

"What do you mean?"

"Bian found out about the watch."

"I didn't tell anyone—"

"Know you didn't." He lets out a choked exhale, like he's stretching. "Turns out Bian's uncle owns the store. Like that damn telephone game, Bian's interpreting stuff her way, tellin' everyone I made the kid steal the watch. And Josefina popped off on me, so we done. Wasn't good for me anyway . . ."

My tongue's glued to the roof of my mouth. I shoot Meowgi a wide-eyed look. He trills, like *hmm?* I unstick my tongue. "But Nixon has CCTV," I say, "I saw the camera."

"Don't matter. People believe what's interesting, not what's true."

"I'm sorry." Meowgi chirrups at me and I stroke his back. It feels good to be doing something with the nervy energy in my hands.

"Well, imma sleep."

"Okay."

There's a pause, but a good one. A comfortable one.

"Appreciate you, Ma."

Before I can respond, Jalen hangs up. I lie there, frozen, till Meowgi sinks his teeth into my hand. I've hit his petting threshold.

Jalen called me *Ma*.

Not *Rafi's sis*. For the very first time.

33

THE NEXT morning, Baba and Dad leave the house early.

Ptero's screeches don't wake me. Panic does.

Mr. A says cortisol, adrenaline, and an increase in body temperature are all responsible for waking us up, but *c'mon*; my evil eye necklace sticks to my neck with sweat and I'm seeing starry squiggles when I prop myself on my elbows.

I remember my dream. A man was in my room. Lips to my ear, he whispered: *With whom do I have the gladness of speaking?* It felt real, like he was here. I get to my feet.

Pull back the hangers in my closet. Look behind Humphrey, my one-eyed giraffe, on the top shelf.

All clear.

But even in my morning steamy shower, my skin flares with goose flesh. Especially after Meowgi, probably hyped because he took a good poop, jumps at the shower door and it *clang-ang-angs.*

———

Before I leave for school, Dad and Baba pull into the drive.

I descend the creaky stairs and warmth touches my skin.

Sunlight spills through the living room windows and onto my face, casting the rugs, statues, and paintings in a gold—

But Baba and Dad walk in with a mission: *curtain raid.*

"Keep them closed, Gojeh." Baba sticks out his gummy lip, closing the drapes on the stairwell.

"Are we vampires now or something?"

"Gojeh," warns Dad. "When the sun rises, we shut them."

"So vampires, then?"

"Enough!" says Baba, smothering all rebuttals.

Vampires it is.

———

Over the next forty-eight hours, Mom and Dad engage in the Battle of the Drapes. Mom opens them when Dad's gone, thinking Dad's paranoia is absurd. I try to agree, but my heart's not in it. Dad's not a vampire. He loves sunshine. Dad told me it's the reason we live in California and not Michigan, where Mom's from.

At school on Wednesday, Jalen gives me the up nod before A&P, stopping me in the hall to ask if I've got gum. Gum's like currency in high school. After I deliver, he *hugs* me; he's so tall he lifts me off my feet, which receives an open-mouthed *"Whoa!"* from Brit.

The D&G-infused hug shoots all silly thoughts of strange callers and curtains and vampires from my head.

Rafi saw, I think. But he walked on. We haven't talked since he's shown where his loyalties lie: *It*, not me and Jalen. *It* is still *Iago*, poisoning Raf's brain. I bet Raf thinks Jalen told Cole to steal the watch, too.

In bed late that evening, Jalen and me text. The convo's

gone from Cole apologizing to Jalen on Twitch to much ran-domer stuff, like: What wud the world look like if bananas were illegal? My cheeks are sore from smiling.

I'm answering Jalen's most recent text: So what wud ur last meal be? when Meowgi lifts his head and sniffs the air.

I don't have cat senses but I *do* hear something: the low whirr of an engine idling. I roll my eyes. Is *It* here? She can't be. It's too late.

I peel back the drapes.

It's the first time I see it.

A sleek black car with tinted windows parked between our house and Cam's, half-shrouded by Mom's azaleas. A shiver slithers along my spine. The warm light from my desk lamp now looks laboratory orange, sinister. In the closet, Humphrey sits on the top shelf, eye lolling from his spotted head. I shut the drapes and the closet door.

I want to find the fuzzy feeling again. It was there a few seconds ago, texting Jalen.

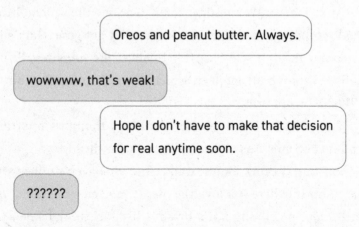

Oreos and peanut butter. Always.

wowwww, that's weak!

Hope I don't have to make that decision for real anytime soon.

??????

The engine revs. I thumb open the curtain a sliver and the car pulls from the curb.

> Just playing.

———

After school the next day, Raf gets a package in the mail from IU and trips up the stairs in his rush for privacy to rip it open.

I don't need to wait long to see what it is.

Because on Friday, Raf parades SMN's halls in his IU jersey like a crowing cock. He makes self-important eye contact with everyone he passes; might as well slap an *Ask Me About My Jersey* Post-it to his chest.

Big Time Recruit indeed.

He wasn't wearing it when we left for school this morning. And I bet he'll take it off before he gets home.

It's minutes till the weekend and Mr. A is just finishing the lecture on nerve endings when Brit jumps up and screams. The sudden burst of motion makes her hoop earrings swing.

"Sorry Mr. A," she says, "but I just found out—*Wiggs lost!*"

"Who's Wiggs?" says Fallon from the back.

I high-five Brit underneath the desk. She's positively buoyant.

Tommy says, "Eff that guy," and he and Jalen bump fists.

———

I push my luck every time I lie and say I'm going to meet Annalie.

So after school, Brit comes over to the house for the first time.

Wiggs is finally back in town, so we've planned the Ghosting for Tuesday. Brit will make sure she's out of Twizzlers at the toppings bar, taking her time replenishing them from underneath the counter. She'll chat up Wiggs while I go outside and let Ptero's toothy key bite into Wiggs's Mercedes.

It feels good to be back here again with somebody. And although I'm not part of a crew, a duo will do.

Still, I can't shake this twisty feeling in my gut . . . First the shoot, now the plane, and the phone call . . . I can't let my Siren down.

I don't want to be *back there* again. Alone.

———

"Hullo?" says Baba, when we walk through the door. He's sitting on his pea-green rocker, holding Habib's donkey. "Is it Annalie?"

"No, Baba. This is my friend Brit." To Brit, I whisper: *"Tell him about Wiggs."* Baba doesn't watch the news till the evening.

"Mr. Shahin, it's so nice to meet you."

"Baba," he says.

"Did you hear about Wiggs?" she asks. Brit waits till Baba gets to his feet. "He *lost*!"

"Oh!"

Brit jumps up and down, and Baba bends his knees with her, without leaving the ground. Then he chants, "Bye bye, Wiggs, bye bye, Wiggs!" and hoists the wooden donkey into the air. Brit giggles.

He grins at me, then at her. Digs inside his vest. "Walnut?"

Brit wags her head. While Baba continues to chant, Brit mouths: *Your baba is so cool.*

"I know," I say proudly.

Before dinner, my phone buzzes.

Come over?

I stare at my phone. Jalen and I have never hung out alone for more than one car ride. Only texting, up nods, smirks, and that one random hug . . .

I doubt I'll be able to anyway. We're about to have dinner, and I'm slicing potatoes and cilantro for bolani.

But I'd be remiss if I didn't try . . . Let's leave the decision to Mom. I go to Mom for things, because like Kate, Dad always looks annoyed when I ask him a question.

"Mom, can I go over to Brit's for dinner?"

"Who is Brit?"

Baba chimes in, "Baba likes Brit."

"She came home with me after school . . . she's a friend."

"Is Annalie going to be there?"

"Mom," I say, "what is your obsession with Annalie? Stop forcing it."

Mom's just thrown the onions into the frying pan, sizzling and spitting in a cloud of smoke. Mom huffs. She always keeps the stove too hot and is surprised when stuff burns.

Baba toddles over to the pan, clucking. "Down, down, *Hey You*. Too hot!"

"Watch how you speak to your mother," Dad says to me, thawing the marinara packet for his mozzarella sticks. Dad's interjection seems to piss Mom off more.

"Go *out*?" says Baba, chewing on a frozen 100 Grand bar, his favorite. The man's gonna break a tooth someday. "What can be better than bolani and Kabuli? Tonight, we celebrate!" He snags a raisin from the cutting board. Mom clenches her jaw.

"Yes, Mama. Fine," Mom says in an exasperated tone. "Excuse me if your mother can't keep up with everything her kids are doing." I think Mom wishes she could leave, too, perhaps to a place where an old man isn't poking his fingers into foodstuffs after visibly hunting for earwax minutes before.

I wrap my arms around Mom. "Sorry I was rude."

"You were," she says, but the humor in her voice tells me I haven't gone too far. She pats my arm. "Be home by nine, before it's too dark. And keep your phone *on*!"

"Yes, Gojeh," says Dad. "Remember—the car is a privilege."

I jog upstairs, feeling shaky footsteps behind me. Because of Baba, the djinn are on my mind. I even run the rubbery stairs at school.

"Where are you going?"

Not the djinn. Rafi. Though he's got an evil spirit vibe right now.

I'm at my vanity table, spraying perfume on my hair to mask the dinner smell.

"To Brit's. You heard."

I grab my purse. Phone. Deodorant—in case. I need to get out of the house . . . fast. Rafi's Titan arm blocks the door.

"*What?*"

His arm tenses like a rope. "I saw you give Jalen a hug at school."

"Good for you."

I karate chop his elbow joint and he buckles. But he steps back and plays defense, blocking the stairs.

"Are you serious right now?" I uncap my deodorant and brandish it in front of his face. "I'll use it, I swear."

"Gross, it's got a squiggly black hair on it." He shrinks against the wall.

I pass him.

"You know he's dating some girl from San Viejo Prep?" Raf calls after me. I'm at the top of the stair landing, staring at my toes, dangling over the carpeted edge. "Rumor is he had sex with her, too."

The deodorant clunks down two steps. I bend, cap, and put it in my purse. I'm not gonna believe something that was likely fed to him by *It*.

But I hurry downstairs before my brother can see my face.

34

I'M SITTING in the car outside Jalen's trying to put on deodorant underneath my hoodie, no easy feat. Being next to the stove for an hour gave me these annoying little flyaway hairs and they're not going away no matter how much I flatten them with spit.

I hope I don't smell like onion.

Jalen's Raptor, with its new bumper—more dark gray than black—is parked in the drive. Mr. Thomas's car is gone. What am I here to do, exactly? Hang out? How do two people who may or may not like each other *hang out*? Oh god, does he expect Netflix and chill?

I'm at war with myself.

I don't wanna be CJ, *Hook-Up Material*, but it's also in my DNA to *want* to hook up. Everything about Jalen turns me on.

Unfair is what it is.

Maybe I'll ask Brit if I actually *can* come over for dinner. My stomach eases with the thought of doing what I'm supposed to—when there's a knock on the roof of the car.

I throw my phone onto the dash in surprise.

"Damn," says Jalen, jumping back. "Didn't mean to scare you."

Heart banging in my rib cage, I get out of the car.

Jalen hugs are the best hugs. He cups my head with one hand and rubs my back with the other. He's so tall my nose burrows into his shirt, but I can still smell his candy necklace. Strawberry.

It's colder out. The wind is no match for his skin, like a heater, even in his T-shirt. It's the Friday before the week of Thanksgiving. After the break, everyone will come to school dressed in beanies and winter jackets. Like the rain, Californians can't handle cold, either.

The sun's going down and my heart's speeding up . . . We're just friends, right? Friends hug. But not like this. Not so long I can count the number of leaves on the sidewalk . . . feel his even breath on my ear.

Jalen gives me a noogie and that settles it.

"You smell . . . like cinnamon," he says, letting go.

"Oh . . . it's—it's Kabuli pulao."

"Kabul what?"

"This rice and . . . raisin cinnamon dish."

And it's awkward for a moment. It's easier to text . . . you can reword things till they sound right.

His nose has healed up now. I eventually texted him to use some antibiotic ointment when he complained it was a pus fest.

"Comin' in?"

"You know it!"

Tone. It. Down.

I follow him to the door, taking the path I've dreamed of walking for years. I pass the Witch Tree, the one beaten by the previous owner's baseball bat. Sap inches down the trunk, like blood.

"That," Jalen says, and he tells me the story I already know, about the baseball kid. ". . . But he moved out. It's dying."

———

We're sitting on his leather couch in the living room. I don't like leather because it makes my legs hot, especially in fleecy sweats.

"Jalen, what's your middle name?" It comes out urgent and panicky, like if I don't find out this instant, the Witch Tree will zap us both into molasses.

All other thoughts—small talk—have escaped me. I almost asked: *Who is weather?*

"Noah. Why?"

"Just wondering."

Noah. *Noah.* Can he get any hotter?

"Woooooow," he says.

"What?"

Jalen shows me his phone. Rafi's texted What r u doin?

"Not a text since he started with Bian, and now Big Time Recruit suddenly turns up?"

"Wow," I echo. A car rolls by, and I imagine Raf in it, and duck.

"Know how I told you Bian's uncle owns that Nixon shop? After practice, Raf had this *how could you?* look on his face. Told me all condescending that I was *Cole's idol*, and to piss him off, I told him *idol don't mean good influence.* Coach pulled me aside after practice, too. Warned me to keep in line. Wouldn't say why, but I knew somebody told him, too."

"Raf's only gotten worse since he started dating *It . . .*" I mumble.

"*It?*"

"Bian Hoa. She's like Iago, whispering lies into his ear."

"Facts. And you took freshman English, you remember how *that* story ends." He raises a brow at me. "Enough about Big Time Recruit and *It*. They made for each other."

I'm happy he thinks so. Kind of.

My eyes scan the motocross paraphernalia, the figurines, the Malcolm Stewart poster on the wall. American flags, too. Lots of eagles.

"Didn't know you were so . . . patriotic?" In truth, patriotic types freak me out. I shift and my arm sticks to the leather.

Jalen looks up from his phone. "That's Pops." He twists his nose stud absentmindedly. "Was in the military. Stationed in Afghanistan, actually. Six years."

The house is dark. Quiet.

The book *Sense and Sensuous* lies on the side table next to me. I wave it in front of Jalen's face. "Tommy's?"

Jalen goes *tshh-tshh-tshh* and it shakes the couch. "Research purposes only. Never tellin' Tommy, but it's actually really good."

I giggle. Put the book down. "So you ride dirt bikes?"

"We do." Jalen rubs his nose. "Been a minute, though . . . don't wanna get hurt. But Pops, he calls it his Throttle Therapy."

"Where is your dad, anyway?"

"School."

Jalen's wish, *I wish Pops would get better,* rings in my head.

Is Mr. Thomas sick? Not so sick that he can't go to night school, but sick enough that he screams in the night and gets into fender benders?

The wailing had to be him. Only Jalen and his dad live here. Maybe he fell that night?

I ask, "What's he in school for?"

Jalen puts a hand on the back of the couch and looks around. "This an interview?" He laughs, and lamplight fills his parenthetical dimples. Irresistible. "Training to be a sonographer. Pops's taking night classes at the career college. The VA pays for his school and living."

"VA?"

"Veterans Affairs."

"Oh. And sonographer?"

"Baby ultrasounds and stuff." *Tshh-tshh-tshh.* "Pops sure loves babies." Jalen leans forward and tosses his phone on the coffee table. When he settles back into the leather, his knee touches mine.

I stare ahead, in awe. *Intentional, or are his legs so long he can't help it?*

He looks at me. "Sorry."

"Hmm?"

"Know it's a mess, Afghanistan."

"Oh."

"Got relatives there?"

I hear Dad's voice in my head: *If anyone asks, say no.*

I shake my head.

"Pops was pissed how the U.S. pulled out like that. Said it was a damn shame."

"Uh-huh."

"What you think 'bout everything that's goin' on?"

What do I think . . . ? I tug at the tag on the inside of my hoodie. I think I'm getting a rash.

"It's, um, whatever." I smile. "Should we order a pizza or?"

Jalen's nose turns up and his knee pulls from mine. *Intentional.* "It's *whatever*? Why d'you do that?"

"What?"

"Pretend it ain't . . . *never mind.*"

For a minute, we look in opposite directions, arms crossed. Sighing, he picks up his phone. "Need some music . . ."

Normally, a boy putting on music is a good sign. But *needing* music means I'm so insufferable he's got to fill the awkward silences.

The Statue of Liberty clock on the wall ticks on, soon drowned out by rap booming from the sound system below the TV.

"So what'd you text Raf?" I ask.

"Didn't," Jalen says. "Ever since he was recruited, been acting like the Big Man on Campus."

"He does that at home, too."

Jalen goes "Haaaa" and the room warms a bit. "Bet."

"He—uh . . ." And I can't stop the words from forming. "He seems to think we've got something, um . . . between us."

Jalen slugs me in the shoulder. "Me and Ma? Neverrrr. You Rafi's sis."

Ma, or Rafi's sis? Which one is it?

My heart drops. It's settled, I'm not *Girlfriend Material.* And after that comment, maybe I'm not *Hook-Up Material,* either. I don't know why I was so worried before.

I single out the clock ticking over the music, a reminder there's an expiration date on this hangout. First hangouts, like first kisses, are the most important ones. Me and Jalen sit at either end of the couch, Jalen texting, me with my arms crossed. I think of Mom and Dad's relationship, undergoing a slow, tectonic shift. They never try. Communicate. So I take a deep breath, and say, "I lied before."

Jalen puts his phone to sleep.

"Okay." He rests his arm along the back of the couch, fingers inches from my shoulder. *"Reveal your secrets."*

"I have family in Afghanistan. My grandpa's brother and his wife. They're stuck there and we've—well—Baba's been trying to get them out."

"Oh, damn. I'm sorry, Ma. Must be hard."

My heart's pounding, but I go on.

"Yeah. And my dad, he's really—um, he doesn't say much, but . . . I dunno. I wish he would. It's so annoying." I hear it, the forced humor in my voice. I take a breath and start over. "I feel like . . . there's stuff he's not telling me. Like I don't *know him*, know him. You know? Aren't you supposed to know your parents?"

Jalen's smirking at me. "You too, huh?"

I lean in. "What do you mean?"

"Pops, he quiet. Biggest supporter of my ball dream and all that, but spends most his energy arguing on the phone with the VA about medical stuff." Jalen chomps down on his candy necklace like it's a horse bit, like he's said too much. "Returning to civilian life, for Pops, I dunno. Wasn't—*isn't*—easy." He looks at me. Half smiles. Then his face gets all serious, and his fingers twitch near my shoulder. "Can I say something, since we're being real?"

"Reveal your secrets."

He chuckles through his nose. Leans his head back on the

headrest. His Adam's apple bobs when he says: "Don't be so hard on your pops."

"Huh?"

"He's got trauma, probably."

"Don't we all?" I laugh, but he doesn't. My humiliation rings in the room.

"Ma. Listen." Jalen takes a deep breath. "Remember when you was my DD? What you heard that night . . . it was Pops. Dealing with *his* trauma. Manifests in different ways."

"Oh."

I think about Baba. How when we looked at photos in the attic, he flipped the page when I asked him who the man in the karakul was. There was trauma there, too, in his face. And in Dad's, the night of the strange caller.

"Jalen, what's this song?" So far, it's been rap, rap, rap. This indie tune bewilders my ears.

"It's 'Float On' by Modest Mouse. Pops's favorite."

When it ends, I say, "Is your dad . . . like, what trauma— or—is he okay—"

Easing my floundering, Jalen says, "For Pops, it's night-mares. Nightmares so vivid he's back in Afghanistan. There's a name for it—"

"PTSD."

"Yuuup." He looks the other way and says in an outbreath, "Dunno why I'm tellin' you all this. Never told anyone. Not even Cole." Or Rafi. Not even in the decade they were friends.

"Maybe because . . . you've held it in so long, it's nice to have someone to talk to." Saying this aloud, I guess it strikes a note for me, too.

Jalen smiles to himself, looking ahead (and is it possible?), suddenly shy. "Bet."

"Can I ask you something?"

"Nah." He chews on his thumbnail, painted pink. I wait. "Just playin'. Shoot."

"What did your dad see that, um . . ." And I stop, because Jalen's gone rigid.

"I"—he sucks in his lips—"dunno . . ."

"Yeah, no, sorry. I . . . hope your dad gets better."

He sighs and props his elbows on his knees. Wrings his hands and looks at me. "Same, Ma. Yours, too."

He gives his half smile and his knee bumps into mine. Once. Twice. *Intentional.*

And it's like those Venn diagrams, and we're overlapping in the middle, wondering why it took so long to realize we had so much in common.

35

ON TUESDAY, I'm the only customer at Fro-Yo Emporium. Brit's been promoted to manager, and she's sent her fifteen-year-old coworker home early. His mom came ten minutes ago.

I was hoping for more hubbub in here. More distractions.

My hands are sweaty and my keys spike me through my sweatpants. This Ghosting's weapon of choice.

"I think he likes you," says Brit, wiping the counter. I've told her about hanging with Jalen. I leave out the dad stuff.

Brit's tone bears caution. Maybe it's the *think* part. If she knew he liked me, she'd say: "He likes you."

"And his middle name is Noah, isn't that—"

"*So hot*, yes. You've told me four times already."

"Sorry." I've already updated his contact card to read *Jalen Noah Thomas*.

I text him. Doing anything fun over break? He texts back immediately. Throttle Therapy with Pops tmrw.

Jalen normally skips the half day before Thanksgiving break. It's an unspoken movie day at school anyway.

I almost regurgitate Jalen's dirt-biking plans to Brit till she says: "Just . . . be careful."

"Why?" I'm already on my second cup of anxiety fro-yo. Did *It*'s poison find her ears? The ball of my foot bounces and I glance from the clock—*8:23 p.m.*—to the parking lot.

"The way he looks at you."

"Huh?"

"Like . . . that one time you gave him gum and he hugged you, he looked straight at Raf."

"So?"

"It was a weird look."

I thought the hug felt a bit long, but I wasn't complaining.

"You *do* study people, don't you?"

She takes a gummy worm from the pile and rips it in half with her teeth. "Yes." She smiles.

"So," I say, crunching an M&M, "what about you?" I like the distraction of talking.

"As you know," she says, "I liked Fallon."

Oh yes. Fallon and his Black Star Canyon blunder.

"And before you say *why*, it's like—ugh, I know. I guess I'm drawn to the wrong guys. But it's also kinda . . . my fault."

"You *can't* be blaming yourself—"

She waves her hand like *that's not it.* Takes in breath like she wants to speak. Stops. Then says, "You know, discrimination against the trans community is terrible, but no one talks about the—like—behind-closed-doors things. Like surgery costs or side effects of hormone therapy. I just—*huh.*" She laughs. "I have no sex drive, Mafi. None. Zilch. On the one hand, feminizing hormone therapy makes me feel amazing, like I'm not so disgusted by my body, but I miss my sexualness. *I miss iiiiit.* Sorry if that's TMI."

"Um, not TMI. And that's a *terrible* side effect." I don't have that problem. Everything about Jalen, from the love in his voice when he talks about his dad, to his veiny arms, to his passion for ball, to that half smile . . . it gets me.

Kate's voice sticks in the back of my head: *Reputations stick. Don't be* Hook-Up Material.

"In sex ed," Brit goes on, "when they talk about those pesky *teenage hormones*, I want to say—*Please! For the love of god! Throw some my way!* Anyway. I'll take this over waking up every morning pre-transition in agony, never feeling like the real me."

"It'll return, won't it? The randiness?"

"Hope so." She smiles, then freezes as headlights shine through the window. Her face drops.

"Oh—the Twizzlers!"

She dumps them in the trash.

———

It's 8:30 p.m. on the dot. Wiggs shimmies out of his Mercedes. He's not followed by his wife this time, and his hair's not slicked back. Neither is he wearing his gray suit. Instead, a holey shirt and sweatpants.

"Oh," I say. I'm blindsided by the wifeless, pathetic look about him.

"Outstanding," Brit says, cat eyes narrowed, "he looks terrible." She gives a happy *ha!*

"I don't know . . . he looks—sad."

"Who the hell cares, Mafi?" she says as he locks his car. "Ew, don't tell me you feel *bad* for the monster."

"But—"

"MAFI!"

Bingbong. Wiggs walks inside. Brit shoots daggers from her eyes at me, like *you better!* But it was never supposed to be like this. I was always the lone Ghost—screwing over deserving class-mates, not politicians with mortgages and grandkids. Maybe Dad's onto something. Maybe putting yourself in the spot-light, in the fire, isn't worth it. This big fish feels *too* big.

"Hi, sir," says Brit, "large cup?"

"Yes," he gruffles, snatching the cup from her.

Brit keeps shaking her head, so disappointed I think she'll cry.

I stand there. Like a fool.

"And a ridiculous amount of Twizzlers," orders Wiggs.

"I'm—I'm sorry, sir," Brit says, "looks like we're out—but I'll do a refill." Her voice is less silvery. It's the first time she sounds scared. Scared I'm backing out.

My heart pounds in my neck. If I'm going to do it, it's gotta be now.

Wiggs exhales, tapping his fingers on the counter. "What's taking so long, girl? Or—" Then he moves his head behind the glass, to see underneath Brit's visor.

"Or what?" says Brit.

"*Aha.* You're not a *normal* girl."

My feet don't wait for her reply. I throw on my hood and march into the lot. Look around. Brandish my car key. Some kid is crying across the lot 'cause his mom's dropped his toy, but the coast is otherwise clear.

Erkkkkkkkkkkkk.

Ptero's tooth drags across Wiggs's Mercedes, hood to trunk.

"Hey! I saw that!"

Crap!

I catch a glimpse of Wiggs's wife, bustling from the walkway into the lot. She's got a doggie bag in her hand.

"Stop!"

I hightail it out of there, legs whirring behind me. She takes chase, waving her purse, but can't keep up. I fly to the back of a grocery store, past a gaggle of smokers on break.

I sneak through the delivery door to the butcher area. Go to the restroom. Throw my hoodie in the trash can. Take my hair down. Splash water on my face.

———

When I finally deem it safe to leave the restroom, I shove my AirPods into my ears, pull up Modest Mouse's "Float On" on Spotify, and walk home, two miles, in the dark. Fear and exhilaration twist in my cells like DNA. I work on my alibi for Dad, a good enough reason why I'd abandon Ptero in the lot. Nothing sounds convincing.

Brit's working till ten. I've texted her, but maybe they've gotten busy. There was a football game that just let out. Cars zoom past. One honks. A man makes a crude gesture from his window. I pull out my key again, for a different reason. My teeth chatter and involuntary *Huhs!* escape from the base of my throat.

"Siri, turn up the volume," I command.

Don't worry, even if things get heavy
We'll all float on, all right

I jog the last quarter mile.

36

AT HOME, playing it cool was easier than I expected. Dad didn't gripe much when I told him Ptero wouldn't start. He says he'll get it tomorrow.

I flop face-first on my pillow.

My phone buzzes with a text.

Brit says: I'm calling you.

When I pick up, her voice is back to its silvery self with a touch of hysteria. "I didn't want to put this in writing, but the cops came and questioned me but they're completely clueless. You're off the hook. Sheesh, woman! You're my hero!"

My ears rise to the sound of the Siren herself speaking those beautiful words, but my heart gives the middle finger. To the both of us.

"Are you okay, Mafi?"

I hadn't answered yet.

"Yeah!" I try to match her enthusiasm: "We caught the big fish!"

———

I wake at three in the morning and can't fall back asleep. At four thirty, I give up hope. I pad downstairs in my slippers to get some PB Cap'n Crunch and find Dad in his robe, reading the Quran on the couch in the dark. Since the night of the strange caller, the deck's not Dad's sanctuary anymore. The living room curtains are drawn, of course.

"Morning, Padar."

Dad yelps and the book flies from his hands like a hot potato, landing with a weighty thump on the floor. Dad utters a string of *scared me, wasn't reading, thought I was alone—*

I take a step onto the Afghan rug, toward him. Why's he guilty about reading the Quran?

Maybe it's because it's not the Quran. It's the Bible.

"Dad?"

He snatches up the book and hides it in his robe. Lifts a finger, like *I can explain.* Then after a moment, says, "Let's go to Starbucks."

———

It's drizzly and gray as Dad pulls the Tesla into the Starbucks lot.

"Chai, please. Thanks, man."

Dad tries so hard, practicing his American. *Dude. Man. Bud.*

He wanted to do the drive-thru but I say, no, that's lazy American behavior, let's sit inside for a bit. He takes it as an insult, harder than he should.

"Uh—tall cappuccino," I say. "Unsweetened soy milk, please." I remember Kate telling me that's a low-cal order. Nothing with pumps of sweet crap or dairy. I've got a big zit on my forehead that's nearing horn territory. I hear dairy makes pimples angrier.

A cop grabs his to-go order at the counter. After committing a legit crime last night, my legs feel like the mint jelly Grandma used to make at Thanksgiving.

"What's the name for the order?"

"Sam," says Dad, at the same time I say "Sarafat." To my surprise, the barista doesn't misspell Dad's name.

Dad clenches his jaw. In the car, I asked him about the Bible and he got quiet again. If America is anything, it's a place to be yourself, right?

Dad pays with his collection of Starbucks gift cards. I wonder if it's the brown suits and bulky black glasses that make his students think he's a big coffee drinker. He's not. Makes him more jittery, paranoid. But it shows his students like him, at least.

The barista asks Dad a question in Farsi. I hear the city *Herat* thrown in.

"I don't understand you," Dad says. "I am from California."

"My bad, sir. I was sure you were Afghan, like me."

Dad grabs my elbow and escorts me to the pickup counter. "Why did you do that? You don't know these people . . ." He peers over his shoulder as if looking for spies.

"Your *name* is Sarafat," I say plainly.

"Shh. Everyone's looking."

I do a 180. No one is looking. Literally no one.

When our drinks are up, we sit at the only open table by the bathrooms. Somewhere outside, there's the hollow scrape of a skateboard on concrete.

Dad nurses his chai. Takes a sip and glances at the barista. Then in a displeased rumble, says: "The worker man, he was looking at you."

"Man? He's, like, my age."

"Afghan boys are men as soon as they learn to walk. They don't age so slowly, like American boys. He said he just moved from Herat two years ago. I don't trust these Afghan men. Especially around my daughter."

"Weren't you once an Afghan teenager, Dad?"

"Yes! So I know. You tell an Afghan one thing in secret, and the next day, you're dead on the street because they've told the wrong person."

I take interest in this girl's Converse, by the window. They're hot pink. I wear my beat-up black ones like a badge of honor. They've seen some stuff.

"You don't believe me, Gojeh Farangi?" says Dad.

"I just think . . . people are people." Caffeine kicks in, and the words spill out: "Padar, why do you try so hard to deny your culture?"

Dad's eyes shoot to mine. Jalen's words play on in my head: *Don't be so hard on your pops. He's got trauma, probably.*

"Whatever I do," says Dad, "it's for you kids."

"And . . . the Bible? Are you thinking about—converting or something?"

"For you kids."

"How?"

Dad adjusts the collar on his American Eagle polo. "Because . . . maybe . . . we would be seen . . . differently." He holds his chai with both hands. Shifts his eyes this way and that.

"Padar."

"Mm?"

"Have you ever thought about . . ." I trail off.

Jalen's wish that *I wish Pops would get better* is my wish, too. But I also know I can't tell Dad he might benefit from talking to someone. I reroute. "How are you and Mom?"

Dad takes a long swig from his chai. Burns his tongue.

"Your mother is fine."

But I asked if he *and* Mom were fine. My mind dredges up the book Mom was considering on her kindle: *Reboot Your Life.* Mom tries to pretend she'd be fine on her own, but would she be, really? Is Kate right? Separate beds first, then separate lives?

Dad gets up.

"Let's go, Gojeh." His eyes sweep the shop. Then he walks outside, head down.

When I don't follow, he turns around. Comes back inside. Sits.

He gives me that look. The one that makes me feel like I'm in a display case, observed. That he's trying to find a reason not to take me home.

"Sometimes, I wonder . . ." I whisper, staring at my hands.

"Gojeh?"

"That maybe I'm the reason you don't like your life."

Dad grimaces. "Gojeh."

"It's this look you give me, Padar. Like. I've disappointed you."

Dad exhales. "Maybe it is something . . ." He fumbles his words, and my heart wilts. His hand moves from his chai and cups mine, and for a split second, my skin's enveloped in warmth. But his hand returns to his cup, and a draft finds me.

"In Afghanistan, when a girl is born, there is much joy," he says. "Like with you, Gojeh. *Much* joy." The joy, I can't find it on his face. He looks out the foggy window, dotted with rain. "There is also pain." His brown eyes peer into mine. "Because as a father, at any moment, you know a gunman can come into your house. Take her. Marry her to—to one of those. And so you worry. *Always* worry."

I'm mid-headshake, ready to tell Dad *Don't worry. We're safe here.* But I shudder as I recall the sickly sweet voice in my ear: *With whom do I have the gladness of speaking?*

As much as Dad tries to distance himself from his culture, he can't.

He can't let it go.

———

In the car, classical music flits from the speakers. A cool breeze wafts through the cracked window as Dad turns on the Tesla.

He takes a deep, diaphragmatic breath. Then—

Rap-rap-rap-rap! against my window. A boy with a lip piercing, sideswept hair, and a skateboard waves at me through the glass. My heart leaps into my neck.

My Ghost. A Ghost I never wanted to see again.

"Oh god," I murmur, shielding my face. Dad looks from the boy to me.

"It's me, Muffy!" Mikey says through the crack in the window. His lip ring bobs when he talks. "From your friend's party!"

This *is* the very Starbucks where me and Annalie met those Viejo Prep skater boys before *the party*. "I'm back for Thanksgiving break, if you wanna—"

Dad puts the Tesla in reverse, swings the car around, and we *euuuuu* off. Mikey's crestfallen face reflects in the rearview. He's not as cute as I remembered. His face is leathery, somehow, and he's got no visible veins in his scrawny arms. But it was Annalie who blabbered all the way home that day about how hot she'd found him. Not me.

"Party?" says Dad, and I'm drawn from the ghosts of my past.

"Padar, it was a long, long, long time ago."

I lift my head and curse the gods. What are the odds that Mikey would be hanging around Starbucks on a Wednesday at 6:00 a.m.?

Maybe he couldn't sleep, either.

"You know this boy?"

"I did."

"American?"

"Yes."

"What does he mean *back*—back from what? College, Gojeh? You are dating this boy?"

"No, Padar!"

Dad digs in the center console for gum. Unwraps the foil with one hand and chews noisily.

We don't talk for two traffic lights. I sip from my coffee cup even though it's empty.

At the turnoff for our neighborhood, Dad goes, "Maybe you are right. Afghan or American—boys are boys. People are people. And *every* boy is a threat to my Gojeh."

"Some boys are good, Padar." *One boy comes to mind.*

"Noooo." And he laughs, a rare sound. I'm reminded of when I was young and I'd fall asleep in Dad's lap while he watched TV, listening to his deep rumbling chuckles. "No boys for Gojeh."

Now I'm cracking up.

I've always been afraid to ask Dad, but here goes . . . "Dad, when can I like—go on a date with a boy? Like in his car and everything?"

Dad's furry eyebrow hitches up. But it settles faster than I expect. "Forty-five seems good."

"*Padarrrr.*"

He sighs. "Seventeen. Same for your sister."

If only Dad knew Kate the escape artist used to sneak out all the time to kiss boys at thirteen.

Dad blows a bubble. Pops it with his teeth. "Okay. Don't tell your baba about the Bible. Or your mother. And maybe I can forget about this . . . party. And this boy, too."

Scoffing at my luck, I say, "Damn, Dad. Deal."

The curse was a step too far. It's quiet the rest of the way home. I don't mind. I stare out the window, the houses on our street whooshing by in a blur of color, and grin.

Maybe Dad is cooler than I thought. Maybe *that's* why he has so many Starbucks gift cards.

My phone vibrates when we pull into the drive. Me, Dad, Mikey . . . Who else can't sleep? It must've been a full moon last night.

Even after all the texts and calls, my heart still vaults every time I see his name.

> Guess me and Pops aren't going dirtbiking after all. He ain't feeling it. We was up all night. Nightmares.

I text Ugh, sorry. Then I'll go! A reflex.

Jalen's typing . . . typing . . .

———

Finally, the text *whoops* in as I'm brushing the cappuccino from my teeth.

> But you a stone cold killer, remember?
> The yield sign . . .

> Hahahahah. Can you teach me? I could
> use some throttle therapy right now.

> U tryna skip school with me tho?

I look up from my phone onto the street. A black-and-white police SUV is outside Cam's. I crane my head and see Cam talking to an officer on his lawn. Their body language is relaxed enough, but my blood runs cold.

I text back: I'll skip.

> K. Meet u at the Ralphs near SMN at 7:30 AM.

And he sends a GIF of a moto dude doing a jump. My stomach's dropping, too. I have twenty-two minutes to get ready. I feel like I'm diving deeper and deeper into danger, but can't stop. Won't.

37

MY FINGERS have never worked so fast. I can't just skip school with no explanation. SMN will call Mom when I'm a no-show at first period. So I create a new email using Mom's name, fiddle with an old doctor's note using my PDF editor (ear infection strikes again), and zap it off to my teachers. Then I confront the next problem: I don't own a dirt bike or a gear set.

Heart ramming in my ears, I text Jalen this and he replies: I got you.

I put my hair up, then down, then half-up-half-down, then up again. I slap on a little makeup so I don't look so tired and head downstairs.

Finally eating my Cap'n Crunch, I text Brit and she says to have fun, tell her everything. And to be careful.

She probably means on the bike, but I'm not asking.

———

"Someone's excited for the break?"

Mom's staring at me, drinking her coffee. Damn. I'm smiling into my cereal.

I attempt to look angry to offset the happy. "Mom, can we go now?"

Jalen said 7:30 a.m. at Ralphs, the grocery store near SMN. After Mom drops me at school, I'll need a few minutes to cut through the woods and get over there.

"Is the smiling about a *boy*?" Mom says, leaning on the counter. She's got this annoying motherly grin on her face.

"No!" My voice squeaks. "I'm just excited about the PB pie you're making me for Thankstaking."

"Thankstaking?"

"You heard me."

With an *I don't want to ask* pout, Mom grabs her purse. "I suppose I'll need to go to the store to get more peanut butter . . ."

"Now?"

"After I drop you."

"Why? Just go later. It looks like it might rain."

"And rain brings out the one-eyed peanut butter monsters, or . . . ?"

"It can!"

"You're a mystery, Mama."

———

We're delayed ten minutes because the car in front is brake happy, stomping at every corner. *The rain and these people, honestly.*

Mom drops me off at 7:25 a.m. I convince her to go to Trader Joe's because they have the peanut butter I like, not Ralphs.

I text Jalen: running a few late! and when Mom pulls from the lot and takes a left toward Trader Joe's instead of a right toward Ralphs, I book it through the woods, emerging on the other side, into the Ralphs parking lot.

The Raptor sits in front of pump four at the grocery's gas station. Two dirt bikes are tethered to the truck bed, one massive green one, and a smaller red one. Is the red one for me? A knot of worry settles in my stomach. Am I really going to ride this beast?

"Hey, Ma." Jalen's wearing a venom-green jersey and black moto pants. His voice is tinged with apprehension. Is he nervous about our outing, too?

He shuts the passenger door and opens his arms in greeting. His wingspan resembles that Jesus statue in Brazil. I go in for a hug, but as soon as I wrap my arms around his middle and his bullet necklace grazes my temple, he stiffens. There's a single thump at my back. Me and Dad hug with more enthusiasm . . .

Jalen clears his throat and turns his head. His hot breath tickles my ear. "Listen, slight change of plans . . ."

"Big Mac, what's the damage?"

A man with a buzz cut marches toward us in a Malcolm Stewart jersey. It's Mr. Thomas, clutching two bottles of Gatorade.

Jalen looks to the fuel meter. "Seventy so far."

I let go of Jalen immediately, instantly living up to my Gojeh Farangi name, *foreign plum.*

Mr. Thomas whistles. "More expensive every damn day."

"Hi, Mr. Thomas," I say. I hope the surprise doesn't show on my face.

"Rafi's sister, right? Mafi?"

I put out my hand, but Mr. Thomas twists the cap on his

blue Gatorade, breaking the seal. He takes a swig and wipes his mouth with his sleeve. "You kids ready?"

Kids. Jalen towers above his dad by at least a foot.

"Oh—well, um—"

Jalen gives me a half-wounded, half-shy sort of look. I'm flummoxed, is all. I attempted Brit's infamous cat-eye makeup today and already feel out of my comfort zone. Now with Mr. Thomas here . . . *No.* It would be impolite to back out now. "Let's do it."

It's a fifty-minute drive to the track.

Mr. Thomas insists I sit in the front while Jalen drives, but I think it's so he can keep an eye on us. I find myself wondering what position he held in the military. But he's seen worse threats than me, I'm sure . . .

The radio's on but Mr. Thomas is on a different frequency, humming his own tune.

It starts to drizzle. The droplets streak backward on my window as the Raptor propels forward on the asphalt.

"More rain," I say, unsure where to direct the thought. Jalen and Mr. Thomas look at me. "More rain than usual. M-maybe it's global warming."

"We need it," grumbles Mr. Thomas.

"Good for track mud," Jalen adds, helping.

Now's the time I'd usually put up my hood. I ignore the urge. Modest Mouse's "Float On" plays from the speakers, and Mr. Thomas sighs.

Ten minutes from the track, he says, "Nicest people you ever meet, Afghans." I half turn and give him a sheepish smile. "News does them wrong, with the guns and all that. That ain't the Afghans I knew. Right, Big Mac?"

"Yup, Pops." Jalen's voice has an edge.

"It's people you *think* are your friends . . ." And I wonder if that's the end of Mr. Thomas's thought, because he doesn't speak for two miles. "*They* the ones you gotta watch out for," he finally says. I feel him staring at the back of my head. "What made you wanna dirt-bike, Mafi?"

Your son. One hundred percent your son. He makes me want to do a lot of things . . . Jalen's window is cracked, and every now and then, I get whiffs of his cologne and need to grip my sweats to re-center.

"It, um, seems therapeutic, Mr. Thomas."

Jalen's foot slips off the gas and we coast for a second. Maybe Throttle Therapy is only okay for Jalen and his dad to say.

"Why you say that?" says Mr. Thomas.

"It probably—takes you out of your body for a bit. You know. The thrill. I haven't been, but . . . I can imagine."

"Mm. Well. You right."

Jalen lays on the gas and loosens his grip on the wheel.

Mr. Thomas says, "The euphoria when you go over them jumps, it's mind-altering. Better than any drug. Puts you in the present. Right, Big Mac?"

"Right, Pops."

A siren wails behind Jalen, and I curse. The car zooms past in a blur of black, white, red, and blue—shaking the Raptor in its haste.

Mr. Thomas eyes me suspiciously.

"I just got my license," I say, gripping my sweats for a different reason. "Cops make me nervous on the road . . . I'm afraid I'll do something wrong." Or maybe it's because I broke the law last night.

"Tellin' me," mumbles Jalen.

I look out the window the rest of the way, tracing the streaming water droplets with a finger.

———

"Pops changed his mind when I was loading up the truck. Hope it's okay."

I wonder if Jalen telling his dad he'd go with me instead made any difference. I keep the thought to myself.

In the dirt lot, Mr. Thomas is unloading the bikes. The green one *is* Jalen's. Matches his gear. I *won't* be riding the red; it's his dad's.

Me and Jalen are in line for a pit-bike rental, which, *thank god*, is smaller. Jalen's annual pass allows one guest to ride free per visit, gear included.

The man at the counter asks for my shoe size, shirt size, pant size in a bored voice, resituating his Fox cap on his greasy hair. Sizes? I've been wearing one-size sweats and hoodies for so long I need to think . . .

"Color preference?" he asks, his final question.

"Anything but purple." On principle, I stay away from anything Gojeh colored.

"What you got against purple?" says Jalen, flashing his half smile. "Hey"—he catches the worker before he disappears into the back—"find her some Barney-ass-lookin' kit. The purplest purple you got."

I try grumbling cutely but it sounds like Baba's snores. *"Thanks."*

"He likes you," says Jalen, while we wait. His tongue rests playfully at the roof of his mouth. "Pops."

"Yeah right . . ."

"No cap! To other girls"—Jalen spins his nose ring—"he, uh, don't speak at all. Just goes to his room."

The thought of another girl on Jalen's couch, on Jalen's bed, gives me a stomachache. I walk it off, feigning interest in blue display boots.

"Did you just *sniff* the boot?" says Jalen, cracking up.

I shrug. "I like that new-boot smell, I guess." *Crap*, I've adopted Baba's habit. He sniffs his shoes before he puts them on.

The Fox dude returns with a purple gear set, chest plate, white helmet, and boots. I don't need to sniff them to know they're rentals; I smell the sweat and—

"Blood?" I ask, surveying a red blotch on the sleeve. "Is that a *blood*stain?"

"Oh, we ridin' dirty out there, Ma," says Jalen. "But don't worry. *I got you.*"

———

Outside, the constant *brepppp breppp!* of bike engines revs my heart into overdrive.

Mr. Thomas is already out there, on the intermediate track. Jalen points him out, airborne in a red suit and black boots. He whips his bike like it's part of his body.

"Pops's doc said Throttle Therapy might be good for him," shouts Jalen, over the rubab-like *neng-neng-neng-neng* of an idling bike. The rider zips off, and I wave away the swirl of red dirt they left behind. "Pops was out here three times a week after that. That was five years ago. He don't go so much anymore because he got homework, like me." He shakes his head with a *tshh-tshh-tshh.* "Now I'm checkin' if *Pops* is posting his homework online at night."

"What does like—Throttle Therapy do for people . . . like him?"

Mr. Thomas is at the other end of the track now, a red speck on the squiggly dunes Jalen calls *whoops.* "Doc says dirt-biking changes how brains with PTSD respond to stimuli."

I like how Jalen phrases it. Mr. Thomas's *brain* is what's ill. Separate from his father.

———

Breathing through my mouth, I change in a porta-potty, cussing as my elbow bangs the narrow sides. The purple jersey is roomy, but the moto pants, tight. It's the first time I've worn something form-fitting in a long time, and my hands shake.

Through the vent by my feet, Jalen's green boots pace.

Pull it together. I absentmindedly reach for the nonexistent hood behind me. I'm wearing a jersey. No hiding.

The longer you stall, the more Jalen'll think you're taking a dump.

I shoulder open the door to the dusty, dry air.

"Yoooo!" Jalen puts a fist to his mouth when I walk out. "Lit kit award goes to . . . Miss Sha*hiiiiin!*"

I bow and smile so big my cheeks hurt.

"Purple's a good look for you, Ma. For real. Especially with the eyeliner you got goin' on, messy hair, and space boots— hmm. *Not bad.*"

I smooth my jersey, rippling in the dusty wind. Maybe being a *foreign plum* on a dusty track isn't so bad after all.

Jalen puts an arm around me and my stomach flips. "Ready to get dirty, Ma?"

Flips again. I'll leave out my ramping hormones when I talk to Brit later.

———

Throttle Therapy is an understatement.

I get the hang of it quickly, probably because I take directions like a champ. Math formulas, IKEA assembly instructions, recipes—following a formula is easy.

Mom breaking me in with the manual Ptero finally pays off; the clutch-to-throttle ratio on a dirt bike isn't so different.

I crash once or twice in the corners but crashing's really not that bad, especially on the kiddie track, where Jalen's giving me lessons. The closely set *whoops* are my favorite; they're where I feel like I'm gonna lose control—but don't.

Mr. Thomas is right. Riding, I'm present. There's nothing else but me and this bike. No disembodied voices in my ear. No worries about cops after Wiggs's Ghosting. And Jalen rides behind me in case I kill the motor and he needs to restart my bike.

I tell Jalen to join his dad on the intermediate track, that I'll be fine here, but he says he won't leave the *purple destroyer* alone in case some *cone* or *yield sign* appears on the track.

After two hours, I tell Jalen I want on the intermediate track.

"Look, Ma. You good—I give you that. Maybe even a natural." He shakes the dirt from his bleached-blond hair. "But . . . the guys out there, they'll eat you alive."

"You underestimate my power, JT." I say it silvery, confidently, like Brit.

Alcohol, eh! Peanut butter on Oreos, that's a drug, sure. Driving a car alone—thrilling the first few times. Riding dirt bikes . . . not *only* therapeutic. Addictive. I can't think of anything better than—

Jalen's grinning down at me, parenthetical dimples engraved into his handsome face. His full lips part as he surveys me with playful disbelief.

What would those full lips taste like? Dirt and sweat . . .

Okay, there might be *one* thing more thrilling than dirt-biking.

———

Euphoria, panic, disbelief.

This is the cycle. I don't soar like the bikes zooming over my head. But there are moments when I push the throttle and leave the ground, just an inch or so . . . *Euphoria.*

Panic as the bike rumbles underneath me midair, threatening to buck me off.

And disbelief as I land, front wheel then back, with a *thump-thump*, unhurt.

It goes like that, cheating death, cheating injury, until Mr. Thomas signals *last lap!* as he zooms by, and I rev the throttle for the last hurrah. "Bit higher!" I murmur into my helmet, to cheat, provoke, push a little more—

But I go a *lot* higher.

The bike vaults off the dirt mound, into the air. I've broken the cycle and the toggle's stuck on *panic*; disbelief won't follow this time.

I've got the handlebars in a bloodless grip but my legs kick out from beneath me, my butt no longer one with the seat—

I wrestle the horns of the motorized beast as gravity pulls it, roaring, to the earth. I shut my eyes on impact, butt touch-and-*go!* on the seat; the handlebars twist and the bike wipes out, tipping on top of me.

"MA!"

Breppppp!

Neng-neng-neng-neng.

Jalen tends to my side, bike idling. Mr. Thomas is there next, and they heave the steel brute off me.

"Think you Superwoman, pullin' a stunt like that on day one?" says Mr. Thomas, furious.

"You hurt?" Jalen runs a gloved hand along my arms, my legs.

"I'm fine, I'm sorry, I'm fine." I pick myself up, just to show them. My head spins in warning. I wait for the three duplicate Jalens staring back at me to revert to the one. And only.

"Goddamn," says Jalen, dusting me off. "Not a scratch! You right, Pops, she ain't human!"

Mr. Thomas examines me, arms folded across his chest. "Got lucky."

My ankle zings where the bike fell on me, but I repeat, "Really, I'm fine."

———

On the way home, we stop off at Chipotle for lunch. Mr. Thomas ordered ahead from the app, and refuses when I offer to pay for my food. He says we'll eat on the drive back. He's beat.

Jalen parks and runs in to get the burritos, leaving the truck door ajar. The door sensor *ding-ding-dings* as we watch

Jalen's tall frame dip into the store. My ankle is tinged blue and swelling, but I won't fuss. Not now.

"You like my boy?" Mr. Thomas says, once Jalen's at the counter. So he *could* tell. Was it the way I trembled when Jalen scanned me for wounds?

"Oh . . . I—um . . ."

"I don't need another Shahin hurtin' my son, you hear me?"

I turn. "I'm not my brother." I'm surprised how fast I say it. How convincing it sounds.

"Hmm."

Jalen's back outside, brown paper bag swinging in his hand. It starts to sprinkle and he ducks in the rain.

"Scoot over, Big Mac," says Mr. Thomas when Jalen hops back in.

"I can drive, Pops—"

"You eat, I'll drive."

"It's cool, I can do both."

"I said I'll drive."

The last one's an order.

Where does that put me? Should I sit in the back, or stay up front? I insist Jalen gets shotgun, and sit alone in the back.

After we eat (Jalen helping to unwrap his dad's burrito as Mr. Thomas drives), father and son talk basketball. I don't understand the jargon: *In the paint? Dropping dimes?* so I use the convo break to steal glances at Jalen. His parenthetical dimples show the whole time he talks with his dad. There's so much love there. I feel a little ping hearing them laugh. Connect. Sometimes, Jalen offers subtle road warnings like, "Look at this clown on your right, Pops, comin' up fast."

One time, I catch Jalen watching me in the rearview, too. But I think he meant me to catch him, because he kinda bites his lip and shakes his head with a smile, like *this girl*. My breath catches. Jalen's never looked at me like that. I smile back, and it takes me a few seconds before I can breathe again.

I sneak a look at my reflection in my phone. Hair's come out of my ponytail and it's flyaways galore. And there's even some dirt on my chin that looks like a soul patch. Oops.

I rest my arm on the door. Then realize not only do I *look* like I've been motocrossing all day, I *smell* like it, too.

I dig in my bag for this body spray Grandma gave me before she died. As her pungent flowery perfumes usually went, this one, I actually like. It comes from a plant in Afghanistan called salvia spinosa.

"What's that?" Mr. Thomas addresses the car, interrupting Jalen mid-sentence. "That smell."

"Oh," I say, embarrassed. I only gave myself a tiny half-spritz! "It's, um—just a spray."

Jalen's nostrils wriggle. "Smells like banana and—"

"Lime," says Mr. Thomas, voice strained. He stares ahead, jaw fixed. Then he fumbles around with the window controls and all four fly down, letting the spray out and thundering of the road, in.

"I'm sorry!" Window down, my hair whips me in the eye. "I shouldn't have sprayed it!"

Something vibrates underneath my seat. The car has veered slightly to the left, off the road and onto the rumble strips.

"*Pops.*" Jalen reaches for the wheel to correct it but Mr. Thomas smacks his son's hand.

"I can do it myself! Sick of your back seat driving, boy."

But Mr. Thomas's breathing is getting heavier.

"Let's switch, Pops, okay?" The concern, the fear in Jalen's voice makes me grip the leather seats with sweaty hands. "Pull over slowly now, and we'll switch." Jalen raises his voice so he's heard, but he never yells. Never.

"I'm"—Mr. Thomas takes a shuddering breath—"I'm fine, I'm okay, I'm fine."

But then he squeezes his eyes shut and gasps, and the car veers once again onto the rumble strips.

Still impossibly calm, Jalen goes, "Pops, you've got to pull over now, okay? Please. Please pull over, nice and easy."

Jalen hits the hazard lights as Mr. Thomas, eyes still shut, turns the wheel onto the shoulder. He stomps on the brake and I'm thrown into my belt. My heart bangs in my ears.

Jalen puts the gearshift into park and the windows roll up. Mr. Thomas hunches over, hands on his knees. Sweat droplets rain from his head. His erratic breathing echoes horribly in the truck.

"Deep breaths, Pops. Okay?" Father's and son's heads are bent together. Jalen's hand massages his dad's back.

Ears ringing, I ask, "Can I do something?" but Jalen ignores me.

I look out the window at a sneaker on the side of the road, laces grimy and twisted.

"Just an episode, Pops. All right? It ain't real, what you see. Stay here, with me."

Eyes squeezed shut, Mr. Thomas keeps repeating, "It smells like her." He looks like a child in Jalen's arms.

"I've got you, Pops. It's just me 'n' you, okay?"

I shrink a little in my seat. I shouldn't be here.

Gradually, Mr. Thomas's breathing slows and he opens his eyes. He looks from Jalen's worried face to mine, then to the road. He wipes the sweat from his head with his muddy motocross jersey.

"Jesus," he whispers. Clears his throat. "Jeeeesus." He pounds the wheel.

He's mad, but not at Jalen. Not at me, either.

"I'll drive," Jalen says. This time, Mr. Thomas doesn't argue.

———

Mr. Thomas sleeps the rest of the way to Rancho Santa Margarita. I ask Jalen if he can drop me at Ralphs instead of home because I need to buy some Oreos. He doesn't ask how I'll get home or anything. Understandably, he's in his head.

I thank him for the day, and he says he hopes I had fun anyway, and he'll text later. I assure him I did, and when we try a hug our arms are like flailing pool noodles trying to find a landing spot. It's our second awkward hug of the day. His dad still asleep when we get to Ralphs, I ask Jalen to thank him for me and hop down from the Raptor. I wait till the truck's up the road before hobble-sprinting through the woods back to SMN. My ankle hurts like heck.

I get to the parking lot just as Mom's pulling in.

Man, that was close. In more ways than one.

I duck inside the Tesla, and Mom asks why I'm muddy and sweaty. I say we ran the outdoor track today because the pool's getting a service—and that my ankle got a beating.

Like magic, Mom buys it. She heard *track* and got excited.

"How'd it feel to be back out there, Mama? Tweaked ankle aside. Ouchie. Think you might—"

"No," I say, and perhaps too excitedly. "I'm taking my talents . . . elsewhere."

"Volleyball?"

I shake my head.

"Tennis?"

"Oh hell no."

"What then?"

I don't think now's the time to ask for a dirt bike.

Mom eyes me suspiciously the rest of the way home.

38

AFTER DINNER, icing my ankle in my bedroom, I text Jalen to see if his dad's okay.

> PTSD episode. Pops said it was the smell of that spray. Reminded him of someone in Afghanistan but he wouldn't say who.

> I'm sorry. I wasn't thinking.

> How could u've known? Never know what's gonna be the trigger. Smell, sound, a nightmare, IDK. Sometimes, the episodes come from nowhere.

> What helps?

> Deep breathing, or a walk. Anything to ground Pops in the present. Damn. Really hate when he drives. Specially alone. It's not the first time it's happened in the truck.

I remember Mr. Thomas's fender bender a while back.

I get that.

How's the ankle?

It's nothing.

Besides Pops and all that, I had a good time wit u today.

Me too.

Purple destroyerrrrr. When can I see u again?

My heart flips. I'm thinking about what to respond when my phone buzzes. Brit's calling.

I pick up and tell her about my eventful day. *Most* events, at least.

Brit laughs, gasps, and hoots in all the right places. She says it *might* sound like Jalen likes me after all, especially when I tell her about the rearview look he gave me. And no, I'll probably *never* be able to wear Mom down about the dirt bike, but I can try.

I leave out the part about Mr. Thomas's episode. It seems insensitive to share.

I'm not ready for Brit's final question when it comes. "Mafi, you never told me you have relatives in Afghanistan."

My heart deflates. "Oh . . . yeah."

"Jalen said something to me a few days ago. Are your relatives okay?"

Annoyance—or is it jealousy?—flares inside of me.

"I didn't know you two talked."

"Not really, but he said he'd noticed we're close in class and asked me to check on you. He said something like you think your last meal is coming."

I think about the man on the phone. The sleek black car. And Wiggs.

"Well, I'm fine." We've talked so long my ear's ringing and the phone is hot on my ear. "Let's not make it a big thing."

"Mafi—"

"I don't want to talk about it! All right?"

Her silvery voice is wobbly, like silicone. "All right . . . I'm sorry."

"Fine."

"Okay."

"I'm going to bed, Brit."

"Okay . . . but if you ever want to talk . . ."

"Thanks. Good night."

———

At nine, the sound of an engine idling purrs through my window. Is it Raf, back from Bian's? No. It's back: The sleek black car sits behind the azaleas between our house and Cam's. This time, anger wins out over fear. Probably leftover testosterone from biking.

Trespassers! Who are they? What do they want? I think about Habib and Yasmoon. How Baba said the Taliban knocked on their door. Painted it with an *X*.

Our house . . . is it marked, too?

The front door opens and Dad walks out in his robe, stopping halfway up the path. My breath catches in my throat. Dad stares at the car. Nods.

The engine thrums and the vehicle pulls from the curb.

———

I wake one hour later with the feeling I'd forgotten something. My phone buzzes, as if to remind me. I fell asleep without texting Jalen back!

He's texted again.

Only this time, the text reads: I'm outside.

I leap to my window.

Everyone's asleep. Everyone but Raf. He's out with Bian and curfew's not for another hour.

Jalen's wearing a Rodman jersey so long it reaches his knees. His bleached-blond hair is almost fluorescent underneath the street lamps. He stands slumped in the shoulders, like he's not all there or something.

"Purple destroyerrrr," he says, attempting a whisper. Jalen's one of those people who thinks they're whispering but shout. Cole's bedroom curtain swishes.

"Jalen!" I whisper from the window. "What are you doing here?"

"Me and Pops got in a fight." Jalen gives a frustrated sigh. "I need you. Come outside."

Headlights stream down the street, illuminating his gigantic silhouette.

"Get out of the street, Jalen!"

It's the Ptero, puttering along.

Jalen watches. And then is so dense as to wave, a silly grin on his face. I duck beneath the window, then pull myself slowly to the ledge, out of sight.

Jalen opens his arms and Rafi drives around him, into the driveway. Hand brake, jingling of keys, and the door slams.

"What're you doing here, JT?" Rafi's voice sounds in the night.

Only crickets for a moment, then—

"What, is it a crime to see my good friend Raf?" Jalen stresses the word *crime*. Raf notices. There's a long silence and I drop to the ground as Rafi peers up at my window.

"Seriously, what do you want?"

"Psh." I hadn't realized it till now, but I think Jalen's been drinking. "Never thought you'd believe I told the kid to steal the watch. But . . . *It*'s word against mine, huh?"

Panic flutters in my chest. Did he just call Bian *It*? Only I do that!

"Watch it."

Leave, Jalen. Just leave. I look for a star to wish on but it's cloudy tonight.

"Ask Cole," says Jalen. "He stole it and *I* was the one they popped off on."

"I'm not gonna take the word of some poor kid who basically worships you. You should know better than to involve him. He's got a bright future and everything."

"And I don't?" Jalen asks. Silence. "Damn. *Raf with the sucker punch.*"

"Stay away from my sister," says Rafi, turning on his heel.

"Which one?" says Jalen.

No. Oh-no-no-no. I don't wanna see *Clash of the Titans* tonight.

"I swear to god—"

"Don't you mean Allah?"

The house vibrates. Light pours onto the driveway as the garage door opens. There's whistling and the gravelly rumble of trash bins being dragged out.

It's Baba, wearing his robe, pakol hat, and for some reason— Mom's fuzzy slippers. I thought he was asleep?

Baba looks up. Stops whistling. "My Kush Giant!"

"Kush Giant?" Jalen howls with laughter.

Rafi seizes Baba's arm. "Baba, what are you doing? It's Wednesday. Trash goes out on Tuesday. These are empty."

Baba scratches his head. "Oh. Your baba had a bit too much to drink, mm?" He slaps Rafi's cheek and shuffles inside, slippers dragging on the driveway.

"You don't drink," says Rafi, but Baba gives him the notorious old-man wave-off with a "Pah!"

"Go home," Rafi tells Jalen, finger raised. He grabs the trash bins and wheels them inside.

"Or what, you'll call the cops?" The provocation makes me shiver.

"I'm not dealing with you when you're like this," Rafi says from the other side of the garage door. It's closing. "If you wanna talk, we'll talk on the bus."

"Whatever, *Kush Giant*," says Jalen, bending low to wave as the garage door lowers.

It clunks shut and I scramble to get under the covers.

Seconds later, my door opens a sliver. Light from the hall pours onto my face. I pretend I'm asleep as Rafi tiptoes past my bed, cursing as he steps onto my eyelash curler (I've been looking for that!) and quietly shuts and locks my window.

Rafi lifts the door handle on his way out. When I hear it latch, I sidle off the bed like the slime Cole used to play with and peek out the window.

There's Jalen, sitting on the curb, head in his hands.

I text him.

> Meet me down the street at Rose Park in ten.

39

IT'S BEEN a long time since I've shimmied down Nutter Butter's oak tree, and it's especially hard to do with a tweaked ankle. But I don't like the idea of Jalen walking the streets alone at night in his condition.

I cross the street and Cole's curtain whooshes open. "Psst! Ma-Ma-Ma! Wait!"

Rolling my eyes, I stalk across Cole's lawn, avoiding the window where I know Melisandre the dog sleeps.

"What do you want?"

"What, uh—what are you doing?"

"Bye, Cole."

"Wait—are you going to see JT?"

"*Maybe.*"

"Why won't he talk to me anymore?"

"He's still angry, okay? You need to let him be."

"Don't leave me behind! I've got notes!"

"Do you?"

Cole shrugs. "No . . . none. But can we hang out soon?"

"Maybe, I don't know." I don't wait to hear if he says anything more.

Jalen's waiting underneath the slide when I get to Rose Park like some gloomy bridge troll. He jumps out, says, "Boo!" and spins me around.

"Jalen—*Jalen!*" My ribs ache and my ankle zings when I put my full weight on it.

I smell it now. The alcohol, spicy and sweet. It wafts from his pores.

"Just saw Cole," I say.

Jalen's face changes as he slopes onto the swing, which protests with a loud *creak*. Sitting, his knees are bent up into his chest. "The kid apologized on Twitch, but I ain't ready yet."

I lower myself onto the swing next to him. "Maybe you've outgrown him."

"Hmph."

"Why Cole, anyway?"

"*Tshh-tshh-tshh.*" He looks over at me, and there's a warm ring to his voice when he says, "He hyperactive, just like Azi."

"Azi?"

"My kid brother."

I stop swinging. "You have a brother?"

He nods, mind somewhere else. "Aminata remarried. Azi'd be . . . eight now."

"Did you ever think about staying in Germany with your mom?" It hurts me to even ask. To not have Jalen here right now.

"Never," he says, at once. "Love her, but . . . they gave me a choice, and it was California with Pops. Better chance to get to the NBA." The sacrifice strains his voice. "How many German ball players you know?"

I run a hand along the bumpy swing chain, wet with dewy dusk. "I can't imagine having to choose between my parents." Maybe one day, I'll have to.

"Was six," says Jalen, "and the hardest thing I had to do. Even then I had this dream. Think Aminata blamed Dad, said he was taking me away from her, putting the dream of ball in my head . . . every free moment we was on the court, shooting. She's fine, I guess, with her new life. But Dad, alone . . ."

"Why's he mad?"

Jalen goes *ughhhh*. "Yeah. Mad I drank. But he was . . . acting up after we got back. Pops made it clear he don't want me . . . uh. Goin' with girls."

He can't mean me.

"You know, never seen him with one woman since Mom. No dates. Nothing."

"Did your mom serve in the military, too?" Baba says most U.S. military bases are in Germany. Maybe that's how Mr. Thomas met Jalen's mom?

"Yeah, they met at the base."

"So you're . . . German?"

"Was born in Baumholder, so uhh, ja?

"That's so cool."

"Or maybe . . . you cool, Ma. Purple destroyerrrrr."

"Ha, cool? Orrrrr the alcohol has something to do with it." I hate that I kind of like the way he smells. The alcohol and the cologne, fanning back and forth as he swings. "Hey . . . sorry about Raf back there."

"Sometimes I wish your bro'd just—like—I don't know."

"Get shoved off his pedestal?"

He laughs. "Yeah. Coach G always treats him like he the MVP. Raf this, Raf that. Me? It's like: *Jalen, run laps. Jalen, do push-ups. Jalen, your hop's weak,* and—*oh my damn.* Woody out!"

I look down. In my rush to get here, I didn't even think to change out of my beaver pajamas.

"Me and Dad had a coffee date," I say.

"For real? He talk?"

"Kind of. He's thinking about becoming a Christian."

"Uhhh?"

"My response, too."

"Huh." Jalen swings back and forth, mouth open. His green Jordans judder in the wood chips. "Pops told me Muslims who convert can face the death penalty in Afghanistan."

"Well," I say, "I don't think Dad ever wants to go back."

"Mine neither," Jalen mumbles. He digs into the chips with his heel. "Pops finally got through to the VA this afternoon. They've agreed to pay for this—gangly treatment."

"Huh?"

"SGB." He rubs his head, thinking. "Stellate ganglion block therapy. Some injection. But Pops say there not enough research on it. Doesn't wanna be no one's guinea pig. Plus, the closest treatment center's in Dallas."

"What's it do?"

"Helps with fight or flight. And pain. But effects are only short-term. I wish he'd at least try, but he's gotta want it for himself, you know?"

That's part of the reason why Jalen's wish—*I wish Pops would get better*—isn't so easily granted.

"Yeah. *I know.* What about Throttle Therapy?"

With a curt shake of his head, it's clear it's not enough. Jalen's slowly teetering from his seat. I steady the chain.

"How much did you drink?"

He pinches together thumb and forefinger. "One, maybe two shots of Patrón." He looks up at me, standing over him, grasping the swing chain, and gives his half grin. "I wanna try something."

"What's that?"

Still smiling, he places a hand on my back. He tries to stand, but loses his balance and curses.

"Hold on," I say, hormones frenzying. "Let me try. Sit."

I swing my leg over Jalen's and sit on his lap. I don't know what's come over me. Maybe it's that our day felt cut short. Before Jalen's dad had the episode, there was that look Jalen gave me. Then the day was capped with an awkward, noodly hug.

When Jalen invited me to go this morning, I was hoping today would be, I dunno. The start of something.

But it still could be.

Jalen utters a surprised "Damn," and I wish I could hear that word repeated infinitely, all breathy like that.

I wrap my arms around his torso, resting my head on his jersey. His heart drums beneath the material. One meaty hand supports my back. Then after it, the other.

We're both shivering as we hold each other, Jalen's chin resting atop my head. We swing slightly back and forth, listening to the calls of the night. Chirruping of insects. Humming of streetlights.

The *dom-dom, dom-dom, dom-dom* of Jalen's heart is loud in my ear.

A dog barks from afar.

After a while, there's a tapping on my spine, starting at my neck. Jalen's hand caresses me, taps every bulb, direction due south. "One, two, three . . ."

"What are you doing?" I murmur into his chest.

"Counting the vertebrae. All thirty-three of them."

Spinal anatomy . . . I recall the pop quiz in A&P. Cervical at the top, thoracic in the middle, and lumbar, tracking to the waist, leading—did he say *all* thirty-three?

He's passed the thoracic and moves to the lumbar, warm fingers tracing the elastic of my pajama pants—

I pull back. Look at him. His Adam's apple bobs. His lips are inches from mine. "Hi," he says.

"Hi," I exhale, giggling and breathy. I'm surprised when my voice doesn't sound like my own.

His hands orbit around to my hips, his long fingers sending ripples across my cold skin.

My face has inched in, but he murmurs, "Ah-ah. Patience."

Jalen's lips are one centimeter from mine. The shivering is uncontrollable. If he doesn't kiss me, I might implode.

He holds my gaze tenderly.

"If we kiss, you gotta know something," he whispers into my mouth.

"What?"

"Your world will be changed." I laugh through my nose, but he doesn't. "I'm not playing. It's like—we can't go back after that. Shit moves. Planets collide."

"Some planets are gas," I say. "Like Uranus. So . . . no colliding."

He cackles and I *shh* him when the dog up the street barks again.

"This wasn't supposed to happen, Ma. Not like this."

"Oh yeah?" I flirtatiously skim my nose across his. I'm drunk with power, for now. Soon I'll be the same blundering girl who hides from her crush in the pool.

"Maybe—I'm a free radical," says Jalen. "The bad kind. The highly reactive, unstable, cell-damaging kind."

"Or maybe the soul-shaking, change-the-world kind."

He smirks, mouth open. The tip of his tongue reaches the roof of his mouth.

Heart ramming at my rib cage, I bring my lips to his.

They're warm and soft. He exhales. A whiff of alcohol fills me up, and I'm drunk. We learned that the lips have more nerve endings than any other part of the body, and I imagine each nerve dancing with his, pirouetting, sparking, moving as one. "Damn," he mumbles into my mouth, and it's no longer smooth Jalen, or sarcastic Jalen. It's vulnerable. It's shaky. *I'm* the one to make him feel this way. He's let his guard down . . . for me.

Jalen opens his mouth a little more, welcoming my tongue. Soon, my hand's resting on his cheek and I'm wondering how it can be so good—I've only done it one other time, with Sandpaper Tongue Blaine.

This is better than the euphoria of bike riding. Much better.

His hands grip my waist, and the next moment, or two hours later—who's to be sure—he's pulled his mouth from mine, lips buzzing.

And I feel like we're two planets that have orbited each other for millennia, now colliding. Colliding, like he said. But not with a crash or a boom.

"You need to get home," I whisper, teeth chattering. It's not the cold. I'm suddenly thirsty and hyperaware my deodorant's working overtime. It smells like fake flowers.

Against every fiber of my being, I swing my leg back, stand on legs like those of a newborn deer's, and pull out my phone. "I'm calling you an Uber."

"I'll call my own Uber," Jalen says, looking like he's gonna nod off. His eyes are still shut.

"You good?"

"Enjoying it." He smiles the biggest I've ever seen.

"Enjoying what?"

"The kiss. It's still going. Don't wanna open my eyes, or it'll end. *Damn.*" The tooth with the diamond stud winks at me.

"Stop saying *damn* like that."

"Damn. Damn. *Damn.*" But these ones are different. Sarcastic Jalen is back.

I shake the swing chain, and his eyes startle open.

"Masha's five minutes away," I say, waving my phone in front of his face. "Promise, no detours."

"Mine," he says, snatching my phone.

"Hey—!"

He tickles me and I fall onto his lap. He opens my camera and extends his arm. "OMG," he says, in his best Valley girl voice, "let's, like, totally commemorate."

He takes the selfie while we're both laughing, eyes half-shut. It's not a cute photo, it's too dark, but that doesn't matter.

He assigns it to my wallpaper before I can, then hands me my phone. I get up, still giggling, still swaying, and he stretches with an *Ungh*. "Told you so, Ma."

"Told me what?"

"Your world would change."

And as he ducks into Masha's Audi five minutes later, I know he's right.

40

THANKSGIVING, KATE'S yakking about medical stuff at dinner. Baba likes it, of course. He asks her so many follow-up questions I'm getting a headache. Mom, too. She's polished off two bottles of Merlot by herself.

Since Mom's sloshed, I figure it's a good time to ask for a dirt bike, and she nearly chokes on her turkey. Kate lists all of the possible injuries associated with dirt-bike wrecks, and I turn my head and mouth *blah-blah-blah*. One day, I'll wear Mom down . . .

I'm itching for more Throttle Therapy. It's the second-best thing I've ever felt.

Me and Raf couldn't wait for the others to finish dinner before tucking into pie.

Raf's quiet because he's not only in the Apple Pie Zone; he's in the Ball Zone. Tomorrow, the team's got an away game in Oakland. Raf needs to be on the charter bus at 6:00 a.m.

I texted Jalen a turkey GIF this morning. I mean, what do you text after you have the best make-out session of your life?

His reply was a Uranus GIF, and I choked on my waffle.

I'm full but I section off another giant wedge of pie. PB pie's mine; no one else in this house eats it.

The landline rings.

Forks clang on plates. Baba wipes his mouth with his sleeve. "Well," he says, getting up.

Kate blabbers about how many calories per gram are in each macronutrient while Baba talks in Farsi on the phone. Dad's trying to listen to Baba's convo.

Me too.

Baba's saying *yes!* And *oh!* And *okay!* in Farsi, waving his hands. He gets off the phone and claps.

"What is it?" says Dad.

Baba answers in Farsi. Dad reminds him to speak in English, for everyone else.

"There is a new plan," Baba begins.

He announces Habib's been speaking to a smuggler. Someone *else* who can get Habib and Yasmoon out. Through checkpoints. Villages. For money.

"In one week, they will take the Kabul–Kandahar Highway and try for Pakistan. Quetta, to the refugee camp. Habib promises to call when he arrives on December seventh, Baba's birthday."

"They will travel the Highway to Hell?" says Dad, forehead dent a crater. He bites potato from his fork and his teeth *shink* against the metal. "A death wish."

Baba says, "My brother will not wait for death like a coward. When the Russians rolled in with their tanks and we escaped in the night all those years ago, was Baba scared? No. Because Baba was already on the Highway to Hell, so much worry, mm?

And when Baba goes through hell, what can he do? *Keep going.*
You forget your uncle . . . Habib is a lion. And Yazzi, she has
two PhDs. Two!"

Dad gathers up his fork and pie. Seconds later, the back
door squeaks open. Shuts.

Baba knocks a baby potato loose from his plate and *whap!*
captures it. "He wants Baba to forget his country. Forget his
family." The spud turns to mush. Baba picks at it. Nibbles.

"He worries," says Mom.

"He is stubborn. Spoiled. Forgets what it was like."

In the humming silence that follows, I'm suddenly wishing
Kate had some medical factoid to blurt out. Or that Mom
would ask if anyone wants tea. I try defusing the tension by
asking Baba a question about the Pythagorean theorem. He
sticks out his gummy lip and grunts. Raf raises his eyebrow at
me, like *read the room.*

It's only the sound of silverware on cartoon turkey plates
the rest of dinner.

———

Before bed, tense whispering travels upstairs from the living
room. I go to the landing to listen.

"Why would you do this to your baba?" Baba's pacing.
"First, you don't want your uncle and aunt to leave, and now,
you do *this*?"

Dad responds, "*Of course I do.* But my main concern is
protecting my family, here, the one in this house."

I hear Baba's fast footfalls; I imagine him squaring up with
Dad. "You cannot forget your roots—who you are! Converting

to Christianity . . . since you were a boy, you were always looking for meaning outside of yourself, your culture. Your eye, it was *always* on the West! Marry an American, wear your American Eagle, eat your hamburgers and cheesy sticks and hot dogs, but you will *never* be like them. You are Afghan. And Muslim. Like your baba."

"Muslim?" Dad says. "All my life, you only pray when you want something."

Baba's voice rasps like wind through a cornfield.

"Baba never wanted to move here. All he wanted was a better life for you and your mom. You grew up in a *very* different Afghanistan than Baba did."

I'm accustomed to the numbing silence between parent and child that follows.

"You can't help everyone," says Dad. "Look what it brought last time, helping those refugees!"

There's a whooshing sound, then a crash. Baba's knocked something off the coffee table. "You dare speak to your baba like this?" My skin crawls with the sheer venom in Baba's voice.

"It was out of line," Dad says. "I'm sorry."

"*Never* treat your baba this way again!" I hear the back door open and close, and the fight's over, but not done.

———

The next morning, I'm woken at an ungodly 5:50 a.m. to honking outside. A chorus of curses sound through the wall. Raf's slept in and his teammate's here to pick him up. Must be all those sleepy turkey enzymes doing their magic.

I roll over, content I'm no longer tethered to track's early mornings. My blanket is fuzzy and Mr. Meowgi purrs next to me.

I burp, and oh, hello, *peanut butter pie*. Okay. The second slice, I *do* regret.

———

So Jalen and Raf are confined to a bus. Then practice, the game, and another bus ride home. *Way* too much time together. Too much potential for Jalen to spill—oh god, what if there's post-game alcohol involved?—that Raf's sister straddled him at the park and kissed him.

I've twirled my hair so much, I think it might snap off. Mom, too, tells me to quit it, and that my hair's dipping into my cereal bowl.

Mom asks what's on my mind and I slurp my milk with a shrug.

Later, in bed, my phone buzzes and warm energy shoots to my heart. I've been smiling so much I'm worried my cheeks will freeze.

> Does it feel like that with other guys you've kissed? Cuz . . . damn. I'm shook.

I squeal and toss my phone. Meowgi places a paw on it; he loves touching screens and laptops. My phone buzzes again, and I rush to meet it, prying off Meowgi's furry, orange paw.

It's Brit.

She's asking if I want to sleep over.

I convince my parents to let me go, saying we need to study for the A&P hike coming up. But actually I'm dying to tell Brit all about the kiss. She lives in Newport Beach, so that means highway time, and Mom and Dad don't like that.

It's been tense after Baba and Dad's spat. Dad's shut himself in his room again, and Baba spent all afternoon in the den downstairs, listening to his music, mumbling in Farsi.

41

WE'RE ON Brit's balcony with our feet on the railing, books open as we study the Krebs cycle. She asks about Habib and Yasmoon and I ignore her, launching into (more) detail about how it feels to kiss Jalen, showing her the grainy photo we took together for the millionth time. "His lips are literally the softest, like *the softest*, and—"

"But your relatives—"

"I told you I don't want to talk about that!"

"Mafi! *Hear yourself!*"

"What?"

"You can't seriously care more about kissing Jalen than your relatives? They could die!"

I push my book off my lap. Stand.

"Mafi, come back!"

I march from Brit's balcony into the living room, past her mom on the couch, and walk outside, not stopping until squishy, cool sand's beneath my feet and any farther would mean stepping into the ocean.

The wind howls. Sand grits stick to my eyeballs.

Brit finds me spinning an old Sprite bottle on the shore.

She plops next to me. Sighs. "I'm worried about you. If you keep repressing stuff, you'll explode."

"Okay, Mom."

Brit curses and gets up. Straightens her skirt.

"Wait," I say, throat aching. "Don't go."

Brit sits again. "The first time I felt comfortable with myself was when I played Alice in *Alice in Wonderland* in the fifth grade. Remember that? I borrowed my cousin's bra, got this blond wig, and wore a dress. It just—felt right. And the next morning, when I dressed how my parents wanted me to dress, I cried. Cried because I couldn't set myself free. But also cried because I knew one day, I *would* set myself free." She slings an arm around me. "Take it from me. Repressing the hard stuff won't do you any favors, Mafi."

"You're brave," I say, wiping my runny nose. "With your activism . . . the way you stand up for who you are. *You're* a free radical, like the suffragettes."

"True," she says in her silvery voice. "I am."

"Jalen asked me how I felt, once. About the whole Afghanistan thing."

"What did you say?"

"I suggested we order pizza."

"Bet he liked that."

"Yup. I guess . . ." I trace a finger in the sand. "I don't feel equipped. Like a fraud. Like I'm representative for a country I've never been to. For suffering I've never felt—only secondhand, through Dad. Through Baba."

"There she is," says Brit, waving a finger in front of my face.

"What?"

"There's the real Mafi."

I laugh.

She hugs me tighter and I nuzzle into her shoulder. I look at my gray hoodie sleeve, sunset swathing the cloth in orange.

———

Hours later, we do a Del Taco run. I tell Brit, "Hold on!" and ask for something to cover the angry red horn on my head.

"I don't own foundation."

"Are you serious? What do you do when you get a pimple?"

She places a regal hand on her hip. "I wear my spots proudly."

"Oh, to be Brit Rossi."

"C'mon, my beautiful unicorn," she says, grabbing my arm.

On the walk to Del Taco, I check Insta to see we've won the away game. There's a video showing Raf sinking the buzzer beater and doing his *cha-ching!* victory dance. I text Jalen: congrats on the win!

I'm left on read.

I try not to obsess. *Try.* And I don't bring it up to Brit, because I'm afraid she'll make me face myself again.

On the way home, we stop at Ralphs for Oreos and tampons, because periods wait for no one. Brit says she's already got peanut butter at home. It's the crunchy kind, but I'll live.

The cashier tells me she likes my hoodie. I bow, because I was never good at receiving compliments. And you know what, the girl doesn't care I've got a red horn on my head and am hobbling, once again, like Quasimodo.

Me and Brit inhale PB Oreos while re-streaming the first season of *Blood Jurors*. Brit pauses on Fallon's ski scene, replaying his pouty attempt to look hard in the shot. When our cheeks hurt from laughing, Brit lets the show play and scrolls through Instagram. Upside down on the bed, she flips over and eyes me sheepishly. "Oh."

"What?"

"Nothing."

I find it fast. Jalen, at some party up in Oakland, hanging on some redhead in a tank top that leaves little to the imagination. She's winking with her mouth open and her pierced tongue's an inch from his face.

Oh. And Jalen's dyed his hair red again. Caption: *Redheads have more fun.*

"Just a party," says Brit. "He's allowed to make new friends. In fact, he's great at it."

"Friends?" I say. "I'm pretty sure I'm straight, and I'd definitely kiss her."

"Yeah," Brit concedes, "I would, too."

I groan. Throw my phone.

"What's your type?" I ask, helplessly. I'm blinking in the light of her phone in about two seconds. "Damn, okay, who's he?"

"An F1 god."

"What show's he from?"

She gawks at me. *"No show. Formula One.* He's a race car driver. From Spain." Brit sighs. "Maybe if I look at his picture long enough, my sex drive will go vroom vroom."

We laugh and laugh.

When I can breathe again, I ask, "Still no luck, huh?"

"The engine's on. But I need a little rev, you know? Oh, wait . . . I'd almost forgotten!"

She hands me a parcel wrapped in silver paper.

I bash my eyelashes at her. "For me?"

"Can't I give my friend a gift?"

I open it. It's a purple Thor motocross jersey.

"For when you wear your mom down . . ."

I smother Brit in a bear hug and she tickles me so that I let go.

42

We never like . . . said what we were.
You n me.

I stare at the text. Open it throughout the day, hoping the wording will have changed, or Jalen will have texted again.

Does *he* think I'm CJ? *Hook-Up Material*, not *Girlfriend Material*? I'm rewinding through the night at the park for the hundredth time, seeing it in a different light. Trying to find where I messed up. Did I kiss him, or did he kiss me? If I'd let him come to me, would he see me differently?

———

By Sunday evening, I still haven't texted him back.

There's a knock at my door. Rafi's back. I'm still mad at him for accusing Jalen like people at school, but I'd be lying if I said I didn't want some company right now.

"I thought you were getting in at five."

He looks at me. "*Thor?* Are you wearing a motocross jersey?"

I shrug. "Yeah."

"Why?"

"Why not? It's comfortable. Brit got it for me."

"Okay . . ." Then Raf goes, "The guys were hungover on the way back. We had to stop twice because Jalen was throwing up. Threw up on Coach the first time. Then Coach threw up, and . . . you know."

Bubbles rise in my chest . . . like the ones in champagne. Happy bubbles. Then I feel rotten for the minor sadism.

"Looked like some party."

"I heard. Didn't go." I know why, too. Bian probably didn't *let* him. Whenever they're back together, Raf skips out on a lot of things. He cheeses real hard. "I'm happy."

"Not Bian?"

"Nothing to do with her. Whenever I feel lost, like I've kinda been lately"—he shakes the loose strand of hair from his eyes—"basketball brings me back."

"Saw you hit the buzzer beater."

Raf hops and fake-shoots an invisible ball. "It was so sick . . . and you know what, Mom showed Dad the vid and he even said *good job* when I got back."

"Serious?"

"Yeah. It was a stiff *good job*, but still."

Before bed, Jalen sends another text. Hello?

I draft a text, or maybe seven, but none of them make the cut. I decide I'll face him in person on Monday.

———

On Monday, the air smells like bonfire.

There's a wildfire somewhere in the hills, in Silverado Canyon. I spend all of A&P watching silver ash rain from the sepia sky, the coast's snow.

Baba explained to me this morning how it's natural. How things need to burn to make way for new things. All the animals and trees and firefighters . . . I can't stop thinking about them. California's not all sun, sun, sun. For most of the year, it's a desert on fire.

Mr. A ends class saying we might need to postpone our field trip hike, and there's a general moan from the group. I think *most* of us were actually excited to go.

———

After A&P, Jalen tells Tommy to go ahead and takes his time packing up.

"See you later," says Brit, hand at my back. She gives Jalen a meaningful look.

"Do you . . . want a ride home?" Jalen asks.

Yes. "No, thanks." I collect my books. The Thor jersey is slick beneath my hoodie.

"Why are you ignoring me, Ma?"

Mr. A looks up from his desk. As I said, Jalen doesn't know how to whisper.

He follows me into the hall.

"Maybe I gave you the wrong impression about me." With each word, I know I'm closer to ruining this, whatever this is, and what I want to say is: *Date me and her and anyone else you want, at the same time, whatever, I don't care! I'll be fine, because it's you!*

But I'm not fine.

"Huh?"

I stop. Turn. "I don't think you know what you want, Jalen. You're so . . . unavailable. And not just like, in the way that you like me one moment, then treat me like *Rafi's sis* the next. I need someone who *knows* they want me. And *only* me."

I wade through the sea of gab, expecting Jalen to follow. He doesn't.

———

Usually when I get home after school on Mondays, I'm the only one in the house.

I drop my bag at the door. Shush Meowgi, greeting me with a reprise of meows. I cradle him and listen.

The feeling's like in *Blood Jurors*, before some vampire punctures their next victim. The air is dense.

Dad's voice carries from the basement. He's supposed to be teaching a class. I go to the top of the stairs to listen. He's talking on the phone, using his *you effed up* lecturing voice. Only—he's not talking to any of us kids.

"I don't care what he said. This is unacceptable. A breach of privacy. You will take it down. *Now.* Goodbye."

He storms up the stairs and I vault into the kitchen. Sensing danger, Meowgi slinks upstairs to seek out my comforter, tail tucked.

"Dad?" I say, all nonchalant as I break off a banana I don't want. "What's wrong?"

He shows me his phone. And oh god.

There it is. A photo of Raf in his jersey, front and center, on the IU athletics website.

When you scroll, Raf spins the ball, like in one of those animated *Harry Potter* photographs. There are two guys behind him in this dramatic backdrop: Liban, from Somalia, and Hajoon, from Korea.

"Click on your brother," growls Dad.

I tap, but it doesn't fetch the site. The screen's all smudged with Dad's sweaty fingerprints. Second click, it goes. I scroll past Raf's photo, and at least it's only the picture of him in his jersey and not the Afghan flag. Name . . . stats . . . incoming year . . . I find the good stuff in the *Did You Know?* section with a light bulb above it, a place for personal player tidbits.

But this tidbit is no tidbit.

It's a comet, a red-hot blaze of fire barreling across the sky, from here to Kabul.

. . . The Shahin family left Afghanistan during the Soviet Invasion in '79. After the recent government collapse, Rafi Shahin's great-aunt, a musician, and his great-uncle, who once worked as a translator for the U.S. military, remain in Kabul. They are one of thousands of Afghan families suffering under Taliban rule.

It's like I've been swept out to sea. *How* did they find out about Habib and Yasmoon, everything down to their professions?

Then I think back to the shoot, the way Rafi was talking to the pretty IU intern . . . *He told her.*

"Did you know?"

I hesitate, and Dad opens his eyes so wide I see those red spindly veins sprouting from his irises, like the toy eyeballs in the punch at Josefina's.

I shake my head. Lie. "No, Padar."

"That boy's done," says Dad. "Enough."

Dad nearly rips the key hook from the wall.

"Where are you going?"

But the door opens before he can get to it. Mom walks in with Baba, his swim trunks sopping wet.

"Baba refused to put on pants," says Mom derisively, hands on her hips, but Dad's blown past them.

Baba grabs for Dad's elbow. "Sarafat, Bachem, what—?"

If Teslas made noise, Dad would rev the engine to all hell.

But the quiet spaceship *euuuuu* is almost worse.

Like *euuuuu* that boy's in trouble.

Me too, once Dad finds out I lied. Raf's stuff is my stuff, like I said. We're in this together.

It's the calm before the storm. Might as well eat the banana. For strength.

43

A TEXT *whoops* in before Dad and Raf get home.

> I know things're weird between u n me, but . . .
> Ma. WTH? Your dad turned up in the middle of
> practice and took Raf outside by the ear. Coach
> just stood there. What did Big Time Recruit do?

I put my phone to sleep. Meowgi's ears prick up. It's the
Tesla, *euuuuu*-ing into the drive.

Dad gets out of the car and slams the door. Raf doesn't
move. He sits there till Dad stomps around the car and opens
his door. It's only when Dad throws up his hands that Raf rolls
himself from the seat.

He looks about five feet tall.

———

I've heard my brother cry a couple times. But I've never heard
him bawl like someone's died. It rings through the vents. My
room. The kitchen. The living room. Baba's lair.

The sound squeezes, tugs, at whatever it is in the body that shoulders a sibling's pain. Kate would know.

Kate *will* know soon. And I hope she doesn't text Raf something like *How could you?*

I go downstairs to see what the adults are doing.

Mom, Dad, and Baba are on the deck, deep in conversation. A negotiation, from the looks of it. Mom's got her arms crossed. Dad pounds the patio table with his fist as he talks. Baba paces, hands behind his back.

Rafi's basketball sits on top of the table. Weighs in the balance. Dad glances at it periodically, and *if looks could kill . . .*

I go back upstairs with a box of Nutter Butters because the unseen Sibling Pain Muscle throbs and I don't know what else to do.

I knock on Raf's door. Feet shuffle underneath. Then the *snap* of the button lock. I sigh. Locks, especially these, are no match for a bobby pin. I root in all three bathroom drawers before I find it.

His bedroom lock's picked within seconds.

My brother's on his bed, facedown, convulsing. Crying so hard I'm scared he'll vomit. His SMN Basketball T-shirt is drenched with sweat.

"Jesus, Raf." I unload the Nutter Butters on his desk and get the trash can. "What—what happened?"

Sigh doesn't cut it; Raf releases air like a dolphin from its blowhole. "He t-took me out of the g-game."

"I know."

He regards me with bloodshot eyes. But me talking to Jalen's the least of Raf's worries now.

More than vomit, I'm afraid he'll dry out, so I hand him his water bottle.

"No," he says, snatching the Hydroflask. *"He took. Me out. Of the game."* He launches the metal bottle at the wall. It leaves a dent.

"Raf—"

"He c-called IU. Told them I'm not eighteen. That they've gotta take my player profile down. And"—he takes a big, panting breath—"that I'm forfeiting my scholarship."

So *that's* who Dad was on the phone with when I got home. *Davis.*

Raf gets to his feet, his bun askew. He does an open-mouthed 360 of his room, staring at the posters. The trophies. The basketball paraphernalia.

The IU jersey.

"Get out, Mafi," he says in a monotone voice, eyes vacant. "Get out . . . now."

He takes hold of his Enes poster with two hands and rips it down. The MJ one, too. Smashes one trophy on the edge of his desk. Then another.

Grabs the trash can. The lighter. His IU jersey.

"Rafi!"

"I said leave!"

I back myself from the room and propel myself down the carpeted stairs. I've got no choice but to interrupt the negotiations outside. "Mom," I say, voice hoarse, "Rafi's burning his jersey!"

At midnight, after Raf's sobs fade from the other side of the wall, the sleek black car rolls up and idles behind the azaleas.

"Leave us alone," I whisper. "Please."

The azaleas wave in the wind, and the car drives off.

44

HABIB AND Yasmoon haven't called since Thanksgiving.

It's Tuesday, the second day back to class, and also the A&P field trip to Black Star. On the news this morning, aerial footage showed a burn scar smoldering on the other side of the canyon. The air's hazy but Mr. A emailed and said it's clear enough to hike.

The bad news is, Brit's scheduled an *alternative* to the alternative exam with Mr. A. The good news is, a security guard escorted Fallon off the bus before we left the SMN parking lot; last night, Fallon rearranged the SMN tulips to read SEMEN. Principal Bugle didn't find it too funny.

After leaving Brit stranded at Black Star Canyon before Halloween, I wonder if Fallon pulled the flower stunt on purpose so Principal B would revoke his field trip privileges.

———

Tommy and Jalen hike together, behind me. After following a long dusty road flanked by electric fences to the trailhead, Mr. A stops and tells us to gather round. He gives his teacherly spiel about sticking together and helping one another, and lists survival info: warding off mountain lions and snakes, detecting various poisonous shrubs, etc.

"What about demons with needle darts? Or ghosts?" says Tommy.

Jalen tells Tommy to shut the hell up. Tommy claps him on the neck and they wrestle.

"These woods have a rich history," Mr. A says, long nose poking from his faded salmon-fishing hat. "Millions of years ago, it was submerged in water. Where we're about to venture"—he gestures to the wall of green beyond two arching trees—"was home to an abandoned Native American village. In 1831, it was the site of a massacre. A dispute over horses."

Tommy gives Jalen one of his cheeky glances and they have a slapping match behind Mr. A's back.

"Indeed, some do believe Black Star to be haunted," Mr. A goes on. "If you believe in that sort of thing—*ghosts*."

Jalen's hand grazes mine and we both flinch. He lets out a hoarse "My bad." Tingles prick all the way up my arm like the strings on a harp.

I wish Brit were here.

A barometer would read *off the charts* with me and Jalen's Awkward Pressure.

And there's another feeling in the air.

Like a storm's coming. And it has nothing to do with the weather.

"Well, into the woods we go!" says Mr. A, waving us on.

We bow underneath the arching trees, Jalen and Tommy stooping more than others. The terrain beyond the Tree Door is nothing like the dusty road we'd followed to get here. The temperature has dropped; cool air whips my pony around my face. Jalen hugs his arms to his body.

"Mr. A, how far this trail go?" he hollers up ahead. When Mr. A replies *two or so miles*, Jalen curses in an undertone, peering anxiously into the canopies. Still the same ol' Jalen; he hates spooky stuff.

The sidewinding trail leads deep into the Orange County wilderness, so far that beaches and oceans seem planets, not miles away. There is no distinct path, but the clear way is *up*.

Mr. A signals for the class to stop after thirty minutes, asking his first round of questions. The purpose of this field trip is a walking oral exam, after all. I think Mr. A's trying to get a one-up on his teacher evaluations this year. But the *idea* of doing a haunted hike on school time and *actually* being here are two different things. Like Jalen, I think I'd rather be back in the warmth of A&P's classroom.

"So, as we begin to take in more air—someone please detail the physiological processes the body undergoes when commencing exercise?"

Everyone stares at the floor. Me and Jalen trip over each other's words.

"Oh, you go—"

"No, go ahead—"

Jalen goes.

He says the blood increases its supply to the brain, blocking pain signals, and depending on the type of exercise, different muscular twitch systems will activate. He runs a triumphant hand over his hair and bites his cheek. *Intelligence is hot.*

I forget I'm in a haunted canyon for a second, watching him. And why I went off on him in the first place.

Mr. A then asks where the biceps femoris is, and I'm able to redeem myself and answer correctly this time (posterior compartment of the thigh). It *still* bothers me that Fallon got the question right on my birthday, not me.

A few more questions and the class receives a nine out of ten.

Tommy asks a question of his own (if we can keep going, because lactic acid hurts his legs) and Mr. A agrees, bending Tommy's ear on lactic acidosis as soon as we start up again. Tommy mouths *help* to Jalen but he shrugs and gives his half smile.

Jalen steps over this little river, but I've gotta give it a good running jump. Soon we're past the riverbed and headed up the shady canyon, bouldering mossy limestone on hands and feet. I look back.

I hadn't realized just how far Jalen and I had gotten from the group. My body's acclimated to the hand-foot, hand-foot motion of bouldering. My lungs don't feel so tight, either.

Till I'm faced with a boulder that's much too tall to climb without performing a pull-up, and by this point, I feel the trembly weight of my arms.

The many skull rings attached to Jalen's hand jut into my line of vision. He pulls me up. His palm is warm and sweaty.

"Thanks."

"I ain't about this place," he says, dodging the low, over-hanging trees. He sucks on his candy necklace, red to match his hair. "So high, and still no sun. Deeper we go, the colder it gets."

Chills run from the tight elastic holding my ponytail to my heel bones.

"You really scared of ghosts, huh?" I ask him.

"Don't like anything I can't explain," says Jalen.

"Maybe not *all* ghosts are bad."

He looks down at me like *ha, please.* "A part of me's got this feeling, like it's only a matter of time till—"

"Till what?"

"I dunno, till I'm Ghosted or something."

"You, Ghosted? You'd have to do something really bad for your name to end up in the SOL tree."

"You've got way too much trust in me." Jalen almost sounds mad when he says it.

"Maybe I'm not so innocent myself," I say. For a guy who's so scared of ghosts, Jalen's sure spending a lot of time fraternizing with one.

"'S that right?" Jalen clears a branch for me to pass but doesn't meet my eye when I do. "Look, Ma, I wanna set something straight with you."

My stomach flips. "Oh yeah?"

"I guess I am . . . *unavailable.*" He sighs. "To be real with you, it's been a hard couple days with Pops."

"I'm sorry."

Jalen gives me another leg up. I no longer see Mr. A's salmon-fishing hat bobbing below, and can't hear the murmur of chitchat or glugging of water in bottles, either.

"Guess I've always been weird about dating and stuff," he goes on—and I don't want him to. I know what he's doing. He's giving me the brush-off.

The trail splits into three different paths—all difficult—all up.

"Shouldn't we wait for the others?" Jalen says as I brush by him. "Looks like poison ivy there—ain't that the one with the three leaves?"

Soon, it's just my breath and the quivering rustle of brambles as I hike on. A glance over my shoulder tells me Jalen took another path. Inevitable.

Always been weird about dating and stuff. Isn't that like *it's not you, it's me*? It *has* to be me, most definitely me. I kissed him too soon. Or maybe he's moved on to the gorgeous redhead. I grab a branch, take a big step, and hoist myself up—

I gasp.

I'm standing on a precipice, the ledge no wider than my foot. Tipping, I cling to the nearest tree. Below my muddy boots is a straight drop into a dark ravine. Thin wisps of fog like spiderweb laze some eighty feet down . . . Behind me, the slope I'd scaled is more vertical than I'd remembered.

My knees rattle and my breath catches in my throat. In the distance, someone cries my name. *Critical thinking skills.* I've gotta crouch, slowly, step one leg back, and descend backward on hands and feet. That's all—

I crouch, but unable to control my limbs, crouch too quickly—

Crack—kk—kk. It's the worst sound in the world, the branch paring from the trunk. Unbalanced, I dip forward, at full tilt to view the obscure mouth of the ravine—

"MA!"

A resuscitating tug around the middle wrenches me backward with impressive force. I heave, gagging. The image of the ravine fades from view as I twirl and—

My nose bumps something solid and warm.

"What the hell, Ma!" In Jalen's arms, my ear pressed to his chest, I feel, rather than hear, the words boom from his lungs. "First the bike and now this? You got a death wish!"

Dom-dom, dom-dom, dom-dom goes Jalen's heart. The biggest muscle of all.

"Shahin! Thomas!" Mr. A calls, head poking through the trees at the bottom of the slope. "That path's not safe. It's crawling with poison ivy!"

"Coming, Mr. A!" says Jalen.

Jalen eventually coaxes me from the slope. We edge sideways and reverse-boulder down.

———

Taking the middle path, our class makes it to the top, to the waterfall.

More like watertrickle. It's been a dry year, so the thin stream makes me have to pee over anything else. It's been a *long* hike.

After we're subjected to one more round of questions (shell-shocked, Jalen and I let the others pull their weight), it's time for lunch break. Tommy's still getting his ear talked off by Mr. A. Jalen thinks Tommy's pleading looks for help are hilarious.

Me and Jalen sit underneath a massive maple tree, on some soggy crimson leaves. I share my PB Oreos with him, smudged in their Ziploc. It's the least I can do after he, you know, yanked me from an untimely death.

Jalen scrapes off the PB with a leaf and eats the cookie. It's a waste of perfectly good peanut butter, but I keep my mouth shut.

Jalen asks about Raf. I tell him Dad's been making Raf follow him around the house.

"Like a dog?" He sounds kinda pleased. "Never did apologize for the Nixon and Cole stuff . . . and now 'cause of this underhanded stuff he pulled with the player profile, the team's gonna suffer. Did *you* know he was doin' this shoot?"

Yes. I drove him there.

Silence. The kind of silence that sets me apart from Brit. Cowardly silence.

I shake my head. "No."

"His attitude is tired. We got the San Diego game coming up . . . Coach says some UCLA scouts are gonna be there, too. Without him . . ." He blows air from his mouth, and notices I'm digging my heel in the dirt. "Too much Raf talk. Gotcha."

"No, it's fine." After what happened back there, I'm happy to be carrying on a normal conversation. Like nothing ever happened. Like Jalen and me are okay again. "So you want to go to UCLA?"

"Yeah," he says, "L.A.'s not too far from Pops, and it ain't so—you know. Old white people."

I laugh. "I know."

"What I tried to say before you took off," says Jalen, lobbing a stick as far as he can throw it (why do boys do that?), "*the dating stuff.* Pops . . . always told me to *be careful*, all cryptic, 'n' I thought it was 'cause he and Mom didn't work out. But last night . . . Pops sweat out the bed. Found him on the floor. He told me what he saw, in Afghanistan."

A shadow draws my eye in the canopies. A crow takes flight, cawing. Did Mr. Thomas see someone get killed? A Hazara, maybe? A convoy on a land mine?

Jalen tells me, and it's nothing like that.

It happened at the base. A fellow soldier, Vanessa, was assaulted in her tent by other U.S. soldiers. Mr. Thomas saw it happen.

He tried to get the guys to stop, but they were too drunk. One put a gun to his head, told him to go. Mr. Thomas reported it and was discharged a week later. Vanessa, too. She never forgave him. Said it wasn't his place; he should've stayed quiet. That he ruined her career.

The night Vanessa was assaulted, she was wearing a scent like the one I sprayed in the Raptor after motocrossing. Salvia spinosa.

Vanessa had discovered the flower and raved about the scent to Mr. Thomas. Days later, he'd found someone selling the oil at the bazaar and gifted it to her.

"Think that's why Pops always say, *put your love into the game, not girls.* Don't want me gettin' hurt." Jalen peers at the trickling waterfall. "Pops and Vanessa was high school friends and enlisted together. Mom used to say Vanessa was his true first love, but Pops denies it. He blames himself for what happened. Says he shouldn't have left her, should've fought them off." Jalen sniffs and looks away.

My eyes are wet. I have the strongest urge to reach up and wrap my arms around those strong, quivering shoulders.

But I don't.

It feels like the wrong time to fall big-time for Jalen Noah Thomas. Again.

We both reach for the last Oreo, but I tell him, *all you.* Jalen crams it in his mouth, pitching the PB into the dirt.

I tip my knee in and graze his. Intentional. His irresistible dimples make an appearance.

We sit like this for a while, on the sodden leaves.

"So," I say after a while, "what've you got against peanut butter?"

Jalen knocks my knee with his and goes *tshh-tshh-tshh.* "After that back there, I ain't pairing Oreos with peanut butter. You said that was your *Last Meal*, remember?"

———

Mr. A says it's time to head back and I stand, offering Jalen a hand. He takes it. His hand is soft and warm. I let go. If I'm going to get back in one piece, I can't be seeing stars.

We start walking down, which feels riskier than the way up. "Speaking of the last meal, thanks for, um . . . pulling me down from there."

"Huh?"

I frown. "You put your arm around my middle and pulled me back . . ."

"No, I didn't." He scowls. "You did some ballerina tutu twirl and fell back."

I disguise a full-body shudder as a downward spurting jog. Jalen eyes me suspiciously, so I go: "You're right, I forgot." I force a hoot. "Whoops."

A throaty scream slashes the air and Jalen curses. Wind's tossed Mr. A's fishing hat into a tree. Tommy's trying to swat it out, but he's an inch or two shy. Jalen's the only one tall enough to retrieve it.

An hour later, we step through nature's awning, the doorway to the dirt road.

To reality.

"You okay, Tutu?" Jalen says, punching my arm.

"*Tutu*? I like *Ma*."

I cast an apprehensive look at the tangled forest behind me. Maybe I *am* right: Not all ghosts are bad.

45

BY THE time I get home, an itchy sensation snakes up my wrist. Damn poison ivy.

I unlock the door to find Mom and Baba at the dining room table. The photo albums are out.

Baba gestures for me to sit.

"Sarafat!" Mom calls. "Mafi's home!"

Since the player profile dropped, Baba's stopped calling Rafi the Kush Giant. He's stopped asking him to do math problems. Actually, he's stopped talking altogether.

Dad moves from the hall to the dining table. Raf follows. When Raf's done with school, he goes straight to UC Irvine to sit in on Dad's math class. And when he's at home, if Dad's got to move the clothes in the dryer, Rafi's his shadow.

Coach G's called dozens of times. Begging. Pleading. To bring Raf back. To reason with Dad.

But there can be no reasoning with Dad once he's made up his mind.

Dad says, "Your brother asks *why*, says that he wants to understand *why* what he did is so devastating, and it is now your baba's will"—eyes closed, Baba nods—"and your mother's, that you know the truth. *Here.*" Dad points to the same photograph Baba showed me in the attic. "Like his father, Baba was a governor in Afghanistan before he moved to the U.S. Baba's known for helping hundreds of Hazaras escape when the Soviets invaded, and the Taliban after that, from afar." Dad points to the man in the karakul hat. "Baba's father, your great-grandfather, refused to leave his country. And—" Baba clears his throat and Dad continues. "After he died, Baba changed our last name to remove all tribal affiliation. Changed it from Yusufzai to Shahin, meaning *falcon*, a free bird in the sky, surveyor of the chaos below but never partaking. This has been my stance. To keep us. You. *Safe.*

"The world is not like Disneyland, kids, with cartoons and duckies and princess stories! Not for anyone, and *especially* not for us. To Afghans, we are deserters. To Americans, we are outsiders. Your relatives have a greater chance if we stay silent. Don't draw attention to ourselves!"

I think about what Jalen just told me. About his dad, and Vanessa. Mr. Thomas could've stayed silent, and then what? Maybe it would've happened again.

Not reporting it, staying silent, would've meant he consented to their barbaric act.

Rafi and I share a look.

Is silence the best way?

———

I'm putting calamine lotion on my poison ivy when Baba totters into the bathroom, clucking.

He supinates his palm, asking for my wrist. He dips a paint brush into the mason jar in his hand and spreads an orange gel over my rash.

"Mm?" he says, inquiring.

It's cooling. Instant relief.

"Thanks, Baba."

The next morning, the rash, the itchiness—it's gone.

———

It's Monday, December 7. Baba's birthday.

Me and Raf have it off because it's faculty development day, where teachers sit around in meetings all day. But Raf doesn't have the day off, not really. He's still Dad's shadow.

Dad surprises Baba with a walk-in pigeon cage, this monstrous wooden construction in the backyard set with five pigeons. Before Mom left for the salon, I saw her arguing with Dad in the backyard about it. She knows she'll be the one cleaning up after the birds, not Baba. Raf sits on the deck, watching.

Meowgi, on the other hand, is simply delighted.

Baba smiles for all of two seconds. Then toddles back to his post by the phone.

Today is the day Habib promised he'd call from Pakistan.

"Happy birthday, Baba." I give my grandfather a hug, but his arms remain limp at his sides. "What time is it in Quetta?"

"Seven thirty," he whispers, "*p.m.*"

Twelve hours ahead.

"They'll call, Baba. They're probably just . . . running late."

Baba sticks out his gummy lip.

There's only one wish Baba has for his birthday. I wish I could grant it for him.

———

Sick of Baba moping by the phone all day, Dad forces him to attend his 4:00 p.m. water aerobics class.

Mom and Dad are too busy arguing again, so at six, it's me and Raf who wait for Baba in the YMCA lot. "Where is he?" I ask.

Raf stretches his legs. Think my bro's glad to be out from Dad's shadow for a bit. "Probably in the Jacuzzi or something. I'll go look."

It's 6:20 and still no Baba.

"He's not inside," Raf says, swinging into the car. "He's been banned."

"Banned?"

"Yeah. *Staff endangerment.* The receptionist said he got mad and pushed his instructor into the pool. They tried to calm him but he ran. Called his emergency contact—me—but my phone's off, in Dad's drawer."

"Baba knows his way home," I say. "Just like before . . . he'll be fine."

"Baba's *never* been fine," says Rafi, incensed.

Baba's phone goes straight to voicemail, a recording of Baba saying *Bakht*, and then asking someone in the background how to *end the mail.*

It starts to pour. Each swipe of the wipers heightens my anxiety.

"You were right," says Rafi. My foot slips off the clutch. I don't think I've ever heard those words come out of my brother's mouth. "I—I should've stood up to Davis. Should've said no. Now, Habib and Yasmoon are probably dead, and Baba's lost in the rain . . ."

I park the car in the drive. He'll turn up—just like before. He's probably snuck through the den door and is watching Peter Sellers movies.

I tell Rafi this, but he lashes out. "Is everyone blind? Baba has goddamn dementia!"

"He . . . he has . . ." I think about it. The trash incident. Cold teas left all over the house. The random bouts of anger. The time he called me *Katie*. But that's what old people do, isn't it?

My phone buzzes. It's Mom. Dad's wondering where you three are?

Three.

Baba's not home.

A vibration travels from my feet to calves as a truck pulls in behind us. The Raptor.

The windshield wipers run on high and headlights shine in the rearview mirror, blinding me.

Thunder rumbles over our street as Jalen hops down from the driver's seat. He walks behind the hood over to the passenger side, unable to avoid muddy grass, ruining his green Jordans. He opens the door.

Out come bare feet, the soles caked with mud. Then hairy legs.

Jalen shoulders the weight of a stooped old man, struggling to hop down from his high seat.

Baba's still wearing his swim trunks and white undershirt, but nothing else. No jacket. No pants—and where are his shoes? There's blood crusted from his nose to his chin, and his white shirt is spattered with the stuff, too.

"Jesus, *Baba!*" I get out of the car and grab Baba's other arm. Rafi's leaning against Ptero, immobile.

"Saw him wandering down Georgetown Lane, about to reach the bridge," says Jalen. "Fell as I drove up. Wouldn't get in the truck. Had to force him."

Rafi stares, calculating. Jalen stares back. Then they both look away.

"He's not said a word in English to me," Jalen says to me, "but when I told him I was taking him to the Kush Giant he stopped thrashin' in his belt so much."

The garage door opens. Dad must've seen us from the window.

"Djinn! Djinn!" Baba says, pointing at Rafi.

"Baba!"

Dad hurries to meet us from inside the garage, taking Baba from me. Mom's standing in the light of the door that leads to the kitchen, ladle in hand. She drops it and helps Dad bring Baba inside, not before uttering a heartfelt *thanks* to Jalen.

Without a look at either me or Raf, Jalen shakes the rain from his red hair and ducks into his truck. *Is Jalen angry at me, too?* I can't see him through the tinted windows, but the truck idles for a moment, and I wonder if he's watching us.

Jalen drives off and the garage door closes. The flag on the doorstep billows and thrashes in the rain.

46

MOM AND Dad take Baba to the hospital. Mom told me she'd call when they knew something. Each rattle of the wind against the kitchen windows or *tink tink tink* of rain makes me shiver, sending a leaden ball of dread into my stomach. The wind chimes on the porch emit a low *dong-dong-dong* in mourning.

I text Brit what happened and she sends a long consolatory text back. I feel guilty that I've only got the energy to read half of it.

While out looking for Baba, I got three texts from Jalen. Probably why he's upset—that I was ignoring him.

> Ma, u home?

> I'm outside. Can we talk?

> Sarafat came out. Didn't seem so happy I was askin for u. Later.

Jalen must've run into Baba on his way home and turned around.

Rafi's in his think tank, listening to some *wahh-wahh* song with a lot of synth that keeps going, *I'm hollow, hollow, hollow.* He can't sing but he hums along. There's something soothing about the bathroom. Once you latch that door, not even a bobby pin can open it. It's the only place in the house with real privacy.

> I got Mom's voicemail. Baba fell again? Are you with them at the hospital?

The text is from Kate. Mom must've told her.

> Are they checking for clumps of beta-amyloid in the brain?

Then:

> Because a high level would suggest Alzheimer's.

I don't text her back. If I do, I'll have to explain why we weren't around to help (again), and Kate's a pro at calling out my lies. It's like her big-sister superpower.

I pick up my phone and wander into Baba's den. My throat constricts as I imagine this not being his spot anymore. Before Grandma died and Baba moved in, it was a game room with a Ping-Pong table. There was a trampoline in the corner to satisfy one of Kate's ridiculous fitness fads.

I sit on Baba's bed next to his vest, draped over his comforter. I search the pockets and—*aha!*—cashews and M&M'S with their usual side of lint.

I stare at my phone background, me and Jalen. Then go through my contacts and click on his name. My thumb hovers over his number. Wincing, I give it a tap.

Don't answer. I want to leave a voicemail—be all breathy and cool . . . upset, and thankful. With a hint of missing him, too. I'm thinking about what I'll say, when—

"'Lo? Ma?"

My throat tenses like a slingshot band.

"Damn, butt dial or what?" There's a sigh, and I hear the *ckk* of him resituating the phone, probably to hit the end button, when—

"Yes! I mean, no," I say in a rush. "I didn't butt dial you."

More *ckk* on the line. Jalen's heard me and put the phone to his ear. "How's he doing?"

"Don't know yet." I sit on Baba's bed, clutching the cashews and M&M'S in my hand till my sweaty palm's blue with food coloring.

Jalen sighs. "I'm sorry, Ma. Why was he wandering down Georgetown with no shoes anyway?"

"He got mad and shoved his water aerobics instructor in the pool."

"Mm." There's understanding in his voice. "Don't sound well."

Then he clears his throat, and says: "Look, me and that redhead . . . nothing happened with her." He sighs. "Was just cool we had the same color hair—that's it. She was just some girl."

"All right."

"You're not just some girl," he says after a moment.

"You neither."

He shoots air out his nose in a half-hearted laugh. "Can't stop thinking about you, to be honest."

"I—really?"

"Ma, I like you. You're funny and kind and we got this connection . . . and it's not just the dad stuff. When we kissed at the park . . . it felt. I dunno." He goes *tshh-tshh-tshh*. "Then you iced me out, and I missed you. Thought about what you said, that you deserve someone who knows what they want . . ." Is he about to ask me to be his girlfriend? "I can't lose you—"

"Oh!"

"—as a friend."

"*Oh*-hh." It comes out as two syllables. "Totally, friends. Hey—my mom's calling. I've gotta go."

———

After I've had time to process, I'm in my bed, on the phone with Brit.

"As *a friend*?" says Brit. "Hm."

It's 10:00 p.m. and all Mom's texted is that Baba had to wait a long time to be seen; there was some issue with his insurance. Something about him not updating his documents or something. Sounds like Baba.

The rain's starting back up. The tree branches scrape against the roof. That, or Nutter Butter is preparing his nuts for winter or something.

"Really love your baba. Hope he'll be okay."

"Me too."

There's a *thwump* outside.

"What's going on over there—?"

"The cat. Er—gotta go, Brit," I say, without giving her a chance to reply, "talk to you later."

I open the window. A surge of cool, rainy air wafts in.

It's not Cole. Not Nutter Butter, either.

It's Jalen.

47

HE'S CROUCHING on the roof and I'm standing there, gripping the curtains—to check I'm not dreaming. He must think I've glitched, because he says, "Yo. I'm Jalen Thomas, your friend. Nice to meet you."

"Hi," I manage to get out. But my head's going: *Jalen Noah Thomas. Jalen Noah Thomas.*

"My daddy longlegs are falling asleep," he says, still crouching.

"Sorry, um—come in, but *shh*. These walls aren't sound-proofed." Something Raf and *It* have proven.

He *does* look like a spider as he pulls himself through the window. Arms and legs shoot in first, one by one, then the head and torso.

At least I'm not wearing beaver pajamas; I'm in a tank and shorts. Braless, so I cross my arms.

Jalen looks around and grins.

"So, this is it, huh?" he whispers (the best he can). "I'd be lying if I said I've never been in here."

"*What?*"

"Few years ago, me and Raf read your diary."

"You WHAT?"

"Hey, *inside voices*." He presses a finger to his lips. Laughs. "Diary under the mattress . . . so obvious."

He takes off his muddy Jordans, lines them up neatly by my wardrobe, then points to the wall I share with my brother and mouths: *Asleep?*

"Should be."

His eyes flick to the heat vent near the ceiling. I hope he can't see my jewelry box.

"Why's it always so hot in here?" he says.

"*Baba*. Loves the heat. Hates AC."

"Ah." He scratches his red hair. The color's growing on me.

"In your diary, you were all about some kid . . . *Sandpaper Tongue Blaine* . . . doesn't he go to Portola now?"

"God."

Jalen laughs. "So . . . what do you write about me?"

"Haven't written for a while." I stopped after Annalie's party.

There's dirty underwear next to his foot. If I had known boys, real boys—not Cole—would visit, I'd clean more often.

"My parents will be home soon," I say. At that thought, I walk over to the door and lock it.

I haven't showered . . . Did I yesterday, even? My hair's a mess after standing in the rain and my makeup, smudged from crying . . .

On the edge of the bed, I stare at my toes. "Jalen, why are you here?"

"You're upset. I'm here. That's what friends do."

I don't know why these are the words that do it, but I turn over and bury my face in my pillow.

"Can I?" His voice is muffled through the pillow but I know he's hovering over the bed.

"Yes."

The bed droops when he sits. He rubs my back with a meaty paw. Even through my shirt, his hand feels warm and comforting. Safe.

I'm warped back to being a kid, when I was crying and Jalen put his arm around me at the park.

He crawls in bed next to me, arm touching mine. Our body heat channels back and forth, and soon I'm warm and cozy. He's falling asleep; his breaths are slow and deep. His lips part, and I'm remembering how soft they felt when we kissed at the park. The rain pitter-patters against the window.

It happens slowly, over many minutes, and I don't know if it's me or him edging in. Soon my face is close to his. I can feel the energy in the gap between our lips, willing us to try again.

My lips touch his.

"Not kissing you," I murmur. "Just—seeing what it's like to be Jalen's lips."

He moves his lips around. "Mm. Mafi's lips are thin and need a lil' ChapStick."

"Hey!"

He laughs, baring his teeth. They feel slick against my lips. "Friends don't kiss, right?"

"No." But I pucker a bit, and after a few seconds, he does, too.

He stops, Adam's apple bobbing as he swallows. "Ma . . ."

"I want this," I repeat, again and again.

"But I can't give you everything you want . . ."

"I want this." And my one-track mind takes over. The one that doesn't care about CJ. Labels. The one that's here with Jalen, in the present. Later, there'll be time to worry about the past. The future. If there's ever a time to be present, it's now, in bed with my crush.

And I'm on top of him. I take off his hoodie and toss it but his undershirt, much tighter, gets caught on his chin. He pulls it the rest of the way off, laughing in between kisses. His skin is hot underneath me. He feels solid, like steel cables.

My brain screams to get closer. As close as I can. I peel off my tank top and kiss him again.

He kisses me back, hard. His bullet necklace grazes cold against my skin. He stops. Grins to himself.

I'm suddenly self-conscious. "Oh god, I'm a bad kisser. I knew it."

"Damn, no, not it at all . . ." His torso swells as he takes a breath, bobbing me up and down. He laughs, and it's a nervous one. "I dunno, Ma."

"What?"

He smiles again. "You're more . . . experienced than me, maybe."

It's then that I realize CJ is in bed with us, too. Shy, I cover my boobs with my hands. "C'mon. You've definitely gone further than me."

He wags his head back and forth in the gloom, teeth glinting in a smirk.

"But I've heard—"

"Mm, so now you believe everything you hear?"

I snigger. "No. Wait. Are you *really* a virgin?"

"Yes. And while we on the Truth Train . . . I think . . . pan as well."

"Pan?"

"Pansexual." And he avoids my eye, waiting for me to judge him, or something.

"Okay . . . that's amazing. But Jalen, you kiss *way* too good to be a virgin."

He sighs, and it's the longest sigh I've ever heard, sending a hot channel of *hhhhhhh* air into my face. It doesn't help. My spine tingles.

He cradles the nape of my neck with a palm, drawing me back to him. He kisses me so tenderly that my hands fall from my boobs and I shudder from lips to toes. The evil eye necklace grazes his chest and he takes hold of it, like he's gonna rip it off.

"Is it bothering you?" I whisper. I run a hand over his pecs, where the necklace touched. He's got goose bumps.

Jalen answers by tugging on the metal, drawing me closer again.

I know it then. His brain's screaming the same thing: *closer.*

He pulls his lips from mine. Hot and bothered is an understatement. Sizzling and tormented is more like it.

Resolute, he places his hands behind his head. He tips his chin heavenward like *whyyy*, at war with himself. "How d'you get me like— No one has—I mean, nothing has ever—" The muscles in his forearms tense, veins like rivers to his heart.

"We'll stop, then," I say, moving to swing a leg off him—

But he holds me close with a *nu-uh*, and milliseconds later, he crows *don't do me like this* and he's kissing me again.

"So we can't," I murmur, and he answers, "No."

But I can feel one part of his body definitely disagrees . . . He fiddles with my necklace, then runs a lazy index finger from my collarbone to my stomach.

I sit up and hug my belly. I hate when people touch it. Always have. Feeling his eyes resting there, I mutter, "Haven't worked out since I've quit track—"

"Pshhhh—get over yourself, Ma."

I snicker. Trace a hand down his core, feeling the smooth square depressions where his abdominal muscles cave. His hand's on mine, and I'm unsure whether he's leading me Down Under or telling me to stop. He whispers, "The other guys feel like this?" and the next thing I know—

"I'm not just Hook-Up Material!"

"Damn."

It's a different kind of *damn*. A *damn* that makes me want to shrivel and die. "I just told you I'm a virgin . . . *damn.* I'm not like that. We're friends. 'Course you're not *just Hook-Up Material.*"

"Friends?" It flies out of my mouth before I can stop it: "But you don't think I'm Girlfriend Material, either!"

"Woooow," Jalen whispers. He's off the bed, looking for his shirt in the dark. He finds it draped across the computer chair. He grabs his shoes, *loops, swoops,* and *pulls* the laces at lightning speed.

I bring the covers to my chest. "You asked if other guys *feel like this.* There were no other guys, Jalen," I say, "none."

He stands up straight. "I heard—"

"CJ? You heard wrong."

My window shuts with a snap and he's gone.

The room hums with an awful silence. There's this whiplashy feeling in my every bodily fiber, between tension and release, like I'm a guitar and my tuning pegs have been twisted, twisted, twisted, strings so tight I might snap. I writhe in bed, tossing the sheets around.

My phone vibrates and I answer without a thought.

"Jay?!" I shout, high-strung.

"Mama, it's your mother."

"Oh."

She seems too frazzled to notice I'm frazzled, too.

"They've done some cognitive tests . . . and an MRI. No tumor, stroke, or buildup of fluid in the brain. But brain imaging shows beta-amyloid is high."

Beta-amyloid. Kate was just explaining the brain protein to me. "High levels suggest Alzheimer's," I say, echoing Kate's text. I hate when she's right.

"We'll be home in an hour. How's your brother?"

"Asleep."

"Good."

No, not good. Rafi's stress sleeping.

When does it happen, exactly? When do parents stop knowing their kids?

48

BABA'S NOT so much upset about the dementia (he's in denial) as he is about his ban from the YMCA. It doesn't help that Baba has zero recollection of tossing his instructor, not exactly a spring chicken herself, into the pool headfirst.

Dad found another YMCA but it's fifteen miles from the house and no one wants to drive Baba. Dad tells us all to keep our car keys hidden, so Baba can't find them and take off in the night. Baba keeps calling Dad a *prison warden* in Farsi. I think Raf silently agrees.

"When Habib gets here, he will take Baba. He will go," Baba tells Dad, again and again, an accusatory finger raised. "Habib loves his brother, and will take care of him, even if his son will not!"

Still no word from Habib or Yasmoon. It's been four days since Baba's birthday, since they were supposed to call.

It's Friday, and Mom's too tired to cook dinner so we order pizza. Raf flicks a tomato around his plate. Mom and Dad sit at opposite ends of the table.

I look to the landline, gathering dust. *Ring. Just ring.*

When Baba tosses his pizza onto the floor, announcing the sauce is *too sugar*, Mom gets up and pitches the pizza box into the sink.

I feel so alone. Everything in my life is unraveling.

I don't even ask Dad's permission. I tell Brit to come over.

———

An hour later, we're lying in the hammock side by side, away from prying ears. Pockets of pollution reveal glittering stars and crickets chirp in the grass.

"Baba any better?"

"Sure," I lie. Next to her, it's the first time I've been able to relax since last night. She's a solid presence. A true, free radical. My friend.

It's a chilly night, but Brit's body warmth and soft cashmere sweater keep me warm.

"And the Jalen stuff? Tell me again?"

"Well, he said he wanted to be friends, then kissed me, which was weird—and then things got heated, and I accused him of . . . only seeing me as *Hook-Up Material*, not *Girlfriend Material*."

Brit hesitates a moment. "So don't get upset, but I've heard rumors . . . is this because of the CJ stuff?"

I stiffen, and she notices. She grabs my hand.

"I'm just going to say it . . . Who *cares* if people think you circle jerked three guys in Annalie's basement?"

"Um."

"Did you?"

"No!"

"So what *were* you doing?"

"Giving one of them a back massage. The other two . . . were playing Ping-Pong."

Brit's giggles morph into a throaty laugh.

"It's not funny!" I pull my hand from hers.

"Seriously? *A back massage?*"

". . . Yeah." She pokes my ribs and I grin in the dark.

"Who put this *Hook-Up or Girlfriend Material* bull in your head, anyway?"

"Kate."

"Aha. Do you want to be Jalen's girlfriend?"

"Of course I do!" I squeal in frustration and fling my arms over my head. "Why does everything need to be so complicated?"

Brit rolls onto her stomach and stares into my eyes. "Says the straight, white-presenting girl to her transgender friend."

"Point taken."

"The only person branding you is *you*." The hammock judders as she flips back over, looks to the sky. "People will talk no matter what you do. Read the comments haters leave on my TikToks."

I groan.

"Do what makes you happy without all these rules, and without hurting anyone in the process."

I screw up my face, eyes following a zigzagging firefly. *Is that so easy?*

49

IN BED two hours later and about to fall asleep, I'm woken by a galumphing crash. Then a snicker.

There's a scratching at my door.

"Mafi . . . it's R-Rafi."

My brother's drunk. He gets catlike when he drinks—scratching, pouncing, rubbing against walls. Not so much marking territory as an attempt to stay upright.

He's still grounded. Was he solo drinking in his room?

"Can you open the door? It's l-locked."

"It's not locked, you buffoon. Just open it." I turn on my lamp.

Rafi swings in with the door, smiling. I bring a finger to my mouth, telling him to be quiet, and he mimics me. "Shh-*shh*. I know, sorry."

God. There are hickeys all over his neck.

"What the hell, were you out?" I say.

"With Bian," he says. "Don't tell the Warden." He sinks onto my bed.

"When are you going to be *done* with her?"

"You're *so* mean," he says, shaking a finger at me. "Her life isn't easy."

"Oh, really?"

"Bian, her little bro, and her dad all live in a one-bedroom in Lake Forest. S-so . . . stop being a meanie." He burps. *"Don't. Tell. Anyone."*

I never would've guessed. "Well, it's still no excuse for being an asshole . . ." My voice sounds small when I say it.

"Mafi." Raf slaps his face. "You're upset." Slaps his face more. "I'm here for it. I'm not completely useless—no matter what the Warden says—so lay it on me." His happy-drunk bubble's been popped.

"I'm fine—"

"No, you're not. Tell me. Tell me what's wrong." He grimaces while pulling a large sheet of plastic from underneath his butt. Chocolate film from the chocolates I was eating before bed. "Oops-a-daisy . . . do I have chocolate on my ass?" He shakes the bed with quiet laughter.

Raf tosses his hoodie strings over his shoulder. "Look, it's my job as big brother to—" But whatever big bro's job is, I never find out, since Mr. Meowgi's pounced on his back—an attack on the flouncing strings—causing Rafi to shriek and do a side flip into the wall.

"Meowgi!"

The bed shakes as Rafi yanks something wedged between the mattress and the wall. Then, he pops his head up. "Ma—*erp!*—fi. What's this?"

He's holding a hoodie. Jalen's.

A poisonous dread seeps through my veins, clotting my blood.

The Kush Giant has a murderous look in his eye when he stands, securing one foot at a time.

Maybe it'll be like the brown bears, and if I stay like—really still—he'll get bored and go away.

Rafi sobers up fast. "Did you . . . I mean, did you two . . . ?" I purse my lips; they're turning white in the mirror behind Raf's head. "I swear, if you don't tell me, I'll call JT right now, and—did he hurt you?"

"No!" But he's not listening. My brother stares listlessly at the wall. "It's between me and him. Got it?"

"Like hell it isn't." He shakes his head. "The dude *promised*."

I stop. "Promised what?"

"After the whole CJ thing . . . Jalen was joking around in the locker room after practice, said *lucky guys* when SV Prep guys came up. I told him if he ever touched you, *looked at you*, I'd end him. He swore he wouldn't. And now—"

My heart jumps into my throat. Descends into my belly. I say, "It doesn't matter." But it does.

It does.

"You've changed since Annalie's party. At first I was worried, then thought maybe the sweats and hoodies and pulling out of track was a good thing, going low-profile till people forgot what you did. Now I find you're *still* whoring around, with JT, *in our house*—"

"Hypocrite!" I launch into a crying fit. "I hate you!"

"Maybe it's time to tell Mom and Dad about Annalie's party. And this, too."

The demonic voice that comes from deep within my chest, my very being, lights up his cloudy eyes. *"Get out. Of my room."*

Hoodie suffocating in his vengeful grip, Rafi slumps out the door. Seconds later, I hear a mighty thump, the telltale sound of a fist making impact with a wardrobe.

"What is the meaning of all this noise!" Dad hisses from downstairs. "It's one a.m.—*you'll wake your baba!*"

"Tripped," Rafi calls out. "Sorry. Night."

"It will be—whenever there is *peace* in this house!" Dad mutters something in Farsi before stalking off.

I corral all three pillows and hold them, rocking myself. When the tears stop flowing, I take out my phone. Text Jalen: Heads up, Raf found your hoodie in my bed.

I sit with my phone open, eyes blurring from stinging tears. No read receipt.

Would Raf *really* hurt Jalen?

Raf's lost his dream. He's got nothing else to lose.

I drift off to sleep and have nightmare after nightmare.

At 2:00 a.m., the sleek black car is back. Idling.

50

IN THE morning, Raf's not in bed.

No read receipt under my message to Jalen, either.

I pad downstairs and poke my head into the kitchen. Mom sits in her robe at the bar, drinking coffee and flipping through something on her iPad. Looks like *Vogue*.

"Mom?" I test the water.

She looks up. "What's the matter, Mama?"

Okay, so Raf's threats to tell Mom about the party, about Jalen, were empty. Next question.

"Where's Raf?"

Staring at her e-magazine, Mom says: "He's gone."

"Gone?"

"On the bus," she chirps. "To San Diego for the away game."

"Wait—what? Does Dad know?"

She sips her coffee. "Nop-*ahh*."

"So—you . . ."

"Rafi is my son, too." She smiles sweetly. It's unnerving. "I told Coach Gordan he *will* finish out the season. It's his senior year, after all. So I woke your brother at five a.m., gave him his phone, and he Uber'd to school. He smiled this morning, Mafi." She looks at me. "Your brother *smiled* at his mother."

"Mom . . . everything okay?" I ask, because her voice sounds simulated, like a recording.

She puts her iPad to sleep. "He *always* holds it against me."

"Huh?"

"When your dad asked me to marry him . . . I hesitated."

"What?"

"I hesitated. And to this day, he brings it up whenever it is convenient for him."

"Mom . . ."

"I've never told anyone that, you know. It's freeing! It's not easy being co-parent, Mama. Because no matter what, the parent-in-command can override anything the co-parent suggests. I fell in love with your dad because he was a force. Strong-headed. Handsome." She shrugs. "I just . . . don't want to mess this parenting thing up, too."

"Too?"

She stifles a sniffle. Is this why Mom hates to bring out the photo albums? Because she wishes she'd never chosen Dad? Never had us?

"Oh, Mama. Oh no no no." Motherly intuition sees the question written on my face. "I wouldn't redo any of it. You three are my life—*the places you will go!*" She clutches me to her.

I'm thinking about the picture of Mom in high school in the plaid pants, and feel a surge of guilt in my chest.

The places we will go.

But what about her?

51

"YOU SEEM superpsyched for this game for some reason, but slow down a bit?"

Brit's convinced her mom to let her take the car to a sleepover at my house for the night. There *will* be a sleepover, but that's after we drive back from San Diego. We're headed to Raf's game.

I'm driving her Jetta because the Siren *does* have an Achilles' heel: She's scared to drive on the highway.

"Sorry." I take it down to seventy. It's easy to speed when everyone else goes a hundred.

I don't tell Brit that Raf found Jalen's hoodie. I'm embarrassed. Afraid she'll think I'm inventing drama in my head. I wanna clean up my mess on my own.

"Can we stop at this dress shop in San Diego before the game?" asks Brit. "They've got a newspaper-themed pantsuit I'm dying to try on."

I stare ahead. "If we have time, sure."

Brit eyes me, and it's quiet for a second. I try to relax and keep my cool.

"What's with you, Mafi?"

"Nothing." I force a smile. "Everything's good, I promise."

But my thoughts reel. Jalen still hasn't read my message. Would Raf punch him on the bus? This is Jalen's big day. The day UCLA scouts are coming.

Nausea surfaces and I shove it down with an *ack*. I think about my birthday. What Rafi told me in the car in the driveway.

How if anyone hurt me, he'd kill them.

———

"That was the turn-off to the dress shop!" says Brit. We're in downtown San Diego.

"Seats, Brit. We need to get there early, you know, for good seats."

"If we get to the high school now, we'll be two hours early. I'm hungry, too."

"Look, I need to—ask Jalen something."

Her silvery voice has an edge to it. "So text him."

My hands remain locked on the wheel.

When we get to San Diego High, SDH players are there in red jerseys, running drills, but there are no yellow SMN uniforms in sight. I glimpse Tommy Lewis on the other side of the court, ducking into the locker room.

"Wait!" I run to catch him up, dodging basketballs, leaving Brit on the other side of the court. I raise a finger like *one sec!* and Brit throws up her hands.

Tommy turns. "Ma. What're you doing here? Game's not for hours."

"I need to talk to Jalen. He hasn't been answering his texts."

He gives me a look, like *you serious right now?* "JT's off the grid. Preppin' for them UCLA scouts. Mr. Thomas is driving him up."

Coach G's voice echoes up the tunnel. I sidestep Tommy to follow the reverb—

"Hey!" Tommy takes one step to match my six. "No females allowed."

"I need to see Raf—"

He rolls his eyes. "Can't believe this girl. Imma tell you one more time, save it for later."

"Look, I don't care if they're naked, I just—"

"We ain't *naked*. Coach G's all about focus right now. So take your"—he twirls his long fingers—"chaotic energy tornado someplace else."

"I have reason to believe my brother has it out for Jalen. That something might go down and ruin Jalen's shot with the scouts."

Tommy eyes me, and it's clear he knows what transpired between me and his friend. "Ain't getting into it with you right now. But listen, I'd never let anything happen to JT. Believe that."

"Okay." I nod. "Okay."

———

As long as Coach G is there, as long as Tommy's by his side, nothing can happen. I tell myself I'll go find Jalen as soon as the game ends. Before Raf can get to him, alone.

I spot the UCLA scouts in the first quarter. They're perched in blue and gold at the top of the bleachers, tapping furiously on their iPads. Jalen looks at them once, expels air from his lungs, and gets on with it.

He's never played so well. After the first quarter, SMN are up ten points. I spot Mr. Thomas in the crowd in a backward hat. He's distracted by this woman's baby, next to him. His smile's just like Jalen's.

At halftime, Jalen's sitting on the bleachers, squirting Gatorade into his mouth. Mr. Thomas sits with him, arm around his shoulder. Jalen keeps nodding.

SMN is neck and neck with San Diego.

Two minutes to go and five points up, Tommy shoots, and Rafi and Jalen both jump for the rebound. The *smack* of skin on skin is audible over the cheering crowd.

Jalen lands on his stomach and Raf on his feet, with the ball.

Brit covers her mouth with her hand. Mr. Thomas stands. Encourages Jalen to get up, but he's wincing.

Raf steps over Jalen. It's Tommy who gives Jalen a hand.

When Jalen gets to his feet, I see it in his face before I hear it: A compressed roar explodes from his lungs, louder than any dirt bike.

Soon, Raf and Jalen are in a shoving match and the ball's bounce-bounce-bouncing off . . .

Short whistle blasts from the refs break up the fight. The UCLA scouts are deep in conversation, nodding toward the court while the refs deliberate. One of them gives a curt nod at the same time Jalen looks up. Raf gets a tech for stepping over Jalen—his second one. He's ejected from the game.

"Head up, Big Mac!" shouts Mr. Thomas.

The game resumes.

San Diego gets a free throw, and the ball. The buzzer *blangs*.

San Diego wins, 66–65.

———

I wanted to catch Jalen before he went in the tunnel, to see if he's all right, but he and Raf were getting yelled at by Coach G.

So I wait outside with Brit, neither of us speaking to each other. I rub my arms. It's cold and I didn't bring a jacket.

Forty-five minutes later, Jalen spots me and Brit as he walks toward the Raptor, idling, behind the charter bus. Looks on.

"Wait—Jalen!"

I can't see Mr. Thomas inside the truck, but I know he's there. Observing. Brit stands at a distance.

Jalen spins around. "You kidding me, Ma?" His voice is smoky with fatigue.

"Just—let me explain!"

"Explain what?" He leans in, smelling of postgame sweat and Icy Hot. "After everything I told you 'bout Pops and Vanessa, and you let Raf believe I *hurt you*?"

"No! I told him you didn't, but he—"

"Why's he telling everyone, then?"

"I—"

Jalen points a finger between my eyes. "Fuck you."

The words wash over me, stinging. Stinging again. The charter bus rattles to life and exhaust fills my lungs. Pollution. A free radical—the harmful kind—that I've become.

Jalen stands there, eyes glistening. A group of giggling girls in SDH jerseys walk by, laughter dissonant.

"A rumor like that—" Jalen hits his chest with a closed fist. Once. Twice. The impact lodges a tear from his eye, falling onto the collar of his jersey. "People like me have been killed for less. Never mind that them UCLA scouts ignored me after the game. Looked at me like I was some—liability. Never. Mind. That."

Avoiding his eye, I whisper, "I'm sorry, Jalen."

"Speak up."

"I'm sorry!"

"Make it right," Jalen says, readjusting his duffel. "You make that shit right."

He spins on his heel and walks, head down, to the Raptor. My hands drop to my knees and I breathe.

Brit rushes to me. I feel a warm, comforting hand on my back.

"Don't do that," I say, as the Raptor thunders off. "Please. Just don't."

52

BRIT'S CAR gets a flat one hour from home.

I told my parents I'd be sleeping at Brit's house. She told her mom she'd be sleeping at mine. We giggled on the way to San Diego that after the game, we'd get a hotel with Brit's Dad's card, or park the car by the ocean, talking all night . . .

Now I'm staring at a flat on the side of the highway, thinking I deserve this. I should've had the big blowout with Raf after the party happened. Had the guts to tell him to stay out of my life, and mean it, no matter the consequences.

Brit's right, I can't repress the hard stuff.

Jalen's curse sounds in my head.

I just want Mom.

———

I text her.

> Are you home?

> At your aunt's in Riverside for a day or two.
> Don't worry. xx

Cars shoot by, none stopping. I cradle my head in my hands. Brit's phone is out. Her hair whips around her face.

She inspects the tire one more time. "I'm calling my mom!"

"No!" I shout over the roar of traffic. A semi trundles past. Trembling, Brit slides into the driver's seat and switches on the hazard lights. I get in, too, and we shut the doors.

The air hums. The car sways with the ghostly *sshk!* of each passing car.

"It's ten p.m., Mafi," says Brit. "I'm not waiting till we get hit—or abducted."

"We'll—figure it out. Don't call her yet!" But her thumb hovers over her mom's number. I lurch for her phone and Brit smacks my hand.

"Mafi!" Her voice pierces. No trace of silver. "Stop it! You've been selfish *all day*! Did you even want to go to the game with me, or were you just using me for a ride?"

White-hot stars burn at the corners of my eyes. "What?"

"You asked me to go to the game because you said it would be *fun*! Have you talked about anything else since you and Jalen hooked up? Or asked *once* what I wanted to do? To eat? You ignored me when I said I wanted to go to the dress shop, and at halftime, you brought me Skittles when I specifically said Snickers!"

"I'm in crisis mode, Brit!" My voice is raspy, wet with tears. "My mom is in Riverside right now—probably thinking about divorcing my dad, and Jalen hates me because—"

"I don't *care* why Jalen hates you. I don't want to hear about Jalen anymore. Friendship is a two-way street, Mafi." She sighs. Her cat eyes narrow into slits. "You know what, CJ aside, you were downstairs with boys at Annalie's that night instead of protecting your friends."

"You're siding with Annalie now?"

Brit rests her head on the window. Breath fogging the glass, she murmurs, "I'm done."

Shhk.

Shhk.

Sighing, Brit picks up her phone at the same time a loud *whoop!* cuts through the whooshing of traffic. CHP, California Highway Patrol, has pulled onto the shoulder behind us.

———

Like oil to water, my brain skims across the officer's cheerful mood, never engaging.

She's shocked when she learns we didn't know to dial 511, California's free roadside assistance number. She says she's got two girls around our age, and waits with us, gabbing away, until a man comes in a utility truck to put on the spare.

After he's done, the officer asks if we need to call someone, and we both stare in opposite directions, till Brit says, "No."

Brit tells me to drive to Irvine. Apparently, Irvine's one of the safest cities in the U.S., and it's only a few miles from Rancho. I'm shocked, when we arrive, to see a jogger at 1:00 a.m. Bicyclists, too. I park underneath a willow tree in a pristine, residential neighborhood that takes obvious pride in its landscaping, its pothole-free roads.

Brit doesn't say good night. She locks the doors, reclines, and turns on her side. I hear her sniffling.

"Brit?"

"I don't want to talk, Mafi." And she means what she says.

Brit would probably hate me for it, but when I turn over, I'm thinking about Jalen. I can't help it. He's always been there, on my mind, since I was a kid.

I think about the panic he'd feel if the roles were reversed tonight. A flat tire. The *whoop* of a police car. Sleeping in his truck in a neighborhood like this. Simple things that for him, are not so simple.

People like me have been killed for less, he'd said.

Before going to sleep, I text him. I screwed up. Epically. How do I make it right?

———

At 6:00 a.m., Brit wakes me. She drops me off, then drives home.

I've got a text from Jalen. It came in at 4:00 a.m.

> You on your own now.

53

COACH G suspended Raf from the team for the rest of the season for his unsportsmanlike conduct toward Jalen at the game. So Dad got what he wanted, anyway.

There was not one peep from Raf; he expected it, I guess.

He's been on his computer all day. And his phone. He tells Dad he's doing research for a big project at school, but I think he's up to something.

Well past midnight, I jog upstairs after watching a movie alone in the living room and am surprised when I bump into something solid.

Bian.

But I didn't hear her BMW, or see it in the drive?

"What are you doing here?" we both whisper in unison.

"I happen to live here," I say. "Do you not even care you could get Raf in more trouble, sneaking in like this?"

She must've come through Raf's window.

"Like you care about him." She flips her hair and flits to the bathroom.

I roll my eyes and open my bedroom door. Weird. I don't ever remember *closing* it. Dad doesn't let us. Inside, the window's cracked open a little. Sometimes a draft'll yank it shut.

I almost want to text my brother, tell him how dense he's being. He's lost his dream, lost Ball. Still on rock bottom. He doesn't care.

I put my phone away. Me and Raf haven't spoken since I told him I hated him.

————

At A&P on Monday, I sit at the front of class while Tommy, Jalen, and Brit sit at the back, like I'm polluting their air. I don't chance a look. I know they're looking at me.

I've lost everyone important to me. Invisible. Again.

————

This week is a half week at SMN before the holiday break. In the evenings, I welcome the cramming of useless facts and figures and physiological processes, of formulas, of things that are objective. I can lie on my stomach in bed, delving into books, till it's time to sleep.

I tell myself that it can't get any worse.

There's knocking on my window every night. Cole. But I never pull back the curtain, not even when he sits for thirty minutes on Monday night. He leaves letters under a loose tile.

I've never gotten so many.

They're all fiction. All hurtful. Every. Single. One.

Jalen Thomas had sex with Mafi Shahin in a Del Taco parking lot and left her naked behind a dumpster.

Rafi and Mafi Shahin are both dating Jalen Thomas and he doesn't know! Ghost the Shahins!

Mafi Shahin forced Jalen Thomas to have sex with her. The witch should be burned at the stake! He can so do better!

This HAS to stop.

Now.

———

It's Wednesday, and a mere few hours till winter break starts. I've noticed more stares in the hallway. More snickering. Whenever Bian passes me, she looks at me like I'm one of those formaldehyde octopi from biology class. I don't think it's because she and Raf are on a break. Walking into the lunchroom, I hear a freshman girl tell her friend: "Yeah, *Mafi Shahin*. The girl who broke Jalen Thomas's penis."

"I didn't!" I growl, startling them. They take off, and it's just the vitriol I need to march myself right onto the small stage set up in the cafeteria.

The choir's just finished singing "The Chanukah Song."

The lunchroom gives their usual half-hearted applause. Someone shouts, "Take off your shirt!" and everyone laughs. My heart beats fast and my eardrums swell with heat.

I reach for the microphone. "I have something to say." When the girl with the mic doesn't hand it over, I nab it from her.

Sitting alone, Raf shoots lasers from his eyes, the spitting image of Kate. The team snubbed him after he stepped over Jalen.

Jalen squints at me from the basketball table. He's right. I'm on my own now.

"Uh." The mic's got feedback. I'm seasick as I peer over the mob. "I just want to set something straight, since—everyone's talking about it."

I think of Brit's comment. Why should I care if people think I'm CJ or not? *Hook-Up Material* or *Girlfriend Material*?

"Jalen Thomas and I never had sex. He *never* hurt me, left me naked behind Del Taco or whatever, and he was never part of any weird love triangle . . . Want the truth? *I liked him* and screwed it up. Hurt him." Jalen frowns at me from his table. "That's it. No trash for y'all to feed on like the maggots you are. It's gone too far now, and I've—"

But there's a hissing over the crowd, like wind over water. Annalie angles her phone at me.

I glance over my shoulder and see what everyone's staring at.

Principal Bugle stands by the double doors. He's flanked by two police officers, one of whom crooks a finger at me.

It's then that I realize it's happened, I've broken my third rule as Ghost.

Ensure justice is served without police involvement.

———

I still hear chants of *Lock her up!* in the hall.

Principal Bugle leads us into his office. A blond woman sits inside. She turns as we approach, and her eyes sprout a dozen more crow's-feet when she sees me.

Mom. She doesn't look mad. More like she might vomit. I'm relieved it's Mom and not Dad in that chair.

Principal B draws the curtain that looks into the secretary's office and shuts the door. Then he and the officers do this *official power play* where each insists the other sit behind the big desk.

The officers end up behind the desk and Principal B stands in the corner, shifting his weight. My knees buckle and I sink into the chair next to Mom.

Arms crossed and leaning back in his chair, the officer on the left looks like he'd rather be watching football. He actually resembles that Formula One driver Brit likes. The other officer has a tidy appearance, with shiny glasses and hair in a headache-inducing bun. I've decided she's the scary one.

She leans in. "Hello Mafi, I'm Officer Gregory and this is Officer Rodriguez. I know this meeting is not pleasant"—she looks from me to Mom—"but here we are. You have been accused of vandalism. After reviewing CCTV footage from one Fro-Yo Emporium on Grand, well—" She swipes through iPad photos, and stored within is incriminating photo evidence: me with my hood up in the fro-yo shop, me keying Wiggs's car. "Is this you?"

Before I can answer, there's all-out banging on the door. Principal B rises, grumbles an apology. "Ms. Rossi—you'll have to come back later, we're—"

Brit pushes her way inside, corset rhinestone top winking and hoop earrings swaying. "I was in on it," Brit says, an unusual frightened edge to her silvery voice. "It wasn't only Mafi."

"Ms. Rossi, was it?" says Officer Gregory. "Seeing as you weren't actually the one doing the keying, might I suggest that you leave, and we'll pretend you never came in . . . okay?"

Brit plays with a hoop earring, thinking. "You're new here, so I'll forgive the ignorance. That's not really me, Officer."

I cover my smile with my hand.

Principal B emits a tired exhale. Brit's no stranger to his office. "Not today, Ms. Rossi. Move along to class, or be removed." He leans across the desk and hovers a finger over the call button.

Like Jalen and Tommy, me and Brit have our own language now.

I've got this. You can leave.

I'm not leaving you here to fend for yourself, Mafi.

Seriously, save yourself. Just go!

Are you sure?

Yes.

Officer Rodriguez is kinda hot.

I know. Just go, okay?

I cap the nonverbal exchange with one final nod that says *sorry*. She accepts my nonverbal apology. With one sweeping look over our waxy faces, Brit sighs. Leaves.

As soon as the door closes behind her, I regret telling her to go.

"Is this you?" says Officer Gregory to me, pointing at the iPad.

"Yes. It's me."

Officer Gregory flips through some papers. "Mafi, can you explain *why* you keyed Rolf Wiggs's car?"

"'Cause he's an asshole," I say in an undertone.

Mom goes, "Mafi," and Officer Rodriguez reroutes a snort into throat clearing.

Officer Gregory then says, "Your father is Sarafat Shahin and your grandfather Bakht Shahin? They are from Kabul?"

Mom cuts in. "What does this have to do with Mafi?"

"And *Mafi*," Officer Gregory presses, "what is your father's known political affiliation?"

"*Don't* answer that." Mom's voice is stern.

"Has your father ever used language or hate speech that might suggest intent to harm Rolf Wiggs, or—"

"Of course not!" I say, face prickling.

"Yet your grandfather Bakht, he has repeatedly destroyed private property—campaign signs from a neighbor's lawn? The very same former electoral candidate whose car you keyed?"

Cam. So *that's* why the police were on Cam's lawn.

I'm tactically quiet now.

Officer Gregory says, "A background check revealed Bakht was flagged for his father Osman's involvement in a terrorist group—"

"No!" Mom looks at me. "Bakht's father, Osman, was murdered by terrorists after Bakht moved to the United States." I frown at Mom. Dad told us Osman died, but he didn't say how. "Bakht—Mafi's grandfather—was a respected governor in Afghanistan. A known activist for Hazaras and minorities. He helped smuggle Afghans out when the Soviets invaded. After Bakht moved his family to the U.S., he was labeled a traitor and Osman was killed. So go on, amend your little file. Tell me how we can resolve the vandalism, but don't sit there accusing my family of terrorism!"

Officer Gregory's jaw is clenched so hard it looks welded shut. Officer Rodriguez steps in. "A settlement," he says. "Wiggs's insurance quotes"—he flips through the file—"one thousand in damages."

Mom makes out the check, slaps it on the desk, and grabs my arm.

54

FOLLOWING MOM through the parking lot, it feels like after I crashed the Honda all over again, a pathetic duckling trailing its mother. Even though she's my height, she's walking at a Jalen pace to the gray Tesla in the lot.

"Mom."

She doesn't answer.

I dip into the Tesla after her. The car doors slam. My ears ring like I've survived a blast. But I know another one's coming.

Mom grabs the wheel and tears spill down her face. Confusion keeps me from crying, too. Shouldn't Mom be yelling? Shouldn't I be grounded? Disowned?

Instead, she says, "I'm sorry, Mama. *I'm so so sorry.*"

"Um."

"Whenever your brother acts out or—or—you hold things in, or lie to me . . . like why on earth you're taking Ubers from Rose Park to Jalen's at odd hours of the night . . ."

Oh, right, the time I ordered Jalen an Uber home after we kissed. Of course it'd show up on Mom's account.

". . . I wonder—where did I go wrong? Is it because of this wedge between you three and your father? We should've told you two earlier about Osman. I'd asked your father many times—to help you understand—"

"*Two?*"

Mom yanks a fraying string from her purse. "I told your sister a few years ago."

"*Mom.*" Confusion mutates into anger. "Why would you—never mind. No, I get it. Kate has always been your favorite."

"Oh, Mama, *never* say that!" Mom blubbers. "Your sister, she just—helps me *understand* you and your brother."

"So ask me yourself!"

"You don't think I've tried?" she says. She brushes my hair back. Brushes, and brushes. Mom looks at me like Dad does, like I'm in that display case. "You're sixteen and I don't have a *clue* who you are . . . why you would be vandalizing politicians' cars with Brit Rossi . . . or quitting track . . . changing your wardrobe . . . tossing your old posters . . . talking on the phone late at night . . .

"When you were little, you used to tell me everything, Mama. I'm not blaming you, you're becoming—who you're becoming. I just . . . want the closeness."

I stare at a leaf on the floor mat. Crunch it with my foot.

"Does Dad know why you're here?" I say after a while.

In my periphery, Mom shakes her head. "The police called the landline. I had a cancellation at the salon and was home."

"Are you gonna tell him?"

She wags her head again. "The questions they asked, it will only upset him."

Mom's right. The questions only confirm what Dad said, how we'll always be deserters to Afghans. Outcasts to Americans. Is

- 320 -

that why the sleek black cars have been parking out front? Does the government have us on some terrorist watch list?

Habib and Yasmoon . . . it all makes sense now. Osman was labeled a traitor and killed after Baba left for the states. Dad and Baba have been terrified that history will repeat itself. I remember the look in Baba's eye when I rescued Meowgi. My grandfather *always* wanted to help others, and my great-grandfather was killed because of Baba's generosity, his inability to leave anyone behind.

Mom rubs the mascara streaking her cheeks. "Can you please, *please* tell me what's going on? What made you do this?"

I look at Mom. Then the woods, in the rearview. "Do you remember the Fairy Tree?"

I can't hold it in any longer. Any of it.

So it tumbles out of me, and as it does, the panic in my stomach lightens. Annalie's party. CJ. How the Fairy Tree became the SOL tree. Ghosting. How Rafi found Jalen's sweatshirt in my bed and stepped over Jalen at the game.

And with a rushing sound like *Oh!* Mom brings me in for a hug, repeating *my girl, my girl, my girl.*

———

At midnight, I open my window to the oak leaves rustling in the breeze.

I climb down, Nutter Butter watching from his perch above me, shaking his tail.

"There're scarier things than you, Nutter Butter." I stick out my tongue, and he does a full-body hop around the branch like a maniac.

THUNK. Meowgi's face presses against my window, teeth chattering.

My backpack jostles on my shoulders as I land in the dirt with a muted *fwump.* I grab my bike from the shed around the back of the house, careful not to let the sliding door squeak.

Invisibility is still paramount, so I stick to the shadows, weaving around pockets of lamplight on the sidewalk.

My final Ghost run.

———

Before Baba moved in, I used to have slumber parties in the den.

Annalie and our crew would pile into the bathroom, the creepy one with the window that's underground and filled with cobwebs outside, and stare into the mirror. We'd spin around three times and shout *Bloody Mary*, hoping to summon some ghostly figure in the mirror. Then we'd scream and hurtle into our sleeping bags.

I never saw anything, but I screamed anyway. What was I meant to see in the mirror?

It was me, all along, scaring myself to death.

Life was easier then, worrying about stuff that doesn't exist, something we may or may not have seen.

———

I descend the leafy hill, feeling—not hearing—footsteps behind me.

"I'm not scared of you!"

I'm not scared of what's real. What I can fight.

"What are you doing here?"

I almost don't recognize the low voice attached to the lanky boy in the Supreme hat behind me. Cole stands next to me, staring over my shoulder. The kid's taller than me now.

"Making things right," I say. The *zrrrr* of my backpack zipper cuts echoes in the forest.

I hand him a pine board, a discarded piece from Baba's pigeon cage. I take out a hammer and four nails from my backpack.

Cole's dark eyebrows furrow. *"Why?"*

"Because people are getting hurt."

It started with menial Ghostings, yes, but Wiggs put it over the top. Because I Ghosted Wiggs, because I broke the law, the police started digging. The sleek black cars out front . . . What if they send my family away?

"I knew you were the Ghost after Josefina's party," says Cole. "I saw you spike that dude's drink."

"Why'd you never say anything?"

"Was afraid you'd stop, or get mad, or—wouldn't need me anymore."

"Oh." I place the pine board over the treble clef tree knot. The crack of the hammer resounds over the forest. Birds caw, taking flight.

Cole's shivering. He's only wearing a baggy white T-shirt and basketball shorts. I don't know why kids pretend they're not cold, no matter the season. "I saw some video, police escorting you out of the lunchroom. What'd you do?"

"Keyed a politician's car."

Cole laughs. "Radical."

I guess it was.

"I'm suspended till January seventh." I line up the final nail over the pine board. Do suspensions show up on college applications? I drive the nail into the wood with a *crack*.

"I'm sad it's over," says Cole. "All those stealth missions you did. That was some sick vigilante stuff. Like a video game, but real."

"You do the honors." I hand Cole the hammer. "Another two hits."

Tongue jabbing his cheek in concentration, the forest echoes with the sound of our liberation. The Ghost-Courier treaty is broken.

———

Cole and I round our street at 1:00 a.m.

There it sits: the sleek black car with the tinted windows, veiled by Mom's azaleas.

"I see it all the time," says Cole, noticing, too. He stops, but I don't.

I'm like Thor in my Thor jersey, hammer in hand. I take off at a run, backpack jolting from side to side. A euphoria similar to dirt-biking ripples across my skin. Cole's shouts are masked by the thumping of blood in my ears. I push the throttle. *Higher.*

Cole catches me up and wrestles the hammer from me. My fist bangs the tinted window. *"Hey!"* The engine fires.

"No! *Who are you?*" I pound and pound. "What do you want?"

The car peels from the curb. Doubled over, coughing exhaust, I peer in the dark for a glimpse of the lighted rear license plate, but see nothing.

55

THE NEXT evening, an orb of light in the backyard catches my eye.

I pad downstairs and find Dad on the couch in the living room, eating cherries. From the look of it, he's eaten a whole carton. Bloody cherry pits stain his white napkin.

Dad spits out another pit.

A faint bobbing light catches my eye. Outside, Baba holds a lantern over the rosebushes.

"What's he doing?" I ask Dad.

"Baba's putting on a funeral."

"What? For who?"

"His brother."

I freeze. Fireflies dance around Baba's head, blinking in turn. "Was there news—? Did he—?"

"No news," says Dad. "But it's been weeks . . . Baba insisted."

Behind Dad's head, Habib's wooden donkey has disappeared from the mantelpiece.

"But—"

"But?" prompts Dad.

"Dad," I say. I've been toiling over this all day. "I think we're being followed."

He spits out another cherry pit. Looks at me. "Yes, Gojeh."

"What—what do we do?"

Dad thinks a moment. *"Be in the world, but not of it."*

"Huh?"

"The Bible says something similar. Don't let events out of your control take over your life, Gojeh. Baba—he is letting go to move on. It is healthy."

I stand there in the dark. Then ask, "Are you really converting, Dad?"

"No, Gojeh." He sighs. "No. But I learn where I can."

———

I pace my room because inaction isn't an option. What about the events that *are*, or *could be*, in my control?

Hours later, when the house is quiet, I shrug into my hoodie and open the window.

I can't just pretend everything's fine, like Mom. Since the interrogation and our talk in the car, she's all smiles today. It's creepy. She spent all day in the kitchen, making four different kinds of cookies. She's in denial, like when she vacuums the rugs over Raf's noisy sexcapades.

Sitting. Waiting. What has that done for my family? For Habib and Yasmoon?

Now is the time to act.

"Don't kill me tonight, oak," I tell the tree, descending gingerly. Nutter Butter does a territorial flying leap from the roof to the tree, chattering. "Chill, dude, *your* home's not at risk."

"Mafi, what are you doing here?"

Brit stands in her silk robe on her doorstep. Her mom calls for her, sees it's me, and tells her to make it quick. I wonder if she found out about San Diego.

"Thanks for what you said—in the office."

"We *did* do it together." Brit shifts awkwardly. "Heard you're suspended."

"You once said . . . if I needed anything, you'd be there."

Brit runs a finger along her hoop earring. Maybe it's too late to summon the Siren. Maybe I've screwed it all up.

"Yeah," says Brit, casting a nervous look inside the house, "but Mafi . . ."

"You don't need to do it for me. It's for my relatives."

"What?"

"When you found that leaf in my hair and said you didn't know if I was the haunted or the haunter . . . that maybe I was both, you were right."

Tears are streaming down my face now. My legs buzz. I hold on to the stair railing.

"I hid behind Ghostings and—ignored everything. All the trauma. All the time. And I'm sorry for being selfish. I want to be better. Do better. For everybody."

Brit stares at me, wide-eyed, torn.

"Britney Marie," her mom repeats from inside, to which Brit snaps: "Just a minute!"

Brit thinks a moment. "How can I help?"

Ten minutes later, we're on the beach. A portable selfie stick is rooted in the sand, holding Brit's phone. TikTok is open, and Brit's finger hovers over the record button.

"Are you ready?"

I hesitate. "The algorithm is finnicky—what if I get fifty views?"

Brit shakes her head. "Please. Have you seen my account? I posted a video of me eating Sidecar doughnuts the other day and it got ten million views."

"Okay." I take a deep breath. "I'm ready."

Brit clicks record and joins me on the log.

"This is Mafi here, and she has a favor to ask of you, world."

"Hi. My name is Mafi Shahin," I say, voice shaking. "And my relatives Habib and Yasmoon, um . . ." But their last name isn't *Shahin*. Dad said Baba changed it when he moved here. What was it? "Yusufzai are missing. They fled Kabul at the beginning of December and were supposed to have arrived in Quetta on the seventh. My family has not heard from them since Thanksgiving. I feel . . ." I take a breath. "Helpless. But still I want to help. I'm sure I'm just shouting into the void, but if you know anything about their whereabouts, *please* comment on this post."

Brit gets in the frame. Points at the camera. "TikTok. Do your thing."

———

After it's posted, Brit rejoins me on the log.

"Proud of you." I normally hate when people tell me that, but not Brit. She holds me. Even though I can't see it, I listen to the ocean. Ebbing. Flowing.

"They're out there somewhere," I whisper after a while.

"Yeah." Brit looks to the sky. "They are."

56

MOM SHOULD get an award for all the pretending she's doing. The smiling. The chipper "It's Christmas tree dayyyyy!" proclamation as I pad down the stairs in my robe. Mom's trying so hard to keep the family afloat.

Family unraveling? Who cares! 'Tis the season. Holiday traditions wait for no one.

Not even the rain. The weather forecaster said this has been the wettest year in SoCal's history. Still, fires burn across the state. And more locally, too.

Kate's down from L.A. and the whole family's packed into her SUV, headed to Twin H Tree Farm. Baba keeps *tsk*-ing at stuff in the road, thinking he sees a dead animal, but it's just palm carcasses, bark stripped off by the wind.

We hit a palm carcass with a *dundun* and my shoe hits Raf's. "Don't touch me," he says.

I ignore him.

Baba's telling a Mullah Nasruddin joke, his favorite Afghan jokester, and Dad's teary with laughter. The joke's kind of sexist, something about a chastity belt and a key.

But I love it when Dad laughs. It's a deep rumble at the back of his throat, like Baba's.

Kate's scrolling through Spotify, picking out the next holiday tune. It doesn't matter what's playing; Kate just talks over the music. She tells Mom that nursing is the only profession where you've got to wash your hands *before* going to the bathroom. Mom laughs, but it's mechanical.

Raf's phone dings. Again and again. He opens Instagram and I briefly see something about Afghanistan—before he clicks over to another message. It reads: *This your sister?*

It's Brit's TikTok. The one we made together. It already has two million views.

"What now?" he mumbles. Raf peers into the rearview mirror at Dad. Then puts in his AirPods and listens to the TikTok, the entire two minutes. I see him scrolling through the comments as he listens. Someone posts that they've got family missing in Afghanistan, too. As Rafi scrolls, I find just how many Afghans are in our situation.

There's a moment where we both just stare at each other. Neutral. Raf swishes his cheek, but says nothing.

I rest my head on the dewy window and fall asleep.

———

The tree, a white pine with long soft needles, is too big. It scrapes the ceiling and Dad has to get the saw out to chop off three inches. Baba tells him he's doing it wrong, to let him do it, and Dad tells him to take his hands off the saw—that he'll lose a finger. It's an unplanned Christmas tradition. That's because Kate likes the biggest trees, and Mom likes to give Kate what she wants.

Kate leaves as soon as we lug the tree inside, saying she wants to get home before it's too dark. I think it's because she has somewhere else to be. The red storage bins have been pulled out from the attic, and within two hours, the house is a twinkling, choo-chooing, sparkling wonderland.

Baba loves Christmas. Ironic, I know. Before bed, he turns off the overhead lights, sets his prayer rug at the foot of the tree, and prays under its flickering bulbs, casting red—green—white over his face in turn. He might joke around with Dad in the car, but his face falls whenever he looks at his brother's makeshift grave in the yard.

Luckily, Baba's settling into the idea about never driving again. He likes being chauffeured around, like when he lived in Afghanistan.

I go up to my room feeling slightly less despondent. With the decor out and the house smelling of pine, I have to admit, my spirits are raised.

57

IN THE afternoon, there's booming outside my window—bass. Meowgi checks out the noise first. I follow, placing my chin on his furry back. He's too nosy to care; his eyes are wide, staring at the shape that's materialized on the street.

Jalen's truck.

Heavy footsteps jog down the stairs. There's a "You're grounded, where are you going?" from Dad and a "Not leaving," from Raf as the front door slams. I crack the window to hear better.

Jalen opens the passenger door from the inside and Raf gets in.

The window's rolled down. Raf tries to do the cool-guy handshake thingy but Jalen leaves him hanging. They sit for a while, Raf talking. Jalen listening. Soon Jalen turns the volume up and rests his head on the window.

Then for a split second, Jalen looks up at my bedroom window and my heart drops with my body—to the floor. Not until the engine roars to life and the bass booms down the street do I look outside.

Raf's standing on the sidewalk, watching Jalen go.

Head down, Raf walks back inside.

———

On Christmas Eve, Mom's singing as soon as I get downstairs. She's already making Christmas Eve dinner. At the Shahin household, the main Christmas feast takes place on Christmas Eve and leftovers are eaten on the twenty-fifth. We eat all the way through New Year's, too. Mom makes food for a troop and a half.

"Need help?" I ask, hoping the answer is no. Brit's asked me if I'd like to go to the Spectrum for holiday crafts.

"No, honey!" It's only 9:00 a.m. and she's already made two dozen (enormous) cream puffs drizzled with chocolate sauce, a cheesecake, and shirpera fudge for Baba. Mom's hardcore compartmentalizing.

I open the fridge. There they are, Dad's kabob skewers, marinating. He always gets up early on Christmas Eve to make them with Baba. The whole refrigerator smells like lemon, onion, and garlic. Dad's skewers are my favorite.

I tell Mom I'm going out with Brit, and she tells me to be back by five.

Baba sits in his green armchair, hands folded over his lap. Come every Christmas Eve, he doesn't say much.

Christmas Eve, 1979.

The day the Soviets invaded Afghanistan.

———

The outdoor mall has set up crafting tables underneath the gargantuan Christmas tree. Me and Brit might be the only people over twelve who have come out for the event, but that doesn't stop us from enjoying it. I'm painting an upside-down ice cream cone with green frosting and sticking on mini M&M'S, like a tree with ornaments.

Brit's finished her tree cone already and is scrolling through Instagram.

She stops on something. Then mumbles, "What the—? Why are you and Rafi on ESPN Stories?"

"Huh?"

I click through the stories. My stomach swoops hard. It's me with the hijab at my side, standing next to Raf. I thought Dad got Davis to take Raf's player profile down last month? *Why* are these photos cropping up?

Tap. They've posted it, the photo that had been left off Raf's player profile, where he's in the karakul hat and patu, bearing the colors of the Afghan flag. The pre-terror flag. The *real* flag.

But not everyone will see it that way.

In the photo, I stand next to Raf, face stony and back foot poised for an escape. They took the photo when I was turning from the shot.

Weak, I lower myself onto Brit's knee.

"What's wrong?" she asks. "You already put yourself out there in the TikTok. Why does this matter?"

"Yes, but Dad doesn't have TikTok, and I lied to him—to Jalen, too—promising I had nothing to do with the shoot!"

"They've tagged Rafi," she says. "They want to interview him."

My phone vibrates.

HOME. NOW.

It's to me and Raf from Dad.

Next in *whoops* a Facebook post from KTLA. They have the same photo. Picked up the same story. The post—it's not just on ESPN.

The winds are spreading the fire.

58

I PARK the Honda, sidle past the Tesla and up our walkway. Raf's there, sitting on the front step. He rises.

"Either you're with Dad . . . or with me."

I can't ice out Raf anymore after a summons like that. "What?"

"I've been talking to ESPN. They want me to tell Habib and Yasmoon's story. It could help them. What you did on TikTok was a start, but we need to do more. All those comments on TikTok, others with displaced family, too . . . It's not just about Habib and Yasmoon. I've got to use my platform to spread awareness, bring the spotlight back to Afghanistan. So are you with Dad or me, because—"

"You, of course!"

"Good, because we're about to go in there and you *know* Dad has his ways of making you feel like a screwup. Like you're wrong. Are you gonna be strong?"

I nod. "I'm not backing out, Raf."

Rafi stumbles up the front steps. He's been drinking. Just enough to take the edge off.

With a deep breath, I unlock the door. A gust of wind takes up the flag and it whips our faces; we push it out of the way and walk inside the lion's den.

——

Mom and Kate are talking quietly in the kitchen, stirring gravy.

"There's the dynamic duo," says Kate, hands on her hips.

"Kate," Mom says, shushing her. Mom looks like she's aged two years in the hours I've been gone. She's no longer got that spring in her step, her hair's frizzy, and there's a half-empty bottle of wine on the kitchen table. "Come with me, you two. Kate—don't let the potatoes burn."

Dad and Baba are arguing in the stairwell to the den. Seeing us standing in the living room, Dad walks up.

He smacks Raf upside the head with a flat palm, and says: "You told strangers on the internet we are still in contact with relatives?" Then he looks at me. "And Gojeh, you said you had nothing to do with the shoot, and *here you are, in the photo*? What kind of—who—" Dad spins slowly in a circle, hands in his hair. "I didn't think I'd have to explain the severity of the situation to you two. Not again!"

"I'm doing an interview with ESPN." Rafi's eyes are wet with resolve. "To help them."

"Interview? What interview—? I've told you for years—"

"Yeah, well, your way isn't working, Dad." Raf towers over him. "You never *told* us *anything*." Emerging from the kitchen, Kate bites her cheek. "We deserve to know where we come from— who we are! Me, and Mafi, and Kate, too—all we've ever done is guess. When you sulk to the deck, we guess. We're lost. Just like you."

Me, Raf, and Kate exchange dark glances. But no one denies it.

"We didn't tell you to protect you! So that you would not have to worry!" says Dad. "When the Talibs knocked on Habib's door, they asked if he was in contact with the Shahins. One of the Skype calls—they were able to trace it. To California."

I think about the sickly sweet voice, like salty caramel. *With whom do I have the gladness of speaking?*

That's what Baba neglected to tell us the day of Rafi's shoot. That the Taliban had made the connection, were asking about us.

"They traced it here?" echoes Rafi, wiping his mouth.

Dad makes an *I told you so* noise, waving his hand. "Habib lied. Said no. Said they disowned us and our Western lifestyle. The Talibs left, but they marked his house with an *X*. That is when they moved in with another family."

"And the sleek black cars staked out in front of our house . . . ?" I say, brain trying to put two and two together.

"Department of Homeland Security. The cars watch to *protect* us, Gojeh. After you confirmed Baba's name to the man on the phone that day, Baba and I alerted the authorities the next morning, worried the Taliban had found us."

That's why when Baba and Dad came back, they shut all the drapes.

"But they can only do so much," says Dad. "We must protect ourselves."

"You should've told us," I say. Raf nods. Kate is still. "We're old enough. We could've handled it! All of it!"

Drumming footsteps sound from the den stairs, and then—

In a whir of fluttery white hair and tweed, Baba pushes past Rafi and yanks on my elbow, pulling me into the hall with impressive force.

"Baba!"

Rafi, Mom, and Dad rush after us, knocking shoulders in the hallway trying to get to me, but Baba's fast.

My skin's white-hot in his grasp. Dad is behind Rafi, ordering Baba off in Farsi.

"They will come!" says Baba, tossing me forward. I fall onto my hands and knees, onto the Daulatabad rug. Baba stares at me on the floor, eyes wide, then turns and hurtles downstairs.

"Baba!" says Dad, not bothering to help me up. Downstairs, there are *bangs. Clunks. Crashes.* It's as if the den has been taken over by a horde of djinn.

Dad disappears downstairs, Mom after him, hand cupping her mouth.

———

I follow, Kate and Rafi behind me.

The pulwar sword is down. Baba is slashing, hacking, and stabbing everything in sight. His pillows are reduced to feathers; wardrobe knobs sliced off; Grandma's old vase shattered on the floor; the rubab split into thirds.

"Enough, now! Enough!" Dad shouts at Baba, but he won't stop swinging.

"No more!" says Mom, hair unraveled from her braid. "I'm calling the police!"

"No, Mom. Don't!" I say, and I attempt to pry the phone from her hands.

"*Rafi!*" Dad bellows, a hand outstretched in warning—

Rafi ducks just in time. The pulwar sword impales the drywall, inches from Rafi's head.

"What the hell?" screams Rafi, yanking the vibrating sword from the wall. "He's not safe, Dad. He's not safe!"

Baba crumples into a heap, sobbing on the floor.

"Leave us," says Dad. He cradles a whimpering Baba. Strokes his hair. "Leave us."

"Rafi, put it down—put that thing down—" Mom says. Rafi tosses the sword to the floor like it's scalding his hands. It hits the tile with an awful *clang*.

Silence.

Baba points at me, then tilts his chin to peer at Rafi through bloodshot eyes. "They will do worse to her!" he says. "And the way they look at your baba! They think we are like—like *them*! The radical ones . . . terrorists! The ice will come. The *ice*! They will—send your baba back! He will be killed by Talibs, just like his habib! You are no Kush Giant, *no*!"

He burrows his head into Dad's chest, crying from the corner of his mouth: "Baba is hurt. Baba is hurt. Baba is hurt." Dad rocks him, tears streaming down his stubbled face.

"Rafi . . . you see how your baba is tormented?" Dad drones, chest heaving. "Baba's father was killed, Rafi. Because Baba left, moved *here*! To start this life for us. For you!"

Rafi's eyes widen.

He's the last to know.

"And still, you will interview? Exposing your family—here *and* there?"

Raf is quiet.

My ears ring.

"Go. *Both of you,*" Dad whispers.

"No," says Mom. "It's Christmas Eve!"

Rafi holds on to me. His torso vibrates with anguish.

"Leave this house, both of you! I will not look at either of you. You sacrifice your entire family for a bouncy-bally thing, mm? I hope it was worth it, my son."

"No!"

It comes from Mom.

"No, Sarafat. You will not order my children from the house! What's it going to take? Baba running one of them through with a sword?"

Baba wails to match the intensity in Mom's voice.

Mom closes her eyes, her back supported by the wall.

"Get out," Dad breathes. "Now."

"Mom?" I say. Tears pool in my eyes. Rafi's, too.

She turns and skirts past Kate, standing halfway up the stairs.

"How could you?" Kate whispers, looking from me to Raf, then follows Mom.

"That's right"—I raise my voice as Kate retreats—"you're the perfect child, Kate. The favorite. Always so goddamn condescending!"

"OUT!" bellows Dad, so loud the glass icicle decoration in the window vibrates against the pane.

I grab Rafi's hand and escort him up the stairs. This time, we don't jog. There's nothing to be afraid of. No djinn to grab our ankles.

In this house, we are the djinn.

Rafi's got the Ptero car jammed in reverse, belt screeching. I hop in as it's rolling; two seconds later, Mom bolts from the house, waving her arms.

"Please don't go." She paws at Ptero's reversing hood. "Please!"

But Rafi's reversed and jammed the stick into second gear, leaving Mom's figure hunched in the driveway.

The curtains swish at Cole's window. A pair of glittering eyes peer into the cold night.

———

All those years, Dad watching out the window, tea in hand. He was waiting for something bad to happen. But it was never ICE, or other Afghans, or Talibs.

It was us, destroying his American Dream.

59

RAFI WAS cursing and speeding so I told him to pull over, to let me drive.

His eyes are closed when I bring Ptero to a shuddering stop.

Have I gone too far? The houses on this street are shrouded in fog. I reverse.

Rafi opens his eyes. He sounds groggy. "Are we on Jalen's street? It looks different."

"Yeah," I say, hitting the brakes in front of Jalen's ranch, "the tree's gone." The Witch Tree. The one battered by the baseball bat. Only a stump remains.

Why did I drive here of all places? Raf's looking at me, probably wondering the same thing.

"Let's go," I say, putting in the clutch.

"Too late." Rafi scruffs up his hair. "He's coming." Old Ptero's rattly idling announced our arrival for us.

Rafi's mood's changed. He's nervous.

Raf uses the oh-shit handle for support as he pulls himself from the car.

I see Jalen's phone before the hand it's attached to, bobbing in the mist. Jalen's face puckers when he sees it's really us.

An excited voice, charged with youth, says, "Bro! How did you even know I wanted this? How?" The voice sounds familiar somehow.

Then I realize: Jalen's on FaceTime with his brother, Azi. "Everything okay over there?" his Mom asks over Azi's squealing.

"Call you right back, okay?"

"Love you, baby."

"Love you, too."

The words are like a punch to my heart. Across the street, a family in pajamas watches TV in front of an electric fireplace.

Jalen's Mom *whoops* off FaceTime, and Jalen goes, "What you want, Shahin?"

Raf stands there for a moment, choosing his words. They cartwheel out. "I messed up, JT. Our friendship, your trust, and I miss you, man—I just. Like I told you in the car the other day. You can date my sister, you can—do whatever you want. And I'll cheer you on, bro, because that's all you've ever done for me, and I've messed up . . ."

Even though my teeth chatter and my knees wobble, I slink out of the car. Jalen frowns at me, then says to Raf: "You heard me wrong, *bro*." He barely opens his mouth to speak. "What do you *want*? 'Cause you'd only be here if you wanted something. You don't care about me."

"That's not true."

"Answer the question," says Jalen.

Raf shifts his weight. Holds on to Ptero for support. "Dad's kicked us out."

Jalen exhales. "Saw you on ESPN, Facebook, Instagram. Knew he'd lose it." Then he looks at me. "You told me you knew nothin' 'bout Raf's shoot, then I see you in the *photo* with him? On top of everything else, you a liar, too?"

My heart drops.

"I'm sorry," I say, voice shaking, "for lying. And for bothering you and your dad on Christmas Eve."

"Pops is in Dallas." My eyes meet Jalen's for a brief second. *Dallas?* Isn't that where the SGB treatment center is? "But he'll be back tomorrow," Jalen adds.

Jalen turns on his heel, toward the ranch. He's in line with the tree stump when Raf calls: "JT—!"

He looks up. Shrugs, like *what?*

"That's how it is?" says Raf, voice breaking.

Jalen shakes his head. "You stepped over me, man." He clicks his tongue and strides into the mist.

60

KICKED OUT.

Alone on the highway.

Homeless, on Christmas Eve.

With every passing headlight that reveals us in a white glow through the windshield, I think about Habib and Yasmoon, in the back of some smuggler's truck on the Kabul—Kandahar Highway . . . How did they feel? Where are they now?

Or is it like Baba said . . . There is no time for fear. *If you're going through hell, keep going . . .*

Float on.

I take the Beach Boulevard exit, some twenty miles from the house. We park next to a band of caravans at Huntington Beach. We won't be out of place here; lots of people sleep oceanfront in their cars. Months, sometimes. The thought makes me nauseated.

I already miss Meowgi. I close my eyes and see Mom scrambling for the hood of the car.

I open the windows. A salty breeze drives the tension from the car. The ocean's good at doing that. Rafi exhales.

"The interview's the right thing to do," I murmur. I can't bring myself to look at Raf. I'm *still* mad at my brother. And myself.

"Then why's it feel like the wrong thing?"

"When's the interview?" I ask.

Raf looks at me. "I dunno if I can do it anymore."

"What?"

"I don't know, Mafia. Baba's dad was killed after he helped those refugees."

"Baba did the right thing!" I wave a hand over the dash, gesturing at the ocean. "We're effectively homeless because of what we did, together—and now you *don't know*?"

Raf's buzz is wearing off.

Mom calls.

My phone.

Raf's.

My phone, Raf's. One phone glows, then the next, like lights on a Christmas tree.

Raf types in his passcode. It's 2-4-2-6. *BIAN* spelled out in code.

He sighs and yanks the lever on his seat. Reclining, he shuts his eyes. When he speaks, his voice is dead. "When you were three, we were at the YMCA pool, and you said, *I can swim, Rafi!* and jumped into the deep end. You'd only had one lesson. You didn't know how to swim, by the way. Mom was setting our towels down, so I jumped in after you. Pulled you out. You thought it was hilarious."

I stifle a smile. "I don't remember . . ."

"Well, I do." Raf sighs. "You were drowning, and you thought it was funny. I was so angry with you after that day.

Your obliviousness, your disregard for danger. But I guess it took too long for me to realize that"—he expels air from his cheeks—"when I told you we'd have our own lives, that I'd be heading to IU, that we're only in the house for childhood and that's it . . . that you have your own life, too. I just wanted it to stop." He looks at me. "*Worrying* about you all the time."

"Oh."

"And you got older, and you and Annalie were always talking about boys . . . I'm sorry about the CJ rumor, Mafi. I believe you when you say you didn't do anything with those guys."

"You don't get it," I murmur.

Raf frowns.

"Whether or not I am CJ shouldn't matter. You should respect my decisions. Even if they're mistakes, they're mine to make. I already have a dad"—I feel a pang in my heart—"but I've only got one brother."

Rafi laces his fingers with mine. He snivels and I shake his hand.

"I did apologize to Jalen," he says. "Set things straight . . . that you said he didn't hurt you."

"Took you long enough."

"I deserve that," he says. "Basketball has been my whole world for so long that I forgot there were other planets out there, too." And I know he's thinking about Habib and Yasmoon.

Me and Raf have a talent for holding things in. Especially when it comes to Habib and Yasmoon.

"We've got to do right by them now," I say.

No explanation needed. Raf knows who I'm talking about.

"How do you know the interview won't make things worse?"

"I don't," I say. "But I don't think sitting around and waiting is the right thing to do, either."

———

On Christmas morning, our phones are flooded with missed calls.

From Mom, asking if we're safe. From Kate. Nothing from Dad.

From Brit, who's recorded a video for me while hiking with her aunt in Sedona. She asks if I'm okay, if I need anything. I say we're fine. I neglect to tell her we're sleeping in our car.

I text Mom two words: We're fine.

The last thing I need is Mom contacting the police . . . she tells us to use her card, but Raf and me agree that's a no-go. She'll look at her statement and find us.

To my surprise, there's a text from Jalen, too.

> Where u guys end up?

Has Mom called him and asked him to find out? I leave it unanswered, for now. It feels good, anyhow, to see his name pop up on my screen again.

"Holy sh—" Rafi's listening to his voicemails. His eyes bug out of his head. "It's Enes."

"What?"

"Enes Freedom. *Enes!*" He slaps my arm. Just then, his phone lights up with a Boston area code. I flap my hands, ordering Raf to put it on speaker.

"Hey, Rafi, Enes Freedom here," Enes's deep, cheery voice resounds from the speaker.

"For real? I'm—wow. I idolize you, man."

"Thank you, thank you. Happy holidays, huh? Look, Rafi—I've seen your great-aunt and -uncle's story on the news. I got your number from ESPN. Hope you don't mind."

"No, Enes Freedom—not at all." Rafi sounds like a giddy schoolgirl.

"So ESPN said you reached out for an interview but now you're unsure?"

Raf scratches his cheek. He must've written to ESPN while I slept.

"Eh, I"—Rafi's voice deflates—"can't. My parents hate me. My dad told IU I'm forfeiting my scholarship and kicked me and my little sister out of the house."

"*What?* Where are you? Do you have somewhere to stay?"

"Erm. We're . . . sleeping in our car for now . . . in Huntington Beach. But we're okay, really . . . some guy in a caravan gave us some doughnuts this morning."

"No good. Let's see what I can do." I hear typing in the background. "Ehm, look, your dad," Enes continues, "he's scared. It must be difficult—a son in the spotlight. In Turkey, they imprisoned my dad, an innocent man, for seven years because I publicly condemned Erdoğan—a dictator. I, too, am considered a dangerous man to many. But without the pressure my fans exerted on Erdoğan, Dad would still be in prison. When people suffer, we cannot sit in silence."

"Yeah, I mean—you're brave, man," says Rafi. "I've followed your story from the beginning. But I'm worried about my relatives. They haven't called in weeks and I don't wanna make things worse."

"You don't think I was worried about what Erdoğan might do to my dad when I spoke out? Never be scared to stand for what's right. In that photo I saw, you're wearing the flag—a beacon of hope for Afghans left behind. Your people need you. And your ball career—you'll play. Just know it'll probably get worse before it gets better. Save my number. Watch for my text—I've booked you a spot at Paséa Hotel nearby. No more doughnuts; room service is on me. If you need someone to talk to, reach out. Happy holidays."

61

"**I KNOW** what you're gonna love," Rafi says as soon we open the hotel door at Paséa later that afternoon.

Is it the view? We're on the eighth floor, and the oceanfront view is unreal. But Raf's looking at the beds. There are at least eight pillows on each.

I sprint over to my very own king and fwump face-first onto the fluffy comforter. There's a latency period where my face sinks farther into the fluff.

"Ah, a toothbrush, thank god," Rafi says from the bathroom. The water splashes. It's then that I feel my fatigue. The aching in my limbs. In my heart.

I'm so tired I could fall asleep right here.

But there's work to do. "Where's the list of questions?" I shout.

"My email," says Raf. "But let's order some food first."

"Are you sure Enes won't mind?"

"He texted that he'll be upset if we don't eat."

Rafi's interview is at two o'clock tomorrow. We eat, then spend the rest of the day at the outdoor pool. I'm jealous 'cause Raf can take off his shirt and use the basketball shorts he's wearing as swim trunks. I roll up my sweats and sit on the edge of the pool, kicking my feet.

We watch hotel guests come and go over the next few hours. Families on vacation. Couples. Me and Raf don't say much to each other. There's too much to think about.

We sit in companionable silence until the sun sets, red-purple in the sky.

One day, when this is all over, I'm sending Enes a long-ass thank-you card.

———

The next day, we pull into the studio and park. I follow Raf's gaze; the building's so tall the antennae on top disappear into the cloudy sky.

"Game face," I tell Rafi.

As we walk up, the automatic doors shoot open. Once I went with Cole to his dad's office. This place smells like that. Official, like books and ink.

After we go through security, we walk into the elevator.

"Thirtieth floor," says Rafi, pressing the button.

We're greeted by men in suits, asking us if we need anything, if they can get us water, coffee, tea.

I say, "All of that," and then ask if they've got any Oreos.

They eye us, Raf, reeking of chlorine in his SMN basketball shorts, his shirt damp with pit stains, and me in my purple motocross jersey. We're showered, at least, but all we've got is the clothes on our backs. That's when my stomach *really* growls. We only ordered room service once. It didn't feel right to rack up Enes's tab.

We're led into some conference room, where they set a char-
cuterie board in front of us, and yes, ten packs of Oreos from the
vending machine. We inhale the food, then serve as each other's
mirror, directing in which teeth cookie crumbs are lodged.

My phone buzzes. Jalen again.

> At least tell me you're safe.

>> We're fine. We're staying at a hotel in HB.

> Can I come thru later? So we can talk?

Rafi growls. He's attempting to wrangle his hair into a bun
but it's not smooth on top.

"Let me do that." I stand behind him, finger-comb his hair.
"There. You're not half-bad-looking now."

I place my hand on his shoulder. He reaches up and rests
his on mine.

———

Within minutes, Rafi's sitting on a swivel chair at the anchor
desk.

He waves me over, but a producer stops him.

"Sorry, it's just you we're interviewing. We're glad to have
your sister—but the questions are for you."

"No," says Rafi. "Me and my sis—we're in this together."

The producer shrugs, then speaks into the mic that there's
been a change of plans.

"Game time?" says Rafi.

"Game time," I assure him.

I take a seat next to my brother.

My eyes adjust to the blinding studio lights.

Our interviewer joins the table. "Hey, kids," she says. Her face looks doll-like, like wax. "Ready?" she says, flashing white, bionic teeth.

Raf's leg bounces. Like me, being called *kid* hits a nerve. Invalidating, somehow. I steady Raf's knee with my hand and in my periphery, he nods, like *thanks*.

The cameraman counts down from ten. Points, showing we're live. There's a lag in my brain; the interviewer's opening comments jumble together.

Focus. I blink. Blink again.

"So, Rafi, you wore the Afghan flag. As an Afghan American, what does the flag represent for you and your family?"

Rafi shifts in his chair, uncomfortable. Takes a drink of water. We had received the list of questions beforehand, but this wasn't on it.

"Well, if you take each part of the flag," I cut in, pulling a page from Mr. A's book (*always break down the question!*), "you've, uh, got black, red, and green." Rafi nods and takes another big swig of water, and even though I'm talking, a bead of empathetic sweat runs down my spine seeing Raf struggle.

"Black symbolizes Afghanistan's dark past—which is now its dark present, actually. The green represents both, um, Islam and prosperity. Red, the blood spilled by those who fought for the country's independence . . . something which the Afghan people have lost. Again. The national flag was—*is*—a symbol for progress. But more importantly . . . for hope."

I smile in disbelief, surprised how much I know about a land I've never visited. My sixteen years with Baba . . . I'd retained so much.

I feel it now. Like maybe I've earned my spot in this chair.

"And your aunt and uncle . . . why did—you two—want to share their story?"

"I didn't," Raf says, answering. "I told someone at IU in confidence I had relatives in Afghanistan and the information was posted to my player profile, and . . ." Raf chooses his words carefully. He knows by telling the truth, IU will receive bad press, and he'll officially say goodbye to his scholarship. Under the table, I place my foot next to his to encourage him, let him know I'm here. "I feel my recruitment was not for my talent, but for IU to use my image as this poor refugee kid—some sob story that wasn't true."

The interview continues for another fifteen minutes.

My heart swells with pride. With love. For my brother. For our purpose. For myself.

———

I don't get mad when I see them, *It* and Raf, sitting by the pool late that evening from the hotel window. For one, they're sitting three feet apart. Second, *It* is crying. Third, Enes has texted to please order room service, and I'm finally full.

There's a knock at the door. I freeze. Did Mom find us?

I look through the peephole. *DEFY* is in my line of vision. Peepholes aren't eye level with giants.

I open the door.

"Ma," he says.

"Hey." Then, "Merry Christmas."

"You too."

"Come in."

Everything feels too formal. Except for the fact I'm in a bathrobe.

"Got a view and everything," says Jalen, crossing to the window. "Oh."

He's spotted Bian and Rafi.

"Yeah, she's here."

He sits on the bed. Holds his breath with bubbled cheeks, like he does at graveyards.

"What're you doing?"

He exhales. Shrugs. "You the Ghost."

"What?"

He shows me his phone. A TikTok reveals all my letters splayed out over a periwinkle bedspread. Then there's Bian's recorded voice, saying she's found out who the Ghost is. Me.

"She stole my jewelry box . . ." I mumble. After I ran into her in the hall, I *knew* she'd been snooping in my room. Now I know why she's outside crying. Is Raf finally standing up for me?

"People are legit scared of you," says Jalen.

"And you?"

"Nah, only scared of stuff I can't explain, remember?" He gives a quarter grin. "There also a rumor going around that you keyed Wiggs's car?"

"Yeah . . ." I say, watching the TikTok again. "That one's true."

Jalen laughs and sits on the bed next to me. "Okay, Ma. Maybe I'm a lil' scared."

I look at him. "I'm sorry I lied when you asked me if I knew about Rafi's shoot at Black Star."

"Well." He sighs. "That wasn't the greatest. But nothin's bringing me down today." He grins faintly. "UCLA passed, but . . . USC called."

"USC?"

"Today, actually. They . . . *expressed formal interest.*"

I fling my arms around him, but he doesn't return the hug. When I pull back, we stare in opposite directions. *Too soon.*

"Listen . . . thanks for settin' everything straight at school. I was mad on Christmas Eve . . . not just at you . . . at everything."

"Is—is your dad back from Dallas? He must be so happy about USC . . ."

He plays with his bullet necklace. "Yup. The doc in Texas got him in after a cancellation. I convinced him to go . . . but Pops backed out when he got there. He say he'll stick to Throttle Therapy."

"Oh. I'm sorry."

Jalen shrugs. He doesn't ask about my dad, and I'm glad. It hurts too much. "But I did ask Pops what he wants for his future, and after a while, he said *to get better. To become a sonographer.* And I think people become what they expect themselves to become. Eventually."

I smile encouragingly, and he swishes his cheek. "Ma, there something else I gotta say. I haven't been completely up front with you. Me and Raf . . . you know our relationship been strained. If I'm true . . . like true to my heart . . . I actually hated him for a while. About a year now. Real nasty stuff up in my head."

I exhale. "Oh."

"Thing is, Big Time Recruit always got what he wanted. Dated Bian when he knew I liked her. Then he got that scholarship, photo shoot, tons of playing time while I got the bench, and a part of me wished he'd trip. Fall. *For once.* Damn . . ."

I hug my knees. My stomach starts to churn.

"So when I asked you to pierce my nose . . . I knew Josefina would get wise. And Raf would find out it was you, too. Told him I was into the girl who pierced me—some made-up SV Prep girl—to get him all riled up.

"Then you got kicked out . . . Raf lost his scholarship. Lost his girl. You got suspended . . . and I've never seen the dude with so many stress pimples. You'd think I'd be . . . I dunno. Happy? But nah. So I guess . . . I'm sorry, Ma. But tell you what, you're not the girl I usually pick, and—"

There's a faint *beep* and the next moment, Raf walks into the room, *It* waiting in the hall. Jalen rises. Bian sees him and her eyes widen.

"Jalen?" says Raf. "What're you—?"

"Visiting my friend Ma, that okay with you?"

"Of—of course it is, I just—"

Jalen says bye, then slides past Raf with an "Excuse me."

"Mafi," says Raf, when the door closes.

"Don't say a word—"

"No, no, I'm cool with that—whatever it is," says Rafi. It's then that I hear the urgency in his voice. "Mom called. We're going to the hospital."

62

HOSPITALS ARE labyrinths and I hate them. I hate the way they smell, like urine and bleach. I hate the phony stock photos they have on the walls. People holding fruit and stethoscopes. The sticky magazines, too.

When we get to the right floor, we find Kate, eyes uncharacteristically puffy. As much as we are at odds, my heart softens at the sight of my sister till she says, "Well?" in that demeaning tone.

The perfect sister. The perfect daughter.

But there's still another part of me that wants to reach out. To hug her. To sniff the guava shampoo in her hair.

She stops, pointing inside a room.

Baba.

He's sitting up in bed staring at his clasped hands. Mom and Dad sit on chairs in the corner, dark circles under their eyes. When they spot us, they rise.

Dad brushes by without a word, but Mom, she hugs me and Raf tight. Kate's upper lip trembles.

"Are you all right?" Mom says, voice shaking. "I was so worried, I've barely slept, and I was going to call the police, but—"

"What happened?" says Raf, cutting her off. Not to be rude. His voice breaks, and I can tell he's short with her so he can keep his composure.

"Baba was hit by a bicyclist," Mom says. Her voice is like the wind. "He's okay, a bit battered, but you know."

We all four look at him. With Baba's dementia, is this how it's going to be? Doctors and hospitals and accidents? I try to stay present.

I ask, "How did this happen?"

"Baba said he was trying to get to the ATM—to get money to fly to Afghanistan. To find Habib," says Mom. "Left in the middle of the night with his suitcase and was hit on the corner. It was a terrible sight . . . his suitcase fell open, and there were clothes everywhere in the street . . . I had to pick them up." She puts her hands on her hips and looks up at the ceiling; she's holding back tears.

Mom finds our eyes.

"I'm so happy you're here now. Just—just wait here, please? Don't go. Don't."

Mom walks off, in the direction Dad went. Kate reaches up and feels Rafi's hair.

"Your hair's gelled," she says. "It's never gelled."

I give Raf a dark look, like *don't tell her.*

"I did the interview for ESPN today," he says.

"Did you?" Surprisingly, the words aren't laced with judgment. "I saw what Enes posted, the petition for Habib and Yasmoon's safe passage. I signed it. *Don't tell Dad.* When will the interview run?"

Rafi nods. "I don't know. Next week sometime? Kate . . . has there been any word?"

Kate looks down the hall, to where Dad and Mom disappeared. "No." She lowers her voice. "Dad leaves the front door unlocked, you know."

"Don't care," says Raf.

Unlocked. Unlocked is big for Dad, the Home Security King. He must really want us to come home.

When we walk into Baba's room, he barely inclines his head to look at us.

I hate to see Baba like this, so fragile.

Kate grabs my arm. "Give Baba and Rafi space," she says, extracting me from the room.

———

In the hallway, I sit cross-legged on the waxy floor and pick at a hangnail. When it doesn't tear off, I gnaw it.

"Don't do that."

I rip it off with my teeth and suck the blood. It tastes like pennies. Kate taps her foot. "Where've you been staying?"

"Under the Santa Ana bridge."

"*Not funny.* You caused me distress, you know," she says. "It was crap what you said."

"What?" I say, sticking a finger in my ear. *Did my sister just curse?* A weak curse—but still?

"What you said at home. That I'm this . . . *perfect* person." She sighs. "It's not so easy for me, you know."

I'm silent. This is a rarity, a Yeti sighting.

"It was always you and Raf growing up. You two on your backyard treasure hunts. Watching *Friends* reruns together. Video games. Bike rides with Jalen." My heart pangs. "Even

the slapping fights in the back of the car. You were always reaching over me to get to each other. I was just—in the way."

Now she's biting a perfectly manicured nail. Venom green. Not a usual Kate color.

"It's not easy being the oldest. Mom and Dad, they had such high expectations for me, and I feel like I paved the way for you two . . . I know how that might sound now, considering." She looks at me. "Mom told me about the advice I gave you about Girlfriend Material or whatever."

"Oh."

"Want to know a secret?"

She bites her venom-green nail. I'm nervous.

Kate leans in and whispers a number into my ear. Then says: "The number of people with whom I've had relations."

"WHAT?"

"It's not my fault I was made randy. I just . . . didn't want to . . . pave the way for you like *that*. And mind you, only *two* of my conquests were at SMN, okay? See here, little cherub. The idea that there's such thing as Hook-Up Material or Girlfriend Material, it's as much a fallacy"—she chuckles in recollection—"as those fairies we used to write letters to as kids."

And I'd like to believe her, but . . . "But you say all that—and still don't have a boyfriend."

"I don't?" She nods, like *hmph, how interesting.*

"Well, for duck's cake!" I say, borrowing one of her half curses. "I should really hate you right now."

"But you don't." I shake my head. Then Kate says three words I've never heard: "Proud of you." We sit there in silence,

staring. "Before Gina died—remember her?" she says after a while.

"Of course I do." The popular girl in Kate's year who died from an overdose.

"We used to smoke together. Party together. Did you know that?"

"Of course I didn't."

"It scared me when she died. That . . . it could've been me, you know."

There's a squeaking noise, a nurse's shoes, as she walks past.

"Everyone's dealing with something, Katey Kat." I wriggle; my butt's asleep.

"Ughhh," Kate says. *"Stop growing up."*

Metal bites my collarbone. It had become a part of me, Baba's evil eye necklace. I'd worn it all along, never taking it off to shower. I pull it over my neck.

I don't need its protection anymore. Who cares what people think. If people don't like me. If people wish me ill.

I'll keep it, though. For Baba.

"Grandma wore that, didn't she?" murmurs Kate.

My big sister's shampoo doesn't smell like guava anymore. The scent's unfamiliar, but I guess it's nice.

———

"Mafi." Rafi's poked his head around the door. "Baba's asking for you."

He looks just as shocked as I am that I'm mid-cuddle with my big sister.

I walk into the room, leaving Rafi and Kate in the hall.

Baba's mouth flickers into a smile. His left eyebrow is sutured with a butterfly bandage and he's got bruises up his arms.

"Mafi," he says, voice gravelly. Not *Katie*. Not *Gojeh*.

Mafi.

He motions for my hand. I give it to him and he grips it tightly.

"Where is my habib?" he says, squinting about the room like his brother's hiding in the corner. "He said we would meet again. That he would come."

"He'll be here." I squeeze his hand. "Soon. I promise." It's a lie, I know it's a lie, but it's like Enes said: Someone needs to keep hope alive.

"Baba's Mafi . . ." He closes his eyes. There's popping coming from the base of his throat as he does a sleepy sort of hum. It sounds like Meowgi when his purring starts to fade.

"Bachem," he murmurs. *My child.* I scoot toward him. Baba opens his eyes, milky and red. "Your baba is sorry, that he hurt his Mafi."

The last time I saw Baba, he'd pushed me down.

"It's okay, Baba. I'm fine." I'm not. Not yet. But I will be.

"Find Habib. Mm? Baba feels like a blind shahin, flying through mist. A blind falcon. Baba cannot see . . . but you can. You and your brother. You will navigate the storm."

His grip eases, and he drifts into sleep.

A tear escapes the corner of my eye and falls onto his hand. I kiss it off.

63

MOM BREAKS down in the parking lot, pleading for us to come home. Dad stands there, arms folded across his chest, lower lip puffed out, silent.

Raf says he wants Dad to apologize for throwing us out, and she says he will, in his own way. In his own time.

Me and Raf share a look. We both know we can't stay at the hotel any longer.

"Fine," we agree. And we trail the Tesla home without a word.

———

It's 5:00 a.m. by the time the American flag greets us. All the Christmas decorations are still up. The tree twinkles, a handful of unopened presents underneath. Ours. It looks like Meowgi's gotten to a few; they're ripped at the corners.

The house smells the same. But somehow everything feels different, like we've been gone a long time, to war and back. No matter the outcome with Habib and Yasmoon, some things won't go back to how they were. That much, I know.

Meowgi, tail up, trills like *hmm?* and saunters into my room, immediately finding my lap. He nips me on the hand to make it clear he's annoyed I left, but soon he's purring and falls asleep on my stomach.

When I wake, he's gone.

———

Two days later, and I still haven't heard Dad speak.

Baba wonders if what Habib and Yasmoon told the Talibs was true: If they have renounced us. If we are dead to them.

I've never seen two people trying to avoid each other more than Raf and Dad. Raf was making a turkey sandwich yesterday and when Dad saw him, he turned around and waited, staring at the wall in the living room, till Raf was upstairs before getting his coffee.

Nightmares roar in like a train. I wake with my shirt drenched. I dream Habib was shot. Or his hand, cut off. Or that Yasmoon was taken. Or worst of all, that they've become names on the endless list of displaced Afghans, never heard from again.

On one particularly bad night, I walk into Raf's room, blanket dragging on the floor, to find he's awake. He's peering out the blinds at the sleek black car parked by the azaleas. The car assigned to us for our protection. But protection or not, it's a reminder that we're not safe here in the suburbs. That we're different from the Dawicki family, or neighbor Cam and his floofy dogs.

Helping us or hurting us—who can really be sure? Maybe I do understand Dad's paranoia a bit more. Officer Gregory's file wrongfully linked our family to terrorism. How deep, how far, does that file go?

Swaddled in a blanket, I sleep on my big brother's floor.

The interview still hasn't dropped. The world's taking a breath. At least, that's what it feels like in the Shahin house. We thought about telling Mom and Dad, but Raf was adamant we wait. Let them watch.

Mom tries to talk to me, to Raf, and I see her mouth moving, but I can't focus on the sounds. What I do hear is: *Just give your dad time. It will all be back to normal soon. Rafi, eat something, you look thin.* She's right. With no basketball and all the stress, Raf's a beanpole with pimples.

Mom hasn't left Dad, not yet. Maybe it would be good for them. Whether vacuuming in her Geometric Daulatabad Dimension of Denial or not, she continues to Just Pretend.

My phone buzzes.

> U OK?

I stare at Jalen's text. I don't want to lie to him ever again.

> Not yet.

——

On the morning of New Year's Eve, the doorbell rings.

We're eating banana yogurt pancakes, fresh off the griddle. In Mom's Just Pretend reality, food is the glue that holds this family together.

So much for *together*; we all eat in different parts of the house. Raf, upstairs. Baba, in his pea-green rocker. Me, at the kitchen bar. Dad, on the deck. And Mom, she took one bite of pancake, said it tasted like onions, and tossed it into the trash. Mom cuts bananas on the wooden board she also uses for onions and the thing never gets clean.

"Who's there?" shouts Baba from his armchair.

"I'll get it," says Mom. She looks down at her batter-stained nightgown, then presses on, like *oh well.*

Through the window, there's an old, insect-spattered moped parked in front of our house.

The door opens. I hear a voice. A man's. He introduces himself as Nasim and asks if he can come in. He sounds like Baba, speaking from the diaphragm.

Baba notices. He rises from the chair and strides over.

"Hazara?" says Baba, and the man says yes.

He shoots rapid Hazaragi at the man and he responds, just as fast.

"But let's talk English," says Nasim, with a look at Mom. The door shuts behind him as he compliments the house.

He is tall, thin, and beams when he passes me. I've never seen a smile so big. With a head bob, he greets me with, "Hello, hello."

The back door opens and closes. Dad emerges.

"They're not great but I've made pancakes, Nasim," says Mom. "Or a coffee?"

"No, thank you."

"Are you sure?"

"Yes, I am fine."

"Very sure?"

"Yes."

Mom knows it's customary in Afghan culture to politely decline any offering a number of times before accepting.

"Who are you?" says Dad, giving Nasim a sideways look.

"My name is Nasim Haidari. I apologize for crashing your New Year's Eve . . . I would have called but your number isn't listed. Erm . . . Does Rafi Shahin live here?"

"No," says Dad.

"Yes," says Rafi, halfway down the stairs. He leans on the railing. "I'm Rafi Shahin."

"Yes! I recognized you from your picture." He casts a nervous look at Dad, then looks at me and goes, "And you, from TikTok. My daughter, she showed me the video a few days ago. I don't use this video thing, but she loves it. Spends way too much time, and . . . well. The girl's account—Bethany, I think?"

"*Brit,*" I say.

"Yes, I watched you speak about your missing relatives, Habib and Yasmoon." Dad's eyebrows knit together. He's *today old* when he finally finds out about the TikTok. "You pleaded for answers, for news, and—my daughter commented on the post, but it must've gotten lost. I wanted to come tell you in person. I know them."

Air rushes from Baba's mouth.

"Or—I know *of* them. Habib and Yasmoon stayed with my sister and her husband in Kabul before they left."

"That was your family?" says Baba.

"Yes, my sister worked for Kabul University. She helped students to escape until it was too late for her."

Baba's face hardens. "Sorry." He paces. "When—when did my brother leave?"

"December fifth."

Rafi sits on the stair. I do the math in my head. They left the day before Raf's initial player profile dropped. Raf looks up. Our eyes meet. *They could be alive.*

"Has—has your sister heard from my habib?" says Baba, visibly shaking. "Have they been in contact?"

"Once, in Kandahar."

"Kandahar! Oh!" shouts Baba, clapping his hands. "When?"

"Four days later, on December ninth."

They were supposed to call on December seventh, Baba's birthday.

Baba's face drops. "So they were delayed . . . but it is only a five-hour drive from Kandahar to Quetta, and that was three weeks ago. By now, they should've called Baba."

"I'm sure they will, Inshallah, once they settle in." The way Nasim says it, he means it. Evidence of smile lines are etched into his now-frowning face. "As you know, the refugee camp in Quetta, it is chaos. Thousands of displaced families. Limited resources. But we must have hope."

Baba moans. He toddles down to the den, likely to find his prayer rug.

"Thank you," says Dad, like *leave now*.

Nasim gets up. "I will pray for good news in the New Year."

"Please," says Mom, two steps ahead of him, "take some cookies. Something. You drove all this way, from—?"

"Santa Barbara."

That's *at least* a three-hour drive to Rancho Santa Margarita, probably more on a moped. Is driving a moped on the highway legal?

"Then you must eat something. Please take them."

"No, thank you."

"I insist."

"I couldn't."

She grabs the tin. "Please, take them."

He grins. "Okay, thank you. I will enjoy them on the way home. If there are any left, I might share one or two with my children." He smiles at me, so big I'm sure his cheeks complain. I grin back.

"Thank you," says Rafi, and moves to shake the man's hand.

Dad is tsk-ing. Raf ignores him.

"No, thank *you*," says Nasim. "My nephew Ali saw your photo with the flag . . . He is your age. Maybe fifteen. He lives in Kabul. He printed the photo, taped it to his wall. He hopes one day to play basketball in America, just like you."

Rafi pulls Nasim into a hug.

Blindsided, Nasim's arms hang loosely at his side. Then he gives a humble laugh and reaches up to hug Raf, real tight.

From the corner, Dad watches.

64

THE INTERVIEW runs later that afternoon.

The sound of Rafi's voice, blaring from the TV, draws us from our rooms. Kate's come back down from UCLA and stands in front of the TV, eating a leftover pancake with her hands like a taco.

Baba's watching from his pea-green rocker, which squeaks every time he rocks. Dad's on the couch. Mom, too.

When we descend the stairs, Kate gives me and Raf a nod.

I briefly place my hand on Rafi's shoulder before we reach the bottom step. We both take a seat on the couch, between Mom and Dad.

Baba's drifted off already. Snoring. His face is still bruised, but he's got color in his cheeks.

We watch on television what I've already experienced in person. The stress signals are the same. My armpits feel damp.

When under those studio lights, I remember feeling nervous talking about the Afghan flag's symbolism. Watching now, I guess I look pretty even. Raf, sipping his water on-screen, looks nervous. But as he answers the next few questions and gets going, loosens up.

When we get to the part where Raf says IU recruited him only to exploit his Afghan heritage, Dad perks up.

"How so?" the interviewer asks.

"I was told having me front and center on the athletics page would attract wealthy international students to the school. I did the research, and last year, public universities in the U.S. brought in more than nine billion in tuition from international students. I didn't want future students to think after seeing my face posted up on the site that the school cares about diversity. Because they don't. Not really."

Dad's leaning forward, lips pursed. Mom's tearing up. Baba's snores ring through the living room.

"So how do you believe schools should foster an inclusive and diverse environment for their students?"

"Practice it," says Raf. He unjumbles his thoughts. "Uh. Like, schools, people—the world—need to not just perform it, but practice it. This whole *let's put a brown face on the front page of our athletics website* sh—stuff—is just . . . a performance. The thing is, I don't wanna be known as that *Afghan* ball player. Just a ball player."

I nod along.

At this, the reporter simpers. "And Mafi, do you have a message for the world—regarding your great-uncle and -aunt, and all the Afghans left behind?"

Me and Raf share a look.

"My great-aunt and -uncle are still missing," I say. "While my baba fled Afghanistan in search of safety and the American dream, the nightmare continues for the people in Afghanistan. Especially its minorities, like the Hazaras. We don't see their plight on the news anymore but we can't abandon them. And if anyone knows anything about the whereabouts of my relatives, please contact us. We need to support the Afghan people in their long struggle against the Taliban."

Dad exhales like a bus releasing compressed air at a stop.

"So what's next for you, Rafi? Still plan on playing for IU in the fall?"

I watch Dad's face. I know what's coming. I can't even hide my smile on television; my poker face needs some serious practice.

"No," Rafi says.

Dad purses his lips, likely waiting for Raf to say his dad won't allow it, to embarrass him on national television. "I've been offered to play at UC-Irvine and I'm gonna take it. Closer to home."

Dad's lips part. He looks down at his hands, then up at the TV again.

As the reporter gives his closing remarks and thanks us for his time, Dad pats Rafi's leg. Once. Then mine.

Mom looks at us, like *it's Dad's way*.

Then he disappears out the back door onto the sunlit deck. He taps the wind chimes. Rests his hands on his hips. His sanctuary.

———

I wake at eleven, twelve, and three a.m. Finally, I realize what feels off.

Just *where* does Mr. Meowgi sleep at night?

Rolling over, I hug my pillows, all of them. But it's not the same.

65

DUSK FALLS on New Year's Eve, which means the beginning of a *boom pop crack hisssss* type of night. Kids chase each other down the street with sparklers, hooting. The Witch Tree's stump is gone. A baby willow sits in its place.

I dredge up the nerve and then rap on Jalen's front door.

I've got something for him.

"Uh—hey, Ma."

My ears ring, filling with blood. "I like the hair." He's gone green. "And is that a Steph Curry jersey?"

"Gift from Tommy," he says.

"Were you—on your way out?"

It's New Year's Eve. *Most people* have somewhere to be.

"Fireworks at Tommy's. But it's early. It can wait." From the kitchen table, Mr. Thomas waves. I wave back. "Wanna get out of here for a bit?"

"Yeah. Don't have long, though. I promised Mom and my sister I'd be back for fireworks."

"You walk here?"

"Mhm. Ptero died. Dad's junking it."

We take the Raptor. We don't talk for a while, just listen to Jalen's new favorite rap song. The rap artist, she really does spit fire.

Jalen turns into SMN's lot.

It's bizarre to see no cars parked out front. An overcast sky shadows the gargantuan manor in shades of gray, and a plastic bag drags across the lot.

It feels like so long ago, now, when Mom and me had that talk in the school lot.

"Wanna show you something," says Jalen.

"You serious?"

I've forgotten my hoodie. I shiver as we descend the leafy hill.

We make our way into the woods, juddering sideways down the slope. From the bottom, only the top of the flagpole is visible. Maybe I *should* have paid Cole more.

We stare at the Fairy Tree, the SOL tree, now just a tree— among the rotting leaves, the detritus of the year. If fairies ever existed here, they're gone now.

Someone's put yellow tape around the perimeter. Maybe Principal B.

"Coleslaw was my messenger," I say. "He brought me the notes."

"For real?" says Jalen. "Makes sense . . . I left your house once after hanging with Raf and saw the kid climbing your tree . . . wondered what you two had going on. Cole never told."

"He wanted to grow," I say.

"Huh?"

"I told him he'd never get to the NBA if he read the notes. Or told."

Tshh-tshh-tshh. I thought I'd never hear that laugh again, not after any joke I'd make.

Leaves rustle across the forest floor, twisting in mini-funnels. Jalen turns, inhaling through his teeth. He's cold, too.

Jalen says, "I should probably tell you something."

"What?"

"I'm afraid of the dark."

I lift an eyebrow. "I specifically remember you walking to my house in the dark, once."

"Facts," says Jalen, "but only after some liquid courage."

Then he says, "You didn't let me tell you the whole story in the hotel that one night. Look, this whole thing started with me wanting to stick it to Raf, but then—I dunno. When you kissed me at the park, it complicated stuff."

"Complicated stuff?"

"Yeah. Wasn't lying when I said I've never felt that with nobody else."

"Oh."

"But imma be straight with you. Another part of me still wanted to see Raf hurt. I like you, Ma, but in your diary, you wrote how much it meant to you when we was kids and I put my arm around you at the park. That you wished I was your boyfriend."

I wish I was wearing a hoodie. I'd tug it over my head in shame.

"And your phone, too, after we started hanging, you'd filled me out: *Jalen Noah Thomas*; number, address, our photo. You liked me so much. Too much. That responsibility . . . *making someone's life*. Not ready for that, Ma. I'm about to go to the NBA." He says it like he's been drafted already. But it's not arrogant.

It's like what he told me: *People become what they expect themselves to become.*

My chest feels sore. I take a deep breath, trying to undo the knots.

"Ma, there's only one thing I *know* I want." He takes my hands in his and gives them a squeeze. Hope rises in my chest, like it does every time he touches me. Talks to me.

His fingertips are cut up from the friction of the basketball leaving his hands, again and again. From hours, months, years of play.

"Basketball," I say, squeezing back. It's not me. Of course it isn't.

"You know, USC is even higher ranking than UCLA?" He jumps up and swats at a tree branch, my hands cold without his. "NBA, that's where it's at. When I ball, I'm me. It's my shot, Ma. It's my shot."

"You're gonna make it," I say.

He swings me around. "Argh! You don't know how much *life* that gives me to hear you say! It's all I've ever wanted, Ma."

He puts me down but doesn't let go. Instead, he wraps his arms around me. I nuzzle my face into his chest. "Me too," I say, muffled by his sweatshirt.

"One more thing," says Jalen, and he leads me around the back of the tree.

"What?"

At first glance, the wooden contraption looks like one of those *take a book, leave a book* stands, but as I get closer—

"Is it a ballot box?"

"Wish box," says Jalen. And as he says it, I see the letters scrawled across the side in his messy handwriting. "Think you and your sis had it right at first. Wishes—it's a better business model than tryna, you know, hurt people with vengeance or whatever."

I let out a teary laugh. "Before I forget, I've got something for you . . ." I dig into the pocket of my jeggings and hand Jalen his wish. He unfolds it and exhales from his nose.

Refolds it. Drops it into the slot.

"Some wishes need a little more time," Jalen whispers.

Wind shifts the leaves in the trees. And I'm glad it's night-time and he can't see the tears streaming down my face.

They're not sad tears. Not at all.

66

AT EIGHT thirty, we roar up in front of my house. I don't tell Jalen to park up the block. I told Dad where I was going before I left and he said, "Alone?" But Mom gave Dad a sharp look and he grimaced, like *if she has to.* Even after all that's happened, Dad still doesn't want me hanging out with boys. Any boys.

But I'll be a junior next year. Seventeen, and according to Dad, old enough to date.

Jalen kills the engine.

At Cole's house, the blinds swish in the living room.

A figure materializes from the bench in front of our door. It's Raf, in sweatpants. He must've been waiting for us.

Jalen gets out of the truck.

"Mafi told me that—eh." Raf yanks up on his sweatpants. "You've hated me for a while. Because I dated Bian and . . . you pretended to like my sister to get back at me?"

"I did," says Jalen. "Wouldn't take it back, either. I pretended till I wasn't pretending anymore. All of that . . . I felt weak. Shoulda told you how I felt when the feelings bubbled up. But you got such a big head and I felt like—like you started forgetting me."

"You're right," says Raf. "I've been selfish."

"You have," I chime in.

Raf punches my shoulder.

"But you two aren't—" Raf looks from me to Jalen.

"No," says Jalen. "Friends."

The words wash over me.

"That's my sister you messed with," says Rafi, in his semi-serious voice.

"Hey, I can handle my own stuff, okay?" I say, and this time, I mean it.

Our laughter rings out over the block.

"Damn," says Rafi, after a moment. He places a hand on Jalen's truck. "I guess . . . Where do we go from here?"

"You get your ass back to practice, that's what."

"I'm suspended."

"Then you better kiss Coach's ass because we need our center." Jalen says, "Is Sarafat gonna let you play again?"

"It's not up to him anymore. I'm the only one responsible for me."

"That's what's up," says Jalen.

Raf says, "Heard USC is looking at you? Congrats, man."

And the boys do their slappy-bumpy-hug.

An orb of light launches into the air and green sparkles rain from the night sky.

"I'm goin' to fireworks at Tommy's," says Jalen. "You two tryna go?"

"*JT!*"

Cole's run outside. By the time he gets to us, he's out of breath. And shy. He wipes his Cheetos-stained hands on his basketball shorts. His mouth is crusted with the orange stuff, too.

"Um." He's peering at Jalen's hair, now green.

"What you want, CD?" says Jalen.

Cole's front door opens, then shuts. Mr. Dawicki watches from the porch.

"Here." Cole's voice is even lower since we hammered up the tree.

He unearths a Nixon box from his shorts. "I bought it for you. I promise—here's the receipt." And Cole curses when he can't remember which pocket the paper's in. He finds it in his hoodie pouch.

Jalen opens the box.

Overhead, another firework booms. Sparks gleam across the watch's blue face as they fall.

"Why?" says Jalen, an edge to his voice.

"I was lucky to have a friend like you . . . never had a brother, and—"

"Can't accept it, Slaw," says Jalen. He thrusts the box into Cole's chest.

Jalen's not trying to be polite like Nasim, turning down Mom's cookies. I try not to fidget in the silence.

Another firework cracks, then fizzles.

Mr. Dawicki calls his son inside. Cole turns to leave. Stops. "Would you—maybe wanna play ball tomorrow?"

"Dunno, kid," says Jalen. "*Shew.* I just dunno."

Cole hangs his head and swivels toward the glow of his house, box in his pouch.

"Yo, Slaw."

Cole stops.

"Never wanted nothin' but your friendship."

Cole turns. Jalen puts out his fist. Cole goes for a fist-bump but Jalen fakes him out at the last moment, leaving Cole hanging.

"We cool?" says Jalen, eyebrow raised. Cole catches Jalen's meaning: *Don't you ever ever ever pull something like that again.*

Cole looks Jalen in the eye. "We cool."

Unsmiling, Jalen gives Cole a fist-bump.

67

I'M ON the deck with Mom and Kate, sitting at the table. I'm nursing a hot chocolate at my normal eighty-twenty ratio. Eighty percent marshmallows. Twenty percent hot chocolate. We can't see the fireworks over the fence in the backyard, but every now and then there's a *pop* and a flash of red or white, and we look up into the sky.

Each boom is punctuated by our pigeons, cooing. I've named them all after *Blood Jurors* characters but I can never really tell the birds apart.

"Have you seen the news?" says Kate. "You and Rafi have sparked a ton of protests . . . people are talking again. The hashtag #ThoseLeftBehind is recirculating. More Afghans are coming out, too. Talking about their missing relatives."

Baba's hiking around the backyard, hopping every few steps and waving an arm. I'm unsure what he's doing.

"Do you think they'll call soon?" I ask Mom.

She takes a sip of her sparkling water. She left the wine in the alcohol cabinet tonight.

"We can't lose hope," says Mom, with a look at Baba. "But you also can't spend every moment of your day worrying, Mama. We have to live in the present."

Mom's gaze follows mine. We watch Meowgi on his window-sill cat perch, doing some cat yoga as he prunes himself.

"Like the cat," Mom goes on. "Do you think he stresses about the past? Or the future, for that matter? Humans love to worry."

"Mom," says Kate, lowering her voice, "how are you and Dad?"

Surprised perhaps by Kate's directness, Mom takes another sip of her water, relaxes her head on the cushion, and says, "Right now is good. We're happy."

I cut in, "So maybe it's a good time to bring up getting a dirt bike?"

"*Mafiiiiii,*" Mom and Kate say in unison.

Baba clomps up the deck stairs, and I decide to shelve the dirt-bike thing for another day.

"Did you see?"

We all peer out into the back garden. "See what, Baba?"

"Magic Man was just here, chatting with Baba—"

"*Babaaaaa . . .*" me and Kate say in unison, like *here we go again.*

"He was, *he was!* Baba does not fib. And he brought something. A gift."

Over the table, Baba uncurls his fingers. Fireflies flicker on his palm, then take off, up into the night sky. "A little magic for Baba's girls."

I get up and wrap my arms around Baba, the smell of after-shave and walnuts tickling my nostrils. He chuckles softly and kisses my head.

Then hums his way inside.

"You're not sending Baba away, are you?" I ask Mom. I can't stand the thought of him in a nursing home.

"No," says Mom. "We're not sending Baba away. He's our Magic Man."

My phone buzzes. A text from Jalen.

> Rose Park tomorrow?

———

A car rumbles into the driveway after midnight. I get to my feet and peek out the curtains. It's only Raf, back from fireworks at Tommy's.

I go downstairs for a glass of water and hear Baba in the living room, cooing. I peek around the corner, careful not to let myself be seen.

Baba's on his armchair with Mr. Meowgi on his lap. He's telling the feline a long-winded Mullah Nasruddin joke. I can hear Meowgi's motor going from here, like a boat. He rolls onto his back, and Baba scratches his orange belly.

In Baba's other hand is Habib's wooden donkey, muddy, but intact.

So *that's* where Meowgi has been sleeping. With Baba.

I'm not crazy about enemies-to-lovers stories, but this one melts my heart. The cat looks like he's *smiling* for god's sake. Meowgi's here because of Baba and he knows it.

Another life saved.

———

Late afternoon the next day, I'm at Rose Park with Brit watching Jalen and Cole play ball.

I'm also writing a note. *The good kind.*

I'm using the purple stationery set Brit got me for Christmas to write Enes Freedom that *long-ass thank-you note.*

"I love this," says Brit, running a hand over the skirt splayed around me. It's the red one Yasmoon gave me. Brit traces the intricate pattern with a finger.

"I figure it's good to get out of sweats every once in a while. *But I do miss them.*"

Brit laughs. Mouths: *Oh my god.*

"I don't know *how* you wear those leg traps," I tell her.

"Jeans?" Brit hugs me to her. "Sweats or skirts or whatever, you're Mafi and I love you."

I kiss my friend's cheek, wondering where Habib and Yasmoon are now. But Mom's right.

We have to live in the present.

That's all we have.

The nightmares still come, but today's been a good day.

Cole's getting pretty good at ball. He beats Jalen during one of their three-point shooting contests. Jalen stares him down, tells him a power forward's not meant to be a great shooter anyway.

"Watch this, Ma!" Jalen shouts, and Cole throws him an alley-oop pass. Jalen slams it home. It's been like that for half an hour, Jalen showing off and the metallic sound of compressed rubber against pavement. I give him the thumbs-up.

Cole runs over with his Gatorade to where Brit and I sit in the grass. The sun is setting and there's a chill in the air. Jalen dunks again, just as the court lights buzz on. "Bang!" he screams. "This is how we do!"

"So," says Cole, "are we good?"

"We will be, Coleslaw."

"I guess . . . no more Ghost stealth missions after break?"

Brit answers for me. "Oh *hell no*."

I laugh, and Cole pulls up some grass, already losing interest in the conversation. Kids Cole's age, they need to be doing ten things at once to hold their attention.

"Can I still come to your window?"

"How about the front door, Coleslaw. As you said, the tree's a liability."

"And don't you think you're a little tall for that tree?" says Brit.

Cole goes, "WOOOOO!" and sprints at Jalen. "She said I'm tall, you hear that?"

"She lyin', Slaw!" says Jalen.

"How are you and Jalen?" Brit asks in an undertone. She cocks an eyebrow as Jalen swishes a half-court shot, shrieking. "You two good? *More* than good?"

I think about it for a bit. "Yeah," I say. "We are."

————

I *had* four rules as Ghost.

Don't get caught rooting around in the SOL tree. Never reveal my identity. Ensure justice is served without police involvement. And most important . . . don't get emotionally invested.

In the fall of my sophomore year, I broke every rule.

And it set me free.

ACKNOWLEDGMENTS

IT TRULY takes a village to launch a writing career. Here's my village.

Thanks to Manny, "Swiss Chris," my love, my life, my forever hype man, who mopped me across the floor by the legs when I got a book deal. My ribs ache from laughter on the daily witnessing your shenanigans. If laughter really *does* add years to your life, we'll probably live forever. Thanks for all the basketball terminology, too. Damn, do I love you.

Thank you to Lola Bellier from CAA for rescuing *Free Radicals* from the slush pile and telling my agent, Mollie, "You need to sign her." Thank you to Mollie Glick, of course, for getting the manuscript into tip-top shape and quickly selling it to Stacey Barney, my editor. Thank you, Stacey, for the initial acquisition phone call, where you said there was "no aspect of this novel you didn't enjoy"—music to a burgeoning writer's ears. Whoever is reading this, whether it be the day of publication or ten years down the line, I probably still can't believe I'm. A. Published. Author. Stacey, you did that.

Thanks to Baba, Father of Fathers, for your strength, packing up your family and leaving Kabul in the dead of night for Indiana all those decades ago. To you, Afghanistan was home. I, like so many others, wouldn't be here without your initial sacrifice. Thanks to Dad for his Mullah Nasruddin jokes and Mom for driving me to those creative writing summer classes and editing earlier work for agent submissions. Thanks to my brother, David, for all the teenage mall runs where we belted Blink-182 and ate greasy french fries in your old Nissan. Lucy, thanks for all the well-mannered frivolity and for forgiving me for reading your diary, throwing your *Titanic* CD out the window, and commandeering all your friends on AIM, and especially for that one walk in Flagstaff one month before I got my agent, where you promised: "You're almost there." Thanks of course to my American, Afghan, Australian, and Swiss families all over the globe for their love and support on this long publication journey of mine. I'm blessed.

I'd be remiss if I didn't thank my best friend of twenty-plus years, Hannah Hershey, who read *Free Radicals* first and provided me with live updates that had me busting. Hannah, my love, you prove Mafi wrong: There *is* such a thing as best friends forever.

Thank you to my dear friends Suzie McGrath and Masha Baher for your love and support, especially during my darkest days. Thanks also to Charlie Tonelli, who reminded me what it was like to be a teenager and kept me up to date on neologisms.

Thanks to Barbara Bogue, my college creative writing instructor at Ball State, who wrote *Let me know when this is published, Lila!* on my final class project. I was seventeen.

This tiny comment was colossal. You made me feel like I *could* do this. Thank you to Richard Bausch, my Chapman University MFA instructor, who assured me after another agent rejection that I had talent and to "yell it into the night sky!" on my darkest days of doubt. It worked.

Thank you, of course, to Julia Walton. I am so grateful for your continued friendship and advice! Thanks to Jeff Zentner, who welcomed me into the writing community with open arms. Because of you, I will never not feel bad for freshly cut grass. Thanks to Sabaa Tahir for her kindness, and this advice: "Friends don't let friends publish alone."

Thank you to Nasim Fekrat, Habib (Adeb), and Homira Rezai, who answered my many questions on Afghanistan and Hazaras. Homira, you are a force, an inspiration to Hazaras everywhere. When I think of strong, intelligent, and beautiful Hazara women, I think of you. I look forward to our coffee date! Thank you, also, to Nico from Puerto Rico for sharing their experience on transitioning. You are a badass, and the inspiration for Brit Rossi's sheer awesomeness. I'm so glad TikTok led me to you.

So many of you have read my writing prepublication and told me, "Keep going!" For that, I am forever grateful. Here's the short list: Thanks to Pattie Morrison, Lori Tussey, Danielle Newhouse, Julie Davani, Helen Sobiech, Dylan and Elvin Deckard, Denisa Vitova, Mario Venanzi, and of course Joanna Zai, for reading all the "other" novels. Thanks also to Brianna Wu and Samantha Larsen, my former English students, for enthusiastically talking up my writing in class. I looked forward to every lecture because of you two.

Thanks to Kristin Boyle for the cover design, Nero Hamaoui for the beautiful illustration of Mafi on the cover, Nicole Rheingans for the interior design, and Via Romano for rush-binding and mailing my book when I couldn't. Thanks to Caitlin Tutterow, Cindy Howle, Liz Montoya, Regina Castillo, and the entire Penguin team for their support every step of the way.

Finally—thanks to all of my readers. I wouldn't be here without you.